PERFECT NIGHTMARE

Also by John Saul
in Large Print:

Black Creek Crossing
Midnight Voices
The Right Hand of Evil
The Manhattan Hunt Club

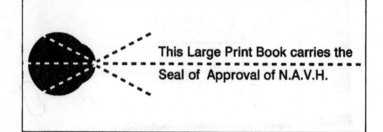

This Large Print Book carries the
Seal of Approval of N.A.V.H.

PERFECT NIGHTMARE

a novel

JOHN SAUL

Waterville, Maine

Published in 2006 by arrangement with The Ballantine Publishing Group, a division of Random House, Inc.

The text of this Large Print edition is unabridged. Other aspects of the book may vary from the original edition.

Set in 16 pt. Plantin by Ramona Watson.

Printed in the United States on permanent paper.

The Library of Congress has cataloged the Thorndike Press® edition as follows:

Saul, John.
    Perfect nightmare / by John Saul.
      p. cm.
    "Thorndike Press large print basic" — T.p. verso.
    ISBN 0-7862-8100-6 (lg. print : hc : alk. paper)
    ISBN 1-59413-131-7 (lg. print : sc : alk. paper)
    1. Girls — Crimes against — Fiction. 2. Mothers and daughters — Fiction. 3. Long Island (N.Y.) — Fiction.
4. Loss (Psychology) — Fiction. 5. Missing children — Fiction. 6. New York (N.Y.) — Fiction. 7. Kidnapping — Fiction. 8. Psychological fiction. 9. Domestic fiction.
10. Large type books. I. Title.
PS3569.A787P47 2005b
  813´.54—dc22   2005020904

For Terry and Judine —

Our parallel lives seem constantly
to be intersecting.
May it always be that way!

As the Founder/CEO of NAVH, the only national health agency solely devoted to those who, although not totally blind, have an eye disease which could lead to serious visual impairment, I am pleased to recognize Thorndike Press* as one of the leading publishers in the large print field.

Founded in 1954 in San Francisco to prepare large print textbooks for partially seeing children, NAVH became the pioneer and standard setting agency in the preparation of large type.

Today, those publishers who meet our standards carry the prestigious "Seal of Approval" indicating high quality large print. We are delighted that Thorndike Press is one of the publishers whose titles meet these standards. We are also pleased to recognize the significant contribution Thorndike Press is making in this important and growing field.

Lorraine H. Marchi, L.H.D.
Founder/CEO
NAVH

* Thorndike Press encompasses the following imprints: Thorndike, Wheeler, Walker and Large Print Press.

PROLOGUE

I prowled through their house for a long time last night before I finally did what I knew I had to do.

I loved the house the first time I saw it — loved it almost as much as I loved the girl who lived there. And last night it was as perfect as it has ever been.

It was the candlelight, I think.

I remember the house being candlelit the first time I saw it — indeed, I think perhaps it was the candlelight itself that drew me to it.

Like a moth being drawn to a flame?

It's a cliché, I know, but didn't someone once say that a cliché is only a cliché because it's true?

And the candlelight did mesmerize me, almost as much as the girl's face.

Her face, and her body.

The first time I remember being in the house, the candles were lit. The family was having some kind of a party.

A birthday?

I don't know.

Now I shall never know.

It doesn't matter that I shall never know, of course, just as it never mattered that I didn't know her age.

All I know is that she was perfect, that I knew I loved her from the moment I saw the candlelight flickering on her face, making her flesh glow as if with an inner light.

A light I have never known.

Could that be why the candles fascinated me? Because of their strange, flickering light that warms as much as it illuminates?

I don't know.

Nor do I care, if I am going to be absolutely honest about it. All I know is that the first time I saw the house it was glowing with candlelight, and her beautiful young face radiated even more heat than the candles, and I was drawn to that heat.

After that first night, I came back to the house as often as I could, slipping into it at night and lighting the candles — just enough for me to make my way around. And the first time I slipped into her room, feeling my way through the darkness of the corridor, moving so silently I could hear my own heart beating — but nothing else — I knew.

I knew she was mine.

She, you see, loved candles as much as I do.

Her room was filled with them. She had them on her dresser and on the table by her chair, and on her desk and on the nightstand by her bed.

Most of them were out, of course, but there was one still burning.

I remember it even now, remember how I stood at her door, which I had opened just far enough to peep inside, and found myself gazing at a flame.

A flame that drew me toward her even from that very first moment.

I slipped into the room, closing the door so silently there wasn't even the softest click to betray my presence. Inside the room — her room — an odd sensation came over me. It was as if I was floating, drifting over the thick rug on the floor, my feet not even touching it.

When I was close by her bed, I looked down and beheld her perfect beauty in the light of that single candle, and knew that we belonged together.

9

I didn't touch her that night. No, I was content merely to hover above her, gazing down on her youth and innocence.

It was a long time before I finally touched her. I don't know how long.

And she didn't mind.

I know she didn't, for she lay still and let my fingers trace her soft contours, let my lips brush hers.

So perfect . . . so very perfect.

I thought it would stay that way forever, that we would share our perfect love, but then one night she pushed me away.

Just like the other one had.

And I knew what I had to do.

I even knew it had to be last night.

Last night, after all, was Christmas Eve.

I'd seen the house once before on Christmas Eve, as I lurked hidden in the shadows, watching the candles being lit one by one, each of them pushing the cold and darkness a little farther away, until the entire house was suffused with a flickering golden light.

Even the Christmas tree, standing in front of the great picture window that overlooked the lake, was aflame with candles, each set in its own holder, clipped to the very ends of the branches so no wick had a twig above it.

It was a beautiful sight, that tree, and last night I lit it once more.

They had all gone to bed by then, of course, and I was alone downstairs.

I only lit that one room, but I lit every candle in it. The ones in the sconces on the walls, and the ones in the uplifted hands of the pair of brass figures — they look oddly Russian, though I don't know why — that stand on the mahogany game table. I even lit the six tapers in the three pairs of sterling silver candlesticks atop the glass-fronted bookcase that fills the wall opposite the picture window.

Then I lit the tree.

For a long time — I don't know how long — I gazed at the tree, knowing it would be the last time I saw it.

Knowing it would be the last time I saw this house.

Then I carefully extinguished every candle I had lit and went upstairs.

As always, she had a single candle lit by her bed, and I gazed at it for a long time, too.

It, and the perfect face it was illuminating.

Her hair was spread around her face like a halo, glowing in the soft light of the candle's flame, and as I beheld her inno-

11

cence, I wanted to touch it one last time.

Touch *her* one last time.

I didn't touch her, though. No, not last night.

Last night I did what I knew I had to do, and as the candle by her bed burned low, I lit the dozen others that she had in her room.

With each match I struck, with each wick I lit, the room grew brighter, washing away the shadows that concealed me.

It didn't matter, though, for after tonight I would never come back here.

Never see this perfect place — this perfect child — this perfect family — again.

When all the candles were blazing, I turned to look one last time on the girl.

She was smiling, content in her sleep.

Did dreams of Christmas morning dance in her head?

I shall never know.

As I stood near the door, a slight breeze came through the window I had opened only a moment before.

A breeze that moved the light lace curtain just close enough to the flame of one of the candles so that it caught.

Caught, as my breath caught in my throat.

The flame on the curtain seemed to die

away in an instant, fading to nothing but a glowing ember, but then another gust of air came through the window, and the fading ember leaped back to life.

Flames climbed up the lace toward the ceiling like a great glittering spider racing up its web. A second later the flames had jumped the gap to the curtain on the other side of the window.

Now the wallpaper was beginning to burn, and I knew it was time for me to go.

I beheld the face of the girl one more time.

"It's all right," I whispered. "We'll be together again someday soon."

I know she heard me, for I saw a smile cross her lips.

I turned away and left before she could awaken.

As I think about it now, I know it wasn't that I didn't want her to awaken and see me — or see what I had done — that made me leave so quickly.

No, it was something else.

I simply didn't want to hear her scream.

CHAPTER ONE

Kara Marshall glanced surreptitiously at her watch and wondered if there were any way — any *tactful* way — to get Claire Sollinger to eat just a little faster. But of course there wasn't; everyone in Camden Green knew that if you had lunch with Claire, it was going to be at least a two-hour event. Not that Kara minded. She and Claire had known each other ever since Claire had turned up as a volunteer for her project to restore the old town square to the park it had been before succumbing to the "modernization" of the post–World War II era when Camden Green, along with a dozen other towns along the north shore of Long Island, had decided to pin their future to the automobile and ripped out the old square in favor of a parking lot. The plan hadn't worked: ten years after the lot went in, so did the mall on the southern edge of town, and parking lot or not,

Camden Green's downtown had gone the way of dozens of others. At least it had until she and a few of her friends decided to change things, and organized a committee to rebuild the square in an effort to revitalize the town.

Claire Shields Sollinger had shown up at that first meeting. A silence fell over the room when she walked in, for no one expected anyone from the huge mansions in the Flinders Beach area along the shore to come to the meeting.

Give money, yes. But not come to the meetings, let alone do any actual work.

But there Claire had been, and after looking around at the shocked faces, she'd raised a sardonic eyebrow and spoken directly to Kara. "It seems my husband has traded me in for his secretary, which means I have a lot of time on my hands. I'm a good gardener, and I don't mind getting my hands dirty. So how can I help?" By directly confirming the gossip that had been running through the town for weeks, she utterly disarmed everyone in the room, and she'd proven as good as her word, showing up at every work party in the square, helping Kara find (and paying for) a landscape architect to re-create the square as it had looked decades earlier, and generally making herself useful. Except that the lunches tended to drag on, and even after ten years, neither Kara nor anyone else had worked up the courage to tell Claire Shields Sollinger that they had other things they needed to do.

Now, Claire's head was cocked and she was frowning, and Kara knew she'd been caught glancing at her watch. "I'm keeping you," Claire said, making it a statement rather than a question. As Kara searched for an answer that wouldn't be offensive, Claire signaled the waiter for the check. "Haven't we known each other long enough for you to tell me when I'm dragging lunch on too long, Kara?"

"You're not —" Kara began, but Claire cut her off.

"Of course I am — I always do. After all, it's not like I have much else to do, do I? And it's all your fault, you know."

"My fault?" Kara echoed. "Claire, what are you talking about?"

"Your committees," Claire said as she dropped her credit card on the waiter's tray without so much as a glance at the check. "You haven't formed a new one in months, and I have to tell you, I'm getting bored. And when I get bored, I keep everyone at lunch too long."

Kara took a deep breath, deciding she might as well come clean with Claire now, rather than put it off any longer. "Well, I'm afraid you're going to have to start organizing things yourself, then. I have an appointment with a real-estate agent."

Claire's eyes widened. "You're moving?"

"To the city. Steve and I just don't have enough time together, and —" Kara cut herself off, remembering the circumstances a decade ago that had left Claire Sollinger with too much time for lunch.

"And you don't want your marriage to end the way mine did," Claire finished for her. "Well, we'll miss you. At least I will."

Kara tilted her head. "That's it? Not going to try to talk me out of it?"

Claire shook her head. "Not after what happened to me. If you love Steve — which I know you do — you need to be with him. At least, if he wants to be with you, which I assume he still does. Unlike Phillip Sollinger." The waiter returned with Claire's credit card, and she added a generous tip and signed the voucher, still without checking the figures. "What about Lindsay?" she said as she stood and picked up her purse.

"She'll get used to the idea," Kara replied. They left the restaurant and stepped out into the bright spring afternoon. "She'll have to."

"Not necessarily," Claire said as they walked to the parking lot tucked well out of sight a block south of the village, which, after a decade of ministrations by Kara Marshall, Claire Sollinger, and a dozen other women, now looked much as it had a century earlier. The last trace of "modernism" had vanished last year when the electric street lamps were replaced with replicas of the old gas fixtures. "At Lindsay's age, a year is a long time, especially when it's your senior year. I remember when Chrissie —"

Now it was Claire who fell silent, but Kara didn't finish her thought, as Claire had finished her own a few minutes ago. It had only been a few months since her niece died in a fire at the Shields's ski cabin in Vermont, and Claire still found it difficult to talk about it. "I'm going to miss you," Claire sighed, just as the silence seemed to stretch on too long. "Anyone else would have tried to find the right thing to say when there is no right thing to say." As they came to their cars, Claire laid a hand on Kara's arm. "If I can help you out with anything, just call, all right?"

"Don't you think I've called you enough over the last ten years?"

"That was for the 'common good,'" Claire replied, emphasizing the last two words just enough to make both women smile. "This is for you. Anything you need, you just call. Just keeping your house straight so it can be shown will be a full-time job, and since I hire people to take care of my own house, I might as well help take care of yours. As long as it's not windows."

"I'll keep that in mind," Kara said. "And thanks." She got into the car, started the engine, and pulled out of the lot, but instead of turning left on the most direct route home, she found herself turning right and driving through the streets of the town she'd lived in for so many years.

The town she'd helped to make what it was today.

The trees were leafing out, and the flowers in the square were coming into bloom. In another month the tourists who had begun discovering Camden Green over the last few years would begin to wander around the street that no longer looked like just another Long Island town full of strip malls and shopping centers, but more like the main street of one of the small New England villages in rural Vermont or New Hampshire that time seemed to have forgotten. In a few years, perhaps, it would become overrun with tourists, and be well on its way to being ruined again. But for right now, it was exactly what Kara had always wanted it to be.

A charming little town, where everyone got along with everyone else, the kids didn't have drug problems, and the streets were safe at night.

The kind of small town that Ronald Reagan had always talked about, but hardly existed anywhere at all.

And now she was going to have to leave it.

And move to the city.

Kara hated the whole idea of it. Hated having to sell her house, hated having to find an apartment, hated the thought of moving to the city.

But she knew it had to be done, so she would do it.

She and Lindsay both.

And the family would survive.

Lindsay Marshall did her best to control the anger that had been building in her since breakfast, but even so, she jerked open her locker to throw her books inside,

20

then slammed it loudly. Her parents were ruining her life, and until she was eighteen and out of school, she had to do what they wanted her to do.

But it wasn't fair.

How could her mother have been so casual about it? "I'm meeting with an agent today," she'd said, like it was no big deal. "Your father and I are thinking of selling the house and moving to the city."

Lindsay had stared at her mother in openmouthed astonishment. "Just before my senior year?"

"It'll be fine," her mother said.

It'll be fine? *It'll be fine?* Lindsay hadn't been able to think of anything else all day. The phrase kept going through her head and she couldn't stop it.

It'll be fine. Life as she knew it was about to be ripped out from underneath her, and no matter what her mother said, it would *not* be fine.

Now she sat on the bench in the locker room, adjusting her sports bra and putting on her white socks and Nikes, unable even to listen to the rest of the girls. Their chatter usually cheered her up, but today it seemed totally frivolous in the face of the disaster that had struck at breakfast.

"Hey, Linds." Dawn D'Angelo opened

the locker next to hers, threw her backpack inside, and pulled out her practice clothes. Dawn's big chestnut eyes — the same color as her long wavy hair — were a perfect contrast to Lindsay's blue eyes and blond hair. But though the two girls had opposite coloring, that was the end of their differences — they'd been best friends since kindergarten.

"Hey," Lindsay sighed, making no attempt to mask her mood from Dawn.

One of Dawn's brows lifted. "What's up with you? You feeling all right?"

"I'm okay."

Dawn looked doubtful. "I hope it isn't the flu. My brother's got it. He puked all last night."

"Not the flu," Lindsay said as she finished lacing up her shoes. The coach's whistle blew from the gym, and she lifted herself off the bench to follow the rest of the cheerleaders out of the locker room, eager to work off some of her anger.

The varsity squad was just back from Florida, where they'd come in second in the regional championships held at Daytona. Until this morning, Lindsay had dreamed of being on that team next year.

Now that was simply not going to happen.

Inside her head, the endlessly repeating chorus of *It'll be fine* turned into *What's the use?* and her anger dissolved into hopelessness. In another two weeks the graduating cheerleaders would choose next year's squad and — most important — name the head cheerleader, but what did it matter now? Even if she performed perfectly today, with the entire varsity squad watching, it wouldn't matter. Her dream of trading in her black JV uniform for the red varsity uniform had been thoroughly crushed at breakfast this morning.

Her mother had been a cheerleader — she should understand how important this was! How could she have been so casual about it? Like it just didn't matter?

Lindsay tried to concentrate on the exercises, but kept losing count and getting off rhythm. Even worse, she was finding it impossible to finish with the grand gesture and big smile that was as important as the stunts themselves. *Smile, girls,* the coach always said. *This isn't just a cheerleading practice, it's smile practice, too!*

Keeping the coach's words firmly in her mind, Lindsay jogged in place, did her best to smile, and tried to find some energy as she waited for her turn to execute the simple flip they always used as a warm-up.

Then it was time. Lindsay smiled, took a deep breath, skipped a couple of steps to get her footing, took a short run, threw her hands down on the mat and began a perfect flip.

And the worst possible thing happened. Just as she was upside down, one elbow crumpled and she collapsed, her shoulder and then her bottom smashing hard onto the mat.

Fire flooded her wrist.

The coach and Dawn were on her in an instant, helping her up.

"I'm okay," Lindsay insisted, horrified that the varsity cheerleaders had seen her screw up a simple flip.

Then, unable to control her emotions any longer, she started to cry.

Sharon Spandler, the coach, helped her up and walked her off the mat. "Okay, girls," she called back as she led Lindsay toward the locker room. "Run through them one more time, then do two sets of backflips. Consuela, you're in charge."

In the locker room, Lindsay took a drink of water and blew her nose. The coach came out of her office with tape and scissors, and they sat facing each other on the bench. The coach gently took hold of her wrist and bent it slightly. "Hurt?"

Lindsay shook her head.

"Just a sprain, then." As she began to wrap the wrist with tape, Sharon eyed Lindsay carefully. "Everything okay with you?"

Lindsay nodded, but the coach could see the lack of conviction in her eyes and tried again. "Boyfriend troubles? Things okay at home?"

"Everything's fine. I'm just not feeling real good. I probably shouldn't even have come to practice."

The coach finished wrapping the wrist, then looked her square in the face. "I'll tell the girls you're sick." Then, thinking she knew what Lindsay was worried about, she said, "A simple fall shouldn't affect the vote. Don't worry."

Lindsay forced a wan smile. What would it matter if it did affect the vote? She wouldn't be back next year anyway. Someone else would be living her dream. The thought brought the hot lump up her throat all over again, but she managed to swallow it. "Thanks," she said.

"Just take it easy," Sharon said. "Rest up."

Lindsay nodded, then wiped her eyes on her soggy tissue.

A few minutes later Dawn D'Angelo came

in from the gym, grabbed some toilet paper from one of the stalls, and sat down in the same place the coach had. Dawn stuffed the wad of paper into Lindsay's hand. "Okay, enough," she said. "What's going on?"

Lindsay started to cry again. "We're moving to Manhattan."

Dawn stared at her in utter incomprehension. "What?"

"Mom says we have to move to the city to be closer to Dad's work." She took a ragged breath as Dawn's expression dissolved to disbelief.

"But we only have one year left," Dawn whispered. "And you're supposed to be head cheerleader next year! And we need to do our senior year together. We have to graduate together. If you leave, who's going to be my best friend? Jeez, Linds — you haven't even gone out with Zack yet! How can they do this to you?"

Lindsay looked bleakly into Dawn's eyes. "They're my parents," she said, her voice hollow with despair. "What can I do?"

Dawn didn't even try to answer Lindsay's question; they both already knew the answer.

There was nothing either of them could do.

Nothing at all.

CHAPTER TWO

Kara Marshall's stomach knotted as she stared at the listing agreement on her dining room table. She didn't even try to stop herself from picking at the already torn cuticle on her left forefinger. Why bother? Though her nails were about the last thing she had any control over, she'd already pretty much ruined them. She could barely believe the low figure the agent had suggested their beautiful home was worth. When Steve saw it . . .

She didn't want to think about what he would say.

A blinding flash of light jerked Kara out of her reverie.

"That should do it." She looked up at Mark Acton, whose professional smile looked phony even as he tried to make it look sincere. "This house photographs beautifully."

She didn't respond, and instead looked

down again at the array of forms and color brochures on the table as the agent put his camera into its case.

"I'll just leave the papers with you," he went on. "I can come back to answer any questions you might have when your husband is home. Do you know when that might be?"

"That's part of the problem," Kara said, looking up, wondering even as she spoke why she was telling this perfect stranger — one she'd already decided she didn't like — things that were none of his business. "I don't know when he'll be home. He commutes to the city and sometimes stays over. In fact, he's hardly home anymore — that's the main reason we're selling. Maybe I'd better just call you after we've talked this over."

Acton nodded. "I'll put these pictures up on our Web site as soon as you and your husband sign the listing." His voice took on the drone of a rehearsed speech. "Our normal procedure is to keep the listing in-house for two or three days. If it doesn't get sold by one of our people, I'll put it into the Multiple Listing Service on Monday and we'll hold a brokers' open house on Wednesday to show it to all the agents in the area. Then we'll have a public open house on Sunday. It's a wonderful house. I think it will sell right away."

Though she'd barely heard him, Kara nodded as if following every word. "Good. Okay. I'll call you."

Mark Acton pulled a sheet of blue paper from the pile and set it on top. "This is the schedule I just laid out for you. Please initial it when you sign the listing agreement and I'll put everything into motion."

Once again she nodded. "Yes, fine."

Acton picked up his briefcase, and she took that as a cue to usher him to the door. "I'm sure you'll be more than happy with the marketing our firm will provide," he said.

That must sound canned even to him, Kara thought. "I'm sure I will," she said. "Thanks for coming."

As she stood at the door, a car pulled up in front and her daughter got out. Kara watched Lindsay wave to her friend Dawn and to Phyllis D'Angelo, who was driving. "Call me!" Lindsay yelled to Dawn, then passed the agent on her way to the front porch.

Mark Acton nodded to Lindsay, then turned to watch her as she walked up the porch steps.

Kara scowled at him, but if he saw her,

he gave no sign. She forced the scowl from her brow, told herself she had to get used to it. Her daughter was seventeen now, and pretty, and men would look at her every day for the next twenty years. Then, seeing the bandage on Lindsay's wrist, all thoughts of Mark Acton vanished from her mind. "What happened?" she asked. "Are you all right?"

"I'm fine," Lindsay said, brushing by her and into the house. She dropped her backpack on the foyer floor, and only then held out her hand for the examination she knew there was no way of escaping. "It's just a sprain. I goofed up a flip at practice."

"Nothing's broken?" Kara fretted.

Lindsay pulled her hand away. "No, Mom. I told you, it's just a sprain." She tipped her head toward the front door. "Who was that?"

"Just an agent," Kara said, shrugging dismissively.

Lindsay winced as if she'd been struck. "Don't I have any say in what this family does?" she asked as she wheeled around and started toward the stairs. Though she'd tried to hide it, Kara saw her daughter's eyes glistening with tears.

"Lindsay, wait!"

But of course, she didn't.

When Lindsay vanished up the stairs, Kara looked again at the listing agreement on the dining room table, and had to resist the urge to pick up the forms and brochures and rip them to shreds. She didn't want to move to the city any more than Lindsay did, but what choice did she have? Being away from Steve so much was destroying their marriage. Still, Lindsay only had a year of school left. Maybe they could find some way to work it out.

But as she unconsciously picked at a different cuticle, she knew there would be no working it out. Not only was the commute killing her marriage, but Steve's promotion, which required him to be in Manhattan even more, hadn't been enough to even cover the cost of the tiny apartment he'd rented. In fact, the apartment had turned his raise into just another liability.

So there wasn't any choice; they had to move.

Kara waited long enough for Lindsay to pour out her tears into her pillow, and as she moved up the curving staircase to her daughter's room, she realized once more just how much she was going to miss this big house. She'd helped design it, and they'd moved in two weeks before Lindsay was born. The entire history of the family was in this house. Whatever they found in Manhattan would not only be much smaller, but an abandonment of their entire past as well. Could they really do it?

She knocked twice on Lindsay's door, then opened it a crack. "Linds? Can I come in?"

She took the silence as assent and went inside. It was a quintessential teenage girl's room, with its neglected but not forgotten stuffed animals and Barbie dolls, new and often replaced posters of buff young men on the walls, stacks of CDs, a computer, and enough makeup to beautify half the women on Long Island.

Kara perched uneasily on the edge of the bed. As she'd suspected, Lindsay's face was turned away, but the emotional storm seemed to have passed. Lindsay was quiet as she lay facing the wall.

"Honey?" Kara smoothed her daughter's silky blond hair. "You know we love it here as much as you do. We'd never move if we didn't have to. I just wish there were another option."

"Just one more year." Lindsay's voice was muffled by the pillow, but her anger was still audible. "Then it won't matter so much, because at least I'll have finished school."

"We can't make it another year like this," Kara said. "We can't keep up both places — it's too expensive. And your father needs us. We need him. *You* need him."

"I know," Lindsay sighed, rolling over to look at her.

Seeing the desolation in Lindsay's eyes, and hearing the hopelessness in her voice, Kara's heart nearly broke. The sight of those red, swollen, unutterably sad eyes bespoke every wonderful thing her daughter was — caring, dedicated, loyal. But as she eased a strand of blond hair away from Lindsay's face and put her cool hand on the girl's forehead, she could see a change in her eyes.

Abruptly, Lindsay sat up. "What if I move in with Dawn's family for my last year?" she asked, her expression brightening. "I could come to the city on weekends and for holidays." Her words tumbled out. "You know, Christmas and stuff."

"We can ask your father, honey," Kara said, knowing that Steve would never agree, "but I know what he's going to say, and so do you."

Lindsay sagged back down on the pillow, her excitement deflating like a collapsing balloon. "Yeah, I know."

Kara took her hand. "We've talked about

this for months — you knew it was coming."

"I know," Lindsay sighed, "but I didn't think it would be so soon."

"It'll be fine," Kara said, squeezing her daughter's hand. "You'll see — it'll be just fine."

But even as she spoke the words, Kara wondered how true they would turn out to be.

CHAPTER THREE

Steve Marshall squinted at the deposition on his desk, but it did no good — he could feel his eyes closing, despite his best intentions. Outside his office window the lights of the city were coming on and the sky had darkened; all that was left of the day was a pale streak at the horizon.

But half the day's work still lay on the desk in front of him.

He reached over to turn on his desk lamp, hoping the bright light would wash away the exhaustion the onset of dusk had brought. Rubbing his eyes, he turned his gaze from the window to the open door of his office. He could see a few lights still on down the hall, but the overheads had long since been turned off, and not even an echo remained of the hum of the departed staff.

Steve sat back in his chair and stretched — no point leaving until he'd at least finished the deposition he was working on. It looked like he'd have to stay in the city again tonight, even though he promised Kara that he'd be home. He dragged his fingers through his hair, ruefully reflecting that right now he far preferred the pressure on his scalp to that of either his job or his family. Still, tomorrow was Friday, and if he got enough done tonight, he'd knock off at noon and go home for the weekend. Maybe there was something the three of them could do together. Go to a crafts fair or something. He knew Kara would love it, and so would Lindsay, and making them happy had always made him happy, too.

Rubbing his eyes again, he turned his attention back to the deposition. There were at least another fifty pages to slog through, either here or in the cramped joke of an apartment that served as home on the nights when he couldn't make it back to Long Island.

Might as well be here.

Just as he was getting back into the dry prose of the blandly worded document, the harsh overhead office light went on. He looked up at the janitor who stood in the doorway, his hand on the light switch. "Sorry, sir, didn't mean to bother you."

Jesus Christ, can't he see I'm working?

But when he spoke, Steve did his best not to betray his annoyance. "Can you come back a little later, maybe?"

The janitor shook his head. "This is my last office. I'll just dump your trash and be gone."

Steve nodded toward the wastebasket. This guy didn't look familiar. "You new?"

The man nodded. "Just started today. Didn't mean to get in your way." He gathered the plastic bag full of trash, dumped it in the large bin he'd left just outside the door, then replaced the plastic liner in the wastebasket. As he straightened up, his eyes fell on the framed photograph of Steve, Kara, and Lindsay at the beach that had been sitting on Steve's desk since last summer. "This your family?"

Steve nodded, not even looking up, wishing the man would just go away.

"Nice. Very nice," the janitor said. "Looks like Long Island."

"It is," Steve mumbled.

"Pretty girl," the janitor said.

Leaning back in his chair, Steve saw that the man's eyes were now fixed on another of the photos on his desk, this one of Lindsay in her cheerleader's uniform.

"Very nice," he said, so softly that Steve

wasn't sure he was even aware he'd spoken out loud. "Beautiful."

He was about to reply when the phone rang, startling both of them. Nodding almost curtly, the janitor disappeared out the door as Steve picked up the receiver.

"Hello?"

"Hi, honey," he heard Kara say, and there was something in her voice that belied her cheerful tone.

"Hi."

"Are you coming home?"

He sighed. "I don't see how — I've got too much work."

"You promised."

He could almost see her struggling not to sound plaintive. "I know," he sighed. "I tried, but I'll get out of here early tomorrow and we'll have the whole weekend. We'll do something — just the three of us."

Kara was silent for a second, then: "I was hoping you could be home before Lindsay went to sleep tonight. She's kind of upset."

Steve sat up straight in his chair. "Upset? Why? What's up?"

"She hurt her wrist at cheerleading practice, and then the real-estate agent was here when she got home. I think we all ought to sit down and talk. You know, like a real family?" Kara quickly added, perhaps at hearing the sarcasm in her voice, "I'm sorry — that wasn't fair. I'm just — well, I just really wish you'd come home tonight."

"What did the agent say?"

Kara chuckled hollowly. "You won't like it."

Steve looked down at the deposition. If he called a driver, he could finish it on the way home. But he couldn't afford a driver — not with what it cost to keep the apartment. "Kara, I'm sorry," he said. "I've got to finish this deposition tonight."

"Okay." Her voice was small now, and he knew she wasn't going to argue anymore, which only made him feel worse.

"Let me see what I can do," he finally said.

"Okay. 'Bye."

" 'Bye."

He heard her say "Love you" just before he put the phone back in its cradle.

Crap!

First the damn janitor had thrown him off his concentration, and now Kara was angry at him, and he couldn't blame her.

And Lindsay was hurt and upset, and that made his stomach churn.

And on top of everything else, he was

going to hate what the agent had to say.

Enough was finally enough. He glanced down at the deposition one more time, then flipped its cover closed, turned off his desk lamp, and headed for home.

Lindsay dialed up the volume on the iPod her father had given her for her last birthday, but no matter how loud the music coming through the headphones was — even if it drowned out the argument going on downstairs — it couldn't cover the tension that filled the house.

And it was her fault — all of it.

She grabbed a pillow and pulled her arm back to hurl it at something — anything — but the warning stab of pain in her injured wrist made her change her mind. She dropped the pillow to her chest instead and hugged it, tears of frustration stinging her eyes and clouding her vision. "Grow up," she told herself.

The song she'd been listening to ended abruptly, and now she could hear her parents' voices drifting up the stairwell.

Though the anger was clear, the words themselves were not. Not that it mattered; she knew perfectly well what they were arguing about.

Her.

In fact, it seemed that all they did anymore was argue. But until tonight, it had been mostly about her father's new job, and the little apartment he had to rent in the city, and the fact that so many nights he couldn't make it home at all.

But their argument now was focused on her, and with every angry sound she heard, she felt worse. All she wanted was for everybody to be happy, and even without hearing what they were saying, she knew that nobody in the house was happy.

She lay on her bed, listening to the muffled words as long as she could stand it. She heard her mother's voice rising, but her father's voice stayed steady. *What's happening?* she wondered. *What's Mom yelling about?* And even though part of her wanted to clamp the pillow against her ears, shutting out the sound of her parents' argument, she knew she couldn't.

No matter how much it hurt, she had to know what they were saying. Putting the iPod on the nightstand, Lindsay got up from the bed, opened her bedroom door and listened.

"You're asking too much of her," Kara said for what she was certain must be at least the third time, if not the fourth or fifth. She was perched stiffly on the edge of the couch, and could see by Steve's expression that she looked every bit as shrill as she knew she was starting to sound. But how many times did she have to go over all this before he would actually *hear* her? "She's only seventeen years old, and you're asking her to give up everything. I know being on the cheerleading squad doesn't mean much to you, but so what? She's your daughter, Steve! And it's not just cheerleading! You're asking her to move away from all her friends — friends she's known since kindergarten — and start all over again in a new school where she doesn't know *anybody*. And it'll be her senior year. Believe me, I remember what it was like when I was her age. The cliques are formed, and they're rock solid. There won't be any room for Lindsay."

Steve spread his hands helplessly. "I don't know what else to do," he said, his own voice starting to rise, though not as much as hers. "There just doesn't seem to be any other answer. We can't afford —"

"Another year," Kara broke in. "Let's stay here just until she graduates." Seeing his expression harden, her voice rose another notch. "For heaven's sake, Steve — the real estate market is down so badly, we'd only get about three-quarters what we would have gotten a year ago, and you know as well as I do that even though the market's dropped out here, it hasn't in Manhattan. We'll be lucky if we can afford a tiny little two bedroom, and you better believe it won't have more than one bath!"

Steve shook his head and picked up the glass that sat on the table next to his chair, downing the last of the scotch in a single gulp. "We've been over the numbers, Kara," he said, his voice taking on a steely edge. "We can't afford to keep this house and pay for the apartment, too. We have to get a place in the city that's big enough for all three of us."

"But we won't get enough for this place," Kara insisted. Hadn't he heard anything she said?

Steve set his empty glass on the end table and ran his hands through his hair. "I thought we'd already had this whole conversation."

"That was before I met with the agent," Kara shot back. Seeing Steve's eyes narrow angrily, she added, "And it was before I watched Lindsay's heart break."

"She's young," Steve said, his voice taking on a tone she'd only heard him use in court when he was trying to make a point to a recalcitrant witness. "She'll survive. In a year she'll be off to college anyway. Frankly, I don't understand why —"

"Don't take that tone with me," she suddenly flared. "This isn't a case you're defending! It's your family! And moving to the city is not the best thing for your family. Remember when we first decided to have kids? We said we'd always put their best interests first."

"And what's best for her — for all of us — is that we start living together like a family again," Steve shot back. "You know — having dinner together every night, with me actually coming home? How many times have we had dinner together in the last week? In the last month?"

"Whose fault is that?" Kara demanded, almost able to taste the bitterness in her voice.

Steve's eyes glinted. "That's a cheap shot, Kara. If I'm going to be the sole provider for this family, then maybe this family needs to rally around a few of my needs, okay?"

Kara felt what little control she still had over her emotions start to slip away. "This family does nothing but cater to your needs," she said, her voice rising yet higher. "All we ever do —"

She was interrupted by a new voice.

A voice even louder and more furious than her own.

"Stop it!" Lindsay yelled. "Just stop it!"

Kara's breath caught in her chest, and Steve looked as if he'd been struck. Both of them looked toward the stairs to see Lindsay, clad in her pajamas, her wrist wrapped in an Ace bandage, tears streaming down her face. "Just stop it!" she cried again. "I can't stand your arguing anymore! I thought —" Her voice broke and she raised her hands to cover her face as her body began to shake.

"Whoa, kitten," Steve said, quickly getting up and going to her. Sobbing, Lindsay fell into his arms. "Take it easy."

Kara thought her heart would break as she watched them, and the anger she'd felt toward Steve only a moment ago dissolved as she saw him comforting their daughter.

"It's just an argument," he said. "It doesn't mean anything at all. Your mother and I love each other and we both love you even more." He held her, stroking her hair as she cried. Slowly, he guided her to the sofa, where they sat down next to Kara.

Kara took Lindsay's hand. "I'm sorry, darling," she said. "We're just trying to work out what's best for everybody."

"Everybody," Steve echoed, looking pointedly at Kara, "because we're a family. And we all agree we need to be together — we're just trying to figure out the best way to accomplish that."

"You need to stop arguing," Lindsay said, sniffling and wiping away a tear with the back of her good hand. "I — I just can't stand it."

"I'm sorry, kitten," Steve said.

"It's okay," Lindsay said, but with a catch in her voice. Beseechingly, she looked first at her father, then her mother. "We can move, okay? I'll adjust. Just don't fight anymore, all right?"

Steve gave her a hug. "Hey, it's not the end of the world, sweetie. It'll be all right, I'm telling you. You'll *like* living in the city. It's an exciting place."

Kara gazed uncertainly into Lindsay's eyes. "You're sure?" she asked. "You're not just saying it's okay because we were arguing?" Lindsay hesitated, then nodded. "Okay," Kara sighed. "I'll call the agent and tell him we're signing the listing. They can start doing their thing, and we'll see what happens."

Steve nodded. Lindsay was sitting with her head down now, her hands in her lap, and as he watched, a tear rolled down her cheek and fell onto her pajamas. "Tell you what," he said, lightening his tone. "Let's go into the city on Sunday. We'll look at some places — maybe hit some open houses and see where we might like to live." He tipped Lindsay's face up so she couldn't avoid looking at him. "We might get lucky and find the perfect place. Something we all love."

"And we can have lunch at that Thai place on West Sixty-seventh," Kara said. "Remember their cabbage salad?"

Lindsay nodded, sniffling once more, but her eyes were no longer flooding with tears.

Kara gave her a nudge. "And we'll go shopping at Bergdorf's."

"Whoa," Steve interrupted. "This is a trip for —"

"Shopping at Bergdorf's," Lindsay broke in, a smile lighting her face.

Steve threw his hands up in mock resignation. "Okay — I get it. I'm outnumbered. Again."

Lindsay shoved her elbow into his side. "You think *you're* outnumbered? How do you think I felt when I was listening to you two fighting about what we should do?"

Kara gave her daughter's shoulders a squeeze, and for the first time in months felt that just maybe things would turn out all right. With a silent prayer of thanks, she smiled at her husband.

He smiled back.

CHAPTER FOUR

I think perhaps I've found her at last!

I can't be sure, of course — not yet.

But when I first got the alert on my computer this morning, I felt a tingling in my belly.

The same kind of tingling I used to feel whenever she was near: a tightening in my groin, and cold fear in my belly.

Though it wasn't strong, it was enough to make my fingers almost vibrate as I typed the keystrokes that took me to the listing.

But not just one listing! No! This morning there were two! My heart beat faster as I went to the first listing, but as the image of the house came onto the screen, the tingling began to fade. It was an ugly house — a kind of squat, shapeless bungalow. Not at all the kind of home I like.

But then I saw the other house, and my

heart started to pound, and when I took the virtual tour, my excitement only grew. It may be the house.

I am almost sure it *is* the house!

A teenage girl lives there, and something inside me tells me she is perfect for me.

I know it. I know it!

I could tell from the first moment I saw the pictures of her room, but I had to be sure. But now I am sure, because I've gone over the photographs so many times that I have every detail memorized. Even as I write these words, I can see the room — her room — as clearly in my mind as if I were standing in it.

Touching it.

Smelling it.

Oh, yes — she is the one.

But I mustn't be hasty, mustn't let my hopes get too high. After all, I've had these thoughts before, and been so often disappointed.

This time, I won't get ahead of myself.

No, this time I'll hold some part of myself aloof, and force myself to wait. After all, the address won't be posted until the house goes into the Multiple Listing Service, and I'll just have to contain my excitement until then. But it's so hard — I am so tempted to get into the car and drive around, and keep driving until I find the house.

The perfect house.

Her house.

I know the idea is ridiculous. I could drive for weeks and never run across it — never find her — yet the feeling is almost overwhelming.

It is as if the house itself — and the girl who lives in it — are drawing me like filings to a magnet.

Yet I have to be patient. After all, it will only be a few days.

In a few days, I shall get the address.

And in a few days, she will still be there. . . .

Still, I'm not used to being patient.

I hate being patient.

But soon . . . soon I shall see her, and touch her, and smell her.

And she will know all the feelings I knew so long ago.

But this time it will be different.

This time all the feelings will go on forever.

CHAPTER FIVE

Manhattan is impossible, Kara thought. Traffic was unaccountably snarled, there were no places to park, and if there was a parking lot anywhere in this part of town, neither she nor Steve had seen it.

"Is something going on?" Lindsay asked from the backseat. "Why is everything so messed up?"

Kara could feel Steve's nerves starting to fray as everywhere he turned the streets were barricaded and traffic hopelessly snarled. She turned on the radio, and Lindsay's question was instantly answered.

"The vice president's motorcade has the entire West Side gridlocked from Forty-second Street north to 125th," a soothing voice intoned. "Motorists are advised to —"

Steve snapped it off. "Who asked the vice president to come to town today?" he grumbled. "I don't recall his office calling to see if it was convenient for me." He scowled, funneling his frayed nerves into a comically exaggerated mask of anger. "And if they had, I'd have told them to keep him in Washington! Who needs him? Especially on Sunday in Manhattan?"

"Bad luck," Kara sighed. If the motorcade didn't hurry up and get where it was going, they were never going to make their appointment with the agent who claimed she had the perfect apartment.

"We should have taken the train," Steve said through clenched teeth, and Kara sighed again, knowing he was right.

And knowing it was her fault they hadn't done it. After all, she was the one who'd thought a drive in the family car would be a better idea.

"I'm sorry," she said, sighing again.

Steve's thin-lipped expression didn't change.

"This sucks," Lindsay muttered from the backseat.

Kara sighed a third time, silently agreeing with her daughter, and checked her watch. Their appointment was in five minutes. The agent wouldn't wait around for long if they were late.

Miraculously, a car pulled out of a parking space just in front of them, and Steve quickly slid their Toyota SUV into it, ignoring the blare of the horn from a Ford Focus whose driver seemed to think he was the rightful heir to the slot. "There is a God," Steve muttered. "C'mon, we've got to hurry."

Just in the nick of time, Kara thought, certain that if the parking space hadn't seemingly dropped from heaven, Steve's temper would have given way.

He locked the car and they hustled along the sidewalk, threading through the pedestrian traffic far faster than they'd been able to maneuver through the car-jammed streets. In less than five minutes they made the three short blocks uptown and the two long ones over and found themselves in front of a tall brownstone. Steve checked the address. "This is it," he said, pressing the bell.

Kara eyed the building and decided it looked presentable, if not perfect. She checked her watch again when there was no response to Steve's buzz. "We're not late. She couldn't have left, could she?"

Steve took a deep breath but said nothing, and Lindsay dropped onto the front step and put her chin in her hands.

"Ring again," Kara said.

Silently, Steve pressed the buzzer a second time.

Still nothing.

Then Kara saw a tall, thin woman in a long black coat striding around the corner, a folio clutched tightly in one hand, a set of keys in the other. "Mr. and Mrs. Marshall?" she asked as she came abreast of the building.

Thank God, Kara thought. She smiled and nodded in response. "This is our daughter, Lindsay," she said as Lindsay stood up.

"I'm Rita Goldman," the agent said, her hand coming out to grasp first Kara's, then Lindsay's, and finally Steve's hand. "I'm so sorry to be late. The traffic —"

"We know," Steve said, his mood lightening as finally something seemed to be going right. "It almost made us late, too. In fact, we were afraid we might have missed you."

The woman opened the front door and held it for them. The building seemed well-maintained, with a clean marble floor in the foyer and contemporary art on the walls. But the dark mahogany moldings and vaguely Victorian light fixtures made it seem older than it was. Still, the elevator moved smoothly and looked modern, with mirrors on the walls.

Kara began ticking items off her mental checklist. So far, so good.

She glanced at her reflection in the mirror, decided her makeup had survived the drive into the city, then noticed Lindsay's unhappy face. Leaning over, she whispered, "Thai salad," which made Lindsay smile.

The fourth floor hall was carpeted and nicely lit.

Two more check marks on her mental list.

The agent, chatting with Steve, walked them down to 409 and used three keys to open the door.

A black mark on the checklist.

Then the door opened, and suddenly Kara felt better. Light. Lots of light, let in by lots of windows.

And hardwood floors and nine-foot ceilings.

Things were looking up.

The living room windows looked down over Amsterdam Avenue, which was okay. Not Central Park, but there was no way they could afford that.

"There's a rooftop garden," she heard the agent tell Steve. "I won't pretend it has the best view, but it's quite charming."

Kara caught Steve's eye, and they nodded at each other. So far, so good.

Then they came to the kitchen. It was

barely big enough for one person to maneuver in, the stove had only two burners, and the tiny countertops were covered with Formica in a particularly ugly shade of brown. It was nothing like the enormous, custom-designed kitchen with granite countertops that Kara had lived with so long that she'd almost forgotten there was anything else. Now the ugly truth hit her.

You can get used to it, she told herself. But even if she could adapt to the size, she knew the kitchen would still need a complete remodeling.

A remodeling they'd never be able to afford if they bought the place.

So she'd just have to get used to it, she decided, hustling Lindsay down the hall, hoping her daughter hadn't noticed quite how bad the kitchen was. "Let's take a look at the bedrooms."

The master bedroom seemed almost as small as the kitchen, but at least it had windows. On the other hand, the windows faced another building, which was barely ten feet away. If the neighbors hadn't had their shades drawn, Kara realized, she would be looking directly at them and see whatever they were doing.

And they could look back, which meant she'd have to keep her shades drawn, too.

The master bath looked like it belonged in an old motel.

A *cheap* old motel.

It's the city, she reminded herself. *This is how people live here. Modern plumbing is not an option.*

"Two blocks to Central Park," the agent was saying as she and Steve followed Kara and Lindsay into the bedroom end of the apartment.

"Hear that?" Steve said to Lindsay. He turned back to Rita Goldman. "What about the schools?"

Lindsay, obviously uninterested, wandered away, and Kara followed her into the other bedroom.

Small.

Tiny closet.

Saying nothing, Lindsay turned, walked out of the bedroom and headed for the front door. Kara, Steve, and Rita Goldman followed. As they left the apartment and moved toward the elevator, no one said anything at all. The silence stretched until the elevator arrived, its door slid open, and they all entered.

As the elevator started down, Kara finally spoke. "Nice light in the living room. I love those big windows."

"Maybe we should have gone up to see

the rooftop garden," Rita Goldman suggested. "Shall we do that?"

Kara glanced at Lindsay and read her daughter's feelings. "I don't think we need to," she said. "I don't really think this is what we're looking for."

The Realtor nodded, her lips pursed, and no one spoke until they were back on the sidewalk. "I'm sure you'll all love the next one," she said, smiling just a little too reassuringly.

But even before she'd finished speaking, Kara saw the expression on Lindsay's face and knew that one of them, at least, would not love anything that Rita Goldman had to show.

And Kara knew there would be nothing she could do about it. Suddenly she felt like crying.

CHAPTER SIX

Sunday morning is when the big edition of the *New York Times* comes out.

Which is why Sunday morning is my favorite time to wake up.

I know Sunday is a lot of people's favorite day, and I know that for a lot of them, it is also because of the paper. But for most of the others, the paper is loved because of the Arts section, or the book reviews or the sports or the editorials.

I love it because it lists the addresses of open houses.

And every open house presents me with a possibility.

An exciting possibility.

Today there were two new listings in the real estate section. I circled each of them with my red felt pen, then located them on my map.

Finding them on the map is especially exciting, because it gives me clues as to the kind of people who live in the houses. Today, both the houses seemed to give promise of the kind of girl I'm looking for, and since they are both convenient, I was at first tempted to visit both of them.

I began my very meticulous routine.

First, I plot my route. In the event I decide to actually go visiting today, I shall rent a car from an agency in Port Jefferson. Perhaps some kind of Chevrolet — the sort of car one sees by the dozens every day but never notices.

Exactly the sort of car I like best for my outings.

Then I plan the route I shall take from the car rental agency to the first house, then to the other, and then back to the agency, always using the busiest — and the most anonymous — roads. Most of the looky-loos (a term I deeply despise) show up in the middle of open house hours, so I shall time my trip to slip in when the houses will be at their fullest.

After all, it doesn't take me long to find out whether I've found the home of the girl for whom I search. . . .

And no one will notice me at all.

I reread the ads, studying them carefully. The first house had four bedrooms. That's a good sign, but its listing agent turns out to be one of those vile, pushy women who darts from room to room keeping track of everyone, babbling inanely, and insisting that everybody sign her book. The last time I saw her, she talked about interest rates and market conditions until I wished I'd never awakened that morning. Now I try to avoid her, but I'm not sure I can today.

After all, the house has four bedrooms, and chances are strong that one of those bedrooms belongs to a girl, although there is no virtual tour of that house on the Internet.

The other house is smaller, but is listed by an agent who is lazy and invariably spends most of his workday smoking on the front porch or the back steps, or the terrace if the house has one, smoking cigarettes and letting the prospective purchasers wander through by themselves.

I shall certainly go see this one.

After all, one never knows what surprises await just around a blind corner.

Still, neither of these listings gave me a shiver of anticipation like the one I saw on the Internet a few days ago.

I just have a feeling about that one.

After plotting my route and planning my day, I doodled on the newspaper with my red felt-tip pen, circling the two ads over and over again. Oddly, the circles around the open houses seemed to turn into eyes.

Two big red eyes that reminded me of something, but I couldn't remember what.

Underneath the eyes, I drew a mouth.

A big, red, smiling mouth under the big, red eyes.

It was absurd, I know, but for some reason, I couldn't stop. The larger and more grotesque they got, the more they made me smile.

Perhaps I won't go out at all today.

Perhaps I'll just spend the day dreaming.

Still, the open houses call me. Oh, I do love Sundays!

CHAPTER SEVEN

"This is the last place I have to show you," Rita Goldman said, and Lindsay silently sighed in relief. The morning, which had started off badly with the traffic jam, just seemed to be getting worse, and even before she looked at her watch, her stomach told her it was at least an hour past lunchtime. But her hunger was only part of it.

The worst of it was that as the morning had worn on, and they'd gone from one awful apartment to another — each of them seeming worse to Lindsay than the last — she'd slowly come to the conclusion that despite her brave words the other night, moving was going to be a lot harder than she'd dreamed, even in her worst nightmares. She hated everything about the city — the crowds, the noise, the traffic — everything.

And now she was starting to get a headache.

As if in response to her mood, a dark cloud had formed over the city and the wind was blowing cold. Still, there was just one more place, and then they could get to the good part of the day.

Lunch and shopping.

It was an open house on the Upper West Side.

Lindsay followed her parents and Rita Goldman into the building. The elevator opened, half a dozen people got out, and even more got in with them.

Crowded.

Lindsay hated that about elevators. People you didn't even know were always touching you, even when they didn't mean to. She pulled her shoulders in, pressed her arms against her sides and herself against the wall of the elevator, but even so, the man next to her brushed against her and she felt a chill pass through her. The knowledge that this would be happening every day after they moved to the city only made the chill worse.

The apartment was on the sixteenth floor, actually had a good view and a big kitchen — big enough to hold a breakfast table. Not so bad.

A nondescript man with greasy hair was the hosting agent, and he had a plate of cookies and a stack of color flyers, which he pushed into the hands of anyone who would take them. There were at least a dozen people standing in the living room in groups of two or three, whispering among themselves and examining every detail of the room.

Lindsay headed for the bedrooms, leaving her parents to listen to Rita Goldman's sales pitch, which by now she was pretty sure she knew by heart: ". . . close to the subway . . . good school . . . great restaurants . . . fan*tas*tic view . . . blah blah blah . . ."

She edged past a young couple coming out of one of the bedrooms. It was a girl's room, with posters on the wall and a pink bedspread. She looked at the jewelry box on the dresser and the cluster of framed photographs that could only be family pictures. A bunch of high school photos were stuck around the edges of the mirror over the dresser, and Lindsay wondered if one of the cute guys was the girl's boyfriend.

She felt a sudden urge to look through the girl's CDs to see what kind of music she liked, but just as she was about to flip through them, she realized there was going to be an open house at her house next week.

An open house just like this one.

With strangers looking through her things.

She jerked her hand away from the CDs almost as if her fingers had been scorched.

She suddenly felt creepy about even having looked at the pictures and wondering if one of them was the boyfriend, and silently apologized.

The thought of this happening in her own room, with anybody at all going through her stuff, made her queasy. Having an agent show people through apartments and houses that belonged to other people was bad enough, but open houses, where anybody — *anybody* — could just walk in and look through her underwear . . .

Lindsay felt her queasiness turn to nausea, and knew that if she didn't get out, she was going to throw up. She hurried back through the rooms and found her parents in the kitchen discussing the apartment with Rita Goldman, who looked just like a raven cawing over a prize piece of garbage.

"Mom?" she whispered, trying to pull her mother aside. But her mother, still listening to the cawing of the raven, put her arm around her shoulders and tried to draw her into the conversation.

"It's only a block to the subway," she heard her father telling her. "That's really terrific, kitten!"

"Did you look at the bedrooms, sweetheart?" her mother asked. "What do you think?"

"I think I've got to get out of here," Lindsay managed, bile rising up in her gorge.

Her mother's smile faded into a look of concern. "Honey, what's wrong? You look a little pale."

"I just need to get out of here."

Kara's motherly instincts came to the fore and she nodded. "Okay." She turned to Steve. "I'm going to take Lindsay out for some air." She looked at her watch. "Oh, good Lord, she must be starving — look how late it is!"

"Why don't we find a little place for some lunch?" the raven clattered. "I can make a few phone calls — maybe find something even better than this — and we can all get a bite."

Lindsay tugged at her mother. She didn't want to have lunch with this woman. All she wanted was the Thai cabbage salad she'd been promised. Then she wanted to go shopping and to forget moving to the city. She struggled against the tears now threatening to overwhelm her. "Mom, please?"

As if she'd read her daughter's thoughts, Kara nodded, then glanced at Steve. "We'll see you downstairs."

The elevator was crowded again, and Lindsay's queasy stomach began to escalate into an anxiety attack. She felt hot and clammy at the same time, and steel bands seemed to be tightening around her chest, making it hard to breathe. As the elevator crept downward, she felt the strange heat rise up through her chest and her neck and into her face, and when the doors finally opened on the ground level, she was unsteady on her feet.

She dropped onto a bench in the foyer and leaned against her mother, who sat down next to her.

"What's the matter, darling?" Kara asked, her brow creased with worry. "Are you sick?"

"I'm hot," Lindsay said. She picked up her mother's hand and pressed it to her face.

"You're burning up," Kara said.

But already the flush was starting to pass. "No, I'm going to be okay," Lindsay assured her. "I just needed to get out of there."

"Then we'll just relax here for a few minutes and wait for Dad. Okay?"

Lindsay nodded, closed her eyes and silently prayed for some kind of miracle that would mean they could just stay in their house and never have to go through this again.

"Did you like this place?" Kara asked. "It certainly seems to be the best thing we've seen — close to the subway, and close to a very good school, and not too far from your father's office." She paused, then added, "And we can afford it. Barely, but we can make it."

Lindsay hardly heard the words, a single thought filling her mind: "Are people going to be going through our house like this?"

Her mother looked puzzled. "Well, of course they are. At the open houses next week. Why?"

Lindsay's eyes widened and she paled. "I don't want anybody in my room," she whispered. "And I don't want to move. Can't we just forget about all this and go home?"

Kara hugged her close. "I wish we could," she said. "But you know we can't! Come on, sweetheart." Turning so she could face Lindsay, she tipped her daughter's head up and looked into her eyes. "It's a new chapter, Lindsay. A new adventure. I know it's scary, but you'll get through it! We've had a wonderful life out on the Island, but we'll have a wonderful one here, too."

"But I hate all these places," Lindsay whispered, her voice breaking. "I hate the city."

"You'll grow to love it. Trust me."

But as the elevator dinged and her father came out with Rita Goldman and a flood of other people, Lindsay knew it wasn't true. She hated the city now, and she always would. "Someone already made an offer on this place," she heard her father say, sounding disappointed. "And it's been accepted." Lindsay immediately felt better.

"Timing is everything," she heard the agent say. "I'll do a little more research, and now that I've got a better idea of what appeals to you, I can zero in. We'll keep looking until we find the place that's just right."

"Thai salad," Lindsay whispered to her mother.

"Thank you so much for your time," her mother said as her father shook the agent's hand. Rita Goldman swirled her black coat like a pair of wings, turned and swooped out of the building with a promise to be in touch soon.

"We'll find something we all like," her father said, but Lindsay knew the truth.

Her parents would find something *they* liked.

The best *she* could do was cope.

But she would do it. Somehow, she would do it.

CHAPTER EIGHT

Kara was just fastening the last button on her blouse when she heard the doorbell. Damn. Was he early? A glance at the bedside clock told her he was right on time — *she* was late. "Lindsay?" she called. "Are you about ready?"

The only response was the sound of the toilet flushing in Lindsay's bathroom, which meant that she was still a while away from being ready.

Kara slipped into her shoes and hurried down the stairs, tucking the blouse into her skirt. "Coming," she breathed, hating, as always, to make anybody wait, and wondering why even the few seconds it took to get to the door made her feel guilty.

Mark Acton stood at the door, briefcase in hand, his agent's smile covering his face like a mask. "Good morning!"

Kara pulled the door wide. "Hi, Mark.

Come on in. We're running a little late this morning."

"No problem. You take your time, and I'll just get started setting up."

Kara put Steve's breakfast dishes in the dishwasher and turned off the coffeepot. "Coffee before I throw it away?"

"No, thanks."

She took a final swipe at the countertops, then looked around to make certain the kitchen looked clean and appealing. Suddenly the yellow paint she'd decided on two years ago didn't seem like such a good choice. Too late now. "Lindsay!" she called up the stairs. "Time to go!" She turned back to the real-estate agent. "How's the response so far?"

"I'm expecting twenty or so agents to caravan through."

"Twenty! I didn't know there were that many agents in town." She wished she'd researched it more thoroughly and chosen a listing agent she liked a little better. Her thoughts were abruptly interrupted by Lindsay's voice.

"Mom?"

"Hi, honey," Kara said, glancing up at her daughter, who had paused halfway down the stairs. "Time to go." Lindsay didn't move, and it wasn't until she spoke that Kara realized her gaze was fixed on Mark Acton.

"Is he showing the house today?"

"It's the agents' open house," Kara said. "Are you ready? I'm already late."

"Where are you going?"

Kara frowned. "I told you last night — I'm going into the city to see some more apartments and have lunch with your father."

Lindsay's eyes followed Mark Acton as he moved around the living room, making tiny adjustments to the furniture and carefully leveling the pictures on the walls. "What time is this open house going to be finished?"

Kara frowned as she watched Lindsay stare at the agent with open hostility. "Honey, where are your manners?" She shrugged apologetically to the agent, but he waved it off.

"I just don't want to come home and have a bunch of strange people here," Lindsay said, her tone annoying Kara.

"Not a problem," Mark assured her, exaggeratedly ignoring the teenager's hostility. "I'll be finished by early afternoon."

"And I should be home by five," Kara said, her voice tightening as Lindsay's expression only darkened further. "Mark will be gone and I'll be home. Will that suit Your Highness?"

Stung by her mother's words, Lindsay turned and fled back up the stairs.

Kara sighed, knowing she'd handled Lindsay badly. But she was late and still had a lot to do, and for once Lindsay would just have to take care of herself. "I'm sorry," she murmured, more to herself and the departed Lindsay than to the real-estate agent.

"Moving is hard on kids," Mark said. "I know."

"It's hard on everybody," Kara said.

Then Lindsay came running down the stairs again, purse slung over her shoulder, book bag in hand. She stopped short and turned to face Mark Acton without a trace of the hostility she'd shown only a moment before. "I'm sorry," she said, almost shyly. "I didn't mean to be rude — I just don't like people in my room."

"It's all right," he replied. "Nobody likes having strangers in their house. Unfortunately, it's just part of the game. No way out of it if we're going to sell this place."

"Nobody's going to go through my stuff, are they?" Lindsay asked, her voice anxious.

"Lindsay!" Kara said.

But once again Mark Acton appeared

unoffended. "It's okay," he told Kara. "It's a fair question." He turned back to the girl whose prettiness was now marred by a worried frown. "The only people who will be here are professional Realtors. Wednesdays are the traditional days for Realtor open houses. There will be a caravan coming through from each real estate office, and they'll be in and out very fast. They probably have fifteen listings to look at today. Believe me, nobody is going to touch anything."

"You're sure?" Lindsay fretted.

"I'm positive."

"And you'll be gone by five?"

He nodded. "Definitely. Probably by noon — one at the latest."

Kara picked up her purse from the hutch and steered her daughter toward the door. "And I'll be home by five, too. Then we can work on your social skills," she added pointedly, earning herself a glare from Lindsay.

"Have a good day," Mark said.

"It'll be a good day when you bring us an offer," Kara replied. As they walked out into a clear cool morning, she squeezed Lindsay's arm. "It's going to be okay," she said.

"I know," Lindsay sighed. "And I'm sorry. I'm trying — I really am."

"I know you are, sweetheart."

"How about if I go to Dawn's after practice?" Lindsay suggested as she got into the car. "Could you pick me up?"

Kara opened her door and got in, too. "Oh, Lord, do I have to?" she pleaded. "Even after I get back from the city, I've got to get groceries and go to the cleaners and half a dozen other things. Can't you just come home after practice?"

Lindsay hesitated, then decided further argument would be useless. "I guess," she mumbled. As her mother backed slowly out of the driveway, she asked, "Are you and Dad going to see the raven again?"

Kara hit the brake and stared at her. "The raven? What on earth are you talking about?"

A grin curled at the corners of Lindsay's mouth. "You know — that woman we were with on Sunday. Between her voice and that black coat, she seemed just like a great big raven."

Kara laughed. "Well, thanks a lot for that!" she said. "Now I'll never be able to look at her again without thinking of a big black screeching bird. And the sad part is, you're right!"

A few minutes later they pulled up in front of the high school. "Just don't buy anything ugly, okay?" Lindsay said before getting out, trying to control the tremor in her voice.

Their eyes met, and Kara knew how hard it was for her daughter to put on a brave face. "I promise," she said, reaching over to squeeze Lindsay's hand. Then she grinned. "Raven!" she repeated deliberately, before both of them would have dissolved into tears. "Mean, but a perfect description. Wait until I tell Dad."

A moment later she pulled away, leaving Lindsay standing at the curb, watching her go. In the rearview mirror, Kara could not see the tear running slowly down her daughter's cheek.

Mark Acton was feeling great. The open house was over, and now he was at Fishburn's — the pub where half the agents in Camden Green seemed to hang out — with his third stein of beer sweating in front of him.

Around him, people he knew were bragging noisily about the huge deals they'd put together, but Mark knew it was mostly bullshit — three-quarters of the people in Fishburn's had never sold a house for over a million, and that included him. And the Marshall place wasn't going to go for anywhere near a million, either, despite the granite countertops in the kitchen and the nice furniture Kara Marshall had filled the place with.

Not that the open house had gone badly — it hadn't. By eleven-thirty three caravans had come through, with Rick Mancuso and the Century 21 crowd as well as the bunch from ReMax.

And it wasn't just caravans coming through, either — there had been a fairly steady stream of independent brokers and agents as well, and he'd done his best to make sure every one of them left their cards in the rosewood bowl he'd set on the table in the entry hall. He gave out a lot of flyers and talked to as many of them as he could, and more than a few of the drop-ins told him they'd be calling for an appointment to show it to a client. The Marshalls would be very happy with his report.

But mostly he'd done what he liked to do best when he was doing a brokers' open: wander around, getting the feel of the place. He had figured out years ago that not only did every house have a unique feel to it, but so did almost every room in every house. The trick was to determine which rooms felt best and which worst, and then plan future tours so you got the bad rooms out of the way early and progressed steadily to the best ones. It was a strategy that had kept him at his agency's Million Dollar Roundtable every year for almost a decade, and it would work perfectly for the Marshall house, because it didn't have any bad rooms.

It was one of those houses that just felt good, and he'd known almost from the moment Kara and her daughter — Lindsay? Yeah, that was her name, Lindsay — had left him alone and he made his first quick tour, that it wasn't going to be hard to sell. He'd adjusted Kara's canisters and then gone into the living room, where he automatically picked a bit of lint from the carpeting and rearranged the pillows on the sofa and wing chairs. And just standing in the living room, he'd known. This was exactly the kind of place he himself wished he lived in.

Nothing in any of the other rooms had changed his mind, especially the kid's — Lindsay's.

He'd stood still in that room for a while, and it seemed he could feel her presence, and it felt good.

Pretty room for a pretty girl.

Then car doors started slamming outside, and he'd straightened the stack of color flyers one more time, checked his tie and his name tag, and put on his professional smile.

He opened the door, and the event began.

The hours had gone by quickly, and he listened to the same comments and answered the same questions, to the point where they almost became meaningless:

"Nice listing, Mark."

"This place'll sell in a heartbeat."

"What's the asking price?"

Over and over again he had patiently repeated every detail to every agent, all the time keeping an eye on the steady stream of agents who cruised through the downstairs, opening every door and checking the cabinets, then glancing quickly into the garage before heading upstairs to get a feel for the rest of the house.

What was it about garages? Mark wondered now as he drained half his third stein of beer. But of course he knew — garages were boring. And they were boring because people didn't live in them. *That's what everyone wanted to see at an open house. The places where people lived.*

After the agents came back downstairs, they'd checked out the kitchen one more time — always the kitchen, because that's

where people spend most of their lives —
then dropped their business cards in the
rosewood bowl on their way out and
picked up flyers.

He knew that the more flyers they picked
up, the better they liked the house.

And today they'd taken a lot.

Over and over, in the lull between each
caravan, Mark went back through the
house, moving things back to the exact
places they'd been, doing his best to
keep the house as the Marshalls had left
it that morning. After all, even though almost everybody loved poking around in
strangers' houses, nobody liked having
strangers poke around in their own. So he
always did his best to make it look as if no
one — not even he himself — had been
there at all. When the Marshalls came
home, everything should look exactly right.

It had been late in the day when Sam
Cousins and Ike North showed up. He
knew they'd be there at the end of the
event so they could all go to Fishburn's together. And he'd been especially pleased
when they came down from their tour of the
second floor and Ike spoke before they even
hit the landing at the bottom of the stairs.

"Is this going to be open on Sunday?"

Mark nodded.

"I'll bring some people by. I wish I could get them in tomorrow, but they're in the city and won't be able to make it until the weekend."

"You'll be lucky if this place is still available on Sunday," Sam Cousins put in.

Music to Mark's ears.

"So," Ike said, glancing around at the house, empty now except for the three of them. "Fishburn's?"

Mark nodded. "Meet you there. I have to lock up, so order me a cold one."

Alone, he'd gone through the rooms one last time, turning out all the lights, checking to see that the doors were locked and everything was exactly as it had been that morning. At the top of the stairs, he went first into Kara and Steve's bedroom, then their bath. Everything looked good. He turned out the lights and closed the door, then did the same with Steve's study and the guest room.

Then he'd gone to Lindsay's room and smiled as he turned out the light and closed the door, knowing that this was the room that would sell the house. It was neat and tidy, and you could almost feel the girl who lived in it. A sweet girl — a girl the Marshalls were fortunate to have.

At the front door, he'd picked up his

briefcase and the rosewood bowl and looked around one last time. Everything looked perfect, and he felt great.

And now, as he drained the third stein of beer and ordered a fourth, he still felt great.

Great, and lucky that the Marshalls had chosen him to sell their house.

CHAPTER NINE

I didn't expect the house to smell so sweet.

Nor was it the fake smell of rose petals in a bowl, or the kind of canned aroma of baking bread that so many agents fill houses with nowadays — as if anybody really bakes bread anymore! No, the house today was filled with the scent of love and harmony, and the moment I walked through the front door, I could feel the warmth of affection as well.

Some houses fairly reek of suspicion or wariness or anger, and in an instant you can feel the misery of the family who lives there.

Even worse, some houses have no fragrance at all — the poison of indifference hangs in the air.

But not the house I went to today — the house I found on the Internet last week that set me to tingling from the moment I went on the video tour.

This house has balance. Wholeness. Wholesomeness. Here there will be no religious icons on the walls, no evidence of secret perversions hidden beneath the mattresses.

That is the wonderful thing about being utterly nondescript; it is almost the same as being invisible. And being invisible is like being God.

Today I had nearly a whole day of being like God, and the feeling was sublime. As I moved from room to room, seeing everything, touching everything, feeling everything, no one noticed me at all.

Though people were milling around me nearly every moment I was in the house, it was as if I was utterly alone.

Alone with her.

And everything — *everything* — was perfect.

A calendar hung on the kitchen bulletin board next to some snapshots. One photo was of a blond girl in a cheerleading uniform, and the moment I saw the picture, I knew.

I knew her.

I'd always known her.

She was so obviously the one who lives in the girlish bedroom on the second floor whose every detail I memorized from the tour on the Internet.

And according to the wall calendar, this coming Sunday there would be an open house.

Below that, written in a slightly different hand — a girlish hand — was another notation: "Cheerleading practice."

And then another notation, written small and by yet a third hand: "House-hunting. Dinner at Café des Artistes?"

So it will be Sunday. What could be more perfect?

After seeing her picture and reading the calendar, I moved with newfound purpose through the first floor rooms just slowly enough to seem nothing more than a mildly interested agent, then headed up the stairs to steep myself in the aura of my new love — my perfect child.

The instant I walked into her room, I knew that she was the focal point, the absolute center, not only of this house, but of this family.

The lovely aroma that imbued the whole house was strongest there in her room, and I wanted to sink into the soft comfort of her bed, to run my hands over the sheets that enveloped her body every night, to feel myself sinking not just into her bed, but into her.

Yet I restrained myself.

I had to be patient.

My digital camera — one so tiny it can be concealed in the palm of my hand — captured every aspect of the room, but when I turned to her bed, I couldn't quite restrain myself.

I let the back of my hand run across her pillow, and as my skin touched the place where her head had lain, I could feel the residue of her psychic aura.

Oh, yes! It was her!

In that moment, I knew that my instincts had been right: this is the one! It isn't just the way she looks, but everything else as well.

After I touched her pillow, I touched everything else, too: the things on her desk, the photos on her dresser, the stuffed animals on the windowsill.

I opened her drawers and touched the soft silky garments she wears next to her skin.

Surely it was only natural to slip a pair of her panties into my pocket, given how they soothed my tortured soul.

With my fingers clutching the silken garment that was hidden in my pocket, I drifted invisibly down the stairs and out the door.

And in all the time I was in the house, nobody spoke to me.

It was as if nobody even saw me.

Indeed, it was as if I hadn't been there at all.

Just as it always has been — no one seeing anything.

As I made my way home, I held those panties pressed to my cheek, barely able to contain my euphoria.

Then, with her image clear in my mind, I crushed her panties in my fist.

Oh, yes — this is the one.

This is the girl, and finally I shall have her.

Soon. Very soon.

I can barely wait for Sunday.

CHAPTER TEN

Lindsay paused on the sidewalk, gazing at the house across the street. From here, it looked no different at all. It was still her house, still the familiar house she had grown up in.

The house that held all her secrets.

Yet even in the bright light of the sunny spring afternoon, something about it had changed. And she knew what it was.

All day long, people she didn't know and would never know had been wandering through the house.

Strangers.

Going through her room.

Going through her things.

Just the thought of it made her shudder, and now that she was across the street, all the horrible thoughts and feelings that had been plaguing her as the day crept by came flooding over her once again.

Except now they were even worse.

Throughout the day, she had been so preoccupied with the idea of strangers milling through her house and her room and her things that she'd found herself behaving completely different than usual as she walked through the halls at school. Where she'd always reached out to everyone she knew, touching their shoulders or their arms or even just brushing against their fingertips as they passed, today she didn't want to touch anybody else.

Then, when she'd gone to Dawn's house after practice and tried to explain how she was feeling, Dawn hadn't gotten it at all.

"They're just real estate people," Dawn said. "It's what they do. They don't even care what's in the house, as long as they can sell it."

"It's creepy," Lindsay declared, thinking of Mark Acton. But then she told Dawn about the Raven and they both started laughing, and for a few minutes she felt better. In fact, by the time she left Dawn's, the whole thing seemed silly.

But now she was home, and all her creepy feelings were back, only there was no place else to go.

Remembering that her mom should already be home, she crossed the street, walked across the lawn and onto the porch, and unlocked the front door.

The house smelled different.

And it didn't smell good, like when the cleaning lady came.

No, it smelled like people.

People she didn't know.

"Mom?" she called. "I'm home." The clothes washer was going, but her mother didn't answer. Lindsay dropped her backpack on the kitchen counter and ran up the stairs.

Her room smelled wrong, too, but not like the rest of the house. It smelled different.

There was a musky odor, and there was something about it that made her skin crawl.

Lindsay opened the window wide, and as she did, noticed that her stuffed animals had been moved. Why would anybody touch the stuffed animals she'd lined up on the sill?

"Mom?" she called out again, almost unconsciously.

She looked around. Everything else seemed to be in the right place. A fresh breeze came in through the window and some of the musky odor went away.

But not all of it.

And it was going to be even worse on Sunday, when dozens — maybe even hundreds — of people were going to go through the house. How could her parents stand it?

Lindsay hated the whole idea of it. *Hated* it.

"Hi, honey," Kara said from the doorway, startling Lindsay out of her reverie. "I was just on the phone with Mark Acton. He said he had twenty-eight people through and thought maybe we'd get an offer or two even before Sunday."

"Good," Lindsay said, feeling a surge of relief.

Kara leaned against the doorjamb and cocked her head quizzically. "That's a change of tune."

Lindsay shrugged. "I just don't want any more strangers in my room." Her eyes met her mother's. "They touched my stuff, Mom, just like I knew they would. They moved things around."

Kara sighed heavily. "Nobody touched anything, Linds. Besides, how could you tell if somebody moved something?"

"I just can," Lindsay insisted, and wrinkled her nose at the musky odor that still hung faintly in the air. "And it stinks in here. Can't you smell it?" When her

94

mother only offered her the kind of indulgent smile that told her she was being humored, not taken seriously, Lindsay felt her face getting red. She wasn't a child anymore, and her mother shouldn't treat her like one. But before she could say anything, her mother seemed to sense her mood and quickly changed the subject.

"Dad's coming home tonight. And we saw some good places today."

"I guess that's good," Lindsay sighed. She flopped on the bed, and the strange musky smell grew stronger.

It was on her pillow!

She jumped off the bed as if it were on fire. "Mom, somebody was touching my pillow. My *pillow!*"

"Honey —" Kara began, but Lindsay didn't let her finish.

"I'm telling you," she said, snatching up the pillow. "Smell this!"

Kara took a quick sniff of the pillow, then shrugged. "Sorry, honey — it just smells like pillow to me. Old pillow, maybe, but just pillow."

When her mother went downstairs to start dinner, Lindsay ripped the pillowcase off and threw the pillow in the corner.

But it didn't matter. Everything had changed.

This room, she knew, would never feel the same again.

Maybe it might be a good idea to move after all.

CHAPTER ELEVEN

Why she woke up, Lindsay didn't know. All she knew was that one moment she'd been sound asleep and the next wide-awake.

Wide-awake and listening.

But for what? The silence of the night was almost palpable.

And then she heard it.

The sound of breathing. She relaxed, certain it was her mom or dad checking up on her. Then she realized the door was closed and the room was dark. Faint light came in around the edges of the closed curtains, and that — along with familiarity — illuminated her room just enough so she knew the room was empty.

And yet she could still hear it: raspy, and uneven.

And now she could smell something, too, and as the scent filled her nostrils, she knew what it was: the same musky odor that had hung in the room when she'd come home this afternoon.

And now someone *was* in her room.

Stay still, she told herself. *Stay still and maybe he'll just go away.* She tried to regulate her breathing, but her heart was pounding so hard it was all she could do to keep from gasping for breath.

Though she still couldn't see him, she felt him move closer, and as the smell grew stronger, she could feel the warmth of his breath on her arm.

He was going to kiss her!

She wanted to scream — wanted to turn on her bedside lamp and flood the room with light, but she couldn't.

She couldn't move at all.

The hot breath moved up her arm to her neck, then something touched her hair.

The musky aroma was so heavy she wanted to gag, but even that was beyond her. She felt paralyzed. She tried desperately to move her mouth, to move her hand, but her lips were numb and her arms had become so heavy that her muscles didn't have the strength to lift them.

She was going to faint! But if she fainted, she wouldn't know what was happening.

What he was doing to her?

She had to know. Had to!

Now she felt a hand snake up under the covers, and she struggled with her paralyzed body to shrink away from it, to strike out, to hit him, to sink her fingernails into his face and rip the skin from his cheek. But her body wouldn't obey her commands. She lay frozen as the strange aroma filled her nostrils and the hands roamed over her body.

How had it happened? How had he gotten in? But she already knew — he'd been there all afternoon, hiding, waiting. . . .

A tiny, helpless whimper finally crept from her lips.

One of his hands caressed her cheek and then covered her mouth while the other hand covered her breast, and once again she willed her body to respond. Once again she tried to struggle, tried to scream, and again succeeded in making a tiny sound, but it was no more than a pitiful gurgle in the back of her throat. Yet somehow it was enough to break the paralyzing fear, and then she took a deep breath and found her voice.

She sat straight up screaming.

The hands vanished.

Then her parents were there, and the light was on, and her mom was smoothing the hair from her sweating forehead.

What had happened? He was there —
she *knew* he was there! She'd heard him
and smelled him and felt him touching
her! But now her parents were with her
and she was afraid she might throw up.

"Honey," Kara said, perching on the
edge of the bed and gently drawing a
strand of hair away from her face. "It's all
right — it was just a bad dream."

A bad dream? She rubbed her face.
Smelled her hands.

The aroma was gone; all she smelled was
the almond lotion she'd used before going
to bed.

Her gaze shifted from her mother to her
father, who stood at the foot of her bed,
wearing his pajama bottoms and a white
T-shirt, his eyes clouded with concern.

"Daddy?" she squeaked out.

Her father came around, sat on the bed
next to her mother and rubbed her hand as
gently as her mother had eased the hair
from her forehead. "It was just a nightmare, kitten."

Her eyes darted around the room as if
they were unwilling to accept her father's
words, but everything looked normal.

So it *had* been a dream — a nightmare.
But she hadn't had one since she was little.
And it had been so real.

She took a deep breath, embarrassed now that she had yelled in her sleep and awakened her parents. "I'm sorry," she whispered.

Kara smiled and kept smoothing her hair. "Nothing to be sorry about, darling — everybody has bad dreams."

Lindsay managed a smile. "I feel so stupid. I —"

"Would you like some warm milk?" her mom asked. "That always cured the bad dreams when you were little."

Lindsay shook her head. "I better just go back to sleep. I've got a science test in the morning."

"We'll leave the hall light on," her father said.

Lindsay nodded, and snuggled under her covers, which smelled just fine now. No strange aroma — just the scent of her own lotion.

Her parents kissed her, then turned out the light and left the room. The hall light went on, and her father came back to close her bedroom door. But he left it open a couple of inches, without her even asking. "Wrap yourself in the wings of your guardian angel, kitten," he said. "She'll hide you from the nightmares."

"Thanks, Daddy." He hadn't said that to

her in years — not since she was in third grade, at least. But tonight the words gave her the comfort she needed.

Her father's shadow vanished from the crack in the doorway, and a few seconds later she heard the master bedroom door close.

She tried to relax, reminding herself that nobody was in her room. Yet she was sure she wouldn't go back to sleep, even with her parents in the next room, because despite their reassurances, she knew that even though her room was empty now, it hadn't been earlier in the day.

Someone *had* been in her room — someone evil — and he'd left something behind; something more than just the vestiges of his strange aroma.

And she knew that no matter what she did, she would never be able to rid her room of his presence.

Suddenly, in the darkness of the night, she wished the house would be sold tomorrow and they could move away. Far, far away, where the man who had been in her room could never find her.

She lay quietly, staring at the silhouette of the stuffed elephant on her windowsill — the stuffed elephant the man had moved.

Getting out of bed, she picked the elephant off the sill and put it in the hall outside her door. She felt better with it gone, just as she'd felt better after she tore the pillowcase off earlier. She got back into bed and again told herself that she was safe.

But she still couldn't sleep.

"I knew it," Kara said as she and Steve got back in bed. "I woke up about ten seconds before she screamed, and I *knew* something was wrong." Steve put his arm around her and drew her close, so her head lay on his chest, and she fell gratefully into the luxurious feel of his warmth. "Remember when she fell off that horse at camp and broke her collarbone?"

She felt Steve's chest move as he nodded.

"I knew then, too. Remember? We were at the Billingslys for dinner, and suddenly I knew I had to get home, even though we'd barely been gone an hour. And by the time we got home, there was a call on the machine. Remember?"

"I remember," Steve said in a tone that told her she'd told the story a few times too often.

But it wasn't just the story that Kara remembered. It was hearing the terrible words: *Lindsay . . . accident . . . hospital* . . . on the message machine. "A mother knows these things," she said. "This move is even harder for her than I thought it would be." She put her arm around Steve and clung to him. "I feel so guilty."

"Hey, it was only a nightmare," he said, pulling her closer. "It'll all be over soon."

"It wasn't 'only' a nightmare," Kara said. "She's upset. She's upset enough that she was absolutely terrified."

"And this afternoon she'd convinced herself that someone moved things around in her room, too," Steve said. "And went through her drawers and rubbed his face on her pillow, and even took her underwear."

"You think any of it could have happened?" Kara asked, her voice sounding to her as young and as vulnerable as Lindsay's.

"Not a chance," Steve replied. "There was no one in the house but a bunch of real estate people. I think she talked herself into that nightmare. You watch — she'll be fine."

"I guess," Kara sighed. "At least she will be once we're out of here and into the city and you can be home every night to take care of your wife and daughter." She snuggled against Steve, and a short while later his regular breathing turned into a light snore.

But there was no sleep for Kara; though Lindsay only had a nightmare, she wasn't prone to dramatics or hysterics. If her daughter said someone had been in her underwear drawer, she believed that someone had.

CHAPTER TWELVE

I believe I dreamed of this morning every moment that I slept. I've slept a lot since Wednesday — after being in her house — being in her room — feeling her presence — filling my nostrils with her sweet aroma — being awake without her seemed too painful to bear.

So I slept. Hours? Days? I really don't remember.

But I remember dreaming of Sunday morning, and when this morning finally came, I think I knew it even before I awoke.

I felt it — a thrill surging through every vein and every nerve of my body. I savored the feeling, delaying the moment when I finally rose. I donned my favorite robe — a black one with a bloodred lining — and my outside slippers before going down to retrieve the paper from the spot the boy always leaves it. It was quiet — I saw no one else, nor even heard a car.

I liked that.

Not that I was the least bit concerned, let alone actually worried — I believe I looked as casual as anyone could look, bringing in a Sunday newspaper. But once I was back inside, I had the paper torn open before it reached the table.

And there on the front page — the front page! — of the Real Estate section was the open house ad. It was a good-sized ad, too; this agent had spent some money to attract a good group of prospects.

And all of this — the placement, as well as the size of the ad — works in my favor.

Not that it was perfect. The photograph of the house was taken from an awkward angle, so it didn't look its best, but there was an intriguing description, the kind that would attract a lot of curious people.

The more the better.

I circled the ad with my red felt-tip pen and felt the excitement and anticipation building inside me.

It is a feeling of which I never tire.

Still, I need to rein it in. I need to be patient.

I need to keep control.

I sipped a cup of coffee while I planned my day. The open house begins at 1:00

p.m.; I would arrive about two hours later, just when the most people would be there. Earlier, people will still be digesting their lunch, and later it will be nothing but the last minute stragglers with an agent trying to shoo them all out.

But not right at 3:00 p.m., either. People tend to be aware when it is an even hour, and remember things more clearly. Perhaps thirteen or fourteen minutes before three would be appropriate.

Yes, I believe that will be perfect.

I've already charted out what time to bathe, what time to dress, and the route I shall take to get there, of course.

And the place to park. I know the garages of the neighbors. I know the alleys that the service people use, and I also know that those alleys are blissfully deserted on Sundays. I can idle quietly down the alley, park, walk around the block, and enter the house as invisibly as pollen on the breeze.

I did all that on Wednesday, and I think I've done it dozens of times since in my dreams.

It is all imprinted in my memory, and nothing will go wrong.

My clothes have been laid out since yesterday morning. I shall wear brown corduroy slacks with a brown and blue plaid shirt. In those colors, I will blend right in with the look of the house — and all the other lookers.

I think of it as camouflage. No one will even notice me.

And with luck, it will rain! Rain means more activity at an open house. Rain means that the agent hosting the open house will spend more time looking at the carpeting to make certain that people are wiping their feet or wearing those stupid little booties than who is coming and going. (Perhaps I should add a brown sweater vest to my costume — it may be spring, but there can still be a chill in the air.) But most important, rain means the house will be gloomier and I will feel more at home.

More at home.

Now why did I say that? After all, I already feel at home in that house.

In that bedroom.

That sweet, virginal bedroom.

I can't wait. . . .

CHAPTER THIRTEEN

"Please?" Lindsay pleaded. "I went with you last weekend and it was awful. And I was awful! I was rude to that real estate lady, and I hated everything, and I almost threw up in the lobby of that one building. Why would you even want me to go?" She saw her father glance uncertainly at her mother, and decided to play another card. "Besides, I have cheerleading practice."

Kara shook her head. "We want to make sure we buy something we can all live with, honey. That's why we want you with us when we look — you need to help us decide."

"But it was all so awful last week," Lindsay repeated.

"I know it was, but today it will be better, and we really want you to spend the day with us in the city."

"With you and the Raven."

"C'mon, kitten," Steve said. "It'll be

fun." He wrapped his toast around two pieces of bacon and bit off half of it, washing it down with coffee.

"You think that's fun?" Lindsay asked incredulously. "Well, it isn't. I don't even know what I'm supposed to be looking at in those places — all they look like to me is a bunch of empty rooms that don't seem like anyone could ever live in them. Can't you guys choose?"

Kara shook her head again. "We are not going to buy a place without you seeing it first. We're a family, remember? And I'm afraid I don't really see the point of you going to practice, either, since you're not going to be on the squad here next year."

"You don't know that," Lindsay said, a note of desperation coming into her voice. "I mean — not for sure. Maybe the house won't sell, and I'll at least get to graduate with my friends. Or maybe you can move to the city right away, and I'll move in with Dawn or something."

Kara looked at Steve, and he could see that she was wavering. "What about that nightmare you had the other night?" he said to his daughter. "I'm not sure what time we'll be back, and you don't want to come home to an empty house this afternoon, do you?"

111

"I'll go to Dawn's after practice and hang out until you get home," Lindsay said, speaking so quickly that her parents both knew it wasn't an idea she'd come up with on the spur of the moment.

Simultaneously, both Steve and Kara sighed in surrender, neither willing to have the argument expand into a full-fledged fight that would ruin the day for all of them. "I guess that works," Kara finally said.

"If it's okay with your mom, it's okay with me," Steve agreed, shrugging. "But I still wish —"

"The open house here is from one to four," Kara interjected, cutting Steve off before he could rekindle the argument. "We should be back by five — six at the latest."

Not if we find a place and decide to write an offer, Steve thought, but refrained from saying it, certain that the idea of buying a place today would only upset Lindsay even more. "If we're going to be later than that, we'll call. Okay?"

Lindsay nodded, feeling better now that she realized she'd won the argument. But then she saw her mother's eyes cloud.

"Oh, Lord," Kara groaned. "I forgot — we're having dinner with the Bennetts."

Steve's brows arched as he turned to Lindsay, seizing the dinner as one last chance to convince her to change her mind. "C'mon, kitten. We're having dinner at Café des Artistes. You'll love it — come with us."

For a moment she seemed to waver. "Who else is going to be there?" she asked.

"Mitch Bennett and his wife."

Lindsay's eyes rolled. "Ooh, that sounds like a lot of fun. A whole evening of watching an old man grope his trophy wife. I think I'll pass."

"Lindsay!" Kara said, even though she didn't disagree with her daughter. Mitch Bennett had dumped JoAnne — and there was no other word but "dumped" — for a girl scarcely ten years older than Lindsay. And since Mitch Bennett was also third in seniority in Steve's firm, no one could say a word about it. All any of them could do was pretend that the new wife was faintly interesting, which she wasn't.

Steve, thankfully, didn't argue, either. "Okay, then. You stay at Dawn's," he said. "Can you spend the night there?"

"I'll be fine!" Lindsay insisted. She rose from her chair, picked up the milk and her dirty dishes and took them to the dishwasher.

"Then we're going to take off," Kara said, glancing at her watch. "We're meeting Rita Goldman at eleven-thirty. Mark will be here soon to go through the house and get himself set up — I told him we'd all be gone by ten. Do you want to stay here until practice?"

Lindsay's brow furrowed. "With that real estate guy? No way. How about if you just drop me at Dawn's?"

"How about if you say 'please' and offer me a smile with that request?" Kara countered.

Lindsay pasted a hugely exaggerated smile onto her face and drawled an equally exaggerated "Puh-leeeeeze?" and suddenly all three of them were laughing.

Maybe the day was going to work out for all of them after all.

Fifteen minutes later Steve stood in the kitchen, waiting — as he always did — for the two females in his life to come downstairs and get in the car. It was already ten after ten, and they would have to hurry if they were going to meet Rita Goldman on schedule. He opened his mouth to yell up the stairs, thought better of it, and decided to kill whatever time they took by taking a swipe at the countertop, adjusting the coffeepot and putting the dishcloth into the laundry. As he came back into the kitchen, he realized just how much he was going to miss this house. He and Kara had designed it themselves, and supervised almost every moment of its construction, and now that it had that perfect lived-in look, and the landscaping had matured into the vision they'd only been able to see in their minds for the first fifteen years, they were leaving it.

For just a moment he was almost tempted to skip the meeting with Rita Goldman, take the house off the market, and figure out some other way to solve their problems. But even as the thought came to mind, he knew there was no other way. The die was cast, and it was time to move on. But if only —

The doorbell jerked him out of his reverie.

"Mr. Marshall!" Mark Acton said, coming through the front door as Steve entered the living room. "I didn't expect you to be home."

Steve uttered a hollow chuckle. "We're trying to get out of here," he said, offering the other man his hand. "You know women."

Mark Acton's hand felt limp in Steve's. "Don't I know it!" he said. "Can't live with 'em, and can't live without 'em!" As the tired cliché lay quivering between them like a dying fish, Steve understood exactly why Lindsay hadn't wanted to be here when the agent arrived. Acton seemed not to notice his reaction. "I just thought I'd get things arranged in the house," he said, "get my signs up and then come back about twelve-thirty."

"That's fine," Steve said. He turned and called up the stairs. "Ladies? Time to go!"

Seconds later Kara and Lindsay came downstairs, Kara carrying her purse and the portfolio she'd been keeping of Manhattan real estate, Lindsay with her gym bag slung over her shoulder.

Steve watched as Acton greeted them. While Kara shook the agent's hand warmly and gave him a few last minute instructions, Lindsay avoided him completely, walking around behind Steve so she wouldn't have to touch Mark Acton's hand or even say hello to him. And he realized he felt more sympathy for his daughter's open dislike of the man than for his wife's apparent warmth.

Not that he didn't understand what Kara was doing. For years he'd watched her treat people he knew she despised as if they were her closest friends.

And as a lawyer, he was even better at it than she was.

"Well, we're in your capable hands now," he said, slapping Acton jovially on the shoulder. "I've got a feeling you're going to sell this place today!"

"I've got that feeling, too," he replied as Steve followed his wife and daughter toward the kitchen and the garage beyond. "I think we've got a good chance of doing just that."

"Excellent," Steve said. *And if you do,* he added silently to himself, *I'll never have to see you again.*

Then he was out the garage door and put Mark Acton — and his open house — out of his mind, focusing instead on finding his family a new home. But as he drove away and glanced at the house in the rearview mirror, he knew that no matter where they went, it wouldn't be as wonderful as the house they were leaving.

After all, despite the problems they'd had lately, it was a house that had no bad memories.

CHAPTER FOURTEEN

Mark Acton glanced at the clock on the mantel: 2:45. Only another hour and fifteen minutes and he could close up the house, head over to Fishburn's, and start unwinding over a cold one. But right now he still had a houseful of people, and more were coming — in fact, they'd started arriving early, and continued streaming steadily in since even before the official one o'clock opening.

Which meant the ad had worked.

As had putting signs up early.

And the weather was cooperating, with a low, chilly cloud cover and threats of rain — just bad enough to keep people from going jogging, playing softball, or heading out on the Sound for a day of boating. But not bad enough to keep them at home. Indeed, it was what Mark thought of as "perfect open house weather," and obviously a lot of people had agreed with him.

The first couple had knocked on the door, then opened it and called out a "Yoo-hoo" before he even had the brochures laid out on the dining room table.

That alone had been enough to tell him this was going to be a good open house. Even if he didn't sell the place today, there would be plenty of opportunities to prospect for new customers. He'd given out a couple of dozen business cards, and almost as many flyers. The worst that could happen would be that he'd pick up a new client or two, and if he couldn't sell one of them this house, he had half a dozen more houses to show them some other time.

"Hi!" The woman's cheery greeting jerked Mark out of his thoughts, and he put on his best smile and started toward her. But even before he was close enough to offer her his hand, she held up her own as if to fend him off. "We're just nosy neighbors."

"Hey, that's fine!" Mark assured them, giving no visible sign that his interest had dropped from high to next to none. "C'mon in and look around." Then he fished a business card out of his pocket. "You live in a great neighborhood," he said. "But if you ever decide you're ready to make a change, give me a call. I'll bet you have no idea what you could get for your own house."

"I think we're starting to," the male half of the couple said as they headed off to look at the kitchen.

As soon as they were gone, another couple came through the front door, but they were very young — maybe newlyweds — and Mark could see at a glance that there was no way they could afford anything like what he was selling today. Still, you never knew what the future held, so he was pleasant enough to them, and by the time he'd given them a quick rundown on the house and turned them loose to poke around on their own, more people were arriving.

The next couple said they were working with an agent across town, and that was a good sign — whoever it was hadn't come up with what they wanted, but they were seriously interested in finding something to buy. Mark gave them a personal tour, pointing out every feature of the house and implying that there was enough interest in the place that they'd better run back to their guy within the hour with earnest money ready in their hands.

Just as he was about to lead them up to the second floor, a single man came through the front door. Mark called out a greeting to him, but knew this wasn't a house for a single man, and that a married man would never buy a house without his wife seeing it. If this guy was previewing it for her, then he probably knew what he was doing, so Mark saw no point in wasting time on the latest arrival unless he came back with his wife. Then, as he was turning away, another man came in, and for a moment Mark reconsidered his appraisal — perhaps the two men were a couple, which was a whole nother kettle of fish. This could be the perfect house in a perfect neighborhood for two well-heeled, professional men. Most of the kids in the neighborhood were growing up, and soon it would be pretty much an adult community, just right for two men who were getting too old for the city.

Mark continued talking to the couple on the stairs while keeping an eye on the two men, but as they moved off in different directions, it was clear they weren't together. His interest in both of them dropped to zero — even lower than was his interest in the neighbors. Refocusing on the couple he was escorting, he deftly moved them toward the bedrooms.

Then, at four o'clock, everything was

suddenly over. The house emptied out quickly. The day had been a success, and he sat down on the couch to enjoy a few minutes of quiet, then opened the guest book and began making notes about as many of the people as he could remember. Already, he'd divided them into those who were prospects for this house, or another house, or just looky-loos to be forgotten, at least until he saw them again at his next open house. Then he began to mentally associate each person in the book with the faces he'd been seeing all day. For the most part it was easy — he'd always had a good memory for names and faces — and today it had mainly been couples, as usual, and only one single man.

No, that wasn't right. He remembered *two* single men.

So one of them obviously hadn't signed in.

The one who had — Rick Mancuso — had introduced himself when they'd run into each other in the master bedroom, and Mark had no trouble recalling what he looked like.

But what about the other man?

The one who hadn't signed the book?

Apparently he'd merely come and gone, not staying more than a minute or two.

Which was okay — it happened all the time.

But the funny thing was, he couldn't remember anything about him.

Nothing.

Weird, given how good his memory for people had always been. Still, it had been a great day. Though no one had written an offer on the spot, Mark was sure that Ike North would bring something in tomorrow or the next day, and he had a couple of follow-up calls to make, one of which he was fairly certain would result in an offer. The Marshalls were going to be very happy that they'd given him the listing.

After a quick walk-through of the house to make certain everything was as it ought to be, he locked it up and headed for Fishburn's.

And didn't give the man he couldn't remember another thought.

CHAPTER FIFTEEN

Lindsay slammed her locker door, liking the sound as it echoed through the halls. She loved being at school when nobody else was there — somehow, it made her feel special. She couldn't quite describe it even to herself, but that didn't matter because even if she could, she'd never say anything about it to anybody. They'd just laugh at her for feeling anything but disgust at having to be at school at all.

But she liked the quiet of the huge, cavernous building that was usually throbbing with noise and activity, and she knew she was going to miss it next year as she walked down the polished floor of the hallway and pushed out through the front doors out into the chilly, overcast afternoon.

Dawn was waiting for her outside. "What are you doing tonight?" Lindsay asked as they began walking home. For the last hour she'd been trying to figure out how to get Dawn to invite her over for dinner — or even to spend the night — without revealing that she was afraid to go home, at least until her folks were back from the city.

Dawn groaned. "I have to go to my dad's for dinner." Dawn's father and stepmother lived across town — not far, but not close enough to walk, either. "He's been on the road for a week, and I haven't seen him for a while, so he's picking me up at our house at five." She checked her watch. "I better hurry — I want to change before he gets there."

"My parents are apartment hunting in the city," Lindsay said, kicking at a pebble on the sidewalk. "They won't be home until late. They're having dinner."

"Cool!" Dawn said, oblivious to the gloom in Lindsay's voice. "You'll get the house to yourself. I love it when my mom takes off — I make popcorn for dinner and play my music as loud as I want."

"Yeah," Lindsay said. "Except I don't feel much like that tonight." She didn't quite know how to invite herself to Dawn's father's, but she didn't want to go home alone. She glanced at Dawn, then decided to take the plunge directly. "Can I come with you to your dad's?"

"I wish," Dawn said. "But it's 'quality' time night." Her voice took on a mocking singsong note as she said *quality.* "He's always wanting more 'quality' time. 'Quality time with my princess,' is what he always says."

"I think that's nice," Lindsay said, cocking her head.

Dawn rolled her eyes. "Yeah, right! If he really wanted 'quality time,' maybe he shouldn't have left us in the first place. Sorry, but I think he and his new wife are total dorks. And she'd pitch a hissy if I brought someone over with less than two weeks' notice." At Lindsay's crestfallen look, Dawn touched her shoulder. "I'm sorry."

"It's all right."

Dawn stopped walking and reached for Lindsay's arm, but Lindsay kept walking to avoid looking her friend in the eye. The problem was, she didn't want to go home to an empty house, but didn't want to tell Dawn that she was afraid, given how stupid she felt about the whole thing.

What happened the other night was only a bad dream — nothing had actually happened.

But still, she didn't want to go home alone to a house where people had been

126

roaming and poking around, going through her things all day long.

And she didn't want Dawn to ask her what was wrong, because she was afraid she'd start to cry.

"You okay?" Dawn finally asked, catching up to her.

"Yeah, I'm all right," Lindsay answered. "I'm just depressed, I guess."

"Depressed? You think *you're* depressed? I have to spend the whole evening with Anthony and *Sheeela* and their little brat."

Lindsay glanced at Dawn, seizing the opportunity to turn the conversation away from herself. "Come on — you like Robert. What is he, two? How can you not like a two-year-old?"

"Yeah, actually, I do. I like having a little brother. He's the only good thing about going over there. I can relate to him. Sheila is beyond me. And what Dad sees in her . . ."

Lindsay tuned out Dawn's rant about her stepmother, wishing she could unburden herself about how scared she was to go home to the empty house, but she couldn't figure out how to approach it without having Dawn think she was being stupid. She began casting around in her mind for somewhere else she could go.

As they approached the corner where they would go their separate ways, Dawn caught Lindsay's arm, stopping her. "Don't be depressed. Please?"

"I just don't want to move."

"I know. Just don't stress, okay? I mean, it hasn't happened yet, has it?"

Lindsay shook her head. "And maybe it won't happen. Maybe we'll figure out a way for me to stay through next year."

"We will," Dawn assured her. "Call me. You've got my dad's number, right?"

Lindsay grinned. "Speed dial six."

"Aren't you the efficient one," Dawn said. Then: "Hey — you did good today."

"So did you," Lindsay replied. "You're going to be head cheerleader next year."

"Unless you are."

"Fat chance. Especially if I'm not even here!"

Dawn shrugged and spread her arms. "Miracles happen."

Lindsay regarded her best friend darkly. "Yeah," she said. "But not to me." She turned away then, crossed the street, and sped up as she walked down the last two blocks toward the house.

Walking slowly, after all, was only going to postpone the inevitable.

Lindsay warily eyed the OPEN HOUSE sign the agent had left leaning against the garage, as if it were a cobra coiled and ready to strike at her. The wind had come up, bringing with it a cloud that was even darker than her mood, and now a few raindrops were falling on her bare arms. It was as if spring had vanished back into winter, with late afternoon darkness closing in around her. She rubbed her arms, shivering, but even as she tried to warm herself, she knew the chill she was feeling came more from the solid evidence the forgotten sign provided that people — strangers — had been in the house all afternoon.

And now, knowing that, she didn't want to go inside.

She wanted to turn away and go somewhere else.

Anywhere else.

She looked up and down the street, but the yards and sidewalks were empty, and nowhere did she see a neighbor with whom she could strike up a conversation, putting off the moment when she would have to go into the house.

Maybe even cadge a dinner invitation, without having to explain. And she wasn't about to tell anyone that, and sound like a little girl too young to be left at home by herself.

Besides, she'd come home to an empty house dozens of times — maybe hundreds! Except that today was different. Today —

"*Stop it!*" she whispered to herself, rubbing her arms again, then walking determinedly up to the front door to let herself in with her key.

And felt once more the urge to turn around and walk away, to go somewhere else — anywhere else — until her parents came home.

Again she conquered the urge to flee, turned the key, and let herself into the house.

Silence.

She scanned the living room, and everything looked exactly as it had this morning, almost as if nobody had been there at all. Feeling calmer, she went to the kitchen.

The agent had left a note on the counter. Dozens of people had been through the house — dozens! But that was a good thing, Lindsay reminded herself. It was what they wanted! And maybe one of those dozens of people would buy the house and she'd never have to go through this again.

She took a deep breath and looked at the clock. Five-thirty, on the dot. Her parents would surely be home by ten. Four and a half hours wasn't a big deal — she'd do a little homework, watch a little TV, and maybe make a plate of nachos. . . .

She turned on the television, more for the background noise than because she wanted to see the news, and made herself go through the rest of the downstairs.

Except for the note from the agent and a few flyers that still lay on the dining room table, the house looked exactly as it always had.

And it would be the same upstairs, she thought.

Everything would be exactly as she'd left it, and no one would have gone through her drawers, and there would be nothing wrong at all.

Except she still didn't want to go up to her room, and found herself gazing at the stairs with the same feeling of dread with which she'd looked at the house itself only a few minutes ago.

And she felt even colder than when she'd been out standing in the chill and drear of the rainy afternoon.

"Stop it!" she commanded herself again, barely realizing she was speaking out loud to an empty room. "You're just freaking yourself out." The sound of her own voice somehow making her feel better, she got a Diet Pepsi from the refrigerator, and then mounted the stairs.

Her room looked exactly as she had left it. She sniffed, and thought she could still smell traces of the strange odor that had hung in her room on Wednesday.

No, she told herself. *You're just imagining it!*

She went to her underwear drawer and slowly opened it. The tiny scrap of paper she'd left balanced on the front edge was still there.

Undisturbed.

Her drawer had not been opened.

See? she told herself. *Nobody went through my stuff.*

She picked up the fragment of paper with a wet fingertip, shook it off into her wastebasket, and felt much better as it dropped away.

The closet door was closed tightly, as she always left it. When she was little, she had always been afraid that the bogeyman was in the closet, and whenever she called out to her parents to tell them how afraid she was of the person in the closet, her father would march right to the door and pull it wide open while she cowered in the big mahogany bed, clutching the covers around her neck.

And of course there had never been anyone — or any*thing* — in the closet.

Now, as she stared at the door, those childhood terrors came flooding back, but she forced them aside, took a deep breath, and did as her father had always done. She walked right over and opened the closet door wide.

And, as always, there was nothing there.

No bogeyman, or anything else, either. She smiled then, realizing how silly her fears had been.

And still were! That was it — she'd been afraid that somehow the bogeyman — who had never been anything more than a figment of her own childish imagination — had somehow gotten into the house when it was open.

Stupid! Stupid, stupid, stupid! There was nothing to be afraid of, and never had been. She was older now — almost grown up. How could she have been so dumb as to let herself be afraid of the *bogeyman?*

Suddenly, things were back to normal, her fears fell away, and she felt so good, she almost wanted to dance. Flipping on the CD player, she took a drink of the soda, then did a couple of pirouettes that weren't quite in time to the music. But who cared? Everything was fine again.

She perched on the edge of her bed and rested one of her feet on the step stool that still stood next to the mahogany four-poster, even though she hadn't had to use it to climb into the high bed for years. She untied her shoes, pulled off her socks, and dangled her feet for a moment, then slid off the bed and took the socks to the laundry hamper.

A second later her shorts and T-shirt joined the socks.

Clad only in her sports bra and bikini panties, she stuck one foot in a slipper that lay by the bed, then looked for the other one, fishing around under the bed with her bare foot, feeling for it. How far could she have kicked it last night?

She got down on her knees and was about to reach under the bed for the way-ward slipper when her cell phone rang. It startled her, and she banged her knuckles against the hard mahogany of the bed frame as she jerked her hand back. With one slipper on, and sucking at her stinging knuckle, she flopped onto the bed and reached over to pick up the phone from the nightstand.

"Hey," Dawn said before she'd even spoken. "You okay?"

"I guess so," Lindsay replied, shaking

her hand, then pressing it against the pillow to try and ease the stinging. "Are you at your dad's?"

"Yeah, we just got here. Sheila's making dinner and Robert isn't up from his nap yet." She hesitated, then: "You sure you're all right?"

"I'm fine," Lindsay insisted. "I just banged my hand, that's all. At least it's the same one I twisted my wrist on last week." She gazed dolefully at her knuckle, which was already turning black and blue. "So what's your dad doing? How come you're not having 'quality time'?"

Dawn groaned. "He's working, of course. Said he had reports he had to e-mail in before tomorrow morning. He'll be finished by dinner, and then we'll eat, watch *60 Minutes*, and then I'll go home. It's so totally stupid. I wish we both could have just gone to my house."

"I do, too," Lindsay confessed. "Ever since Mom and Dad decided to sell it, I hate it here. I —"

"Oops," Dawn interrupted. "I've got another call. Want to hold?"

Lindsay hesitated, then: "I guess not — I need to change and figure out what to do till Mom and Dad get home. I just wish —"

"Okay," Dawn said, and Lindsay could tell by her voice that she was already thinking about the other call. "See you tomorrow." Dawn clicked off, and the cell phone went dead in Lindsay's hand. She put it back onto the charger on her nightstand, feeling bleak at how far away they were moving and the difference that would make in her friendships with Dawn and everyone else.

She looked down at her feet. One slipper on, one slipper off. Somehow, the lost slipper suddenly seemed appropriate — one of her slippers was just as lost as she felt, and the other was right where it was supposed to be.

Just like her. Supposed to be right here in Camden Green, but half of her already feeling lost in New York.

Sighing, she knelt down once more to fish the other slipper out from under the bed.

And smelled it again.

That awful, disgusting, musky odor that had filled her room on Wednesday, but that her mother hadn't been able to smell.

Now it was back, and stronger than —

With sudden, horrifying certainty she knew, and all her terror came crashing back in on her.

He was in her room.

Now.

Under her bed — the bed that had always been her final refuge, the one place where she felt utterly safe.

And he was there.

Waiting.

Paralyzed, Lindsay knew she had to move, knew she had to scream, to run, to get out.

Get out!

Now she could hear him breathing.

Her heart pounded so hard, she thought it was going to explode, and her mind raced. But panic was already overwhelming reason, and her terror seemed to have utterly sapped her of the ability to move or even cry out. . . .

CHAPTER SIXTEEN

"I liked the place on West Eighty-eighth," Kara said as Steve pulled onto Route 25A and headed out to the north shore of the Island.

"What wasn't to like?" Steve asked, turning on the windshield wipers as rain began to dribble from the clouds that had been gathering. When the wipers did little more than smear the city grime across the windshield, he sprayed them with cleaner, which barely helped. "Except that we can't afford it," he sighed.

"I know, but —"

"No buts, Kara." He glanced over at her. "I knew we shouldn't even have looked at that one. It's out of our price range, and I don't see the advantage in trading one bad situation for another."

"You got a raise," Kara argued, but Steve could hear more hope than certainty in her voice. "If we get a good price for the house and give up your city apartment, I don't see why —"

"Maybe after a year or so," Steve interrupted. "Maybe after I see how my promotion works out, and get another raise, and we're back on our feet again."

"After a year?" Kara echoed. "What would be the point? By then Lindsay will be off to college and we won't need anything that big. And the way prices are going in Manhattan, we could sell it at a big enough profit to buy ourselves something really terrific!"

Steve sighed. He'd liked the apartment, too. It was big and bright and airy and had everything they'd hoped to find. But it was a quarter of a million more than the absolute outside limit of what they'd agreed they could afford. "I just don't see it. I mean, it's perfect, but so what? We just don't have the money."

"But it has granite countertops in the kitchen —" Kara began.

"Granite countertops — or the lack of them — aren't going to make the difference in our *family!* Besides, we've already had those, we'll have them again. Just not right now, okay?"

Kara sighed in defeat and closed her eyes. She had a headache from looking at too many apartments that were just too small, too dark, too old-fashioned, too modern . . . too . . .

Too *not* their house on Long Island.

Steve slammed on the brakes and her eyes snapped open again. A river of red taillights flashed ahead of them, reflected on the wet pavement, and a hand with an uplifted middle finger was waving at them from the small sports car that had cut in just ahead of them, forcing Steve to dodge to avoid rearending it.

And now the jerk was flipping *them* off!

"This commute is something I'm not going to miss," Steve said through clenched teeth. "It's a wonder more people don't get killed out here." He glanced at Kara, then reached over and patted her knee reassuringly. "Hey, things are going to be okay — we'll find the right place, and we didn't get killed just now, and in the end everything's going to be fine." When Kara made no response, he squeezed her leg, then returned his hand to the steering wheel. "Why don't you give Lindsay a call?" he suggested. "Tell her we'll be home in another half hour or so."

Kara dialed Lindsay's cell phone, but all she got was Lindsay's voice mail. "Hi, honey," Kara said, leaving a message. "It's nine-twenty and we're on our way home. We should be there around ten." After a slight hesitation, she added, "Call my cell when you get this, okay?" She clicked off.

Steve, frowning, looked at her. "Isn't she supposed to keep her cell phone on?" Kara nodded, but Steve wasn't sure she'd heard him. "That was the deal, right?" he pressed. "We'd pay for the phone if she'd leave it on so we could reach her?"

Kara chewed at her lower lip, then pressed the speed dial digit that would connect her to their home phone.

On the fourth ring the answering machine picked up, and she pressed in the code that would let her listen to any messages that might have been left.

Nothing.

"She's probably in the shower," Steve said. "Or maybe she left us a note."

"Maybe," Kara agreed, but she didn't believe it. In fact, she had a feeling that something was wrong. "Maybe I ought to call Dawn's," she said, as much to herself as to Steve.

He glanced over at her again, hearing the worry in her voice. "Hey, come on, honey — nothing's wrong."

"She's not home, and her cell phone's not on," Kara replied. "That means —"

"That means she's seventeen," Steve broke in, hearing a note of panic creep into his wife's voice. "She could be at Dawn's, or she could have gone to a movie, or she could be any number of other places. Her phone might even be on but she's just in some dead spot — God knows, half the time I can't get any reception at all in Camden Green."

And I know when something's wrong, Kara told herself. *I always have.* As traffic thinned and they picked up speed, she looked out into the dark countryside, rain sliding past the window, and tried to tell herself she was wrong, that it was just the cumulative discouragement of the entire day that was getting to her. And it wasn't just the apartment hunting, either. It was the prospect of having to turn into an urban corporate wife, spending more and more time with people like the Bennetts, who had managed to make even a dinner at Café des Artistes a miserable experience. Maybe she was just tired, and upset with everything that was going on in their lives, and there was nothing wrong at all.

She closed her eyes and tried to quiet her mind.

But it didn't work.

Something was wrong.

Something was terribly wrong.

Suddenly all she wanted was to be home.

Home with Lindsay.

CHAPTER SEVENTEEN

I must write down every detail of what happened, lest I forget even the tiniest fragment of this perfect day.

My planning was flawless, of course. The spot I'd found for the car was as secluded as I'd remembered, and as deserted as the rest of the area. People are so predictable.

When I entered the house, it was also exactly as I had anticipated. People were wandering through every room, thinking they were seeing everything, but in actuality seeing nothing. When I first entered, I saw the agent in charge standing on the stairs, talking to two people who were of absolutely no interest to me — too young to have children yet not old enough for any other role. The agent looked right at me, but I knew even as his eyes scanned me that he was dismissing me.

As they always dismissed me.

If he held any memory of me at all from that disinterested glance, it has long since faded utterly away.

Perfect.

I drifted invisibly through the house, awaiting my opportunity, and when I finally came to her room, it was empty. It was less than a second before I had slipped under the bed.

Under the bed!

It is such a cliché that I knew the moment I saw the huge old-fashioned mahogany four-poster on Wednesday, it would make the perfect hiding place.

The trick, I had been afraid, would be to stay awake as I lay waiting for her, but as I smelled her delicate fragrance, I could almost feel her all around me, and it was enough.

I knew I would not sleep.

And it was marvelous, hiding under her bed. Marvelous to lie hidden only inches away as people wandered through the room. I watched their feet and listened to them talk about the house and the family who lived there. I was particularly thrilled when someone mentioned her — talked about how well she kept her room, how pretty she was in her photographs. It was exactly as people described the others, thinking they were perfect when I knew what they really were.

I found one of her bedroom slippers. Pink, it was, and well-worn. I held it to my cheek, feeling the softness of its silk, and filled myself with the scent of her feet.

And as I pictured her perfectly formed foot nestling into that glove-soft slipper, I crushed the slipper in anticipation of crushing the foot itself, just as I crushed her panties on Wednesday last.

And heat poured through me.

As the hours passed, I fantasized that she was sleeping in the bed above me, mere inches away, with no idea how close I was.

And then at last the house fell silent, and I was alone.

Alone with my passion and my fantasy, and the knowledge that soon the fantasy would become reality.

I'm not sure how long it was before I finally heard the front door close, but the moment it did, my heart began to pound so hard that I found it hard to breathe.

She turned on the television.

I don't like that.

I felt my groin begin to ache as I heard her slowly come up the stairs, and as I watched her feet as she padded into the bedroom, opened a drawer, and sighed, I felt myself begin to harden. . . .

A moment later she sat on the bed, and the mattress sagged and touched my chest. It was incredible — I could almost imagine it was her fingers themselves touching me. Then a shoe dropped, and then the other, falling to the floor with a carelessness that I like no more than the sound of the television. Once her shoes were off, she stood up, turned on her music and danced a few steps, her naked feet only inches from my face.

I could have reached out and taken her then.

Next her blouse dropped to the floor right before my eyes, and then her shorts as well!

It was as if she knew I was there, and doing what she's always done.

There she was, only inches away, and clad in nothing more than her bra and panties.

Thin, light green bikini panties, I imagined. Or perhaps the ones with butterflies on them that I'd seen in her drawer on Wednesday.

As I watched, she slid one of her feet into a slipper and put the other foot under the bed, feeling for the second slipper. I wanted to touch her foot so badly I could barely rein in the urge, but I held fast!

Patience! That is the key to everything.

A moment later her hand came snaking under the bed, and for an instant it seemed she was reaching out for me.

I shrank away, of course. The moment of capture was not yet at hand, and I was about to nudge the slipper closer to her grasp when the telephone rang.

In an instant her hand vanished and the mattress sagged above me once more.

As she talked with her friend, I felt the moment draw closer and knew I wouldn't have to wait much longer.

Though the torture had been sublime, it was time to take her home.

I began to slip out from beneath the bed, and knew the exact moment when she became aware of my presence.

It was a moment we shared together — the first of what I know will be a lifetime of such moments.

Before she could even speak, I seized her, my fingers closing on her ankles. If she screamed, I have no memory of it.

Perhaps she didn't scream at all.

Or perhaps the music drowned out her scream.

Certainly, any scream she might have made would have been like music to my ears.

Would have been, and will be for a very long time to come . . .

I held her tightly, covering her body with my own.

Then I covered her lips with mine, and this is when I nearly lost control in the feel of her skin against my body, in the smell of her that filled my nose.

And in the terror I saw in her eyes.

I wanted to lie atop her for hours, feeling her submitting to my power, but the glue on my fingertips — the glue that saved me from leaving my fingerprints anywhere in this house — now prevented me from touching her cheek or her lips or her eyes the way I wished.

Once again I drew upon my patience; there would be time for all of that later. But first there were chores to be done.

Chores must always be done before pleasures are to be taken.

Just after the sun set, I took her home. Everything about that brief trip was entrancing — not just the fear I felt from her, but everything else as well.

Her ineffectual struggle against the bindings on her hands and feet — a silent struggle, given the gag in her mouth. But the struggles won't last long. Certainly no longer than my own.

Soon.

Soon she'll submit to me, just as I submitted to her.

As she struggled and trembled, I wrapped her snugly in a blanket from her bed and kissed her forehead.

Then I carried her home so that we may begin.

All will be once more as it was the last time we were together.

But it will be different, too. Oh yes! This time it will be different.

This time I'll be saved.

CHAPTER EIGHTEEN

The house was ablaze with light as Steve and Kara pulled into the drive. "See?" Steve said. "She's home."

Kara remembered turning all the lights on in the house when she had been a nervous teen left home alone for the first time, but also knew that it didn't mean anything.

Lights on didn't mean anyone was at home.

She jumped out of the car before Steve even turned the engine off. "Lindsay?" she yelled as she burst through the door from the garage into the kitchen.

In the living room, the television was blaring, and she switched it off, then went through every room, turning off half the lights even though she was barely aware she was doing it. "Lindsay?" she called out again when she came to the bottom of the stairs.

Now Steve was in the house, too,

standing in the dining room holding the note Mark Acton had left on the table. "Well, this looks good," he said. "Seems like there were a couple of dozen people here today, and this guy Acton seems to think he might have an offer by tomorrow!"

Kara ignored him, heading upstairs, but even as she approached Lindsay's room, and heard no music drifting from her daughter's open door, she was all but certain what she would find.

Something was wrong — she could feel it. And the feeling hadn't started in the car when Lindsay didn't answer the phone. No, she'd first felt it at dinner, but told herself it was nothing — that there was no reason to think Lindsay wasn't exactly where she'd said she'd be — first at cheerleading practice, then at Dawn's. She should have called then — she should have excused herself from the Bennetts' less than scintillating company, gone to the ladies' lounge and called her daughter.

Instead she'd ignored her feeling and finished her meal.

And now, if Lindsay really was in trouble, Kara knew she would never forgive herself.

"Lindsay?" she called yet again.

No answer.

Feeling her panic rising, Kara stepped into Lindsay's room, found it as empty as she'd known it would be, then quickly searched the rest of the upstairs — her own bedroom, the bathrooms, the guest room, even the office that doubled as a sewing room, which Lindsay had always hated because it meant mending clothes she'd rather replace.

No Lindsay.

"She's not here," she called down to Steve. "I'm going to call the police."

"The police?" Steve echoed, emerging from the kitchen with a drink in his hand to peer up the stairs at his wife, whose face looked ashen. "Why? What's going on?" He hurried up to Kara's side.

"I'm telling you," she said, her voice trembling, "she's not here, and something's wrong."

With Kara behind him, Steve went into Lindsay's room. To his eye, everything looked perfectly normal, but when he turned back to Kara, she was biting at a fingernail, something she only did when she was extremely upset.

"Honey, what's going on?" Steve asked. "She probably just went over to Dawn's, like she said —"

"I'm telling you," Kara cut in, "something's wrong." She opened the laundry hamper and pulled out shorts and a T-shirt. "Look! These are what she wore to practice today."

Steve shrugged. "So she came home — it's obvious she came home. She turned on the TV and every light in the house. And there's her cell phone."

"So where is she?" Kara demanded. "If she came home, where is she?"

"Call Dawn," Steve sighed, wishing now he'd let her do it from the car. "That's where she's got to be."

They went back to the kitchen, where Kara pulled the address book from the drawer. But even as she looked for the number, she knew Lindsay wasn't at Dawn's.

No, something had happened.

Something bad.

And every second they delayed in calling the police was only going to worsen whatever danger Lindsay was in. Now Kara was furious at herself for having ignored Lindsay's fears about coming home after the open house.

As she dialed Dawn's number, Steve moved quickly through the house, intending to check the doors and windows, more to put Kara's mind at ease than because he expected to find anything amiss.

And nothing was.

All the doors and windows were locked.

Going back to the kitchen, he turned on the patio lights and looked out into the yard.

No Lindsay, but nothing else, either.

Everything was perfectly normal.

"She's not at Dawn's," Kara said as she hung up. "Phyllis said that Dawn told her Lindsay was upset after practice today, but that she came home because Dawn was going to her father's house."

"Upset about what?" Steve asked. He picked up his drink, started to take a sip, then thought better of it. After they found out exactly where Lindsay was, there'd be plenty of time for a drink.

For him, and for Kara, too.

"Upset about the move, of course," Kara said as she picked up the phone again. "And probably about coming home alone after an open house." She looked away from Steve as someone answered at Dawn's father's house. "This is Kara Marshall. May I speak with Dawn, please?" She talked for a moment, then hung up and faced Steve again. "She was here. Dawn talked to her, but only for a minute." Kara's voice began to rise. "But

155

she did come home, and now she's not here! I'm telling you, something's wrong!"

"Settle down," Steve said. "Let's reason this out."

"We need to call the police," Kara said, reaching for the phone once more. "Something has happened."

"Nothing has happened," Steve said, trying to stop her hand before she could pick up the receiver.

Kara pulled her hand away. "She never leaves the house without letting us know where she's going. Never! She'd leave a note or a message on the machine —"

Steve shook his head. "Maybe she left in a hurry — she left all the lights on, the television on. Maybe one of her friends came by and she took off with them."

Kara nodded and took a deep breath, telling herself that what he said could be true. She stood, opened the address book again, and began to call Lindsay's friends. Steve watched her, feeling helpless and almost more worried about Kara than Lindsay, and already rehearsing the speech Lindsay would get when she finally showed up.

Kara might ground her for the rest of her life.

But by the sixth call that yielded

nothing, Kara was crying, and now Steve, too, was beginning to worry.

"I knew it," Kara said, struggling against a sob that was threatening to strangle her. "I knew it at the restaurant, Steve. I had a feeling something was wrong." She glanced around, shivering though there wasn't the slightest chill in the room. "Someone was in the house, Steve. We should have listened to her. Somebody has her." Her voice rose. "*Someone has her!* And it's my fault. It's all my fault."

"Now just take it easy," Steve began. "Let's —"

"No!" She grabbed Steve's wrists. "Will you listen to me?" Suddenly, Kara was rigid with a rage born out of the terror that had seized her. "Someone has her! Someone has been in here! *We have to call the police!*"

"I'm not going to call the police," Steve insisted, making one last attempt to reason with her. "What are they going to do? She's not even missing — she's just not home. And it's barely even ten-thirty!"

"Then *I'm* calling them," Kara said, brushing his words aside and picking up the phone again. But now she was trembling so badly she wasn't sure she could dial, and she couldn't even read the numbers on the phone through the tears flooding her eyes.

Steve tried to take the phone from her hand. "I'll do it."

Kara steeled herself and refused to give it up. "No," she said. "You don't believe anything's wrong, so you won't be able to make them understand." She wiped the tears from her eyes with the sleeve of her blouse, focused her mind, and dialed 911.

Sergeant Andrew Grant sat on the Marshalls' sofa, a clipboard on his knee. His partner, younger and even bigger than Grant, sat next to him. Kara wasn't sure if it was their no-nonsense, just-the-facts-ma'am attitude or their navy blue uniforms, handcuffs, and guns that had imbued the house more with an aura of danger than of comfort from the moment they walked in. Nor had she taken any comfort from their search, which hadn't taken more than fifteen minutes, both inside and out.

Then, for fifteen more minutes, Steve — all his lawyerly training coming into play at the moment the officers arrived — had made Grant read every note he made out loud, as if afraid that the officer, if left to his own devices, might skew his report to make Lindsay herself look like a criminal.

Now Steve was perched on the arm of Kara's chair, one arm around her, the other holding one of her hands while the fingers of her other hand twisted a damp handkerchief into a shapeless wad. Every one of her nerves felt as raw as those in her nervously working fingers, and she thought the muted but constant squawk from the officers' radios might very well elicit a scream of frustration and annoyance from her before their questioning was over.

Seemingly oblivious of Kara's state of mind, Sergeant Grant glanced over his notes, then shifted his attention back to her. "Does Lindsay have a boyfriend?"

"No," Steve said before Kara could reply.

Grant's brow arched skeptically. "She's a cheerleader and she's not dating anybody?"

Kara shook her head.

"Could she be dating someone you don't know about?" Grant pressed.

"No," Steve said, forcefully enough that Grant's partner — whose name Kara couldn't remember — recoiled slightly. "Lindsay's not the kind of girl who keeps secrets from her parents." Then, as if to underscore his words: "She's not the kind who has to."

"Bad breakup with an old boyfriend?" Grant went on, utterly unfazed by Steve's words. "Maybe dumped someone recently, or vice versa?"

Kara shook her head, but even as she denied the suggestion implicit in the policeman's question, she realized that she didn't know for certain. Lindsay never talked about boys; was it possible she could have a boyfriend, or an ex-boyfriend, whom she knew nothing about?

"Internet chat? Does she engage in a lot of that?"

Kara shrugged helplessly, realizing that she had no idea whether Lindsay chatted on the Internet or not, at least with anybody but Dawn D'Angelo, with whom she seemed always to be exchanging instant messages. "I guess I don't know," she finally admitted. "She spends a lot of time on the computer, but she gets straight A's, so I've always assumed she was doing her homework."

"Straight A's?" Sergeant Grant said. "That's a good sign — not consistent with drug use."

As Grant made a note, Kara's nervousness morphed into indignation. "Drug use?" she began. "Lindsay would nev—" Before she could finish, Steve squeezed her

160

shoulder gently and she lapsed into silence.

"Anything been bothering her lately?"

Grant looked expectantly at Kara, as if certain she would give him at least three or four things to add to his notes, and though Lindsay's resistance to the prospect of moving instantly occurred to Kara, she wasn't about to admit it. Instead, nervousness and frustration welled up inside her and she abruptly brushed Steve's hand from her shoulder and leaned forward, her eyes fixed on the officer.

"Listen to me," she began, her voice low and under total control. "I know my daughter. She is a perfect student, has dozens of friends and no enemies — male or female — and has no secret life involving drugs or anything else. She shares things with us — she talks to us. I'd know if she was sneaking around doing things, but she isn't, hasn't, *wouldn't!* Then, last Wednesday, she thought someone had been in her room. Not just going through it the way people do at an open house, but going through her things. And today she's missing. I didn't believe her at the time, but now I do, and I'm telling you, someone was in this house, and now he's taken her."

As a great wave of emotion began to rise

161

up inside her, her voice trembled, but she steeled herself, and went on. "Someone has taken her," she said, enunciating her words carefully, lest they begin spilling hysterically from her lips. "And the longer we sit here, the —" Her voice cracked, and she couldn't bring herself to utter the thought of what might be happening to Lindsay as they sat there talking. She looked at Steve, then took a deep breath. "We need to stop *talking* and start *looking* for her!"

The policeman offered Kara what she knew was supposed to be a reassuring smile, but it struck her as patronizing. "I'm not discounting any of what you've said," he said in a tone that clearly told her he wasn't counting it for much, either. "I understand exactly how you feel." He turned to Steve. "But I still have to ask: *has* something upset her lately?"

As Kara glared at him, willing him not to respond, Steve nodded. "We're moving to the city," he said. "That's where we were all day, apartment hunting. She was at cheerleading practice."

Now Grant's brows rose as if he understood everything, and he closed the metal lid on his report. "And she's just finishing her junior year," he said, and, when Steve nodded, leaned forward. "I think we've just figured out what's going on here. You've got a seventeen-year-old daughter who wants to graduate with her class. Which means she's pretty upset right now. And when kids that age get upset, they do all kinds of things. Some of them turn to drugs, but, frankly, it doesn't sound like yours is that kind of kid." As he began listing all the possible things Lindsay could be doing or places she could have gone, Kara saw what he was leading up to.

He wasn't going to do anything.

Nothing.

Nothing at all!

And sure enough, just as her fury grew to the point where she was about to demand that he get to the point, he did just that.

". . . that's why we don't consider them missing for twenty-four hours," he was saying as she tuned back in to his words. "Mostly, nothing's happened to them at all — they've just taken off for a while."

"Not Lindsay," Kara said coldly. "She would have left a note and taken her cell phone."

"Not necessarily," Sergeant Grant argued. "Not if she's feeling like she wants to punish you. It's the only power they have

163

— get their parents as upset as they are." He glanced at his watch. "It's not even midnight, and the odds are good she'll be home in an hour or two, but frankly, I wouldn't be surprised if you don't hear from her until tomorrow."

As Kara opened her mouth to object to what she knew was coming next, Grant spoke again, quickly enough to cut her off.

"Tell you what — I'll call you in the morning." He handed Steve a card. "If she shows up, give me a call at this number, no matter what time it is."

"That's it?" Kara said, staring at the officer. "My daughter's been abducted and all you do is take a quick look around the house and ask us questions for half an hour?" Though his partner had the decency to redden at Kara's words — presumably in embarrassment — Sergeant Grant only took a deep breath.

"I'm afraid there's not much more we can do right now, Mrs. Marshall," he said. "Given that there aren't any signs of a forced entry or a struggle — or anything else that would suggest she was taken against her will — I'm afraid we have no choice but to wait twenty-four hours. And I have to tell you, the odds are overwhelming that she'll come home, or at least call you." As Kara started to interrupt him, he held up a hand — as if no matter what she was going to say, he'd heard it all before. "Look, I know what you read in the papers and see on TV about how many perverts there are out there, but I have to tell you, it's not nearly as bad as everyone thinks. If we went chasing after every kid that took off for a night or two, we wouldn't have time to do anything else."

"But she said —" Kara began, and once again Grant didn't let her finish.

"I know. There was an open house, and she thought someone was going through her stuff."

"And there was another open house today," Kara insisted. "Which is why I don't understand why you're so interested in looking for signs that someone broke in. Anyone could have just walked into the house, hidden, and waited for Lindsay to come home!"

Grant and his partner exchanged a glance, and then Grant frowned and re-opened the clipboard he'd closed as he stood up. "I guess it wouldn't hurt to talk to the agent," he said. "Do you have his home phone number?"

As the two officers left the house a minute or two later, Kara wondered if they

165

were going to talk to Mark Acton or whether they'd just taken his number to appease her.

She strongly suspected it was the latter. And she hated it.

CHAPTER NINETEEN

Pain.

Pounding pain, hammering at her head like a great mallet.

Pain so overpowering that it was all Lindsay felt as she slowly rose up through the layers of consciousness.

She tried to shrink back from it, tried to sink back into the blessed nonreality of unconsciousness, but the pain wouldn't let her.

And with consciousness came the memories.

Memories of *him.* Except they were barely memories at all, for she had no face to put to them.

Only impressions.

Hands closing on her ankles.

Then he was on top of her, scuttling out from beneath the bed like a rat from the sewer, his weight pinning her to the floor, crushing her.

Then there had been something over her face, pressing down on her, and she couldn't breathe and tried to struggle but she wasn't strong enough and she thought she was going to vomit and —

Nothing.

She opened her mouth to scream, to cry out against the blackness and the throbbing pain in her head, but before any sound could escape her throat, she cut it off.

Quiet, she commanded herself. *Be still and make no sound and maybe it will go away. Maybe the pounding will stop.*

Maybe it's just another bad dream.

Lindsay tried to take a deep breath, but her heart was racing harder and faster, which made her head hurt even more, and she knew it wasn't just a bad dream.

She moaned, and heard the sound of it echo hollowly.

Where was she?

Panic rose up now, and she tried to move, but couldn't. It was like the terrible helplessness of nightmares in which her feet felt mired in mud and no matter how hard she tried she couldn't escape whatever terror pursued her. But this was even worse.

Her wrists were so tightly bound to the

arms of a hard chair that she couldn't move them at all, and her hands felt numb. Both her ankles were bound to the front legs of the chair, and something in front of her neck held her head utterly immobile — even the slightest movement made her feel as if a blade was about to slash into her throat.

As the wave of panic threatened to break over her, Lindsay suddenly knew with terrible clarity that if she gave in to it and began thrashing against her bindings, she would surely die, her neck laid open by the razor-sharp edge she could feel against her larynx. Forcing the panic down, holding it at bay by nothing but her will, she pulled against her bonds.

And flinched again as fire shot through her right wrist, the one she'd injured at practice.

The pain in her wrist penetrated the throbbing in her head, and more memories came slinking back into her consciousness.

He had been under her bed all along!

She felt sick as she remembered peeling off her shorts and T-shirt.

He'd been under her bed, watching her all along.

Watching her, and listening as she talked to Dawn.

Listening and waiting and —

She breathed as deeply as she could against the wave of panic suddenly looming over her again.

Where was she? The air smelled moldy and damp. Like Dawn's basement.

With each deep breath, her head cleared a little more. He'd covered her face with something, and then her nostrils had filled with fumes that made her sick.

She'd fought — fought as hard as she could — but he was heavy, and her wrist had hurt and —

He'd said something — whispered something.

Angel. He'd called her Angel.

Then nothing.

Blackness.

Quiet.

Unconsciousness.

Now there was still blackness around her, and quiet, too. But she was no longer unconscious. She was alive, and awake, and whatever had happened, it wasn't a dream. She began going over her body, trying to feel every part of herself. Nothing seemed broken, nor was she bleeding anywhere, at least not badly.

So she wasn't hurt.

Just bound to some kind of chair, with a terrible taste in her mouth.

She tried to think, to tell herself it was going to be all right. She was smart, and strong, and somehow she would get out of this.

She'd escape.

Just the thought of finding a way out somewhat calmed her, and as her pulse slowed and the agony in her head finally began to recede, she concentrated on the blackness around her.

She was in a room, and it was dark and cold and damp.

Her wrists were bound to the chair with something.

Not rope.

Duct tape?

Yes, that had to be it — duct tape.

And something was pressing against her throat, holding her head in place.

She licked her lips, trying to get rid of the bad taste in her mouth.

Then, out of the darkness, she heard something.

A whimpering sound.

She froze.

What was it?

A dog?

She heard it again, and even in the darkness, Lindsay was certain it wasn't a dog.

Was it possible she wasn't alone?

She wanted to call out, to cry for help from the unseen person in the darkness.

But what if it was *him?*

Then the sound came again, but this time she was almost sure it wasn't just a sound.

This time it sounded like a word.

And then it came again, still almost inaudible, but clear enough for Lindsay to hear: "H-Help . . ."

The voice trailed off, and Lindsay's mind spun. She wasn't alone!

There was someone else here!

Someone who could help her? Without thinking, she spoke into the darkness. "Who is it?" she whispered. But her voice emerged from her throat as little more than a low croaking sound, the words barely comprehensible even to herself.

There was a silence for a moment that seemed to go on forever, and then she heard another sound.

"Shh . . ." the voice said, quivering in the darkness. "Shhh . . ."

More silence.

As Lindsay began to wonder if she'd actually heard anything at all, the voice spoke again.

A fragile voice, barely audible.

A girl's voice.

"Shannon . . ."

The voice fell silent, and once again the silence — and the darkness — closed around her.

CHAPTER TWENTY

"This is crazy!" Kara exploded. "We're sitting here, helpless, waiting! Waiting for what? Waiting for nothing. Waiting for no reason!"

"Kara . . ." Through red-rimmed eyes, Steve looked at her from the shadows of his wing chair. Tiredly, he rubbed his unshaven chin.

"It's seven o'clock," she said. "The sun's been up for an hour and I'm not waiting any longer! I'm calling the police again — they have to do something!"

"Honey, it hasn't been anywhere near twenty-four hours —" Steve began, but Kara cut him off.

"I have to *do* something. I can't just sit here and wait for the phone to ring. I've called everyone and every place I can think of, and she's not with anyone she knows and she's not in any of the hospitals — not on Long Island, anyway — and I can't just sit here and wait for a ransom note or somebody to find a body —" Putting voice to that thought for the first time was like a punch in her own chest, and Kara sagged back. But a second later she rose from the couch and began to pace.

And to pick at her last remaining undamaged fingernail.

"Make some coffee, babe," Steve said, searching for something — anything — to distract her.

He didn't have to ask twice.

"Coffee," she said, her voice taking on an almost hysterical edge. "Okay, I'll make coffee. And I'll wait. I'll wait until eight o'clock. But at eight o'clock I'm calling Sergeant Grant."

Too tired to argue, and every bit as frightened and exhausted as his wife, Steve nodded.

Kara put the coffeepot on, then came back to fidget once more on the edge of the couch. "I feel like I want to go do her laundry. I want to change her sheets and clean her room and — and —" Her voice faltered and she fell silent. "I'm so scared," she finally whispered. "What if —" she began again, but now her voice dissolved into a helpless sob.

"*Shhh,*" Steve said, rousing himself from

his chair and going to her. He put his arms around her and drew her close, and a moment later thought he felt some of the tension in her body ease.

Kara rubbed the tears from her cheeks, pulled away from him and went back to the kitchen. She returned with a cup of coffee for each of them. "At eight o'clock I'm going to call the police, and the newspapers," she declared. "And then I'm going to make flyers and start taking them around. Somebody must have seen something!"

"Kara —" Steve began, but she shook her head, cutting off his protest.

"What do you expect me to do, Steve?" she asked. "Sit here like a helpless idiot while nobody does anything?"

"The police —"

"This is not Sergeant Grant's daughter we're talking about," Kara said, her voice taking on an edge. "He thinks she ran away, remember? He's not going to do anything." She felt a mixture of panic and anger begin to rise inside her, and in the end it was the panic that won out. "Oh, God," she sobbed, and collapsed onto the couch again. But as quickly as the panic overcame her, she forced it back. Taking a deep breath, she steeled herself and stood up. "I've got to do *something.*" Taking her coffee cup, she headed upstairs, leaving Steve sitting alone in the living room.

In the silence, Steve's exhaustion from the sleepless night began to overtake him, and despite his worry about Lindsay, his eyes drifted shut.

And then Kara screamed.

Steve sat bolt upright in the wingback chair and for one terrible instant thought that Kara must have found Lindsay.

And she was dead.

Then Kara yelled again. "It's gone, Steve!"

"What?" he called back, taking the stairs two at a time. When he got to the top, Kara was waiting for him, her face ashen, a slipper — one of Lindsay's slippers — clutched in her right hand. "Her blanket's gone!" Kara said. "The one she always kept folded at the foot of her bed. And I can't find her other slipper." She gazed at him, her eyes wide, her voice bleak. "Where's her other slipper, Steve?"

Steve ran his hands through his hair and massaged his scalp. "Did you look in her closet? Under the bed?"

Kara's look told him she had. "I'm calling the police again," she said, her tone leaving no room for argument. "Right now."

Steve nodded and followed her back down to the kitchen, feeling utterly useless. All night he had tried to convince Kara that the police were right, that Lindsay had just taken off somewhere and would come home when she cooled off.

And not once had he taken the time to go upstairs and look around the room for himself — to look at it the way Kara just had.

Now, seeing that single worn and forlorn-looking slipper in Kara's hand, he was finally as terrified for his daughter as his wife was.

But it might already be too late . . .

Mark Acton and Sergeant Grant arrived at almost the same time. Steve poured each of them a cup of coffee while Kara introduced the two men, then told Grant what she'd been doing all night, from calling every one of Lindsay's friends — and every one of *their* friends — to calling every hospital and police department on Long Island, and then she told Grant about finding the slipper and the missing blanket. But even as she spoke, she could see in Sergeant Grant's eyes that he didn't feel nearly as certain about what had happened as she did.

Mark Acton, apparently stunned by what Kara was saying, handed his logbook to Grant. "Your girl is missing?" he kept repeating, over and over again, as if the concept were somehow evading him.

"She isn't technically missing yet," Grant said, "given that it hasn't been twenty-four hours since she —" He hesitated, saw the look of cold fury in Kara's eyes, and smoothly shifted gears. "— that she's been gone," he went on, glancing at the names in the book as he spoke. His eyes shifted to Acton. "Did everybody sign in?"

The agent shrugged. "It was busy — I was talking with people the whole time. I'm pretty sure everybody signed in, but —" He spread his hands helplessly. "I always ask them to, but I guess I can't be sure."

"Did you see everybody leave?" Grant asked, more to appease Kara Marshall than because he thought there might be any merit to the idea she'd expressed last night and repeated again this morning.

Mark took the guest book back from the policeman and looked down the list of names. But now his hands were sweating and he was trembling, and he was sure the sergeant knew just how nervous policemen made him.

Kara Marshall noticed it as well, and her eyes bored into Grant, willing him to see what she was seeing. But if he was aware of Mark Acton's nervousness, he gave no sign.

"Rick Mancuso was at both open houses," Acton finally replied. "He's an agent with Century 21. I remember him coming in yesterday, but I'm not sure I remember seeing him leave." He pointed to the name near the bottom of the list.

Kara fixed her eyes on Acton. "Did anybody —" She hesitated, searching for the right word, then settled for the first one that came to mind. "— *strange* come through?"

"Strange?" The question seemed to catch him off guard.

Sergeant Grant took back the logbook and, to Kara's relief, picked up the thread of her question. "Anybody who seemed out of place? Nervous?"

"It's a public event," Acton said, shrugging. "We get lots of strange people." He paused, reflecting. "Nobody who stood out."

"And what did you do afterward?" Grant asked.

"Afterward? After the open house?"

Grant nodded.

"Went to Fishburn's, like I always do.

Had a couple of beers, ate a little something, went home and watched television."

Grant eyed the agent speculatively for a moment, then seemed to come to a decision. "Thanks for your time," he said. "If I have any more questions, I'll be in touch with you."

Mark Acton shot off the couch and almost ran toward the door.

"I've got some things to follow up on, Mrs. Marshall," Grant said, rising to his feet as the front door closed behind the real estate agent.

"And I've got a reporter from the *Sentinel-Gazette* coming over at ten," Kara replied, her eyes fixing on the policeman as if daring him to ask her not to talk to the press. To his credit, he only nodded, and then she pressed a wallet-sized school photo of Lindsay into his hand. "She's our only child," she said. "Please — you've got to find her. I'm begging you."

"She'll be home," Grant assured her, but she could see in his eyes that he wasn't as certain as he'd been last night.

"Only if we find whoever took her," Kara said.

Grant looked at her appraisingly, clearly taking her measure. Then: "I'll be in touch." He shook hands with Steve, who opened the door for him, and when the door closed behind him, the house again was quiet.

Too quiet, and too empty.

"No," Kara said softly, "I'll be the one in touch."

CHAPTER TWENTY-ONE

Everything about the place had changed, and though Claire Shields Sollinger knew exactly why it had changed — and when that change had come — she still wasn't used to it. Until last Christmas, she'd always felt a sense of peace fall over her as she waited for the big estate gates to swing open. Today, though, her fingers tapped nervously on the steering wheel of her Range Rover as the gates moved back. She looked again at the newspaper on the seat beside her and firmed her resolve as Lindsay Marshall's eyes seemed to look right into her own.

The crunch of the gravel on the quarter-mile-long driveway gave her no comfort as she approached the house, and as she pulled to a stop in front of the immense Tudor pile her great-grandfather had built, the title of a book she hadn't read since her days at Miss Porter's suddenly popped into her mind.

Bleak House.

That was what Cragmont had become. There was a melancholy air about the place that even the bright spring morning and the fresh breeze off Long Island Sound couldn't wash away. It was as if the house itself somehow knew that for the first time in its history, it was occupied by a single resident.

A single, very unhappy resident.

She brought the car to a stop at the front door, and by the time she stepped out, straightened the skirt of her suit, and tucked the morning paper under her arm, the front door had opened and a figure had appeared on the porch. For a moment Claire felt a flash of optimism, but then realizing it wasn't her brother on the front porch, her optimism faded.

"How is he today?" she asked, though Neville Cavanaugh's dour expression had answered her question even before she asked it.

Neville, never long on words, shook his head gravely. "He spends all his time in the library these days, with the curtains drawn. He even sleeps there. I do my best, but . . ." The servant's voice trailed off and he spread his hands in a gesture of helplessness.

Claire sighed heavily as she looked at her

brother's factotum, who was, as always, impeccably dressed. His long face reflected the sorrow every member of the family felt, but as she always did, Claire wondered if Neville truly felt the pain of Patrick's loss, or whether he was merely playing the role of the devoted servant. Even after having known the man for most of her life, Claire had never warmed to him. Still, her father had trusted him, and so did Patrick, so now she carefully masked her antipathy. "Thank you, Neville. I don't know what he'd do without you. How is his leg?"

"Completely healed," Neville said. "Even the scars are beginning to fade, but he insists we put ointment on them every night. It's as if he wants to keep them as wounds."

"Is he eating?"

"Some soup last night."

Claire took a deep breath. "Well, he'll eat today. Would you bring us some coffee, please?" She strode to the heavy double library doors and knocked with what she hoped sounded like authority, then tried the handle. The door was locked. "Patrick? Patrick, it's Claire. Open the door."

Eventually, she heard noises from the room beyond. The lock clicked and the door opened a crack. The unshaven, pale face of her brother peered out at her.

Claire pushed the door open and walked into the darkened library, shaking her head at what she saw. Nothing — absolutely nothing — had improved since the last time she was here. She went to the windows and opened the heavy velvet draperies to let the bright morning sunlight flood the room. Patrick squinted, but raised no objection to the light. "Neville tells me you're sleeping in here," she said, and wrinkled her nose at the sour odor that hung in the room. "It smells like it."

Patrick merely shrugged, and in the bright light of the morning sun, Claire realized how much he'd changed. A mere shadow of the robust brother who until a few months ago had still, even in his early forties, played the occasional raucous game of rugby with his friends. Now his thinning, sandy hair had gone as dull as his spirits. He appeared not to have shaved for a couple of days, and his linen slacks needed laundering, as did his polo shirt.

"I can't sleep in our bedroom anymore," Patrick said. He sat, sagging into one of the leather chairs that flanked an ornate chessboard. "I reach for Renee in the night and —" His voice caught.

Claire steeled herself against the whirlpool of her own grief. Renee had been like a sister to her, and her nieces — She distracted herself by opening the French doors and letting in the cool, fresh spring air. As she did, Neville arrived with a tray. Claire poured her brother a cup of coffee and sweetened it with enough sugar and cream to give him some instant energy.

As he took an almost reluctant sip, Patrick gazed out at the old boathouse that stood at the foot of the lawn that rolled from the house down to the Sound. "I'd be taking the girls sailing on a day like this," he said, his eyes glistening with tears.

Claire moved around the room, folding the blankets and setting them on the table next to the door and putting the pillow on top of the pile. There would be no more sleeping in the library if she had anything to do with it.

Then she saw that all the family photographs had been turned to the wall. She turned to face her brother. "I don't believe you've done this," she said.

"I can't look at them," he replied, seeming to shrink even deeper into his chair.

Claire strode across the room, dropped into the chair across from her brother, and reached across the chess table to put a hand on his arm. "You can't pretend they never existed, Patrick. The fire was a terrible thing — a horrible, tragic thing. And everybody feels it — everybody we know loved Renee and the girls. But the rest of us aren't trying to shut them out. They loved you, and you loved them, but you can't bring them back. Life goes on."

Patrick finally met her gaze, and the pain in his expression tore at her heart. "I'll never get over it."

"You will," Claire replied. "You're not the only person terrible things have happened to." She laid the morning newspaper on the table.

Patrick hesitated, then picked up the paper, flinching as he saw the picture of the girl on the front page.

"Her name is Lindsay Marshall," Claire said. "I know her mother. Kara and I worked together on the town square renovation and a dozen other projects. Now her daughter is missing — either a runaway or she's been abducted. Kara believes the latter."

Patrick said nothing, but Claire could see his eyes scanning the article. She sipped her coffee, giving Patrick time to finish it. "When I saw this, I went to Kara's. Do you know what she was doing?"

Patrick looked up from the paper. "She must be terrified," he said softly.

Claire nodded. "She is. But she's not just sitting there, Patrick. She's calling people. She's organizing a search. She's printing up flyers and calling the paper, and doing everything she can to find her daughter. She's not just sitting around feeling sorry for herself."

"The girl looks like Jenna, doesn't she?" he said, and Claire saw the tears well up again in his eyes.

Claire nodded. "And her loss is just as tragic."

Patrick dropped the newspaper to the floor. "It's hardly the same," he said with a harshness bordering on anger. "She's just missing. Your friend's whole family didn't —" He fell silent, unable to complete the thought.

"That's true," Claire agreed, then leaned forward, her eyes fixing on him. "But at least you know where your family is — know what happened to them. Kara doesn't have the slightest idea where her daughter is, doesn't know whether she's even alive. But she's not just sitting around feeling sorry for herself!"

Patrick recoiled as if he'd been slapped. "I just want to be left alone."

"Well, that's not going to happen," Claire said. "As of today, you won't be left alone anymore. If Kara Marshall can deal with her reality — without even knowing yet what it is — you can start dealing with yours." He seemed to cower from her words, but Claire continued. "Would Renee want to see you living like this?" she asked. Before he could answer, she went on. "Of course she wouldn't." She stood up. "You need to get out of here," she said, taking his hand and pulling him to his feet. "You need fresh air, and you need to eat. So we're going out for lunch."

Patrick seemed on the verge of panic. "I — I can't —" he began, but Claire cut him off.

"Of course you can." She pointed to the shoes he'd dropped on the floor at the end of the sofa. "Put them on."

Before Patrick could object, Claire went to the library door and called for Neville to bring one of Patrick's jackets.

A few minutes later Patrick reluctantly passed through Cragmont's huge oaken door for the first time since his wife and children had been interred back in December and he'd returned to the house after seeing their coffins disappear forever into the family crypt.

"Where would you like to go?" Claire asked.

"I'm not hungry," Patrick whispered.

"Then we'll go to Julia's," Claire decided, ignoring his tone. "If you're not hungry, you might as well not eat good food as bad." She put the car in gear, rolled down Patrick's window so he could feel the wind in his hair, and drove down the long drive, passing through the gate and turning toward town.

Neville Cavanaugh surveyed the veal cutlets in the butcher's case, decided they looked decent, and turned his attention to the bacon.

Too fatty.

And the roasts seemed a little grizzled.

So it would be veal tonight, and waffles for breakfast in the morning.

He fingered his paper number, glanced up and saw on the digital counter that he was now fourth in line. He waited impatiently by the rack of bottled sauces and marinades, and when a voice spoke to him from behind, he didn't even have to turn around to know it was Martha McGinn, who had cooked for the Ashcrofts at Beech House even longer than he'd worked for the Shieldses at Cragmont. And he disliked

Martha almost as much as he despised the cuteness of the name of the estate at which she worked.

"So good to see you," Martha gushed, taking his hand in her plump fingers and holding it despite his best efforts to extract it from her grip. "How is poor Mr. Shields?"

"As well as can be expected," Neville said, masking his dislike of the woman and finally freeing his hand from hers. Then, knowing that whatever he said — or didn't say — would spread along the north shore even faster than the food poisoning after Martha McGinn's unfortunate experience with the salmon mousse two summers ago, he added, "Actually, I believe he's doing better."

"Such a tragedy," Martha McGinn said, shaking her head with enough emphasis that some powder shook loose from the broad expanse of her bloated face.

Neville hated to think that this woman considered him her peer. "Yes," he said, starting to turn away.

Martha McGinn's fingers closed on his arm, immobilizing him. "He's fortunate to have you to see him through this, Neville."

"I believe I'm the more fortunate," Neville replied. "Having loved Mrs. Shields and the children in my own way, it's a privilege to be able to look after Mr. Patrick now."

"Yes, of course," Martha said uncertainly.

"Number forty-seven!" the butcher called out.

Neville held up his number. "You'll excuse me?" Without waiting for an answer, he turned away and moved to the counter, and moments later stepped into the bright spring sunshine, white paper bag in hand. He checked his mental list and headed toward the drugstore in the middle of the next block. But halfway down a door opened and Patrick Shields and his sister emerged from Julia's Dining Room, a restaurant that Neville found even more repulsively cute than the name of the Ashcrofts' beach house.

"Neville!" Claire said. Then her eyes fell on the white bag from the butcher shop. "Oh, dear, I hope you haven't bought something wonderful for dinner."

Neville's brows lifted uncertainly. "As a matter of fact, I have," he said. "The veal cutlets look excellent today."

"Well, I'm afraid they'll have to hold," Claire said, not so much as a hint of apology in her voice. "My brother has agreed to dine with me tonight."

"Better even than the veal," Neville said, betraying no hint of annoyance. "And it's good to see you enjoying the day," he added, turning to Patrick. For the first time in months, he saw a hint of a smile play around his employer's lips.

"When Claire makes up her mind to something, there's no stopping her," Patrick said.

"Indeed. Well, I'm off to the drugstore, then the cleaners."

"Thank you, Neville," Patrick said. "I don't know what —"

"My pleasure, sir," Neville said before Patrick could finish.

"And enjoy your evening off," Claire said.

As she was passing him, Neville stopped her with a gentle touch on her arm. "You're a godsend," he whispered. She flashed him a quick smile and followed Patrick down the walk, and Neville felt his mood lighten considerably. He'd finish his errands and then have the rest of the day and the entire evening to himself, and his employer wouldn't be home until after dinner, which, knowing Claire, would be very late indeed.

So he could spend the afternoon and evening doing anything he wanted.

Anything at all.

★ ★ ★

The Range Rover pulled to a stop before Cragmont's massive front doors.

"Are you sure, Patrick?" Claire asked. "All you have to do is say the word and I'll just keep going. You can spend the night at my place, get up, have breakfast with me, and I'll bring you home."

Patrick smiled at his sister but shook his head. "I'll be fine," he assured her, knowing the words were a lie even as he spoke them, but knowing too that Claire would see through the lie. Both of them, after all, had been raised in a culture of social platitudes, where little truth — emotional truth, anyway — was ever spoken. "I might even try sleeping in my own bed tonight."

"Well, *that's* a good sign," Claire said, leaning across to kiss his cheek. "I'll call you tomorrow."

Neville was waiting in the foyer with a scotch and soda, but for the first time since the fire, Patrick left the drink on the tray. "Shall I draw a bath?" Neville asked, his brow lifting.

Patrick smiled wryly. "Actually, leaving the house seems to have worn me out. I think I'll just go to bed." He climbed the staircase to the second floor, and as he started along the corridor to the master suite, steeled him-

195

self against everything he was about to see. But when he finally passed through the door into the small sitting room and saw the portrait of Renee that had hung over the fireplace since the day they were married, his resolution nearly failed him. Then he determinedly tore his eyes from the portrait, went through to the bedroom itself, stripped off his clothes, and slid between clean, fresh sheets. The soft bed, after months of sleeping on the library sofa, felt delicious.

But the feeling was short-lived, as all the memories of his wife and children rose out of the darkness, and he felt once again the overwhelming urge to reach out to them, to take them in his arms, to protect them.

But he hadn't protected them. Instead, he'd failed them, and as long as he lived, that failure — and their faces — would haunt him.

He sat up and switched on a light to clear the darkness and the memories from the room, and as the images of his family faded, the words Claire had spoken over dinner echoed in his mind.

There are groups you could join, Patrick — groups of people who've gone through what you're going through.

But who else had lost everyone they loved on Christmas Eve?

As the pain of his loss threatened to overwhelm him once more, he picked up the remote control and turned on the television.

And was instantly confronted with the face of the girl whose image had dominated this morning's front page of the newspaper.

Kara Marshall's daughter.

Lindsay — that was her name.

Patrick clicked off the television, but the image of Lindsay Marshall — who looked so much like Jenna — lingered.

The silence grew almost as massive as the house itself, and Patrick found himself straining to hear the little cry that Jenna used to utter when a bad dream had awakened her in the night.

It was a cry so soft that it rarely woke Renee, but it had always pulled him from sleep instantly.

Except on Christmas Eve . . .

And then he heard it! He heard Jenna!

In an instant Patrick was out of bed, out of the suite and rushing down the hall to Jenna's room. Was it possible? Would he open her bedroom door and see her face puffed with sleep and surrounded by tousled hair?

But when he pushed open the door, the bedroom was dark and cold and its emptiness chilled him even more than the cold itself.

He turned on the light. It was exactly as Jenna had left it when they went to Vermont for the holidays.

Her bed was covered with stuffed animals, her walls with posters.

Her schoolbooks were stacked on her desk as if she might pick them up tomorrow morning.

The sound of her voice had, indeed, been nothing but a dream.

Patrick sank down onto her bed and ran his hand over her quilt.

The pain in his chest felt as if it might actually burst through his ribs, and with a strangled cry, he grabbed an armful of her stuffed animals and hugged them to him.

He curled up on Jenna's bed then, aching for one more hug from his little girl. Just one more hug.

Just one more good-night kiss.

But it was not to be.

It was never to be again.

At last Patrick released his grip on his daughter's toys, uncoiled his body from the tight ball into which he'd curled up, and forced himself to stand.

This could not go on. Claire was right — somehow he had to learn to deal with what had happened, to accept that his family was gone and get on with his life.

But how?

Leaving Jenna's room, he went back to his own suite. As his eyes swept the room — and the door to the bedroom beyond — he knew that he could not sleep here tonight.

As long as the rooms were filled with Renee's things, the memories would only return to haunt him once again.

He went downstairs to the bathroom off the library and opened the medicine cabinet, picking up the bottle of sleeping pills the doctor had prescribed three months ago. He shook two of the tiny tablets into his hand, washed them down his throat with a glass of water, and made a mental note to ask Neville to begin removing Renee's things from the master suite tomorrow morning.

Then he switched off the bathroom light, made his way through the darkness to the hard sofa, and lay down.

He'd try his own bed again another night.

And in the hall outside the library, Neville Cavanaugh waited for his employer's breathing to fall into the even rhythms of sleep. . . .

CHAPTER TWENTY-TWO

The sharp pain of Kara's nails digging into the flesh of his upper arm jerked Steve out of the semistupor to which he'd finally succumbed after forty-eight nearly sleepless hours, but it still took a moment or two before his mind — and his vision — cleared enough for him to recognize the image on the television at the foot of the bed.

Lindsay's face, smiling at him.

Her junior class photo.

". . . search continues for missing seventeen-year-old Lindsay Marshall today," the anchorwoman was saying. "She was last seen Sunday afternoon about four-thirty, walking home from Camden Green High. Lindsay is five feet six inches tall, one hundred twenty pounds, blond, with blue eyes, and her hair is shorter than in this picture. If you have any information regarding Lindsay's whereabouts, we urge you to call the Camden Green police department or this station." Two phone numbers were now superimposed over Lindsay's photo, then her photograph was replaced with the face of the anchorwoman, flanked by the sportscaster and the weatherman, all three of them wearing the kind of empathetic expressions Steve had never seen anywhere but on TV. They clucked with sympathy for a moment, but their expressions shifted quickly back to bland smiles and the anchorwoman began speaking again. "On a national level —"

Kara turned away from the television. "That wasn't enough," she said. "They had more! They had me telling them what happened, and they had . . ."

Steve barely heard her, the memory of Lindsay's face on the television screen still filling his mind. Somehow that image made the whole surreal experience all too crushingly real, and her absence from the house came crashing down on him like a blow from a sledgehammer.

Lindsay was not at camp.

She was not spending a few nights with Dawn's family.

She had not gone out of town to a cheerleading competition.

None of those occurrences had ever made the house feel as empty of her presence as it felt now, for before, he always knew where his daughter was and when she'd be home.

But this time was different.

This time they didn't know what had happened.

Had she left with a boyfriend — a boyfriend he knew nothing about — in a fit of pique?

Had she run away to spite him and her mother?

He didn't know.

All he knew was that she was gone, and that he'd never felt so helpless.

"They should have shown videos of her," Kara was saying, her voice taking on the edge of hysteria that Steve had grown all too familiar with over the last two days. "I gave them video footage from our trip to Disney World. And what about the reward? They should have said we've posted a reward!" She picked up the phone from the bedside table, pulled a phone book from the nightstand drawer and dialed, her fingers jabbing furiously at the buttons. Steve turned down the volume on the TV as she began to speak.

"This is Kara Marshall," she said, her voice quavering. "I want to speak to someone at the news desk." He watched as Kara drew dark arrows pointing to the telephone number in the book. "Hello?" she finally said after nearly two full minutes had gone by. "This is Kara Marshall. You just ran a short — really short — piece about my daughter who has been abducted? Yes, well, it was too short. I gave your people all kinds of pictures, and they talked to me on camera, and we're offering a reward —" Abruptly, she fell silent, listening, and a moment later her shoulders sagged. "Yes, all right," she said, her voice cold now. "I understand. Okay. I'll call back in the morning." She hung up the phone and set it back on the nightstand.

Steve's stomach knotted as he watched her glare at the television screen, and he could almost see the wheels turning in her head.

"I'm going to have to call them every day," she said. "Tomorrow morning we'll have the police here and we'll hold a press conference. I'll need fresh flyers, ones with a different photo of Lindsay on them, and the reward information. And I'll put them on bright yellow paper." She turned to look at him, her eyes filled with desperation. "She's somewhere, Steve. Someone has to have seen her! Someone has to have!"

She got out of bed then, wrapped herself in her robe, and left the bedroom without a word. Steve knew where she was going — to the room next to the master bedroom, from which the sewing equipment had vanished on Monday so it could serve as a full-time office.

A moment later he heard her fingers tapping the computer keyboard, and he knew she was making lists of things to do in the morning.

He had nothing on his own list of things to do in the morning. There was no point in going to work — he wouldn't be able to concentrate on anything. So someone else was shouldering his load, which wasn't good. But what could he do? He was useless in the face of the possibility that someone had actually taken Lindsay, and though he'd been clinging to the hope that the police were right — that she'd just taken off and would be back within another day or so — there had been something about seeing Lindsay's face on the television screen that told him Kara was right.

Lindsay hadn't just run away.

Someone had taken her.

Ignoring the tiredness in his muscles and forcing his mind to overcome the numbness that had gripped it only a few minutes ago, Steve heaved himself to his feet and pulled on his own robe.

As the sound of Kara's fingers tapping at the computer keyboard kept the silence of Lindsay's absence at bay, Steve went down to put on a pot of coffee. It would be another night without sleep.

CHAPTER TWENTY-THREE

Flames!

Flames so virulent they threatened to suck the breath from Patrick's lungs even as their crackling whispered in his ears with a seductive passion. Its heat, warm and comforting when he first felt it, made him feel as if he was melting an instant later.

Flames so beautiful he wanted to embrace them.

Flames that sang to him, beckoned to him, urged him closer.

No! The flames were evil! They were destroying his home, devouring his family, consuming his very life! Now their soft lullabies were drowned out by the screams of his wife and children, and though he wanted to rush to them, to reach into the flames and pull them to safety, he couldn't.

He couldn't even see them. All he could see were the flames dancing in front of

him, mocking him, laughing at him, torturing him.

And drawing him closer . . .

It wasn't too late — he could still save
them, could still rush into the flames and
find them and —

But their screams were fading, and he
knew they were dying and there was
nothing he could do and —

As if to punish him for his helplessness, a
tongue of flame lashed out at him, and he
jerked back just as an alarm bell sounded.

Patrick's head slammed into a wall, and
the fire abruptly vanished, its heat instantly
replaced by a terrible cold.

The cold of death itself.

Yet the alarm was sounding again.

But how could that be? If there was no
fire —

He groped in the fading amber light that
was all that remained of the glow of the
flames, and his hand met cold concrete.

His left leg felt numb, and when he tried
to move it, he discovered that it was
twisted around, pinned beneath his right
leg.

As the last vestiges of the nightmare
faded from his consciousness, Patrick
opened his eyes and found no fire, no heat.
Rather, he was in near darkness, in the

cold, his muscles cramped, his joints aching.

His left leg, though, was beginning to come back to life and tingling painfully. He groped again, but found only a pair of concrete walls coming together into a corner.

A corner in which he was huddled like some kind of vermin trying to hide from a predator.

The fire! That had been the predator! It had hunted down and devoured his entire family, and all he'd been able to do was cower helplessly, just as he was cowering now.

But where was he? He tried to concentrate, to think of what he last remembered, but his mind was still filled with the memory of the flames, flames that even now seemed ready to leap at him once more.

The alarm sounded again, but now he knew he was awake, and the sound seemed unnaturally loud in the small confines of the concrete room.

He flailed about, and slowly his mind cleared until he recognized the alarm for what it was: the ringing of his cell phone.

And the phone was in the pocket of his robe.

As it rang again, he realized he was wearing only his robe and his pajama bottoms and was no longer in the house.

Then he recognized the amber light slanting down through a small stained-glass window above a heavy door, and he knew.

He knew where he was, though he had no memory of how he had gotten himself there.

The mausoleum.

The huge concrete structure in which generations of Shieldses were interred. In front of him was his wife's crypt, and below were those of their children. He could see the brass plates with their names engraved. He could see the wilting flowers in their teardrop vases.

And he could see the still empty crypt next to Renee where he himself would someday be entombed.

The cell phone rang again, and with fingers that seemed to be operating under their own volition, he found the key that would answer it. "Yes?" he asked, his voice sounding distant even to himself.

"Patrick?" an unfamiliar voice said. "It's Alison Montgomery."

The name meant nothing to him.

"We met once, through Claire, though I doubt you'd remember."

He did not remember.

"Claire tells me that you're having a difficult time getting through your grief."

Patrick stared numbly at the empty crypt next to the one that held his wife's remains.

"Patrick?"

A faint grunt emerged from his throat.

"Grief is a hard thing to handle," the woman went on, and he could tell she was choosing her words carefully, as if he might bolt if she said the wrong thing. "Especially the feelings of guilt that always go along with it. I lost my son last year, and I don't think I'd be here today if it weren't for the weekly support group."

Suddenly he understood.

"How about if I pick you up this morning and take you for a cup of coffee?"

Patrick ran his fingers through his hair. He wasn't sure he could make his way back to the house, much less dress and go to coffee with this woman. And how could he tell her — or anyone else — that he had awakened this morning in the mausoleum, and not for the first time?

How could he describe to her what he was feeling? How could he explain that it wasn't just the grief — it was the guilt.

She'd just said something about guilt,

but how could anyone understand the guilt he felt at not being able to save them?

"Patrick?"

"Yes."

"Are you having some trouble?"

A small strangled sob erupted from his throat.

"I'll pick you up at ten o'clock," Alison Montgomery said, seemingly having understood every emotion that had been packed into his single sob. "That's an hour from now."

"All right," he breathed, and without waiting to hear her response, he closed the phone and put it back in his pocket. Maybe Claire was right — maybe he did need help. Certainly he couldn't go on much longer the way he was.

If he hadn't seen Claire's Range Rover parked in the drive when he came back from his meeting with Alison Montgomery, the massed yellow tulips that greeted Patrick would have come as far more of a shock than they did. Still, he felt his heart race when he saw them — the first perfect blooms of the season — arranged in Renee's favorite vase on the circular table in the center of the great foyer.

Exactly as Renee herself would have arranged them.

But it wasn't Renee who had cut the flowers — it was Claire.

With a surge of energy he hadn't felt in a long time, Patrick strode through the hall to the kitchen, where Neville was disposing of the leftover stems and leaves, as well as the dozens of not-quite-perfect blooms that Claire had rejected for the foyer's centerpiece. Through the windows, he could see Claire in a blue sundress with hat to match.

Leave it to Claire to be dressed for a garden party despite the lack of even a single guest. And now she was filling yet another basket of blossoms, most of which he was sure would be as firmly rejected as the blooms that now stuffed the wastebasket. He went through the butler's pantry to the dining room, pushed through the French doors and walked down the path to her.

"Planning to cut every flower we have?" he asked, taking her basket.

"But the tulips are glorious," Claire replied, surveying the now decimated bed. "I just had to come over and see them!" She turned, shears in one gloved hand, and gave Patrick such an appraising look that

212

he wondered if she was planning to cut him, too, and add him to the basket. Then a hint of a smile played at the corners of her mouth. "Well, look at you," she said. "All dressed up, and looking human!"

Patrick rolled his eyes. She was going to gloat.

Instead, she turned back to her task. "So I assume it went well?" she asked.

Patrick understood, then, that her visit had nothing to do with the tulips. "What went well?" he countered, deciding to make her pull the details of his meeting with Alison out of him one by one, if he chose to give her any of them at all. He took the flowers she handed him and laid them carefully in the basket.

"Coffee with Alison," she said, making it a statement rather than a question, and still not looking at him.

"Well enough, I suppose," he said, masking his true feelings. In fact, it had been almost impossible trying to talk to a near-total stranger about what his life had been like since Christmas Eve. And yet, after the first few minutes, he had seen something in Alison Montgomery's eyes that told him that she did, indeed, understand exactly how he felt, and how hard it was even to talk about it, let alone deal with it. "I'm going to a meeting with her tonight. She's picking me up."

"That's marvelous," Claire said, then stood upright, rubbing her lower back with one gloved hand as she handed Patrick the shears with the other.

"I'm not so sure it's *marv*elous at all," Patrick said, putting even more emphasis on the first syllable of the word than Claire had.

If she noticed the hint of sarcasm in his voice, she ignored it. "Of course it is," she said, pulling off her gardening gloves and eyeing the heap of tulips in the basket. "I think those should do it. Come along — I've told Neville to make his raspberry iced tea." She brushed his cheek with a kiss as she passed him, and he followed her back along the path toward the house, until he caught a glimpse of the mausoleum and stopped dead in his tracks. Embers of last night's nightmares were still smoldering in his memory, and when he turned away from the mausoleum, a flash of reflected sunlight from the windows of a yacht on the Sound seemed to fan the embers into hideous flames.

"Patrick?" he heard Claire say, but her voice seemed far in the distance. "What is it, darling? What's wrong?"

He squeezed his eyes shut against the bright sunlight and shook his head as if that could rid him of the images. When he finally reopened his eyes, he made himself focus on the basket of flowers in his hand.

Brilliant color.

Beauty.

Life.

"Nothing," he said, finally answering Claire's question. "I'm all right." Then he continued to follow his sister up the path.

Claire pulled her sun hat off as they went in the French doors and left it on a sideboard as they passed through the butler's pantry into the kitchen. "We'll have our iced tea in the library, please, Neville."

Patrick shook his head. "Not the library."

"Why not?" Claire asked, and Patrick thought he detected a hint of steel concealed in her blithe tone. "Let's open it up and air it out."

"Not the library," he repeated.

Her eyes glinted for a split-second, and then she shrugged. "Very well. The conservatory, then." She selected two vases from the half-dozen Neville had set out for her and began to arrange the tulips into perfectly symmetrical bouquets. "I think we should open the house today," she said as she worked. "It needs fresh air and sunlight. Spring is here, and it's time this old rock pile started looking like it."

Patrick said nothing.

"Including the library," Claire went on. This time Patrick opened his mouth to protest, but she stopped him with a gesture. "In time," she temporized. He followed her out of the kitchen, and held the door to the drawing room for her. "Why you even want to keep living in this old sepulcher is beyond me," she said as they moved on into the conservatory, where she set the flowers on a table and looked straight at him. "Why don't you sell it, Patrick? Why don't you get out of here? Buy something new, something fresh! You could get one of those fabulous condos in the city, overlooking the river or something."

He stared at her. "You're kidding, right?"

"Kidding?" she echoed. "Of course I'm not kidding." And he could tell by her expression that she was, indeed, serious.

He shook his head, still barely able to believe it. "How could I ever sell this place? All my memories are here — all *our* memories. Our childhood, our parents. And Renee, the girls . . ." His voice trailed off and he shook his head again. "I'll never sell this house. Ever."

Claire's eyes fixed on him, but before she could say anything else, Neville appeared in the open door with a tray bearing a silver pitcher, two glasses, a bowl of sugar, napkins, spoons, and a vase containing one single perfect tulip. As he set the tray on the table, Claire nodded toward the two vases she'd placed on it only moments before. "One of those is for the sitting room, Neville. And I'd appreciate it if you'd open it up and air it out. The other should go into Patrick's bedroom." Her gaze shifted to Patrick, but when she spoke again, her words were still for his servant. "And maybe tomorrow we'll air out the library and fill it full of flowers, too."

A silence hung over the conservatory for a moment, and then Neville took the two vases, offered Claire the smallest of nods, and left the room.

Claire's eyes still coolly fixed on Patrick, she lifted the pitcher from the tray.

"Tea?" she asked.

CHAPTER TWENTY-FOUR

Patrick dropped into his leather recliner and closed his eyes for a moment. His head sank into the headrest, but tonight — for the first time since Christmas Eve — it wasn't despair that had drained him to the point of exhaustion. No, tonight it was something else: a faint sense of hope; hope that perhaps, after all, he might find a way to survive the grief that until now had seemed utterly fatal.

Granted, that sense of hope was faint, little more than a tiny pinpoint of light piercing what seemed an infinity of darkness. He opened his eyes as if to see the faint glimmer of light better and found himself gazing at a vase of daffodils that Claire had somehow managed to sneak into the library while he was gone. They glowed on the mantel like a beacon, each of them perfect, each of them seeming to infuse the library with a feeling of life.

Claire had been right to fill the house with flowers this morning.

And she'd been right about the support group tonight, too.

Alison Montgomery had said little as she drove them the two miles or so to Shelley and Gordy Castille's house a few hours earlier, and he'd had no idea what to expect. What he found were a half-dozen cars — ranging from a battered and rusty old VW beetle to a brand new Mercedes-Benz — parked in front of the kind of house that looked as if it would be owned by someone with a Ford Explorer.

Inside, nine people were murmuring over glasses of wine. All of them smiled at him, but no one offered any of the sympathetic words he'd heard so often over the last months that they'd become nearly meaningless. As they sat down, Shelley Castille turned to a wan-looking young woman who seemed to be melting into the corner of the sofa. "Beth?" she said.

It seemed that the young woman had not heard her name, but then she stirred, tried to speak, and pressed a sodden tissue to her eyes with one hand as she clenched the other into a fist of frustration at her failed attempt. After a moment she took a deep breath, then another, reached for her wine, then seemed to think better of it. "My husband ought to be here," she finally said. "I think that's what's killing me the most." She took another ragged breath, and her eyes moved to Patrick. "Our baby died —" she began, then choked on her own words and pressed the tissue to her nose and mouth. "Oh, God, it's so hard to say that."

"Take your time," Shelley said, gently touching Beth's shoulder.

Patrick found himself leaning forward in his chair, holding his own handkerchief out to the young woman. "Thanks," Beth whispered, managing a hint of a smile, which vanished as she began to speak again. "Our baby died last week. She was only four months old. We'd been trying to have a baby for ten years. Ten years! And then —" Her voice broke and she spread her hands apart. "And then she died. She just died in her crib!" Her voice began to rise, her pain palpable. "Our lives revolved around getting me pregnant, and then being pregnant, and then having this baby, and now she's — she's gone — and David —" She choked again, took a deep breath, and forced herself to finish. "David just went back to work."

Patrick stared at her, trying to comprehend her words and failing. What kind of father could have done that?

"I mean, I don't get that," Beth went on. "I really don't get that at all." Her voice took on an edge as her grief coalesced into anger. "Is it like our baby was such a small part of his life that he could just go back to work like she never happened?"

"I'm sure it's not like that —" Shelley began, but Beth didn't let her finish.

"I know!" she cried. "I know it's not like that! But I just don't see him hurting — not like I hurt."

"You know he does," someone said.

Beth nodded, but she looked so forlorn, so vulnerable, that Patrick wanted to hold her, to comfort her.

Her eyes darted from one face to another. "I'm so angry at him," she said. "I'm so angry about everything, but I know I shouldn't be. I should —" She broke down again, and now Shelley took her hand.

"You should feel whatever way you feel," Shelley said. "There's nothing wrong with being angry — we've all been angry. Most of us still are."

A slight man with thick glasses — a man whose name Patrick hadn't caught — cleared his throat and began speaking in a voice etched with as much pain as Beth's.

221

"I lost my boys," he said. "My twins. They were in an accident with my wife." He bit his lip. "My *ex*-wife," he went on. "She had them for the weekend, and after the accident there wasn't a scratch on her. But the boys weren't in their car seats, and they both died. She'd fastened her own seat belt, but couldn't be bothered to strap her own sons in! Talk about angry! I was furious at her, and furious at God, and furious at everything. All I could do was sit in the dark and plot revenge. I didn't know what I wanted more — to kill her or just curl up and die myself."

Patrick barely heard the murmurs of understanding that ran through the room, so transfixed was he by the words he was hearing.

Words that expressed perfectly how he himself had been feeling the last months.

The man spoke again. "After a while I started losing track of time. Whole afternoons would pass and I couldn't remember them. It was like I'd have blackouts where I'd find myself at the grocery store and couldn't remember how I got there or even why I was there at all." Patrick's focus had narrowed until there might as well have been no one else in the room. "I was losing my mind over it — I

222

don't know which was worse, my grief or my anger. But they were both killing me." He paused again, collecting his thoughts. "Then I came here, and found out I wasn't the only person who'd ever felt that way." His eyes roamed over the room and came back to Beth again. "You've got a right to be angry," he said softly.

Beth's eyes were so bleak, they tore at Patrick's heart. "Will I ever get past it?" she asked.

The soft-spoken man smiled gently. "In time," he said. "If you want to."

"How?" Beth asked, her voice hollow. "How can I ever get over it?"

The man spread his hands in a wry gesture. "We all find our own way," he replied. "I finally decided to join Big Brothers, and now I have a dozen kids who seem to need me just as badly as I need them. Seems like that's what always does it — find someone else who's hurting as bad as you are, and try to give them a hand."

Now, in the silence of the library at Cragmont, the nameless man's words echoed in Patrick's mind.

. . . find someone else who's hurting as bad as you are, and try to give them a hand.

223

Patrick ran his hand over his face and felt the little scab on his chin where he'd cut himself shaving that evening. At the time, he hadn't even felt it. In fact, he hadn't realized he'd cut himself until he noticed the trickle of blood running down his neck. He'd stared at the reflected image of the cut for nearly a full minute, but felt nothing. Then his gaze shifted to his own eyes, where he'd seen only blankness.

The same kind of blankness he'd seen in Beth's eyes tonight.

. . . find someone else who's hurting as bad as you are, and try to give them a hand.

His eyes fell on the newspaper that lay folded on the table next to his chair, and on the photograph of the girl who had vanished.

The girl who looked so much like his Jenna.

This morning he had used that newspaper to fuel his grief. Now he picked it up and looked at it in a new light.

Lindsay Marshall. A nice name.

More of the nameless man's words came back to him.

. . . I started losing track of time . . . I was losing my mind . . . curl up and die . . .

Only that morning, he had awakened in

224

the mausoleum with no knowledge of how he got there.

And he didn't want to lose his mind.

. . . find someone else who's hurting as bad as you are, and try to give them a hand.

His eyes fixed once more on Lindsay Marshall's image.

What could he do?

What could he offer?

He wasn't sure.

But the point of light that had pierced the vast darkness in his soul began to brighten.

CHAPTER TWENTY-FIVE

Rick Mancuso handed his fake Mont Blanc pen to Ellen Fine, and watched disinterestedly as she read every line of the fine print on the listing agreement, knowing that in the end she would sign. This was a nice little listing; he wasn't sure Ms. Ellen Fine and her daughter were going to be prospects for another house, but at least he'd make a nice commission on this one.

She hesitated, looking up, but before she could say anything, his cell phone rang.

"Sorry," he said, pulled the phone from his pocket and looked at the caller ID. Instead of a single name, or just a phone number, four words were scrolling across the screen.

CAMDEN GREEN POLICE DEPARTMENT.

Crap.

Mark Acton had told him they'd be calling, but why did they have to call now, just as he was about to get this woman to sign on the dotted line?

He'd talk to them later.

Keeping his expression impassive, he switched the ringer to vibrate and dropped the phone back into his pocket. "Will you be relocating in this area?" he asked, his voice betraying none of the concern the phone call had caused.

Ellen Fine shook her head as a little blond girl — maybe five years old, he thought — appeared at the kitchen doorway.

"Mommy?" the child piped, sidling over to her mother while her eyes remained suspiciously on Rick.

"Hi, honey." Ellen wrapped an arm around her little girl. "This is Mr. Mancuso. He's going to help us sell our house."

"Hi," Rick said, and held out his hand.

The little girl kept her own hands firmly behind her back. "Nice to meet you," she said. "I'm Emily."

"You're very pretty, Emily."

The little girl smiled shyly at the floor.

"What do you say?" Ellen prompted.

"Thank you," the girl whispered, her eyes still avoiding Rick's.

"Sweet little girl," Mancuso said. Ellen frowned, glanced at Mancuso, and felt a

227

sudden urge to end the meeting right then. A moment later, though, she remembered her financial plight, dismissed her misgivings about the agent, and signed the listing. "We'll get a good price for this house, Ellen," Mancuso went on. "You and Emily can —"

His cell phone vibrated in his pocket, and though he tried to resist it, he couldn't help pulling it out and looking at the screen. The police again, and obviously not about to give up. "Sorry," he said, throwing his new client an apologetic smile. He opened the phone and turned away from Ellen Fine. "Rick Mancuso."

"This is Sergeant Grant from the Camden Green police department, Mr. Mancuso. We're investigating the disappearance of Lindsay Marshall."

The real-estate agent nodded as if the officer were in the room with him. "Listen, I'm with a client right now. Can I call you back in a few minutes?" He scribbled the sergeant's name and phone number in his notebook, then folded his phone and tucked it back in his pocket. "I'm sorry," he said, turning back. "Where were we?"

"I think you were about to pitch us another house," Ellen Fine said. "But I'm afraid we'll be moving out of the area entirely."

"I'm sorry to hear that."

"We're moving to Missouri to live with my grandmom," Emily said.

"Lucky her," Rick said. He picked up his paperwork and put it in his briefcase. "I'll get this right into Multiple and we'll start showing it." He stood up.

Ellen hoisted her daughter to her hip and walked him to the front door. "The sooner the better," she said. "Thanks for your help."

Rick opened the back door of his black Mercury and threw in his briefcase, then got into the driver's seat, wondering how long he could postpone his call to the cops. Not long at all, he decided. Might as well get it over with. He pulled out his phone and punched in the numbers.

"Sergeant Grant," a gruff voice responded after the first ring.

"This is Rick Mancuso."

"Thanks for getting back to us so quickly," the officer said, somewhat moderating his tone. "We're just following up on a few things. You were at the Marshalls' open house last Sunday?"

"Mark Acton's open house in Camden Green. Yes, I was there."

"You were there with clients?"

Rick frowned. "That was the plan, but they had to cancel."

"But you went anyway?"

"I was meeting them there, and they called at the last minute. I was already there, so I took another look at the place, with them in mind. And it's perfect for them, by the way."

"You were at a broker's open house there the previous Wednesday." It was a statement, not a question, and Mancuso thought he detected an edge to the cop's voice now. Where was this going? "Yes," he said, remembering his father's advice never to volunteer anything.

"And you went back again on Sunday by yourself?" Sergeant Grant pressed.

"Yes."

"Have you taken your clients to see the house yet?"

"No," Rick said, but the definite edge in Grant's voice told him he'd followed his father's advice long enough. "I called Mark to schedule a showing, but he said the house had been temporarily taken off the market because of what happened to the girl."

"What did you do after Sunday's open house?"

Rick told himself this call was nothing

personal. The police were just following up, calling everyone who had been at the open house. "Let's see," he said. "I dropped by the post office to get my mail, went to the grocery store, drove to my sister's place to take her some ice cream, but she wasn't home, so I went home and grilled myself a steak."

"Can anybody vouch for any of that?"

Rick's heart began to pound. The post office had been closed — he'd just picked up the mail from his box.

He'd paid cash at the store.

His sister wasn't home, and he lived alone — her ice cream was still in his freezer.

So he hadn't talked with anybody. There was nobody to corroborate his story.

"Mr. Mancuso?"

"I — I guess not," he finally said. "Unless maybe someone at the store remembers seeing me."

"And what time would that have been?" Grant asked.

Rick hesitated. "I'm not sure. Five? Five-thirty? I remember getting home in time for the six o'clock news."

Grant thanked him and hung up, but even after the phone went dead in his hand, Rick sat there, staring numbly through the windshield of his car.

Maybe he ought to stop by Fishburn's, he thought, and see who else the police had called.

And it wouldn't hurt to show his face after leaving Ellen Fine's place, either.

That was the other thing his father had always told him:

You can't be too careful.

"I heard we were the last to see her alive," Tina McCormick said, tossing her blond hair in the way she thought was so sexy but that Dawn D'Angelo thought was just kind of slutty. Both of them, along with the rest of the cheerleading squad and their coach, Sharon Spandler, were sitting at a table in the cafeteria, facing the policeman who had called them all there.

"Well," Andrew Grant said carefully, ignoring Tina's flirting, "you were certainly among the last to *see* her."

"And we're sure she's still alive, Tina," Sharon Spandler said, fixing her eyes disapprovingly on the girl. Tina tried to pretend she didn't notice the coach's glare, but reddened in spite of herself.

"*I* was the last to see Lindsay," Dawn said. "We walked home together Sunday after practice. And she's still alive," she added, glowering at Tina. She could hardly believe Tina had said that. If the policeman and Ms. Spandler hadn't been sitting with them, she would have thrown her water bottle at Tina. But the coach was there, looking almost as tired as she herself felt, and the cop was there, so she hadn't. Not that doing anything to Tina would help her feel any better, Dawn thought. She hadn't been able to eat since last Sunday night, when Mrs. Marshall had called, saying that Lindsay was missing.

And she couldn't stop feeling it was her fault. If she'd only asked her stupid stepmother if Lindsay could come with her — or better yet, not asked at all and just brought Lindsay with her on Sunday night — then Lindsay would be fine, and everything would be good again, and none of them would have to be sitting here talking about her.

"I heard she ran away," Becka Saunders said.

"I heard her parents were taking her to the city and putting her in a private school," Heather Blaine offered.

Grant's eyes swept over the group. "Anybody hear anything else?"

Dawn sat silently as every rumor that had swept through the school was repeated,

233

each of them with new embellishments. She sat with her arms crossed, and with every new theory that was aired, the dull ache in her belly grew worse.

And it would continue to get worse until she saw her best friend's face again.

"Did Lindsay have a boyfriend?" Sergeant Grant asked. "Maybe somebody who didn't go to school here? Somebody older? Somebody she didn't talk about too much?"

All the girls shook their heads.

"She was kind of hot on Zack Sorenson," Tina McCormick said, "but I don't think he even knew about it."

"They never went out?"

Tina shrugged, but Dawn rolled her eyes. "Zack is going with somebody," she said, wishing Tina would shut up, since she barely even knew Lindsay.

"No boyfriends?" Sergeant Grant pressed. "Don't you all have boyfriends?"

The girls all nodded except Dawn. "Lindsay didn't have a boyfriend," she said firmly.

"At least not one you knew about," Tina McCormick taunted.

"Is she gay?" Sergeant Grant asked, making a note of what the McCormick girl had said.

Dawn rolled her eyes. The other girls only giggled.

"What about drugs?" Grant went on.

The girls glanced at each other, and Dawn could see three of them blushing. "Not Lindsay," she finally said. "Lindsay was as squeaky clean as you can get."

"Not as squeaky as you!" Tina McCormick threw in, and Grant began to wonder if Dawn D'Angelo knew Lindsay Marshall as well as she claimed she did. But when he looked at Sharon Spandler, the coach shrugged.

"I never heard any talk about Lindsay using," she said.

Grant raised his brows noncommittally. In his experience, most of the teachers were as ignorant about kids' drug use as their parents were. "So the thing that was upsetting her was that her folks wanted to move her to the city?" he asked, his eyes once more sweeping the group.

And once more it was Dawn D'Angelo who responded. "She was really upset about that. She didn't want to go — she wanted to spend her senior year here, and be head cheerleader and then graduate with all the rest of us." She glanced around at the other girls, who were nodding in agreement. "I mean, we all grew up together — she hated the idea of going someplace she didn't know with a bunch of kids she didn't know."

"How unhappy was she about that?" Grant asked.

"Very," Dawn said. "Very, very, extremely."

The other girls nodded again, and so did Sharon Spandler.

"Unhappy enough to run away?" the policeman went on.

A long silence fell over the group gathered around the cafeteria table — a silence that told Grant as much as anything the girls had actually said out loud.

They didn't know.

They didn't know anything at all.

Sergeant Grant took business cards from his shirt pocket and handed them around the table. "If you can think of anything, no matter how small, or if you hear something, call me, okay?"

"Do you think she's all right?" someone asked.

"I hope so," he said, standing up and closing his notebook. The girls watched in silence as he turned away from the table and walked out of the cafeteria.

Sergeant Grant sat quietly for a moment in his warm car with his eyes closed.

There were no red flags in this case.

No sign of forced entry to the home.

No hint of anyone who Lindsay might have gotten on the wrong side of — no boyfriends, no drug dealers.

Apparently no enemies at all.

But unhappy.

Very unhappy, and probably very angry at her parents.

He sighed, picked up his notebook, made a few notes about his interview with Lindsay's friends, then radioed his office.

"I still think she's a runaway," he said. "We'll keep our eyes open and keep talking to people, but I'm thinking she'll show up by the end of the week. Give her some time to cool off."

Still, as he started his car and pulled away from the curb in front of Camden Green High, he wondered once more about that real estate agent. What was his name?

Mancuso — that was it. Rick Mancuso.

Something in his voice just hadn't sounded right.

CHAPTER TWENTY-SIX

Lindsay's eyes opened slowly.

She was still bound to the chair, still surrounded by darkness. Darkness hiding terrors she could feel, even if she couldn't see them. But even closer than the terrors concealed in the darkness were the ones inside her.

Pain.

Numbness.

Exhaustion.

And thirst.

A thirst so terrible it threatened to consume her. Her lips were swollen and cracked, her tongue dry. She ached for water. Visions began to dance in the darkness around her — brief glimpses of the water her body craved: herself, swimming in the school pool; birds, flitting in water fountains; cold ocean spray breaking over rocks; glasses of chilled soda; lawn sprinklers soaking cool green grass. She wanted to reach for the visions, touch them, feel the water. But her body had long ago gone from mild discomfort to aching and twitching, and now it felt coldly numb. And the thirst was so overwhelming that even her eyelids felt like sandpaper as they moved across eyeballs gone dry from lack of moisture.

If she cried, she knew she would shed no tears — the thirst made her feel as if every drop of water had been leached from her body.

She tried to whisper to Shannon but no sound came from her parched throat. And was Shannon even there anymore? She strained to listen, searching in the silence for the sound of the other girl's breathing, but heard nothing.

She let her eyelids close, and silently prayed for unconsciousness.

A sound.

A scraping sound. Then bright light — a light so dazzling she reflexively twisted her head away. Then she slowly opened her eyes, and her heart pounded as she felt whatever evil that had locked her in this dungeon come closer.

Steeling herself, she twisted her head around to face the evil looming over her, but all she saw was a black silhouette in the blinding light.

Then she heard a voice — Shannon's voice — moan a single word: "No."

Now, in the glow filling the chamber, Lindsay could see her crouched on a mattress on the floor of what seemed to be a long, narrow, unfinished basement. Shannon's back was pressed to the wall and her knees pressed against her chest, as if they could somehow protect her from the evil presence that hung against the bright light. Her long, dark hair was matted, and the deathly pallor of her face made her look far older than Lindsay, though her voice sounded much younger.

As the dark silhouette took form and became the figure of a man, Shannon moaned again and hid her face against her knees.

The man passed Shannon and came directly toward her. Lindsay's heart pounded so hard she could hear it throbbing in her ears, and her breath caught in her lungs.

He came close enough so her nostrils filled with the same musky odor he'd left in her bedroom.

He set something on the floor, then touched her.

Touched her breast, squeezing the nipple so hard it hurt.

She reflexively tried to jerk away from

his touch, but the object pressing against her throat kept her from moving her head more than a fraction of an inch.

Then he was holding something in front of her, and for an instant Lindsay was certain it was another hallucination. But then he gently fed the straw emerging from the neck of a water bottle through her parched lips.

Reflexively, she began to suck.

Water!

Fresh, cool water!

She greedily drank as fast as the straw could deliver the soothing liquid across her tongue, certain that at any moment her captor would snatch it away.

And all too soon, he did . . .

Lindsay licked her lips and peered up at him.

A scream rose in her throat as she saw the leering grin that hovered above her, but it died away to little more than a helpless gurgling sound as she realized that he wasn't grinning at all.

He was wearing a mask.

A white surgeon's mask upon which two huge and lascivious lips had been drawn with some kind of red marker. Above the surgeon's mask his face was covered with a black ski mask, his eyes glinting almost invisibly from deep beneath the eyeholes.

His body was cloaked with a black raincoat.

Then her thirst broke through her terror and her head tipped up, almost against her own will. "Please," she whispered, her voice sounding as if someone else must have uttered the single word.

"Quiet!" the man commanded. He reached for her breast once more, and though every fiber of her being wanted to shrink away, her need for water was stronger. She made herself hold still beneath his touch, and finally he held the bottle to her lips once more.

He bent down, and when he straightened, he held a bowl and spoon.

Lindsay's eyes fixed on the bowl, and her exhausted mind groped to understand what he might be doing.

But it didn't matter: if he drugged her, she would at least fall into the bliss of unconsciousness.

If he killed her, she would be forever released from his prison and her own terror.

She opened her mouth and let him feed her.

Oatmeal! Oatmeal, sweetened with brown sugar and cinnamon.

And milk!

She swallowed and opened her mouth for more.

Part of her was revolted that she was letting him touch her just so she could have water and food, but the food itself ignited a hunger she hadn't realized was there.

She swallowed every morsel he offered, and sucked down as much water as she could manage when he held the bottle to her lips again.

She felt her body begin to tingle as its numbness gave way to the infusion of energy the food and water provided.

"Please," she whispered quietly to him. "Please let us go."

"You never let me go," he said, but a moment later she could feel him ripping the tape away from her ankles.

She could barely move her knees, and couldn't feel her feet at all, nor move her ankles.

Then he tore the tape from her wrists, and her arms dropped from the hard wood into her lap. She moved her fingers and tried to get one hand over to the other to massage her throbbing wrist, but it was too much.

Her joints screamed with pain and her muscles refused to obey the commands of her mind.

The man untied the object that had pressed against her throat, and she finally saw what it was — a metal bit, the kind she'd seen on horses. Tentatively, fearfully, she rotated her head on her neck. But it was all right; nothing pressed against her throat, nothing strangled her breath.

He peeled the blanket away from her, then grabbed her by the arms and pulled her to her feet. Her legs still numb, Lindsay stumbled and fell against him, and as her body came in contact with his, her nostrils filled with the musky odor she'd first smelled in her bedroom on Wednesday afternoon.

Could it have been that recently? The time when every muscle in her body hadn't ached and her soul hadn't been filled with terror was a memory so dim it seemed years ago.

Could it only have been a few days?

She tried to resist her captor, tried to pull away, but she couldn't even straighten her back, let alone find the strength to twist herself out of his grip. He half carried her away from the chair to a mattress on the floor, where he shoved her down, hurling her body with enough force that she could feel the hard concrete even through the thick padding.

A low wall separated her mattress from the one a few feet away, on which Shannon cowered. But the wall was just high enough so she could no longer see the other girl.

The man closed hard, cold, metal handcuffs around Lindsay's wrists, then chained the cuffs to the wall behind her.

From the pocket of the raincoat, he produced a packet that looked vaguely familiar, but Lindsay didn't quite recognize it until he tore it open and pulled the contents loose from the foil.

Baby wipes.

The kind she had seen mothers use on their infant children in the restrooms at the mall.

She cringed, and had to force herself not to give him the satisfaction of uttering even a single sound as he pulled her panties away and began cleaning her.

"How do you like it?" he asked as he worked. "Do you like it as much as I did?" Tossing the wipe aside, he put what looked like a dish towel between her legs, pinned it like a diaper, and covered her with a ragged blanket.

He vanished behind the low wall, and a few seconds later Lindsay heard Shannon's chains rattling. "No," she croaked. "Please . . . no . . . please . . ."

Then Lindsay saw him again, straightening up, pulling Shannon to her feet and half leading, half dragging her across the chamber floor. Naked, Shannon was so thin Lindsay could see the knobs of her spine and hollows between her ribs.

"Please . . . no . . . please . . ." Shannon whispered again, the words coming like a mantra. ". . . No . . . please . . . no . . ."

Every muscle in Lindsay's body tensed, and she wanted to hurl herself on the man and tear Shannon from his grip. But her wrists were cuffed and chained to the wall, and she knew her body was too weak anyway.

She watched helplessly as he opened a door on the far side of the long room, half carried Shannon through it, and closed it behind them, abruptly cutting off Shannon's whispered pleas as a terrible, hollow silence fell over the dungeon.

Lindsay was alone.

She felt like crying, but refused to give in to the urge, knowing even through her terror that it would do no good.

She closed her eyes against the threat of tears and stretched her legs out to their full length.

As the oatmeal and water fed the tiniest bit of strength back into her body, and the numbness and tingling in her legs and arms finally began to ease, she tried not to think about what was happening to Shannon, and what might soon be happening to her, too.

And there was no way out.

No way out at all.

CHAPTER TWENTY-SEVEN

The sound of the door echoed oddly as Steve Marshall closed it behind Sergeant Grant.

Sergeant *Andrew* Grant, he thought as he sank back onto the sofa next to his wife. How had it happened that until tonight he'd never even thought of the cop in terms of having a first name, let alone wondered what it was?

Not that it mattered, for knowing Grant's first name hadn't changed a thing. Not one single thing. His beautiful, wonderful, perfect wife still looked every bit as hollowed out and ashen as she had before the policeman arrived to fill them in on his progress.

And Lindsay was still gone.

And no one — not her friends or the police or Kara, or he himself — had any better idea of what happened to her than they had on the day she vanished.

The only thing new was that he now knew Sergeant Grant's first name.

And he and Kara were once again sitting side by side, not talking, feeling the emptiness of their home. As the silence threatened to overwhelm them both, faint echoes of Sergeant Grant's visit seemed to whisper from the walls of their home, and Steve reached out to take Kara's small, pale hand in his own.

"She's not a runaway," Kara said, as if responding to the same echo Steve had heard.

He hesitated, wishing he could offer her some scrap of evidence — anything — to share with her the same faint hope he was still clinging to that Sergeant Grant was right and at any moment the phone could ring, or the door could open, and their daughter would be with them once more. But he couldn't. All he could do was hold her hand.

"What did he mean, there was no evidence of foul play?" Kara asked, her voice as hollow as the house had been since Lindsay vanished.

"He meant that teenage girls do things when they're upset," Steve said, choosing his words carefully. "You know that. Remember when you were seventeen? Remember what the girls in your class were thinking about? How many of them were constantly angry at their parents and threatening to run away? You know what he was talking about, Kara."

It was as if she hadn't heard him at all. "He said there was no evidence," she whispered, almost to herself. "But she's gone. Her blanket is gone. What kind of evidence does he want?"

"Kara —"

Finally, she looked at him. "Where would she go? With who? Oh, God, we've been over this a thousand times, Steve. You know as well as I do that Lindsay's no runaway!"

"Honey, maybe he's right," Steve began. For the last hour, as Andrew Grant had gone over every tiny scrap of information he'd garnered about Lindsay's disappearance — which was essentially nothing — Steve had allowed himself to hope that maybe the sergeant was right — that Lindsay had just taken off in a fit of anger, wanting to punish them the same way teenagers everywhere wanted to punish their parents. And if he could hang onto that, he could hang onto hope that when she cooled off, she would, indeed, come home.

At least it was something.

Kara pulled her hand from his. "All he really came to tell us," she said, "was that they're not going to do anything."

Steve put his arm around his wife. "They are," he told her. "They're just doing what the police do — they're the experts in these things. We have to be strong and have faith."

She paid no attention to him. "They ought to call the FBI. But they won't, because —"

"Because we don't know it's a kidnapping," Steve broke in, and immediately wished he could retract his words.

"Not to them, it isn't," Kara flared. "But I know better." She picked at a cuticle that was already seeping blood, and when she spoke again, her voice had hardened. "I know better." She turned to face him. "Tomorrow I'm going to organize a group to post flyers all over Long Island. I've already blanketed the town, but it's not enough. And I'm going to call the FBI myself, if Sergeant Grant isn't going to, and then I'm going to start distributing flyers in the city. And you can —" She fell abruptly silent and her eyes searched his. "What is it?" she asked when he looked away.

Steve hesitated, then, realizing there was no point in waiting until morning to tell her, said softly, "Honey, I have to go back to the office tomorrow."

It was as if he'd struck her. "Your office? *Tomorrow?*"

He reached out to her. "I have to. There are so many things no one else can take care of, and —"

"You believe him," Kara said, her voice suddenly flat. "You believe Sergeant Grant." Her voice rose. "You think that if we don't do anything, Lindsay will just come home!"

"No," Steve whispered, but even as he said it, he knew it wasn't quite the truth. He pulled her close, and though at first she resisted, her exhaustion and grief and terror for their daughter overcame her and she folded into him as she used to before Lindsay vanished and their lives had fallen to pieces around them.

He rocked her gently, and slowly felt the anger drain out of her body. "I'll call you," he promised. "I'll call you every hour if you want, and you can call me as often as you want to."

She nodded.

"And I'll be home every night — I can promise you I'll never stay in the city again."

She sniffed.

"She's my daughter, too," Steve whispered, drawing her even closer. And then they were clinging together with an intimacy they hadn't felt for years, an intimacy he knew she had been missing as much as he.

If only it could have come in some other way.

CHAPTER TWENTY-EIGHT

She is truly the devil — it isn't just her looks, though of course it was her looks that first told me what lurked within her soul.

I was almost afraid to bring her here, but now that I have, I know I've done the right thing; I shall keep her in exactly the condition — and the environment — she deserves. And the time will come when she will understand why she is here, what she has done.

I wish I could visit her more often, but I know I cannot. I must be patient. But patience is so hard when I feel this desperate hatred inside me.

Did she feel what I felt when I touched her body? Her skin is even softer than mine, and her fragrance — a fragrance that holds me still in thrall — lingers on the tips of my fingers and in the depths of my nostrils, and even as I sit writing these simple words in the loneliness of my chamber, I can smell her once again — even see her, stretched out on her mattress, lying in the darkness. Does she sleep at all, or does the evil inside her keep her as wakeful as it does me?

Is she dreaming of me as I shall dream of her tonight when at last I put aside my pen and drift into my own dark sleep?

Perhaps our dreams will come together, and we shall touch again.

And if we do, I hope she feels the pain I shall feel.

Perhaps I should deal with her — with both of them — right now. But patience must be my watchword. Everything must be done correctly, everything perfectly planned, all things executed in precise order.

It must all be done right.

But it's so hard — so hard to keep away from her, now that I have her within my grasp.

She looked frightened when I visited a little while ago. She needed water, and she was terribly hungry, and I gave her just enough to give her hope.

She moaned, of course, and pretended to turn away, but I know it meant nothing at all, for even as she made her feigned protests, she gazed at me in a way that showed me her true desires as clearly as if she were pressing her naked flesh close to my own.

I stripped away the soft material that covered her loins and slipped it into my pocket.

It's still there as I write, and even though I hold a pen in my fingers right now, the simple knowledge that in a moment I will once again clutch that foul fabric — will once again press it to my nose to breathe in the evil scent that emanates from the secret places of her body — makes my own body shiver with an anticipation that verges on ecstasy.

She will know. Soon she will know.

Soon they both will know.

But I shall not give in to my desires, not until the time is right and all of them are here. Then, after her scent has reminded me one more time that I now hold her in my power, I will press that fabric into these pages and keep it here forever.

As I will keep her here forever . . .

Kara Marshall gazed unseeingly out the train window, the clacking of the wheels on the tracks — a sound that normally lulled her into a half doze within moments of

leaving the Camden Green station —
doing nothing at all today to calm the tur-
moil of her mind.

She had to *do* something! And she was
going to do something, the moment she
got to the city.

Unconsciously, her hand closed tighter
on the bag filled with the posters she'd
made up last night. Except they weren't really posters — they were just sheets of
standard size copy paper showing an image
of Lindsay and pleading for any information about where she might be.

And Kara's phone number.

Not that it was going to do any good, for
deep in her heart she knew — knew with a
terrible certainty — that Lindsay hadn't
simply taken off for a few days.

Someone had taken her.

Turning away from the world racing by
beyond the train window, she remembered
that there were people around her. People
who might have seen Lindsay.

Pulling one of the posters from her bag,
she began to circulate through the train,
showing it to anyone who would look at it.
Half the people simply turned away; the
rest shook their heads sadly and looked at
her with pity in their eyes.

When Kara had reached the last car, she

collapsed into a seat and stared vacantly at her daughter's image.

And felt utterly helpless.

Was she going to show the poster to ten million people? And even if she could, what good would it do? *It doesn't matter,* she told herself. *You have to do something, and there isn't anything else you can do.*

She got off the train at Grand Central and took the subway south to Spring Street, emerging from the station into the streets of SoHo. And everywhere she looked — on every kiosk and lamppost — she saw masses of posters just like hers, advertising everything from rock groups to performance artists to housecleaning services to free kittens. On some of the kiosks, the posters were layered more than an inch thick. Even if she put hers up, how long would they remain uncovered? A day? An hour? Five minutes?

Steeling herself, she began. She went into every shop, every store, every gallery and restaurant along Spring and Prince and Houston. Wherever they let her, she taped a poster in the window, and sometimes taped one to the outside if they wouldn't let her put one inside.

But none of them would let her show Lindsay's photo to their customers. Not in the restaurants, not in the shops, not in the galleries.

When her stomach finally told her she had to eat something, she bought a hot pretzel and a bottle of water and walked up to Washington Square to eat the makeshift snack. The pretzel seemed to have no flavor at all, and she could barely swallow the water. Finally, she threw the last bite to the pigeons, stood up, took a deep breath and began her work again.

By four o'clock she was numb from repeating her questions. She was almost out of posters, and had seen some of the ones she'd put up earlier already covered by posters for other things.

How many girls went missing in New York every day, apparently with no one giving a damn about any of them, let alone her own daughter?

Kara felt like crying, but would not. Instead she took another deep breath and looked around to get her bearings.

She was on the corner of Bleecker and Lafayette, only a few blocks from where she began. She'd been in the city nearly all day, and had covered only about twenty city blocks.

Manhattan had almost seven thousand city blocks.

She had not even made a dent. She felt exhausted, broken, and almost overwhelmed with hopelessness.

She wasn't going to find Lindsay this way.

So what was the use?

Before she could decide what to do next — call Steve or start back home — her cell phone rang. She glanced at the display, didn't recognize the number, but pressed the key to accept the call.

"Kara?" a woman's voice caroled. "Hi! It's Rita Goldman!" For a moment Kara couldn't quite place the name, but then the woman spoke again, and Kara remembered who she was. "I've found the perfect apartment for your family. It's a three-bedroom, two bath with a great view on West Eighty-fourth. Lots of light, and you'll love the price. The sellers are highly motivated —"

Kara clicked the phone off without speaking at all.

Rita Goldman. Their agent in the city. And she didn't even know about Lindsay.

With everything that had happened — the TV coverage, the stories in the paper, the dozens of calls she'd made and the hundreds of posters she'd put up — even their own agent didn't know that Lindsay was missing.

The world was just too big, and there were too many places someone could hide a girl.

Finally it all caved in on Kara. She sank to the curbing on a corner in the middle of the city, put her head on her knees, and began to cry.

CHAPTER TWENTY-NINE

All things come to he who waits.

I do not know who first said that, but I have always found it to be true.

I wait.

I am observant.

I am able to see the signs.

And this morning another one came.

Yet even now, as I write this, I couldn't say exactly how I know that this was what I have been looking for.

Waiting for.

Searching for.

At first glance there was nothing special about the ad at all.

A seemingly innocuous little ad for an equally innocuous-sounding house.

And yet something about it kept bringing my attention back to it, and soon it stood out from all the other ads like a brilliant signal shining out of darkness.

262

A beacon, reaching out to me, drawing me to it.

I have circled the ad in red, of course, and I suppose I must admit the possibility that I could be wrong.

Which is why I circled a few other ads, too, and though I shall go and look at all the houses, I have a feeling about this one.

After I've been to the house, and assured myself that it is, indeed, the place where she lives, I shall paste the ad into this journal, just as I have the ads for both the girls' houses.

I could probably paste the ad in now, so strong is my feeling, but again I must remind myself to be patient and wait until everything is proven and everything is right.

Still, things are coming together perfectly — far more perfectly than I could ever have imagined.

It won't be long now.

I can be patient.

I must be patient.

I will be patient.

But it is hard, and my cravings are so strong. . . .

CHAPTER THIRTY

Mama.

Lindsay focused on the word that had become her mantra, silently repeating it over and over again in the suffocating darkness. Sometimes it helped her slip off into a restless sleep.

But mostly — as now — it was the only thing that kept hope alive.

Somehow her mother would find her; would know what had happened to her; would come to her rescue.

Mama.

She had to come soon, before the man — the *monster* — turned from Shannon to her.

Shannon.

The other girl's name echoed in her mind. How long had she been here? Where had she come from?

And what had the man done to her?

Lindsay didn't want to think about it,

but no matter how hard she tried, images kept forming in her mind — terrible images cobbled together from scenes she'd seen on television and at the movies.

Images of the man looming over Shannon's emaciated body. In her mind's eye, Lindsay saw Shannon tied down, her body stripped naked, the man's fingers running over her skin, touching her arms and her legs, then moving over the contours of her body. Lindsay's own skin crawled as she imagined how Shannon must feel, and as she imagined his hands caressing Shannon's breasts, then moving lower until his fingers slipped between her legs, her own groin began to tingle and she found herself trying to twist away from the touch that wasn't even happening.

Not, at least, to her.

A faint groan escaped her parched lips — so faint she wasn't sure she'd made it at all — and now her thirst finally wiped away the terrible images of Shannon's torture her mind had conjured up. She fantasized now that her captor had left the water bottle on the floor, that somehow she could get to it, but even as the fantasy lured her, she knew it was only that: a fantasy.

The man had taken the bottle with him.

There was no water.

No water even to long for, let alone water within her reach.

Mama . . .

Lindsay closed her eyes, hoping to drift off, but was suddenly jerked back to full consciousness by the creaking of hinges and the blinding light from the doorway.

A low moan came from Shannon, the only indication she'd had in hours that the other girl was still alive. Then Lindsay heard Shannon's chains jangling, and a moment later she could see the terrifying figure clad in black lift her body — as limp as a broken doll — and take her through the door into the darkness beyond. Just before he vanished, the figure turned back to gaze at Lindsay for a moment, and the bloodred smile painted on his surgical mask leered at her.

Then he was gone.

Lindsay lay quietly, trying to still her heart.

There was a way out. There had to be! She was an athlete. Her body was strong — much stronger than Shannon's. If she could find a way to loosen her bonds, find a way out of her prison, she could outrun this man, whoever he was.

For what had to be the millionth time,

she tested her strength against the bonds that held her.

And for the millionth time they held her fast.

Then, too soon, he came back through the door.

He was alone.

Lindsay cringed as he knelt next to her and stroked her hair. "Drink," he whispered, his lips so close that she could feel his breath on her cheek. "Drink, or you might die too soon. . . ." He held the water bottle before her and put the straw between her lips.

Lindsay sucked the water into her mouth before the meaning of his words quite registered, swallowing as much as she could, knowing he would pull the bottle away in only a few seconds. She tried to drain it, sucking hard and fast, trying to shut out the sound of his voice and the touch of his fingers. Too soon — far too soon — a gurgle from the straw told her the bottle was empty. It had not been enough — not nearly enough to soothe her parched tongue, moisten her lips, end the dryness in her mouth.

Now he was cleaning her the way he had before, and Lindsay cringed, shutting her eyes tight, as if blocking out the sight of him could also block the vile touch of his fingers on her skin.

Mama . . . she silently cried. *Come find me, Mama.*

"Come with me," the black figure with the grotesque mask said when he was finished wiping her skin.

Lindsay felt the shackles around her wrists loosened, and for just an instant, hope surged. But a second later, as she realized she was too weak even to attempt to flee, that brief flicker of hope died away.

The fingers of his right hand closed on her arm like the jaws of a vise and he pulled her up from the mattress, pinning her easily to the wall with a single arm. She tried to resist, but the last of her strength seemed to have drained away and all she could do was force a scream that emerged as little more than a nearly inaudible whine.

"Quiet," he commanded. "I've brought you something new to wear."

With utter incomprehension, she gazed at the scrap of cloth he was holding in his free hand then realized that it was a dress.

A dress for a doll.

Using a string he'd run through both arms of the tiny dress, he tied the garment around her waist.

The skirt of the dress barely covered her groin.

Holding her up as if she were an invalid, he walked her to the door through which he'd carried Shannon a few moments ago. If he let go, she knew she would fall.

And she knew that if she fell, he would simply drag her along behind him as if she were a broken doll whose dress was all she now wore.

But he didn't let go. Instead he steered her through the door, and into a dark, damp, cold tunnel that reeked of mold and mildew and rot.

Lindsay tried to keep up, tried to keep her legs moving with him, tried to keep her feet on the ground, but half the time they seemed to drag on the floor as he hauled her along.

They came to a set of wooden stairs, and he surged up them, his viselike fingers still closed on her wrist in an unbreakable grip. Her legs and feet banged on the treads as he half dragged her up the stairs and through a trapdoor, into another room.

It was here that Lindsay saw Shannon stretched across a low table, her wrists and ankles taped to its legs. She was bone thin, her long brown hair matted into tangled strings. A filthy scrap of a doll's dress that must once have looked like the one she herself now wore was all that covered her.

Shannon's eyes stayed closed, and Lindsay didn't know if she was even conscious.

Her mouth was covered with shiny silver duct tape upon which the man had painted the same grotesquely leering red smile that was spread over his own mask.

"See how much she likes it?" the man whispered. "I'm going to make you like it, too." As Lindsay gazed at Shannon in mute horror, the man forced her down onto one of the child-sized chairs that circled the table.

He bound her wrists together behind her, and her ankles to the chair legs with the same duct tape he'd used to bind Shannon to the table. Finally, he put a wide strip of tape over her mouth.

He pulled a red marker from one of the pockets of his black raincoat, and Lindsay knew without being told that soon her mouth would look like Shannon's and his own.

"It's important for us all to smile at each other," he said softly as he worked. "It's how we know we love each other, isn't it?"

When he was finished, he capped his red

marker, then roughly brushed a tear from her cheek. Crouching down beside her, he looked into her eyes. "Isn't this fun?" he said, his voice now so cold it made her shiver. "All of us playing, just like we used to!"

Then he rose to his full height and stood behind her. He ran his fingers over her cheek. "So sweet . . ." His fingers roamed down her neck and shoulder to her breast. "So pure . . ."

Lindsay wanted to scream, wanted to twist away from his touch, wanted to lash out at him. But she was bound helplessly to the chair, and even if she could scream, there would be no one except Shannon to hear her.

So she did nothing at all. She held absolutely still, refusing to acknowledge his touch, refusing to give him the satisfaction of any reaction at all.

Abruptly, he pulled his hand away.

He gazed at her for a long moment.

And finally he spoke.

"You'll learn," he said softly. "You'll learn the same way I learned."

He turned away from her then and knelt down close to Shannon.

And as Lindsay stared in shocked horror, he began to do to Shannon all the things Lindsay had only imagined him doing a few minutes before.

She turned away, and an instant later, his hand slashed across her face. Her mouth filled with the coppery taste of blood as one of her teeth sank into her cheek.

"Watch," the man commanded. "How can you learn to love me if you don't watch?"

Her cheek stinging, her eyes flooding with tears, her soul gripped in a terror worse than anything she'd ever known, Lindsay watched in utter silence as the man went about his "lesson."

Finally finishing with a sigh that seemed more a release than any kind of ecstasy, he rose back to his feet and loomed once more above her.

"You see?" he asked, holding her chin and tipping her face up so she couldn't avoid looking at him. "We love each other. That's why we're smiling. Because we all love each other, and we like playing together." He slit the tape that bound Shannon's ankles and wrists with a pocketknife, then lifted her up like a rag doll. With one arm around her waist, the other holding Shannon's arm around his own neck, he dragged her to the hatch leading to the stairs.

Lindsay knew that in a few moments he would be back.

He would be back for her.

Mama, she silently cried one more time. *Come and find me, Mama. . . .*

CHAPTER THIRTY-ONE

Neville Cavanaugh put the first of the garden's lilies in a vase and set it gently on the breakfast tray. Even though Mr. Shields was still sleeping in the library, at least he seemed to have finally regained a little of his appetite. Perhaps if he rapped on the library door — But before he could finish the thought, let alone pick up the breakfast tray to act on it, the kitchen door opened and Patrick Shields himself walked into the kitchen.

And this morning he wasn't wearing his pajamas and bathrobe. Rather, he was freshly showered and shaved, wore a pair of loose-fitting white linen trousers and a black polo shirt, and was looking fitter and more chipper than Neville had seen him in months.

Since the day before Christmas, in fact.

Wherever Patrick had gone two nights ago, Neville thought, it must have done him a lot more good than he himself would have thought possible.

"Good morning, Neville," Patrick said. "Think I'll eat in the conservatory this morning. It's such a beautiful day."

Neville took the tray to the conservatory, where the remains of his own breakfast still littered the table. He set the tray down and then began to tidy up.

Patrick Shields picked up the newspaper that Neville had taken to reading himself since his employer had shown little interest in it in months.

Neville set out his employer's breakfast, then piled his own dishes on the tray and waited for the paper. Patrick glanced up at him.

"I think I'll just read it, today, thanks." His eyes went back to the story Neville himself had been reading half an hour earlier. The story about the girl who had disappeared, Lindsay Marshall. "Have you heard anything else about this girl?" he asked.

"No, sir," Neville responded as he dusted crumbs off the table. "Just what I've read in the paper."

"Claire knows the girl's mother," his employer replied. "Said we actually met once at a fund-raiser. What a horrible thing."

"I can barely imagine what they must be going through," Neville murmured.

Again his employer glanced up, his lips compressing into a hard line. "No," he said. "I suppose you can't. But I can."

Neville felt himself flush as their eyes met once again. Then he picked up the tray and left the room, and Patrick, alone, turned back to the paper and focused on the story. It had been almost a week, with no word. The girl's family was frantic, and understandably so.

Unlike Neville Cavanaugh, Patrick could more than imagine what they must be going through.

He knew exactly what they were feeling.

And then, as he read the story one more time, he remembered the words spoken two nights earlier by the man who had lost his twins.

Find someone else who's hurting as bad as you are, and try to give them a hand.

Picking up the phone Neville had left on the table, Patrick dialed information, asked for the number of the Camden Green police department, then waited while the connection was made.

Moments later he'd gone through several people before the person he was seeking finally came on the line, his voice flat. "Sergeant Grant."

"Sergeant Grant, this is Patrick Shields."

"Mr. Shields," Grant said, his voice immediately losing its neutral tone. Though he hadn't actually spoken to Patrick Shields since they were children, the policeman was as aware of who Patrick was — and what had happened to his family — as everybody else in Camden Green. "It's been a while. How are you holding up?"

"I'm getting along," Patrick replied. "Thank you for asking. But I'm not calling about myself. I'm wondering about the Marshall girl. Has there been any progress on the case?" He heard the sergeant hesitate. "I'm thinking I'd like to try to do something for her parents," he explained. When Grant still made no reply, Patrick told him, "I think I know how they must be feeling." Another silence, and now Patrick wondered if maybe he shouldn't have called. "I guess maybe —" he began, then forced himself to go on. "I thought perhaps if I posted a reward . . ." His voice trailed off, and once again he wondered if he'd made a mistake, if he should just keep to himself after all.

Then Andrew Grant responded. "You

never know," he said. "Sometimes rewards bring out new leads. That's very generous of you."

"Then consider it done," Patrick said. "Do you think ten thousand would help?"

"It would sure get me calling," Grant replied. "You'll have to run that by the family. They're the ones who'll have to decide. But if they go along with it, it's fine with me." Now it was Patrick who was silent. "Is there a problem with that?" Grant asked when the silence went on too long.

"I — Well, I think I'd prefer the source to remain anonymous. So if you wouldn't mind, perhaps you could inform the family?"

"I understand," Grant said. "Of course. I'll get back to you."

Patrick clicked off the phone, set it down on the table, and took a blueberry muffin from the basket Neville had left. As he broke it open and spread butter on its steaming halves, he looked out the window toward the Sound.

It was, indeed, a beautiful day.

In the kitchen, Neville Cavanaugh quietly set the extension phone back in its cradle.

CHAPTER THIRTY-TWO

When will I learn? When will I ever learn?

When I'm patient — when I'm in control — things happen exactly as they are supposed to happen.

Even magic happens.

Things fall into place seemingly without any effort on my part at all.

But when I'm impulsive — and today I was impulsive — disasters happen.

I barely escaped one this afternoon, all because I was both impatient and impulsive, which is the worst combination.

The odd thing is, I'm still not entirely sure how it happened. I found myself in the neighborhood of the house I saw in the newspaper, but I have no memory of going there. No conscious memory, at any rate, though I suppose if someone were to dig deep enough into my psyche — well, never mind!

The point is, I would never have gone

there without the proper preparation, without the proper planning, without thinking the entire event through.

And yet, when I found myself in the general vicinity, I was seized with a sudden desire to see the house right then. I couldn't wait until the time was right.

Then, to compound my error, I threw caution to the wind and parked across the street from the house, though at least I had the sense to park two doors down.

It should have been harmless, of course. All I wanted to do was take a quick look.

Get a general impression.

Find out if the feeling that came over me when I found the advertisement was genuine.

I must have been insane.

Worse, I was stupid — totally stupid.

The house, though, was perfect. Small and tidy, with a lovely border of flowers along the walk.

But it was the aura I felt most strongly. It was almost a visible thing, enveloping the house with a wonderful feeling of love and tenderness, though I also sensed a mild undertone of sadness — perhaps even of tragedy.

Instinctively, I liked the people who lived there, and deep in my soul I knew that someone who lived there had a role to play for me. Yes, there was a reason the house spoke to me even from that tiny ad in the newspaper, and when I was actually there, gazing at it, it spoke even louder, more clearly, calling out to me.

I should have left then.

I didn't.

And then the first thing happened: a small truck coming down the street swerved away from me and the driver blasted his horn as if it were my fault that he almost hit me, when it was obvious he hadn't been paying attention to where he was going. He missed me — by perhaps a fraction of an inch! — then slammed on his brakes and backed up until his windows were even with mine. Then he proceeded to glare at me, again as if it were somehow my fault! Without thinking, I slid down in my seat in an automatic attempt to avoid being seen, but of course to him I looked like a coward, and he took a good, long look at me. A moment later he stomped on the gas and his tires screeched as he raced around the corner.

I should have left then and there and

crossed this house — and its occupants — off my list of prospects, but before I could even start my own car, another car pulled up directly in front of the house.

First, a young girl — an absolutely adorable child — got out of the car. Tiny and sweet, perhaps five years old, wearing a little pink dress with matching bands around her ponytails. She ran up the walk and up the steps to the front door and waited.

Then her mother got out of the car, and I knew! I had not been wrong. Tall and lithe, with an easy grace, I knew in an instant that my instincts had once again proved flawless.

The mother said her good-byes to the driver of the car, closed the door, and started toward the front door of the house. Then, in a second stroke of bad luck, she stopped to pull a weed from her beautifully tended flower bed.

When she did, she must have felt the intensity of my gaze, for she turned her head and looked directly at me.

Her eyes are brown — dark, dark brown — just as they have to be.

There was no way I could avert my gaze, and our eyes met. For a moment I felt a perfect connection with her, but then she straightened up and hurried her daughter into the house.

And turned to look at me one more time before following her daughter inside.

I stayed where I was for another seventy-seven seconds, knowing it was better to act as if I were waiting for someone than to drive immediately away. But when I finally started the car and pulled slowly away from the curb, I saw the curtain in the house move.

I know she watched me leave.

This is not good. This is not good at all.

Stuff!

Everywhere she looked, Ellen Fine saw *stuff.* Nothing valuable. Nothing she even wanted. In fact, she couldn't remember where it had all come from. But there it was, the accumulation of five years in this tiny house, now piled on the floor in a mound that seemed to be getting bigger instead of smaller. She'd already filled three garbage bags with junk that was being consigned to the dump, and nearly a dozen boxes had been filled with Emily's toys, shelves of books, and stacks of file folders.

For a moment she almost wished she'd married Emily's father — at least then she would have had someone to help her sift through everything and make the hundreds of tiny decisions about what to keep and what to throw away. Of course, if she'd married Danny, this little cottage would have been far too small for the three of them. And in the end, she was sure, Danny would have wound up taking off with Brenda Lansky anyway, and nothing would have been any different than it was right now.

Danny — along with Brenda — had vanished, and with them had gone the monthly support checks for Emily. Which made perfect sense when Ellen thought about it; after all, Danny certainly couldn't be expected to support his daughter and his girlfriend, too, could he? So now she was moving back to Missouri, back in with her mom and dad, because she simply could no longer afford Long Island.

Not even this tiny little cottage in Smithton, which wasn't even half as nice as Camden Green, just a couple of miles farther out Route 25A.

Today was Goodwill and garbage day, and Saturday would be estate sale day. That was a laugh, thinking of this tiny house as any kind of an "estate."

What wasn't a laugh was that she was having second thoughts about the "estate" sale, which would be a "selling off every-thing I have left in the world" sale, with all kinds of people tramping through her house, making her ridiculous offers for what little furniture she had. And she would take the offers, because she couldn't afford to ship anything back to Missouri, where her parents already had a houseful of furniture. But the truth was, it wasn't the loss of her furniture that was bothering her. Instead, it was the idea of all those strangers tramping through the house. And even that wouldn't have bothered her until this morning, when someone had been sit-ting in a car across the street and down the block, watching Emily and her.

She felt the eyes on her as soon as Marla Williams dropped her off, and for a second she'd almost asked Marla to stay. But then she'd decided she was being silly, that who-ever was in the car probably wasn't watching her at all.

So she'd said nothing.

And felt the eyes tracking her right up to the front door of her house.

She'd pretended to pull a weed and looked at the man in the car, and for an in-stant their eyes met and she felt a cold terror go through her. She'd turned away and gone into the house, and in about a minute he drove away, leaving her still shaken from that brief moment when their eyes had met.

Her first instinct had been to call the police, but even as the thought occurred to her, she dismissed it. What was she going to say? That there had been a man in a car who looked at her? She'd sound like a loony tune. Besides, she couldn't even remember what the man looked like. Of course, he'd been in his car, but the weird thing was, even though she'd looked directly at his face, she couldn't recall a single thing about it. Whether his cheeks were fat or sunken, or his lips thin and his nose thick, or vice versa.

In fact, she couldn't even remember the color of the car, let alone the make, model, or year.

So much for calling the cops.

After that, she'd tried to dismiss the whole incident from her mind, but that had been no more possible than remembering what the guy had looked like, especially since that cold feeling of terror she'd felt when their eyes met was still with her.

What had he wanted?

And what if he came back?

What if he came to her estate sale and walked right into her house?

She told herself she was being silly, that absolutely nothing had happened or was going to happen. But no matter how long she argued with herself, she couldn't shake the creepy feeling she had. Maybe she should just cancel the estate sale and let the open house happen on Saturday and Sunday with all her ratty furniture still there. Then she and Emily could simply pack whatever they wanted into her little Honda and drive back to "I told you so" land, and the heck with the furniture. Maybe the agent would be able to sell the house for enough to give her a new start, and she wasn't going to get that much for the furniture anyway.

She picked up a worn, floppy-eared rabbit with a yellow ribbon around its neck and a yellow bow sewed to one of its ears. Emily hadn't touched this rabbit in a year or more. She tossed it into the Goodwill box and picked up the next item for evaluation. A music box. She turned the key, trying to remember where it came from, but no music came out.

Broken.

Garbage.

Emily came down from her bedroom with an armful of books. "These, Mom."

Ellen took the picture books from her

daughter. "Oh, honey, this is too many books to take to Grammy's. Besides, these are too young for you — why don't we give them to some little kids who don't read as well as you do?"

"No," Emily said. "I want them." Then she picked the rabbit out of the Goodwill box and hugged it to her chest.

Ellen sighed. If Emily had never seen the rabbit, it would never have been an issue, but now it would be. "Emily, honey, everything that we take has to fit into our car. We'll get new stuff in Missouri. Better stuff."

"I need Mr. Spanky," Emily said, hugging the rabbit.

"Honey —"

"*Daddy* gave him to me."

Ellen gently put the books into the Goodwill box and let Emily keep the rabbit. Since Danny had vanished, he had become a god in Emily's eyes, and even though she was sure a time would come when Emily would see him for exactly what he was, that time was not yet at hand. For now, she was not going to interfere with her daughter's idea about her perfect father.

"Okay, honey, if Daddy gave him to you, you can keep him, but the books have to go."

Emily turned without a word and carried the rabbit back up to her room, climbing the stairs exactly the way she'd climbed the front steps earlier.

The memory of the man in the car — blessedly absent for the few moments she'd been talking to Emily — leaped back into the forefront of her mind, and she suddenly knew that it hadn't just been herself the man in the car had been watching.

It had been Emily, too.

And with that realization, all thoughts of the estate sale vanished.

After the open house, they would come back just long enough to pack their bags, and then she and Emily would be gone.

Gone from Smithton, and gone from the memories of Danny and what might have been but hadn't, and gone from this house. And gone from the man in the car.

CHAPTER THIRTY-THREE

I'm going to die.

I'm not *going to die,* Lindsay silently insisted to herself. But even as she uttered the mute denial, the terrible, hypnotic chant rang in her head again.

I'm going to die . . . I'm going to die . . .

Lindsay had lost all track of time; she no longer had any idea how long she'd been held in the dank confines of her prison or in the strange child's room, let alone whether it was day or night.

All she knew was that the man who had taken her from her home was crazy.

He was crazy, and he was going to kill her just like he was killing Shannon.

She was back in the surreal little child's room, the windows papered over, the room illuminated by candles set on every flat surface she could see. She was bound to one of the undersized chairs with duct tape, and it was all she could do to keep breathing through her nose, slowly and steadily, to keep from gagging on the cotton her captor had stuffed into her mouth before placing duct tape over her lips. So hard was it even to breathe that she'd been unable to struggle when he brought her again through the tunnel from the dank chamber where she and Shannon lay on damp mattresses during the hours when their captor didn't want to "play" with them.

But now they were back, taped to their chairs, with those hideous parodies of smiles painted on the tape over their mouths, while the man who tortured them moved around the room like a figure in a nightmare from which Lindsay couldn't awaken.

There was a teakettle boiling on the little stove — a stove only half the size of the one at home. She had assumed it was a toy, until she saw a flame emerge from one of the gas burners, and though at first she had no idea what the man had in mind, it became clear as he started laying out a miniature tea set on the tiny table that stood between her and Shannon. The table itself had been covered with a stained and tattered tablecloth that must have been beautiful when the linen, with its meticulously hand-embroidered pattern, was clean and new. Now, though, it only added a final macabre touch to the scene.

Though she sat perfectly still, Lindsay's eyes followed every move the man made as he placed a cup and saucer, along with a tiny silver spoon, exactly in the center of each place at the table.

What would happen when he poured the tea? Was he going to at least take the tape from her lips — and the cotton from her mouth — so she could drink?

If he did, she knew exactly what she would do. She would scream. She would scream louder than she had ever screamed in her life, hoping that somewhere outside the playroom, someone would hear her.

Meanwhile, it was all she could do not to choke on the batting in her mouth.

Across the table from her, Shannon's head lolled on her chest, her eyes closed.

Had she finally died?

No. Lindsay could see a slight movement in the other girl's chest as she breathed. So she no longer had enough energy to hold her head up.

Then the man was looming over the table. "Good morning, my ladies," he said in a strange, almost singsong voice. "How nice of you to come to tea."

In his hand he held the steaming kettle.

Was it morning? It looked like night, but how could she be sure with the candles burning and the windows covered up?

"Aren't we going to have fun today?" the man intoned. "All here together?" He poured the boiling water into the tiny teacups that sat in front of the girls. In the center of the table, the empty sugar bowl and creamer matched the chipped and cracked china set. "Don't I set a lovely table?" He put the kettle back onto the little stove, then squatted down to perch on the tiny chair between Shannon and Lindsay. He picked up his cup — his pinky held carefully straight — and brought it up to his mask.

He pretended to sip.

"Mmmmm. That *is* good. An orange pekoe — my favorite in the morning." He pretended to sip again, and Lindsay saw his eyes flash from Shannon to her, then back to Shannon.

"What's the matter?" he demanded. "Isn't the tea to your liking?" His voice began to rise like that of a petulant child. "Why aren't you drinking it? This is a tea party! *My* tea party! You have to do what I want you to do." Once again his eyes darted from one girl to the other. "Isn't that right?" he demanded. "Isn't that the way it works? Isn't that the way it always was?"

Though she was terrified by the tone of his voice, Lindsay saw an opportunity to be rid of the tape over her lips and the cotton in her mouth, if only for a moment or two. She forced herself to nod at the man, looked at him with what she hoped were beseeching eyes.

But he wasn't watching her; he'd turned to Shannon. "Drink your tea," he ordered her, but Shannon seemed beyond even hearing. The man's voice rose querulously. "I'm not having a good time," he said. "Perhaps I shall have to discipline you."

He rose from his chair, went to Shannon, and picked up her cup of hot water. Then he lifted her head by clutching her hair and tried to pour the scalding water into her mouth. It dribbled down off the tape and ran — red with the ink from her grotesquely painted smile — onto her chest.

As the scalding water hit her skin, Shannon's body convulsed and her eyes snapped open. A muted moan penetrated the cotton in her mouth as she tried to scream, but the tape over her lips all but silenced it. "Drink your tea," the man demanded. "Drink it!" Abruptly, he shoved Shannon, and her chair went over backward. "And you," he said wheeling around to glower at Lindsay. "I thought better of you — I thought you had manners!" He came toward her, moving slowly, and Lindsay's heart started to hammer. She couldn't get enough air through her nostrils, and for a moment thought she was going to pass out.

"Drink your tea," he demanded.

There was nothing she could do but nod eagerly, doing her best to communicate that she would.

She would if she *could.*

"You will play with me!" the man cried. "You will play whatever I want to play. Don't you understand? You have to *play with me!*" Suddenly, he was behind her, cutting through the tape around her wrists and ankles, and with a terrible clarity, she knew what he was about to do.

Then, exactly as she had foreseen it, it happened. He hauled her to her feet and threw her onto the little table. She felt shards of china cut into her as she landed on the tea set, and the sugar bowl and creamer shattered beneath her weight.

As he loomed over her, she saw her chance. While he fumbled with his pants, she brought her foot up, smashing it directly into his crotch with a kick so hard its strength surprised even her.

She saw the shock and pain in the man's eyes as he doubled over and fell to the floor, writhing and groaning.

Instantly, Lindsay rolled off the table, scrambled to her feet, and raced to the chamber's tiny door.

Too late, she saw the hasp and padlock.

As he struggled to get back to his feet, she darted to the trapdoor, stumbled down the stairs, and plunged through the darkness of the tunnel until she came to the room where he kept them when he wasn't toying with them in the playroom.

Now she heard him stumbling behind her, and tore the tape and cotton from her mouth as she tried to make herself move faster. But she could hardly see in the gloom, and if she tripped —

Her thoughts were suddenly cut off by a sharp pain in her back. She whirled, and there he was, right behind her, holding a ski pole as if it were a fencing sword. As Lindsay cowered, he jabbed at her, the point at the end of the pole jabbing first her leg, then her stomach. She squealed and tried to turn away, only to feel the next jab in her side.

He was working his way higher, moving toward her face.

Her face, and her eyes.

"No!" she begged, hunching over, trying to protect herself.

The point of the pole was dancing around her now, and then she grabbed the end of it, trying to jerk it away from him, but he pulled back hard and she lost her footing.

Crying out in terror and agony, she crumpled to the floor. A moment later the man had her and was dragging her toward her mattress.

Then she was lying on her back, gasping and staring up at the terrible smile painted on the mask.

"I'm angry," he said. "So angry I'm going to punish you. I don't want to, but I have to."

"Just let us go," Lindsay said. "Please, just leave us alone."

He gave no sign of even hearing her as he cuffed her to the wall. Then, as she watched helplessly — hopelessly — he held her water bottle high above her and let the water slowly pour out of it onto the floor.

"Bad girl," he said, as if talking to a re-calcitrant puppy. When it was empty, he tossed the bottle into the corner and disappeared back into the tunnel.

As she lay panting on the mattress, fighting the pain in her body and the terror in her soul, Lindsay heard the terrible words begin to echo in her mind yet again.

I'm going to die . . . I'm going to die . . . I'm going to die . . .

And slowly, as the rhythm of the words took over her mind, Lindsay realized that maybe she no longer cared.

Maybe death would be better than whatever the man was planning to do with her next.

For the first time, she began to sob.

CHAPTER THIRTY-FOUR

Useless, Dawn D'Angelo thought. *It's all useless. We should all be out* doing *something!* The problem was, there wasn't anything else *to* do, so she and the rest of Lindsay's friends were gathered in Sharon Spandler's office, getting everything ready for the vigil tonight. *A vigil,* Dawn thought. *Like she's dead.*

She gazed down at one of the three hundred copies of Lindsay's junior class picture — three hundred copies that she'd been pressing one by one onto buttons to pass out at the vigil tonight — and struggled not to start crying again. Crying, she reminded herself, wouldn't do Lindsay any good at all. And maybe — just maybe — the vigil would attract enough attention from the TV people so that someone, somewhere, would recall seeing Lindsay sometime during the last week.

Taking a deep breath, she carefully

placed one of the miniature pictures facedown onto the button blank, placed the back piece onto the picture, then leaned her weight down on the lever that crimped the pin together with Lindsay's image protected beneath a layer of transparent plastic. She pulled the pin from the machine and assessed her work.

Straight.

Perfectly centered.

Lindsay looked beautiful, her hair long, her makeup perfect, her face surrounded by dark green letters that read FIND LINDSAY along with the 800 number the Marshalls had set up. She added the pin to the box holding the hundred-odd others she'd already completed and set up the next one.

The rest of the cheerleaders were gluing Lindsay's photograph to signs, and as she watched them, Dawn wondered if they felt as frustrated as she did that there wasn't something more they could do. Somehow, all this seemed . . . she searched her mind for the right word, and finally one came: *useless.* While Lindsay was going through whatever horrible thing had happened to her, all she and the rest of her friends could do was make buttons and posters and hold a candlelight vigil.

Like a vigil was going to find Lindsay!

Tina McCormick sighed, put down her last poster, and looked at Dawn as if she'd read her thoughts. "This isn't going to do any good at all, is it?" she said.

Oddly, hearing her own thoughts spoken out loud instantly transformed Dawn's frustration into anger. "Don't be stupid, Tina. Of course it is. The problem is, we can't do enough!"

"We can only do what we can do," Sharon Spandler said, setting six boxes of candles on the table between Tina and Dawn. "At least that's what my grandma's always saying. Can you start passing these out, Tina? Consuela says there's already almost a hundred people in front of the gym."

As Tina left and Dawn began putting together another pin, Hugh Tarlington, who had taken over as principal of Camden Green High only last fall, peered into the room from the doorway. "How are we doing?"

"We're ready," someone said.

Dawn pressed down on another button.

"Good," Tarlington said. As the rest of the girls began trooping out the door past the principal, their arms full of posters, Dawn felt him eyeing her. He seemed on the verge of saying something before changing his mind and pulling the door closed. Less than a minute later, however, it opened again and Sharon Spandler came in.

For almost a full minute the coach stood silently watching as Dawn continued to work. Finally, as the silence threatened to stretch on forever, she spoke. "Dawn? Aren't you coming?"

Dawn couldn't even bring herself to look up, let alone go outside and face all those people and all those candles, knowing that almost everyone secretly thought Lindsay was dead.

She just couldn't do it. "You go," she said, and as she spoke, the hot lump of pain in the back of her throat made her voice break.

"You come with me," the coach said quietly. "Come on, Dawn. We'll do more buttons later."

Dawn was about to shake her head when it occurred to her that compared to whatever Lindsay was going through, the vigil was nothing. And it wasn't about her anyway, she thought, it was about Lindsay, and even though she still didn't want to go to the vigil — didn't want to think all the thoughts the candlelit prayer meeting would raise in her mind — it suddenly didn't matter how hard it might be for her.

Lindsay needed to know she was there, praying for her, with everyone else.

She finished the button she was working on, tossed it into the box, and picked the box up.

She would hand the buttons out herself, and ask every single person to wear one. Little as it was, at least it was something.

She stood and walked out of the office and through the girls' locker room, followed by the coach. Lindsay's gym locker, like her regular one on the second floor of the main building, was covered with notes and hearts and yellow ribbons, and just the sight of the tributes made Dawn want to cry all over again.

But she didn't.

Instead, as they passed the decorated locker, Dawn kissed her fingertips and pressed them to the cold metal. "We'll find you, Linds," she said. "We'll find you, and you'll be home soon."

Sharon Spandler put her arm around Dawn's shoulders and gave her a squeeze.

Kara Marshall stared in astonishment at the mass of cars crowded into the high school parking lot. She'd expected no more than twenty people — maybe thirty at most — to show up for the vigil Dawn D'Angelo and her friends had organized, but the lot was so full, there were cars blocking other cars, and still more spilling out of the parking lot onto the front lawn. She was about to give up and try to find some place on the street to park her Toyota when she saw someone waving frantically, beckoning her to drive to the end of the parking lot closest to the gym. For a moment she almost backed out into the street anyway, but when she saw it was the principal, Hugh Tarlington, waving, she followed his direction to a spot that had been roped off with a sign that read RESERVED FOR STEVE AND KARA MARSHALL. She bit her lip as she pulled into the spot, wishing once more that Steve was with her.

Indeed, she wasn't sure exactly how she was going to get through the evening without him.

One minute at a time, she told herself as her eyes burned with sudden tears. *Just one minute at a time.*

She got out of the Toyota, shook the principal's hand, then let him guide her toward the crowd that had gathered in front of the school.

Not twenty or thirty. Not even forty or fifty.

No, hundreds of people had shown up. Hundreds of people, many of whom she recognized, but even more whom she'd never seen before.

And all for Lindsay.

She fished in her purse until she found a small packet of Kleenex, pulled one out and dabbed at her eyes.

On the steps of the school, all the cheerleaders were gathered, wearing their uniforms and holding signs that bore Lindsay's picture — the same picture Kara had been putting up on walls and lampposts and windows every day since Lindsay disappeared. "Here comes Mrs. Marshall," she heard one of them call, and suddenly everyone turned toward her and started to applaud as Hugh Tarlington led her up the steps.

At the top, she turned around and looked out at the mass of people who had gathered, and at the television cameras, and at the candles that were already lit, and suddenly she didn't have the slightest idea what to say. Or even what to think. Her mouth worked for a moment, and finally she heard herself utter the only two words she could possibly speak: "Thank you."

As if sensing her inability to say anything

else, Hugh Tarlington led her back down the steps, and then the crowd was all around her, everyone reaching out to her, speaking to her, gently squeezing her hand or kissing her cheek. Her mind reeled as she moved through the crowd, recognizing old friends, and neighbors and acquaintances, and people she hadn't seen in years.

All of Lindsay's friends, along with their parents, and their teachers, and everyone else from the school.

Even Sergeant Grant was there, wearing khakis and a golf shirt.

Soon Kara was using the last of her tissues, but the outpouring of love and support kept flooding over her, and at last she let her tears flow unchecked.

Then Dawn D'Angelo was there, and Kara gathered the girl into her arms, hugging her close. "Thank you," she whispered. "You have no idea what —" Her voice broke as her emotions once more overwhelmed her, but Dawn obviously knew what she'd been about to say.

"We'll find her," Lindsay's best friend whispered, and for a magical moment, Kara believed her.

Then Claire Sollinger appeared out of the crowd, her patrician features softened by her concern. She kissed Kara on the cheek, then held both her shoulders and looked directly into her eyes. "How are you holding up?" she asked.

Kara, choking back a sob, managed a weak smile. "Well enough," she said. Her eyes swept the crowd. "I'm overwhelmed."

"It's exactly what I expected," Claire said as she drew a man only a couple of years older than Kara forward. "I'd like you to meet my brother, Patrick Shields."

Patrick took Kara's hand and leaned in to gently kiss her cheek. "I'm so very sorry about what's happened."

Their eyes met, and Kara could see the pain of his months of grief deep in Patrick Shields's dark brown eyes.

Exactly the kind of pain she herself was suffering.

"And I'm so sorry for your loss —" she began, then fell silent as she realized how hollow the words must sound to him and how often he'd heard them before.

Patrick gave Kara's hand a gentle squeeze, and as their eyes met again, she knew she needed to say no more; what they were going through could never be described with mere words. But in that brief moment when their eyes met, Kara felt a glimmer of solace. He understood exactly what she was feeling.

Suddenly the crowd fell silent, then the principal began to speak. As he began his litany of thanks, first for Lindsay's friends, who had organized the vigil, then for the people who had come, more and more candles were being lit in the gathering night, until finally their warm glow seemed to hold the darkness at bay.

"I've also just been told that the reward for any information leading to Lindsay Marshall's safe return has been increased to fifteen thousand dollars."

A murmur passed over the crowd, and Kara looked around, wondering who had put up the money. But of course it could have been anyone — maybe even a group of people. But why remain anonymous, and give her no one to thank?

Steve should be here.

The thought brought fresh tears to her eyes, but now she concentrated on the principal's final words, refusing to let herself break down again. "All of us here offer our love and support to Kara and Steve Marshall," Hugh Tarlington said. His eyes moved over the crowd until he found her. "Kara, please know that all of us hold Lindsay gently in our thoughts and hearts and prayers tonight, tomorrow, and every moment until she comes home.

And now, let us take you home."

As someone began singing "Amazing Grace," the crowd moved across the lawn toward the street, and as more voices joined in, Dawn D'Angelo and Patrick Shields fell in beside Kara. Each of them linked an arm in one of hers, and the slow march from the high school to the Marshall home began.

CHAPTER THIRTY-FIVE

When Steve Marshall had accepted Russ Doran's invitation for a quick drink after work, he fully intended to take only a moment at the end of a hectic day and unwind with a good friend. But the martini had both cooled and soothed him, and when Russ ordered another one, Steve figured one more wouldn't hurt. While they waited for the second round, he excused himself, went to the men's room, and while at the urinal, caught sight of himself in the mirror over the sink.

He didn't just look tired — he looked at least ten years older than he had a week ago, and in the space between his eyebrows there were deep creases that barely vanished even when he stretched the skin with his fingers.

He didn't need another martini; he needed to go home.

The problem was, he didn't want to go home.

Home, in the last week, had become so completely different from the wondrously happy place he and Kara and Lindsay had shared since the day Lindsay had been born that it no longer felt like a place of refuge at all. Lindsay's absence hung over it like a suffocating blanket, and every moment he was in the house reminded him of his terrible impotence in the face of what had happened.

He should have protected his family — his little girl — and he had failed.

Failed so utterly, so paralytically, that Kara had taken charge, focusing like a laser on doing whatever she thought would bring their baby back.

But Steve had a deep, gnawing feeling about Lindsay, a feeling so bad that he couldn't even confide it to his wife.

Instead, he had to keep it inside, where it was not simply festering, but now consuming him. And he was certain that if he breathed even a word of his feeling to Kara — that they were never going to see their daughter again — she wouldn't simply cry or try to talk him out of it.

No, she would be furious at his lack of faith, and call him a traitor, and a bad father, and a terrible husband.

And deep down inside, he knew she was right.

He *was* a bad father, and he *was* a terrible husband, because no matter how hard he'd tried to do everything he could for them, to make their lives as perfect as possible, he'd failed.

He'd failed, and Lindsay was gone, and the part of him that didn't already feel dead didn't really want to go on living, either.

Russ Doran knew about Lindsay's disappearance, of course, and he had let Russ think he was doing a nice thing by taking him out for a drink and a little distraction before he went home.

But there it was again: he didn't want to go home. And that one simple fact left him hating himself.

He returned from the men's room, telling himself to lay down a couple of bills, take a sip from the final drink, and go home to Kara, no matter how painful it might be. Yet by the time he reached the table, the martini looked so frosty in its fresh glass that he found himself unable to resist it.

Steve sat down.

Before he knew it, that martini was gone and another was in its place.

This wasn't good. If he didn't leave now, the last train would be gone, and there would be no choice but to spend the night in the apartment by himself.

When Russ Doran ordered still another round, Steve said nothing, and slowly the alcohol began to numb him. And then, in the middle of the fifth martini, Russ pointed up at the television screen above the bar.

"Look at that," he said softly, then frowned at Steve. "Shouldn't you be there?"

Steve looked up to see Lindsay's photograph splashed across the television screen, and a moment later the camera pulling back to show a great mass of people, each of them holding a candle, walking slowly down a street in Camden Green.

Kara.

Dawn D'Angelo.

The cheerleading coach — what was her name? Spandler.

And all his friends and neighbors, plus at least half the rest of the town.

And he'd completely forgotten that the vigil was tonight.

He stood up so fast he almost tipped over his stool. He fumbled in his wallet and threw a couple of twenties down.

"Gotta go, Russ. See you tomorrow."

"Whoa, wait a minute," Russ said, grabbing onto his wrist. "Are you going to *drive?*"

"I've got to get home," Steve said, and gently but firmly pulled away from Russ's grasp.

Five minutes later he was in the Hertz office on West Fifty-seventh Street, and ten minutes after that he was on the road.

Maybe — just maybe — he could get there before it was over.

CHAPTER THIRTY-SIX

Kara stood in her kitchen, closed her eyes and listened to the sounds of talking, laughing, eating, and drinking.

The sounds of life.

The sounds of normality.

The sounds she hadn't heard since Lindsay vanished.

And the sounds that Steve should be hearing but wasn't.

A flicker of anger ignited inside her; a flicker she instantly doused, reminding herself that Steve was dealing with the situation the only way he could, that she couldn't help him, and neither, she suspected, could any of the people who had gathered here tonight. But it still would have been better for him to be here.

But he wasn't.

She opened her eyes to see the roomful of friends — and people who until tonight had only been acquaintances — and suddenly, gratitude replaced the fear that had all but overwhelmed her; calm replaced the frenetic anxiety that had gripped her since the moment of Lindsay's disappearance. If only Steve were with her. . . .

Steve gripped the steering wheel and hunched forward in the driver's seat of the tiny rented Hyundai, his frustration growing by the second. He needed to get home, and he needed to get home *now*. But traffic wasn't moving.

Someone who must have found his driver's license in a Cracker Jack box was holding everything up on the on ramp to the Sagtikos Parkway — maybe he should have just taken 25A all the way and not even bothered with the Long Island Expressway. But this time of night the expressway should have been clear, and he'd figured —

Who cared what he'd figured?

He pounded the horn, then cut around to the on-ramp shoulder, right of the lane of stalled traffic. Sure enough, at the top was an old man afraid to merge into the lane of northbound traffic.

Steve gunned the little car and darted from the shoulder into traffic.

But traffic was even worse when the

Sagtikos turned into the Sunken Meadow above Northern State Parkway. It seemed as if every oversized SUV on Long Island was trying to get to Camden Green tonight, and Steve took a fresh grip on the steering wheel, bore down on the gas pedal, and swerved into a gap between two huge vehicles, each occupied only by a driver. One way or another, he was going to get home to Kara.

What had he been thinking, going out drinking with Russ while Kara walked in the vigil by herself?

He slipped between two more SUVs and hit the horn as he passed yet another one on the right, then veered back into the left lane and hit the accelerator as he saw the highway finally open up ahead of him.

Finally free — at least for a minute or two — he fumbled in his coat pocket until he found his cell phone and flipped it open. With one hand on the wheel, he punched the thumb of his other hand on the speed-dial key for his home number.

Raindrops began to splat on the windshield.

Where was the wiper control?

Just as Kara answered, a town car came out of nowhere and passed Steve on the right, sending a cascade of mist over his windshield, blinding him for a second.

Where the *hell* were the wipers?

"Hello?" Kara's voice crackled in his ear.

"Kara?"

"Steve?" Though the crackle was momentarily gone, her voice was now muffled by voices in the background. "Honey? Where are you?"

"I'm on my way home," he said, raising his voice against the cacophony of the rain on the roof of the car and the crackling in the cell connection. Holding the steering wheel with his knees, he twisted a switch on one of the stalks protruding from the steering column.

The headlights went out, and Steve swore under his breath as he tried to switch them back on.

"Honey?" he heard Kara say, her own voice now rising, too. "I can't hear you. You're breaking up. Are you driving?"

"I'm on my way home," he said.

The rain turned into a pelting downpour, and every light beyond the windshield turned into a dazzling blur.

"Steve?"

The last of the alcohol from the martinis he'd consumed surged into Steve's bloodstream, and along with the alcohol came a wave of guilt. "Kara, I missed the vigil," he said, his words slurring. "I'm sorry, honey, I'm so sorry —"

"Steve? You're breaking up — I can't understand you!"

As a Humvee suddenly loomed out of the darkness ahead on the right, the phone fell from Steve's hand and dropped to the floor between the front seats. Instinctively reaching for it, Steve missed the beginning of the Humvee's movement into his own lane, and by the time he looked up again, red lights were flooding his windshield.

His headlights! He'd never turned them back on!

Jerking the steering wheel and slamming on the brakes, he felt the car start to the left out of the oversized car's path, and for an instant thought he was safe.

And in that instant, the tires lost their grip on the rain-slicked highway. The car spun out of control, hit the concrete divider, and flipped into the air.

In a moment of terrible clarity, Steve hoped Kara wouldn't be able to hear what was coming next.

Then his windshield exploded as the car slammed against the support columns of an overpass and dropped to the ground upside down, its roof collapsing. Steve felt a terrible pain in his spine, and an instant later was surrounded by a dazzling white light —

And another instant later, the light, too, was gone.

When the phone went dead, Kara moved into the laundry room, away from distraction and noise that only a moment ago had sounded so good to her and tried to call Steve back.

She got nothing more than his voice mail.

Maybe he was trying to call her again.

She hung up, waited almost a full minute, and tried again.

And again she got his voice mail.

Questions churned through her mind. Why was Steve driving home this late? And what would he be driving, anyway? He'd taken the train to work.

Maybe he caught a ride with someone else?

She set the cordless phone down on the washing machine and tried to sort out the pieces of words she'd heard him speak. She thought he'd been trying to apologize.

But there was something in his voice, even through the static . . .

She walked back into the living room but could no longer concentrate on anything anyone was saying to her; there were too many questions tumbling inside her head.

What was it he'd been trying to say? Where was he? Why was he driving?

None of it made any sense. There was something about the whole situation that wasn't right. . . .

"Kara?" Phyllis D'Angelo's voice penetrated her thoughts. She and Dawn were putting on their coats. "I'm sorry, but we've got to head home."

Kara managed a smile. "Of course. Thank you so much for coming." She turned to Dawn. "And for everything else, too."

"We're praying for Lindsay," Dawn said.

"We're praying for all of you," Phyllis echoed.

"I know you are." Kara walked them to the door, and as if their departure was a signal, everyone else began to drift out. Within five minutes everyone was gone except for Patrick Shields and Claire Sollinger, who remained seated on the living room sofa, apparently deep in conversation, which meant that despite her desire to sink down at the kitchen table with a hot cup of tea and wait for Steve to come home, she couldn't.

Not as long as Claire and Patrick remained.

As soon as the door closed, though, Claire looked up and gave her an apologetic smile. "I think we're overstaying our welcome," she said, rising to her feet. "Come on, Patrick. Kara needs some peace and quiet."

A moment later Kara found herself accepting yet one more hug and one more kiss on the cheek, this time from Claire Sollinger.

Then Patrick took her hand, and as she looked into his eyes, suddenly she knew. "It was you," she whispered.

He frowned in apparent puzzlement, but his sister smiled knowingly. "I'll meet you outside," Claire said, and let herself out.

"You're the one who put up the reward," Kara said.

"What makes you think that?" Patrick asked, but his expression told her that she was right. The pain of his own loss was still clear in his face.

"Because you're the only other person in town who understands. You're the only one in town who could. You're the only one who would."

"I just want to see Lindsay come home to you," he said.

"I don't know how to thank you."

"Seeing Lindsay home safe will be plenty

of thanks." Patrick impulsively leaned forward and put his arms around her. "Helping you helps me," he went on. Then he released her, held her at arm's length and forced a smile. "I'm really quite a selfish bastard."

"I'll never believe that," Kara replied, but now she was smiling, too, though her tears were still flowing.

"Claire awaits," Patrick said, and opened the door.

Claire stood on the front porch. "I just realized that you don't have your car," she said. "We'll take you to it."

Kara started to protest, then thought better of it. Better to get it now than wait for Steve or try to deal with it in the morning.

Five minutes later Claire dropped both of them at the high school, where Patrick insisted on following Kara home in his own car, just to make sure. She got into her cold Toyota, turned the heater on full blast, and waited until she saw the headlights of Patrick's Mercedes go on. Then she put her car in gear and headed home.

A strange car waited in front of the house.

Had someone left something behind? Or maybe it was Steve, being dropped off?

As she pulled into the driveway, she saw the shield painted on the door of the parked car.

Not Steve, and not someone from the vigil.

The police.

They've found Lindsay.

With barely enough patience to put the car in park and turn off the lights and ignition, Kara opened the door and met the policeman on the walk. "What is it?" she demanded. "Have you found her?" By now Patrick was at her side, taking her elbow as the policeman walked them up to the door.

"Let's go inside," the officer said in a tone that instantly told Kara that whatever he had to say, it wasn't going to be what she wanted to hear.

"Tell me," she said. "Tell me what's happened."

Once inside, the policeman nodded them to the sofa, then pulled over a dining room chair and sat facing them. "This isn't about your daughter, Mrs. Marshall," he said. "This is about your husband."

Kara's heart skipped a beat. "Steve? What about him?" She felt Patrick's hand on her forearm, and unconsciously covered it with her own. "What's going on?"

"There was an accident," the policeman

said. "On the Sunken Meadow Parkway." Kara felt a terrible chill fall over her as she realized what the officer was going to say next, and when he spoke the words, it sounded like an echo of her own thought. "I'm so sorry, Mrs. Marshall. A one-car accident. Your husband was killed instantly. He didn't suffer."

She sat numbly for a minute — or ten? — or an hour, or only an instant? — then turned to Patrick. "I can actually feel the blood draining from my face," she said, her voice sounding as surreal to her as the words themselves. "Did that happen to you, too?" But before Patrick could reply — even before the terrible reality of what had happened could close completely in on her — Kara sank into the blessed oblivion of unconsciousness.

CHAPTER THIRTY-SEVEN

Kara rose slowly through the levels of consciousness, feeling first dizzy, then nauseated, then reluctant. When she finally let herself wake up, she knew she had some terrible, unfinished business — something too terrible even to remember yet — that she would have to take care of.

Go back to sleep, she told herself. *Just don't wake up.*

But something was holding her back, something she couldn't quite put her finger on.

Then she knew.

The scent of Sleepytime tea.

Her favorite.

Slowly, awareness came to her.

She was on the sofa, covered with the quilt her mother had made. Had she and Steve fallen asleep watching television?

No.

Then it all began coming back.

Lindsay — the vigil — Patrick Shields — and Steve . . .

Steve, and the policeman.

Steve.

An ache came alive in her belly, an ache that threatened to devour her.

Steve.

Steve and Lindsay both.

Oh, God. No! There was no way — no way at all — that she could survive this! Sleep! Just go back to sleep, and when you wake up again, everything will be different. Steve will be alive, and Lindsay will be home, and it will all turn out to be nothing but a nightmare!

Kara took a long, deep, slow breath and tried to clear away the emotions that felt as if they were on the verge of destroying her mind entirely.

And then she heard it.

Lindsay's voice, as clear as if her daughter was in the same room.

"Come and find me, Mama. Come and rescue me. Please."

Kara's eyes jerked open. She expected to see Lindsay standing in front of her, but there were just the remains of the reception.

Lamps were still on in the dawning light and Patrick Shields was kneeling in front of her, a steaming cup of tea in his hand.

"She's alive, Patrick," Kara whispered. He held the cup to her lips, steadying it as she managed a sip. She set the cup on the coffee table. "Lindsay's alive."

"I'm sure she is," Patrick said softly, reaching out to gently brush a stray wisp of hair from her brow. "I'm sure she is, and I'm sure we'll find her."

In the silence that followed, both of them were acutely aware of what neither of them had said since Kara had awakened. Still, despite their silence, Steve's death hung over both of them like a shroud.

CHAPTER THIRTY-EIGHT

I'm very good at what I do. Better, probably, than anyone else. But then again, no one else knows what I do, and thus it shall remain, precisely because I'm so good at it.

The open house went well, even though it was a Saturday. I was perfectly prepared, and slipped into the house with the same silence and invisibility as the air of poverty that permeates the neighborhood. The difference, of course, is that while I could sense the air of poverty, I'm quite sure no one sensed me at all.

At least, not the danger inherent in my presence.

The interior of the house was much as I imagined — a sweet little cottage that had once known love but had grown shabby and taken on the look that houses do when no one cares about them anymore. Someone had given up

on the little house — I could feel it immediately.

Perhaps someone had given up on
love, something I know something of.

After all, I have much love to give.

Her bedroom was that of a sweet
woman, exactly the sort I always dreamed
of. A wonderfully feminine paper covered
the walls, and the ceiling was painted a
soft peach.

A shade of peach I remember well.

I could sense her — feel her — know her
— despite the fact that most of her life
was already packed away in the stacks of
boxes that were piled against the walls.

The kitchen cabinets were almost bare,
and what little they held was the sort of
boxed food that people who live in that
kind of neighborhood invariably eat. A
shame, really: nutrition is so important to
healthy brain activity, and perhaps if they
ate better, they would find themselves
able to live better.

Regardless.

The poverty of the household did
nothing to dampen my spirits; indeed, it
confirmed for me that this woman will
provide the perfect completion of my
little tableau. Knowing that the days until
I could make her mine would be in-

complete without something to remember her by, I slipped a family photograph from the dresser into my pocket.

And I began to make my plan.

There is a fine line between adventure and recklessness. Parking in front of this house last week was pure recklessness, but after I examined the house more carefully today in the company of a dozen or so other people (each of the agents more ineffectual and each of their clients less observant than the ones who went before) I engaged the host agent in the sort of bland conversation that no one — no one except me — remembers five minutes after it has happened. I have no doubt that the agent will remember no more of what we said than of what I look like. Still, the encounter gave me an adrenaline rush, as toying with people who think they are manipulating me always does.

Having taken his listing sheets, I consistently nodded as if I were interested in everything he had to say. When he finally ran out of platitudes and pitches, I eventually made my way to the basement, where I discovered a perfect hiding place behind an old armoire. Indeed, I tested the niche by hiding myself there for nearly two hours, and listened to the conversations of everyone else who came and went. After the house grew silent and the host agent had come down to check that everything was locked — never, of course, bothering even to glance behind the armoire — I closed my eyes and breathed deeply. I stood quietly, my anticipation under control, and waited.

CHAPTER THIRTY-NINE

Ellen Fine pulled her sweater across her shoulders and looked at her watch for at least the millionth time. Finally, blessedly, it was four o'clock.

The open house was over and at last she and Emily could go home. Rick Mancuso, whose appearance right after lunch to set up the open house had served only to remind Ellen of the strange feeling she had when he was watching Emily the day he'd taken the listing, would be long gone, which was fine with her. She'd almost changed her mind about even listing the house with him, but when he showed up with his signs precisely when he said he would, she decided she was just being paranoid.

The man was a real-estate agent, not a child molester, and she had to stop seeing monsters lurking inside every man she ran into.

Still, she'd been glad to escape to the

park with Emily, and for the first half hour it wasn't too bad. But then the sky began clouding over, and she started worrying about rain and the fact that she hadn't brought raincoats.

As it turned out, her worries proved groundless: it hadn't rained and Emily had a perfectly good time wearing herself out. Meanwhile, she'd been so busy watching Emily that she hadn't managed to read even a single page of the paperback book she brought along, though the afternoon seemed to stretch on forever. Now, as she put the bookmark back exactly where it was when they arrived, she realized this might well be the last time she and Emily would be in this park.

She put her book into her bag and started toward Emily, who was playing on the merry-go-round with several other kids, most of whom appeared to be in the park in the company only of their fathers. And most of the fathers seemed to have as little interest in their children as Emily's father had in her.

But at least they're here, Ellen chided herself. *At least they didn't just take off and vanish like* — She cut the thought off, not wanting to get bogged down yet again in her fury toward Danny Golden. *Danny Golden, indeed! Danny Anything-But-*

Golden was more like it! "Emily!" she called, putting Danny out of her mind once more as she pulled her sweater tight against the chilly breeze that had suddenly sprung up. "Let's go."

Emily leaped off the moving carousel, stumbled dizzily for a couple of steps, then ran toward her, flush-faced, excited and giggling. But not even Emily's happy chatter could lift Ellen's spirits as they walked home together.

The For Sale sign still stood on the front lawn, but all the Open House signs were gone, and the house was as dark and quiet as Ellen had hoped it would be.

Clearly, the agent who had given her the creeps was gone.

"Go jump in the tub," Ellen said as she unlocked the front door. "I'll fix us some dinner."

Emily ran upstairs, and Ellen's eyes roamed around the living room. Nowhere could she see any sign that anyone had been here at all. Did that mean nobody had showed up for the open house? The thought gave her a sinking feeling, for once she'd made up her mind to leave not only the house but the area as well, she wanted it to sell quickly.

Still, she knew she was going to miss this

little house. She and Emily had been happy here for a long time, and it was the only home Emily had ever known. *Oh, get over it,* she told herself. *It's too late. We can't afford it, and there will be plenty of other little houses in the future. And they'll be a lot more adorable than this one.* Putting the moment of sentimentality firmly behind her, she went upstairs to change her clothes.

As she took off her jeans and pulled on a pair of sweatpants, she noticed that the framed photo of herself with Emily at the top of the Empire State Building was no longer on her dresser. All the other photos had already been packed into boxes to be shipped to her parents' house in Missouri, but she'd deliberately kept that one in its usual place, partly so the house wouldn't look quite so ready to be abandoned, but mostly because it was her favorite and she liked looking at it every morning when she woke up and every night before she turned off the light.

"Honey?" she called. Emily padded into the bedroom, ready for her bath, wearing only her Power Puff Girls underpants. "Did you borrow the photograph that was here on my dresser?"

Emily shook her head.

"Okay," Ellen sighed, frowning and deciding the picture must have fallen behind the dresser. "You better go turn off the water in the tub. And don't forget to wash your hair," she added as Emily trotted off toward the bathroom.

Ellen waited until she heard the water stop running into the tub before looking behind the dresser.

No photo.

Strange.

She was sure it had been on the dresser this morning. She even remembered winking at Emily's image as she rummaged in the top drawer for a clean bra.

And she didn't remember packing it in any of the boxes. But maybe she had — she *must* have, since the picture was no longer on the dresser.

Not for the first time, Ellen found herself wishing the move were already over. But that wasn't quite right — if she was going to be completely honest with herself, what she really wished was that it had never started in the first place.

That Danny were still here, and that they were still a family.

Then, from the depths of her memory, her mother's words came to her. *Not the kind who will ever make a good father.*

Thank you for sharing, Mother.

But she'd been right. It wasn't long after Emily was born that Danny took his leather jacket and his gym bag and moved in with a girlfriend of whose existence Ellen had been utterly clueless.

Get over it, Ellen.

Hearing splashing and the squeak of Emily's rubber ducky, which told her all was well in the bathroom, she turned her attention to dinner. Putting the missing picture out of her mind, she headed downstairs to the kitchen, where almost everything had already been packed away. But she'd left two glasses, two plates, two knives, two forks, one small pan, and her paring knife.

The barest of the bare essentials.

Taking the last two potatoes from the refrigerator, along with an onion and the carton of eggs, she decided a meal was possible. Not totally desirable, perhaps, but possible.

She clicked on the television in the living room for the news, started to peel the potatoes, and once more felt her spirits — and her energy — sag as everything in her life once more began to close in on her.

Single mom.

Moving back in with the parents.

Packing.

Leaving.

Failing.

338

And now cooking two potatoes, an onion, and some eggs for dinner. It was too much.

She closed her eyes for a moment, resting her wrists on the sink. *One day at a time,* she told herself. *One hour at a time, one minute at a time. This, too, shall pass.*

Suddenly, the words emanating from the television penetrated her thoughts.

"The search continues for Camden Green High School student Lindsay Marshall," the newscaster said. Ellen turned to look at the television, where a photo of a pretty blond teenager filled the screen. "Lindsay disappeared almost two weeks ago after an open house . . ."

After an open house!

Now that wasn't even safe.

And then the missing picture came back to her.

The picture of Emily!

Ellen rushed out of the kitchen, her heart in her throat. "Emily? Emily!"

No answer.

She ran through the little living room, dodging boxes, and started up the stairs. *"Emily!"*

And still there was no answer.

CHAPTER FORTY

The bathroom door slammed hard against the wall as Ellen burst in, but she was oblivious not only to the noise, but to the deep gash the doorknob dug into the plasterboard.

The tub was still filled, the rubber ducky still floating.

But her daughter was gone.

A surge of panic rose in her, and for a moment she felt totally paralyzed. Then a scream began to form in her throat, a scream she formed into a word as it emerged from her lips. *"Emily!"*

Nothing.

As the image of the missing picture of her daughter recurred to her, Ellen wheeled away from the bathroom door and rushed to her daughter's bedroom. "Emily, where are you?" she cried, and heard the tremble in her own voice. *She's hiding,* she told herself. *She's got to be hiding!* But a quick glance in Emily's closet and under her bed only made her panic grow.

No Emily.

Now her mind was churning with all the things that could have happened to Emily, and the thought that Danny — the jerk Danny Golden — had come back to claim his daughter was the least terrifying. Instead her mind was consumed by the missing photograph of Emily and the report she'd seen only minutes ago of a girl disappearing from home after an open house.

Could some kind of maniac have been hiding in the house?

Or even that creepy agent? Once again she recalled Rick Mancuso watching Emily a few days ago.

And she hadn't even checked the house to make sure everything was all right when she brought Emily home. Instead she'd taken a quick glance at the living room, then let Emily take a bath while she blithely went downstairs to fix supper.

Her fault! Whatever had happened to Emily was all her fault!

Stupid! Stupid, stupid, stupid.

Leaving Emily's room, Ellen dashed into her own, hurling the door open with even more force than she'd applied to the one in the bathroom. "Emily!" she yelled. "Please, God, please! *Emily, where are you?*"

And then the closet door opened and Emily burst out, stark naked.

Stark naked, and giggling. "Surprise!" she said, a huge grin spreading across her face.

Her terror instantly dissolving into relief, Ellen dropped to her knees and gathered the little girl into her arms. "You scared me," she said, barely managing to muster even the tiniest edge of anger into her voice.

But then the two memories that had set off her panic came back once more. "Get dressed and put on your coat," she said.

Emily looked confused. "What?"

"Just do it," Ellen said, trying not to let her own fear infect her daughter.

"Why?"

"Just do what I say, all right?" Hustling Emily into her room, she grabbed the first clothes that came to hand, helped Emily into them, then stuffed her arms through the sleeves of her little pink parka. Her own raincoat was still hanging in the coat closet by the front door.

Picking Emily up, Ellen lurched down the stairs, seized by the necessity to get out of the house.

To get out right now, until someone could check the house and make sure it was secure.

She pulled on her raincoat, grabbed her bag from the hook by the door, then remembered she'd left the stove on.

With Emily heavy on her hip and her bag in the hand that wasn't supporting her daughter, she made her way through the maze of boxes into the kitchen, fumbled a moment, then managed to turn off the stove. As she turned, her eyes scanned the room. . . .

The knife she had used on the potatoes was no longer on the drainboard.

Fresh panic surged through her.

"Come *on,*" she said, whirling and running out of the house, pulling Emily after her.

After glancing first one way, then the other, she headed toward Ralph Larson's house next door. Too late, she noticed that his draperies were closed and remembered that he was going to visit his daughter upstate.

She rang his bell anyway, and pounded on the door.

Sensing her mother's fear, Emily started to cry.

"*Shhh,*" Ellen said. "It's all right."

"What's wrong?" Emily sobbed. "I was just trying to fool you, Mommy!"

"It's okay," Ellen said. "Everything's okay." But her quavering voice gave the lie away.

"It's not." Emily began to sob, clinging heavily to Ellen's neck. "Mommy, I'm scared!"

"Shhh." Ellen tried to smooth Emily's hair, then jabbed at the bell one last time.

No answer.

Shit. Shit, shit, shit.

Abandoning Ralph Larson's porch, Ellen cut across his yard to the next house, again pulling Emily along with her. She didn't know the couple who lived there, but they had always looked nice.

Surely they would help.

They would help if they were home.

Praying silently, she pressed their bell.

CHAPTER FORTY-ONE

For just a moment Kara wasn't sure she had the strength to walk from Claire Sollinger's front door to Patrick Shields's Mercedes, even though the car was parked directly in front of the house, no more than fifty feet away. She was utterly devoid of energy; both her mind and body were imbued with the strange sensation of being absolutely drained. Still, this was at least better than the depression — the feeling of utter desolation, of incomprehensible despair — that had all but paralyzed her for an entire week.

A desolation and despair that had overwhelmed her inclination to argue when Patrick and Claire insisted she move into Claire's house until she felt capable of taking care of herself.

"We'll pick up some of Kara's things and be back in less than an hour," she heard Patrick tell Claire. He put a folder of papers in the backseat, got in, slowly pulled around the circular drive, and headed for Kara's house. "I made all the arrangements at Summers Funeral Home," he said as Claire's house disappeared from sight. "I chose a mid-range urn — perfectly nice, but not too expensive — and we can schedule Steve's funeral whenever you feel up to it." He glanced at her out of the corner of his eye. "Which right now, I suspect, feels like exactly never, correct?"

Kara took a deep breath, let it out, and nodded. Patrick, once again, knew exactly how she was feeling. "And certainly not until Lindsay comes home," she said. A sob caught in her throat: just hearing the words "funeral home" and "urn" made her eyes burn with tears. But how was it even possible? It seemed all she'd done in the last week was cry. Shouldn't she be out of tears by now? She felt completely dehydrated, and her eyes were swollen and sore, but still she could see her vision blurring as more tears welled up from somewhere. "I'll give you a check when we get home," she said, determined not to give in to yet another bout of sobbing.

"No rush," Patrick said. "But there are a lot of other things you're going to have to start thinking about. Steve's will, his life insurance —"

"Steve's office is full of lawyers," Kara broke in. "They can do it."

Patrick remained silent the rest of the way back to her house while Kara stared, unseeing — barely even thinking — out the window.

When they pulled up in front of the house, it looked exactly the same as it had a week ago, when Patrick and Claire had led her out of it. But how could it look the same? How could anything about it ever look the same again, when everything about the world it contained had changed?

But of course that was it — it was only her world that had changed. The rest of the world had barely even noticed what had happened to her.

And it all seemed inconceivable.

Patrick set the brake and shut off the engine, grabbed the folder from the backseat, then came around to her door and opened it. Taking her hand, he helped her out of the car, and she stood unsteadily for a moment, wondering if she was going to fall. Then, in the instant before her knees gave way, she steadied herself and started toward the front door.

Patrick took her elbow, then her keys,

and opened the door. Steering her inside, he led her to the sofa.

The sofa she had neither seen nor sat on since the night she'd perched on its edge while she heard the news that her husband was dead. Now she lowered herself onto it gingerly, as if somehow it might be preparing to inflict yet another blow on her battered spirit. Then she sat staring straight ahead.

"I'm going to make tea," Patrick said, moving a box of tissues to within her reach.

Kara managed a nod, and as Patrick began rummaging in the kitchen, her eyes were drawn to the dark green folder he'd left on the coffee table.

Left where she couldn't help but see it.

For almost a full minute she gazed at the gold letters that were embossed on the front of the folder: SUMMERS FUNERAL HOME.

An odd name for a funeral home. Wouldn't "Winters" have been more appropriate? And how had she chosen it? She couldn't remember, just as she couldn't remember much of the last week.

Maybe she hadn't chosen it at all; maybe it had been Patrick, or perhaps Claire.

Patrick and Claire.

Two weeks ago Claire had been nothing more than an acquaintance, really, and Patrick even less than that: a person she'd been aware of mostly because of what had happened to him, rather than as Claire's brother. But Claire had opened her home to her without a thought, and Patrick had tended to her as if he were her brother rather than Claire's. Without them, Kara wasn't sure she could have gotten through this week at all.

Except for Lindsay.

That was what had kept her going. Clinging to the hope — no, the *knowledge* — that Lindsay was still alive, and needed her. And when she finally came home and found out what had happened to her father —

Kara flinched at the thought, then put it out of her mind. They would get through it. Together, she and Lindsay would find a way to rebuild their lives.

When she found Lindsay.

And how was she going to find Lindsay if she kept sitting numbly letting Patrick and Claire take care of her?

"Here we go," Patrick said, setting a steaming cup of chamomile on a coaster in front of her. He lowered himself next to her on the sofa and blew on his own cup, but Kara was barely aware of his presence, her eyes fixed now on Steve's favorite wing chair.

The chair he would never sit in again.

How was it possible?

Yet, inconceivable as it seemed, it was true.

And suddenly, as the full reality of it all finally sank in right here in her own house — a house that was so full of Steve and so full of Lindsay that she could actually feel their energy — she began to regain some of her own. Sitting up, Kara reached for the cup, sipped the tea that was sweetened with exactly the right amount of honey, and felt her mind begin to shift from neutral back into gear. "I hardly know where to start," she murmured, almost unaware she was speaking out loud. "There's so much to do."

"Let other people handle it for a while," Patrick said softly.

Kara turned to look at him. "I can't. I have to start handling things myself." Patrick was about to say something, but Kara shook her head. "Thank you for everything you've done, Patrick, you and Claire both. I can't begin to tell you what it's meant to me."

He took her hand and squeezed it.

"Helping you helps me," he said.

Now Kara nodded, understanding, and knowing what she had to do. "I'm not going to go back to Claire's tonight," she said. "It's time I got back to work. Lindsay needs me."

"Maybe in a couple of days," Patrick countered. "But not tonight. It's too soon. Let's just pack a few things and head back to Claire's, where you can rest."

Kara felt her energy surge and her resolve strengthen. "No," she said. "It's time for me to get on with it. If I don't get back to work on finding Lindsay, nobody else will. I know the police think she just ran away, but I know that's not what happened. She's out there, Patrick, and she's depending on me, and I have to find her. I *have* to!" She looked up at him, expecting to see doubt in his eyes, and braced herself for an argument. But instead he nodded.

"If that's the way you want it, then I'm with you."

"You don't have to," Kara said softly. "You've done far more already than anyone could have expected."

"But we won't be done until we find Lindsay."

As they gazed at each other, Kara's mind was already at work.

351

★ ★ ★

Ellen stared numbly at the badges pinned to the two policemen's shirts. O'Reilly and Murphy, like some dumb B-movie they wouldn't even show on TV anymore. Irish cops, smiling at her and telling her they were sure everything was all right. But everything wasn't all right — the picture of Emily was gone from her house, and so was the knife she'd left on the kitchen counter when she'd gone up to find Emily. And now Emily was sitting on the floor in the Sanchezes' house two doors up, watching TV under the vigilant eye of Angela Sanchez, and she was standing in front of her own house with Ramon Sanchez and two cops named O'Reilly and Murphy.

"You didn't actually hear anything?" O'Reilly said as they approached the front door.

"I didn't have to hear anything," she said for what seemed like the hundredth time. "The knife was there when I went upstairs and gone when I came back down." She fixed the officer with a cold stare. "Which means someone took it, which means someone was in my house."

"All right," O'Reilly said in a tone that clearly told Ellen he wasn't buying her story. "You and Mr. Sanchez stay here, and

Murphy and I will have a look around." Then he spoke quietly into the microphone attached to his shoulder. "We're going in."

The door was not locked — indeed, Ellen was surprised it was even closed, given the way she and Emily had fled only half an hour earlier. As she and Ramon waited on the front lawn, O'Reilly and Murphy took positions flanking the door, then O'Reilly reached out with a foot and pushed it wide open.

Again, just like a B-movie. What did they expect? A blaze of gunfire? For a moment Ellen thought she was going to laugh out loud. But when they both disappeared into the house, the urge to laugh evaporated.

Seconds ticked by.

The seconds turned into minutes.

Twice she saw shadows in the upstairs windows, and both times her heart skipped a beat before she realized it was only the policemen, doing their jobs.

And then, after what seemed like an hour but was less than five minutes, O'Reilly appeared in the doorway. "You want to come in here, Ms. Fine?" With Ramon trailing after her, Ellen crossed the small porch and went into the house. "How's it look?" O'Reilly asked. "Any different from earlier?"

Ellen glanced around at the nearly bare room and the boxes stacked against the wall. How could she know if anything was any different? If nothing had been packed, if the house was the way it had been before —

Before.

She put the thought out of her mind. Before didn't count. Only now, and next week, and next month, and the rest of her life counted.

"I guess it looks the same," she sighed.

"And there's no one here," O'Reilly assured her. "Not upstairs, not in the basement, and not here."

"But the knife," Ellen protested. "And the —"

"This knife?" It was the other cop, Murphy, and as Ellen turned to him and saw what he was holding, she felt like a complete idiot.

"Where was it?" she breathed. "Where did you find it?"

"On the kitchen floor," Murphy replied. "In the kick space right under the counter where you were working. You musta dropped it when you went upstairs."

Ellen took the knife, examining it carefully, part of her wanting it to be the right knife, but part of her hoping it was a different knife and she would be vindicated.

But it was the same knife she'd been using, and there was no vindication, and she could almost feel the egg on her face and barely heard what O'Reilly was saying.

"I've searched the basement, and it's secure. There's no one there. There's no one in the house at all."

Ellen sighed. "Okay. I guess I wasted your time."

"That's what we're here for," O'Reilly assured her. "If you hadn't called, me and Murphy probably would've eaten two more doughnuts each, and neither one of us needs that." Ellen nodded distractedly, still barely hearing him. How could she have been so stupid? She'd probably packed the picture and forgotten about it, and of course she'd just dropped the knife! Why hadn't she at least looked for it? "Anyway," O'Reilly went on as she tuned back in, "I'll write up a report, and if you have any other problems, you give us another call, okay?"

Ellen managed a faint "Okay" as she saw them to the door.

"I'll call Angela and have her bring Emily home," Ramon Sanchez said as the door closed behind the two officers.

"You don't have to," Ellen replied, "I'll just walk down with you. I feel like such an idiot!"

"You did just what you should have done," Ramon told her. "And you're not going anywhere. I'll wait here with you, and Angela will bring Emily. Or you can both stay with us tonight if you want to."

Ellen shook her head. "You've done enough, and we'll be fine."

But ten minutes later, when she and Emily were back in the house, she wondered if she'd made the wrong decision.

It still didn't feel right.

Emily's piping voice interrupted her thoughts. "Mommy?"

"Hmmm?" The little girl was still nursing the juice Mrs. Sanchez had given her, and staring up at her through wide eyes.

"Will you sleep in my bed with me tonight?"

"C'mere." Ellen dropped onto the sofa and pulled Emily up onto her lap, wrapping her arms around her warm, sweet-smelling little girl. *It's going to be all right,* she told herself. *Just a few more days and we'll be out of this house, and out of this town, and back in Missouri where we belong.* "How about instead of me sleeping in your bed, you sleep in mine?"

Now Emily was struggling to get loose, and reluctantly, Ellen let her go. Her daughter stood in front of her, noisily sucked down the last of her juice and handed her the empty box.

"I'm hungry," she announced, and Ellen realized she had forgotten all about dinner.

And now it was far too late to start frying potatoes. "How about P.B. and J.?" she asked.

"Yes!" Emily jumped up and down a couple of times and clapped her hands. "And then I'll sleep with you tonight so you won't be scared!"

"P.B. and J. it is," Ellen said, standing up and putting the last of her misgivings out of her mind. If Emily could get excited about something as simple as a sandwich, so could she. And if she didn't stop worrying about every little thing, her fears would quickly infect Emily, and then they'd both be quivering masses of exactly the kind of jelly she was about to spread onto the bread that was waiting in the kitchen.

As Emily skipped ahead, Ellen followed. Yet as she began making the sandwiches, she found herself thinking yet again about the missing picture.

It had been there on the dresser this morning.

She was sure of it.

And now it was gone.

CHAPTER FORTY-TWO

The front door wouldn't stay closed!

No matter what she did, it kept on opening again.

How many times had she tried, and what was she doing wrong? Once again she firmly swung the heavy wood panel closed, and once again heard the lock click into the keeper.

Maybe this time it would hold.

But even as Ellen started to turn away, the door swung open yet again.

And she went through the process again, closing it once more, locking it once more, this time even throwing the dead bolt.

That was it! Before, she hadn't thrown the dead bolt.

That was all there was to it!

She twisted the heavy latch, felt the bolt shoot home, and finally relaxed.

But as she turned away, she heard the

door creak open and felt the draft of cold air on her back.

She turned, and this time didn't look at the door at all. Instead she gazed into the darkness that lay outside, a darkness in which she could feel danger lurking.

A darkness that wanted Emily.

But she wouldn't let it happen! Whatever was out there, whatever was hidden in the blackness of the night, it wouldn't take Emily.

Not her little girl!

"No!"

The volume of the single word she'd uttered was enough to startle her awake, and for a moment she lay still in the bed, her heart pounding, a clammy sweat covering her forehead.

Outside, she could hear the wind blowing, but that wasn't what had awakened her. No, it had been something else.

A door.

The door that wouldn't stay shut in her dream!

Was that it? Was that what she was listening for? The sound of a door?

Then she heard it.

A noise. A squeak and a bang. Something loose in the wind?

Or something downstairs?

Disentangling herself from the sheets, and careful not to awaken Emily, who was still sound asleep beside her, Ellen pulled back the blanket.

She felt the cold wood of the floor beneath her bare feet but ignored the chill as she slipped quietly out of the bedroom.

She silently pulled the bedroom door closed behind her.

At the top of the stairs, Ellen paused, listening again. The wind outside had risen, and now she heard rain pattering on the roof.

Was that all she'd heard? Wind and rain?

The sound came again, and it wasn't from the roof at all.

It was from somewhere downstairs.

The kitchen?

She moved down the staircase like a wraith, slipped through the darkened living room and paused again, listening.

Nothing.

Reaching through the kitchen door, she turned on the light.

The peanut butter was still on the counter. The butter knife — with jelly still on it — was in the sink, exactly where she'd left it. The paring knife was also in the sink, the raw potatoes still in the cold frying pan on the stove. Milk glasses hadn't even been rinsed; by the time they'd finished their sandwiches, she'd been too exhausted to deal with dirty dishes.

Maybe she'd do them now.

She started toward the sink, then froze.

The noise!

It was coming from the basement. But hadn't O'Reilly or Murphy said that everything was all right down there?

She hesitated, part of her wanting to go back upstairs, get Emily, and get out of the house again right now. They could go back to the Sanchezes' and take Ramon up on his offer.

Except that it was almost two in the morning, and Ramon would insist they call the police again, and then she'd look like a fool once more.

Maybe she should just go back to bed.

Thunk!

She jumped at the sound, and now the urge to get Emily and flee the house was almost irresistible. She turned and took a half step toward the door to the living room when she heard it again.

Thunk!

And now she knew what it was! One of the little windows that opened into the three light wells that were spaced around

361

the perimeter of the cellar! That was it — that had to be it.

She opened the door to the basement, felt the draft, and silently cursed O'Reilly and Murphy.

The basement's okay, my ass! A window was open, and they hadn't even noticed it.

Now she could hear it. *Squeak, bang — squeak, bang!* The wind was blowing it open and closed, open and closed.

She was about to go down and close it, then hesitated.

She had never opened a basement window, not as long as she'd lived in the house.

Could the cops have opened it?

Why?

Maybe they'd opened it while checking it, and just forgotten to latch it again.

The stairs were dark. A string hung from the lightbulb, but when she pulled it, nothing happened.

Damn. Was she going to have to go down there in the dark? She had no idea where her flashlight was. Packed away somewhere, probably, along with every spare lightbulb, which meant she couldn't even change the burned-out one.

She should just go back to bed and

forget it. But there were boxes in the basement, too, and the last thing she needed was for rain to come in and ruin them.

Taking a deep breath, she started down the stairs. The dim shaft of light from the kitchen door illuminated nothing more than a narrow area at the bottom of the stairs, and barely lit even that. Still, it was better than operating in total darkness.

She went down one stair at a time, slowly, almost lost in her own shadow, careful not to lose her footing. A broken leg or twisted ankle was something she needed even less than a bunch of rain-soaked boxes. She tried to visualize where everything was on the floor so she wouldn't step on or trip over something. But no visualization came to mind — all she could remember was that she'd stacked boxes everywhere.

The concrete floor was far colder on her bare feet than the wood floor of the bedroom had been, but she ignored the chill and followed the sound to the far corner. Sure enough, barely visible in the faint light leaking from the top of the stairs, she saw a window flapping loose.

She closed it and locked the handle down securely.

Then she turned and made her way back

through the maze of boxes in less than a quarter of the time it had taken her to get to the window.

She ran up the stairs, taking them two at a time, and firmly closed the basement door behind her.

And it was over.

The banging was silenced and she could go back to bed.

She took a deep breath, crossed the kitchen and turned out the light.

Then, in the darkness of the living room, she heard another sound.

And heard it a second too late.

The arm snaked around her neck from behind, and before she could make a sound, a hand clamped something over her nose and mouth.

Something soft, and wet.

Something with a scent that made her want to vomit.

She struggled now, struggled for breath, struggled to yell for Emily, struggled to run, to kick, to rip the hands away from her face.

But like hearing the sound itself, it was all too late. She was already out of breath, and against her own will she inhaled the fumes deeply into her lungs.

She felt her knees weaken, and with a

last thought of her baby sleeping so peacefully upstairs in her bed, Ellen began to drop away into the darkness.

A *way out!*
There *had* to be a way out.
Kara's breath rasped in her throat as she raced barefoot through the tunnel.
A tunnel so dark she couldn't see its walls. But she could feel them, feel them surrounding her, closing in on her. And where was the tunnel's end?
Maybe it had no end! Maybe she was going to race on forever through the blackness but never get anywhere. Nor could she turn around, or even stop, because the man was behind her. The man in black, who was chasing her. So she had to keep going, keep going forward, forward through the tunnel that had no light at its end.
She could only hope — *pray* — that it did end, and that there would be a way out when she finally got there.
Suddenly — impossibly — the tunnel narrowed. It was getting smaller, colder. Now she was running crouched over, her head brushing the ceiling, her back burning with pain, every muscle in her body screaming in agony.

Out, she told herself. *Have to get out . . . please get me out. . . .*

The tunnel narrowed still further, and now her shoulders scraped against its cold walls as she dragged herself onward.

Then she heard him behind her — close behind her. "Angel," he whispered, his voice a gentle, almost seductive breeze that flowed over her like cool water. "Come to me, my angel. . . ."

"No!" she yelled, but her voice sounded muffled even as it echoed back to her from the still-narrowing walls.

The cold walls that were pressing against her now.

Moaning almost inaudibly, she forced herself on, but now her feet felt so heavy she could hardly move them. But what did it matter? If the tunnel had no end, she would never get there anyway.

Hope began to fade.

And now she needed water. She needed —

Abruptly, she stopped short, sensing something ahead of her, blocking her way.

The man? No! He was still behind her.

The darkness began to lift, and in the faintest of gray light, she saw it.

A door! A huge door, unimaginably

large, made from planks as big as tree trunks, bound together with thick iron straps.

And a latch! A latch she could touch, that fit perfectly in her hand.

But a latch that would not open!

Behind her, she felt the man drawing closer, smelled his fetid breath on the back of her neck.

Her fingers felt numb as she fumbled with the latch. Panic was threatening to overwhelm her now, and she could feel the man's hands reaching out to her. In another second his fingers would close around her throat and then —

And then she had it!

The door swung open, and beyond it lay a room filled with light so bright it momentarily dazzled her.

In the center there was an object, something she almost recognized, but not quite.

She moved closer.

It was a twisted mass of metal from which faint wisps of smoke were rising.

A car!

That was it — a wrecked car! But —

Something rolled out of the smoldering wreckage, coming to rest only inches from her bare feet.

A ball?

No, not a ball.

A head.

Steve's head!

She opened her mouth to scream, but nothing came out. Then a voice echoed in the vastness of the room. "He didn't suffer," the policeman said as he leaned down to pick up Steve's head.

Steve's eyes opened as the policeman raised his head up so it was even with her own. "Playing house," he said. His dead blue lips twisted into a grimace of a smile, and blood oozed from between his shattered teeth. "She's playing house."

A scream welled up in Kara's throat and she opened her mouth to set her anguish free.

And sat straight up in bed.

Utterly disoriented, stunned by the vividness of the dream, Kara put her hands to her head in an attempt to still the dizziness that had seized her. Feeling the lentil soup she'd had for dinner begin to rise in her gorge, she hurled herself out of bed, and barely made it to the bathroom before the soup spewed through her throat and out her mouth.

She crouched, gasping, next to the toilet, and finally her head began to clear. The porcelain felt cool against her burning cheek, and she stayed where she was, slowly emerging from the shadows of the nightmare. Finally, when her breathing returned to normal, she stood up, moved to the sink, and cupped her hands under the faucet. She rinsed her face, washed out her mouth, then drank thirstily from her cupped hands. Only when she was sure the nausea was completely over did she straighten up and stare at herself in the mirror.

"I'll never survive this," she whispered to her reflection. But even as she formed the words, the response rose in her mind: *Why would I want to?*

Wrung out, Kara shuffled back to the bedroom. A late night infomercial was on the television she hadn't bothered to turn off when she went to bed, and now it provided just enough background noise to muffle the echo of the emptiness of the house.

Kara crawled back under the covers, still wearing the pajamas, the bathrobe, and the thick pair of fuzzy socks she'd put on before going to bed the first time, but they did nothing to protect her from the cold knowledge that Steve would never again reach for her in the night.

He'd never rub her back after getting up to go to the bathroom.

He'd never pull her close for a cuddle in the darkness of night, murmuring in her ear.

If she could wrap an insulating quilt around her bathrobe under the covers, she would have, but there were no more quilts, so instead she wrapped her arms around her chest and gave in once more to the terrible agony of her loneliness, and the fresh crop of tears that came with it.

In the emptiness of the house, the tears were her only company, and she let herself sob until even that comfort was exhausted.

When the crying was over, the numbness came back.

But so did the answer to the question that had come into her mind as she'd gazed into the mirror a few minutes ago, considering her own survival: *Why would I want to?*

Because of Lindsay, of course.

She had to survive for Lindsay.

And Patrick Shields had survived worse.

He had survived, and she would, too.

Clinging to that belief, Kara picked up the remote and switched off the television.

The silence of the empty house closed around her, but as she closed her eyes, she knew that tonight, at least, she would dream no more.

★ ★ ★

Emily had to go to the bathroom.

She climbed out of bed and walked, half awake, out the bedroom door and turned left, just like she had a million times before.

And ran smack into a wall.

By the time she was awake enough to realize what had happened, she was sprawled on the floor, crying.

"Mommy?" she called. "Mommy!"

No answer.

For the first time in Emily's short life, there was no answer.

But she didn't really hurt, either. Not enough to make her cry, anyway. She hiccuped a couple of times, then rubbed her eyes and gingerly touched her forehead, where a new bump had grown, right in the middle. Then she rubbed her bottom where she'd landed after her forehead had hit the wall.

Her bottom didn't really hurt, either.

And she still needed to go to the bathroom.

She looked around, peering into the darkness, trying to figure out what had happened. Then she remembered: she'd gone to sleep in her mother's bed.

So the bathroom was the other way.

She turned around, found the bathroom, and sat on the toilet until she was sure there was nothing left. Then she wiped herself carefully, flushed the toilet, and went back to her mother's bed.

It was empty.

"Mommy?" Emily called, more puzzled than frightened.

No answer. She climbed back into the bed, found the warm spot where she'd been sleeping, and snuggled down.

But where was her mother?

She sat up and called out again, a lot louder this time. *"Mommy!"*

Nothing but the sound of the wind and the rain outside.

"There's nothing to be afraid of," Emily said out loud, repeating the words her mother had spoken to her so many times when she'd awakened from a bad dream, or heard thunder outside, crashing so loudly it shook the house. Now the sound of her own voice speaking her mother's words comforted her. "She'll be back in a minute," she went on. "That's what she always says, 'I'll be back in a minute.' "

Then she remembered what had happened earlier, when her mother had been really scared and they'd gone to the neighbor's house. But the police came, and then everything was all right. So now, if she got really scared and her mom wasn't home, she knew what she would do. She would go back to the neighbor's house, and they'd call the police for her.

But not right now, because she wasn't really scared. She was a big girl, a brave girl, and besides, her mother would be back in a minute.

The minutes ticked by, each one of them feeling like forever, and Emily began to feel like she was going to start to cry if her mom didn't come back to bed pretty soon. She stuck her thumb in her mouth — something she never let her mother see her do — and snuggled down right in the middle of the big bed.

Somehow, it didn't feel quite as lonely there.

Then she decided to tell herself a story, the way her mother did when she couldn't fall asleep.

"Once upon a time," she whispered to herself, "there was a brave little girl. . . ." Her voice trailed off, and she decided to start over. "Once upon a time . . ." she whispered, but once again her words trailed off.

A moment later Emily's thumb slipped back into her mouth, her breathing grew slow and rhythmic, and her eyes gently closed. . . .

And in her dreams, her mother was cuddling her close, just the way her mother was supposed to.

In her dreams, everything was perfect. . . .

CHAPTER FORTY-THREE

Rick Mancuso sank the spike of the Open House sign into the soggy earth at the corner, two blocks from the Fine house, tamped the mud with his foot, then stepped back. The sign tilted a couple of inches but held; good enough for the few hours he needed. If it fell over by four, so be it. Satisfied, he checked his watch.

Ten of two, which meant he was running late. Normally, he liked to be at his open houses at least half an hour early, just to make certain everything was in order. And Ellen Fine had a little girl; kids in a house — even just one — usually meant the house wouldn't look as good as it should in order to sell quickly, and since Rick liked quick sales, he didn't mind spending half an hour putting a place straight.

Not today — there wouldn't be time, so he'd have to trust that Ellen Fine had done her job. Giving the sign one last desultory adjustment, an adjustment that failed almost as soon as he made it, he slammed the trunk of his car, then drove the two blocks to Ellen Fine's house and parked across the street. Even though it was small — real small — the house still had good curb appeal, looking more like the "cottage" he'd described in the ad than he actually remembered. The grass was nice and green and looked freshly mowed, and the trees that lined both sides of the street were almost fully leafed out. There were even a few daffodils still blooming along the walk. Nice — very nice: the rain last night had made everything fresh.

As he crossed the street, he saw Emily looking out the upstairs window. He waved at her, but she had already disappeared, leaving only a wisp of swaying lace to show that she'd been there at all. Rick punched another Open House sign into the lawn, picked up his briefcase and the folder of flyers, and headed up the walk.

Usually clients were so anxious about open houses that by the time he was on their porches they were at the open door, waiting. But not this time. He rang the bell.

Nothing.

He pressed the button again, then once more.

Nothing.

No sound from inside at all; no music, no "I'll be right there" call from the bedroom or kitchen.

Just silence.

But Emily was there — he'd seen her. Feeling faintly uneasy, Rick knocked hard on the door. "Ellen?" he called out. "Ellen, it's Rick. For the open house?"

And still he heard nothing at all from inside the house.

He tried the door.

Locked. And today was the day she'd promised to have a key for him so he could put a lockbox on. What was going on? Ellen Fine hadn't struck him as the kind of mother who would leave her child alone in the house. Besides, her car was in the driveway.

The basement! That was it; she was down in the basement doing laundry — the last thing he needed at an open house — and she just hadn't heard the bell or his knock or heard him when he called out.

He walked around the side of the house and tried the kitchen door.

Unlocked and unlatched.

Standing ajar, in fact.

Rick pushed on the door and it swung wide. He stuck his head in. "Hello?" No answer. "Ellen? It's Rick Mancuso."

Now the silence from inside felt eerie. And then the stories he'd heard, about some agent or another — always nameless, of course — being shot by a homeowner who had forgotten about a showing appointment, came to mind.

Gazing around the kitchen made him even more uneasy. There were dirty dishes in the sink and uncooked potatoes in a cold frying pan on the stove. A carton of eggs sat on the countertop along with a jar of peanut butter and another of grape jelly.

He didn't think Ellen Fine would have left this kind of mess in the kitchen, even if no open house had been planned.

His sense that something was wrong escalating, Rick stepped into the kitchen, put his briefcase down on the kitchen table, and walked into the living room. "Emily?"

For a moment there was no response, but as he was about to call out again, a small voice drifted down from the top of the stairs. "You better go away."

"Emily? It's me, Rick. You remember me — I'm supposed to be here today to meet your mommy. Is she here?"

He saw pajama legs at the top of the

stairs. Then, one careful step at a time, Emily appeared, her hair touseled and her thumb firmly planted in her mouth. Halfway down the stairs, the little girl sat down, staring at him.

"Hey, Emily — remember me?"

She nodded. Her face was blotchy, and he could tell she'd been crying. "Is your mommy here?"

She shook her head.

"Where is she?"

She shrugged, then sucked in a long, ragged breath. "I — I don't know," she finally stammered, and as she spoke, her voice broke and her eyes filled with tears.

Jesus Christ, Rick thought. What did she do, just take off last night? But Ellen Fine hadn't seemed like that kind of woman.

Not at all.

"I'm going to come up and look, okay?" Emily nodded, and now the tears overflowed and began to run down her cheeks. "Hey, hey, hey," Rick said, flustered. "Don't cry, sweetie." He moved up the stairs and sat on the step next to her, and instantly Emily scooted close to him, climbed into his lap and put her arms around his neck. Now, with her face buried in his shoulder, her sobs began in earnest.

Rick froze, with no clue what to do —

never before in his life had a five-year-old girl clung to him, let alone one sobbing as if her heart was breaking. "C'mon, honey," he finally said, standing up and supporting her with one arm. "Let's find your mommy."

But Ellen was not upstairs, nor was she in the basement, nor was there any sign of her anywhere else in the house. Back in the living room, Rick lowered Emily onto the couch, fished in his pocket for his handkerchief, and helped her blow her nose and wipe her eyes. Then he squatted down in front of her so their heads were on the same level. "When was the last time you saw your mommy?"

Emily's little face screwed up as she concentrated. "Bedtime," she finally said. "Mommy was scared, so I slept with her."

Whatever this was, it wasn't good. "What was she scared of?" he asked.

"She was scared someone was in the house."

Ellen Fine had been afraid someone was in the house, and now she was no longer in the house herself. "I'm going to call the police," Rick said, almost more to himself than to Emily.

The little girl instantly brightened. "They're nice!"

Rick Mancuso cocked his head. "You know the police?"

Emily nodded again. "They came last night."

"Because your mommy was scared?"

Emily nodded a third time.

Rick pulled out his cell phone and dialed 911, and in less than two minutes had explained exactly what he'd found when he arrived at Ellen Fine's house ten minutes earlier.

"An officer will be there in less than ten minutes," the impersonal voice of the 911 operator said when he was finished.

With Emily clinging to him like a burr in a puppy's fur, Mancuso pulled the Open House sign from the lawn, then went back inside. He didn't particularly want to babysit — didn't know how — but he sure wasn't going anywhere, at least not until the cops arrived. "Why don't you show me your room?" he finally asked. It wasn't going to kill him to play with dolls for a half hour or so, was it?

Besides, there was still the hope — faint though it might be — that Ellen Fine could still show up, clean the kitchen and make the beds, and between the two of them they could save the open house.

Yeah, right.

★ ★ ★

A nightmare. It had to have been a nightmare. But if it was only a nightmare, why did she feel burning scrapes on her legs as if she'd been dragged over the cracked and pitted asphalt of the alley behind her house?

Why was her nightie still damp from the rain?

And why was the panic that had always before been at its worst at the moment she woke up from a bad dream not now falling away? Why, instead, were its tentacles closing tighter around her with every second that passed as her mind slowly cleared?

Because it hadn't been a nightmare at all.

As the last vestiges of unconsciousness lifted, Ellen felt not only the stinging abrasions on her legs, but the stinging in her feet, the aching in her joints, and the agony of a headache whose throbbing threatened to overwhelm her with every beat of her heart.

Her neck hurt.

Her wrists hurt.

Her shoulders hurt.

She tried to move, hoping to ease some of the aching.

Then, from somewhere behind her, a voice whispered: "She's waking up . . . Mommy's waking up!"

Ellen's eyes snapped open to behold a nightmare even more horrifying than the one from which she'd thought she just awakened. A strangled scream rose in her throat, but when she opened her mouth to vent it, nothing happened; instead of filling the chamber around her with her howl of anguish, she felt like her mouth — her cheeks, her eardrums, her very head — was about to explode. As the scream crashed against her taped lips, her lungs tried to suck in new air to replace the mass they'd just expelled, and a new panic seized her.

She couldn't breathe!

She couldn't breathe, and she was suffocating!

Yet another scream rose in her, but she found one tiny corner of her mind that had not yet given in to the overwhelming panic.

Nose! that tiny fragment of her mind commanded her. *Breathe through your nose!*

She caught the second scream as it was rising in her throat, and forced it back down into the pit of terror from which it had arisen. Focusing her mind — blanking out the pain, the burning, the terror, even the images she'd seen when she opened her eyes — she focused her mind on a single thing.

Breathing.

Breathing through her nose.

And breathing slowly, so the rhythm could do its part in staving off the mind-numbing panic.

Almost miraculously, air began to fill her lungs.

In . . . out . . . in . . . out . . .

As the oxygen began to flow through her, Ellen's mind began to clear and the panic to subside.

Then the memories finally came flooding back.

Real.

It was all real. Waking up . . . hearing a noise . . . going downstairs . . . checking everything, even the basement. And thinking it was all right, thinking she'd been wrong, that there was nothing in the house at all. And then, just as she was going back upstairs —

Even now she could still taste some kind of drug in her mouth, smell it in her nostrils. But there hadn't been quite enough to keep her completely unconscious. So it had all seemed like a dream. A dream from which she would awaken. But now she was awake, and the reality was even worse than the dream that hadn't been a dream at all.

She struggled against the bonds that held her hands behind her, struggled against the tape that bound her ankles to the legs of a chair — a chair far too small to hold her body.

Across from her sat two girls. One of them she recognized immediately — the girl from Camden Green who had vanished after —

An open house! An open house just like the one that had been held at her home.

The other girl was younger, emaciated, with a grayish complexion that told Ellen almost as much as the blank look in her eyes. It took Ellen a second or two to realize that the bright smiles on both the girls' faces were nothing more than lipstick clumsily drawn onto the duct tape that covered their mouths, and each of them was bound to an undersized chair, just as she was.

All three of them were sitting at what looked like a child's tea table, a table that was already set for tea, though the crockery was stained and cracked, and the silver dented and badly tarnished.

A flicker of movement caught her eye, and Ellen twisted her neck to see another person, a figure clad all in black except for a white surgical mask upon which was drawn an even bigger, redder, and more grotesque smile than those the two girls wore.

Then, as she turned back to the two girls, she remembered her own daughter.

Emily! Oh dear God, Emily!

Emily . . . Emily . . . Emily, Ellen chanted in her head. She had to know if Emily was all right. Had this — this *monster* taken Emily, too? But maybe not — maybe he'd left her at home in bed. Maybe it was just her he wanted, and not her daughter.

That was it — that had to be it. It wasn't Emily who had interested him in the picture. It had been her.

She had to believe that. She *needed* to believe that.

Once again her panic subsided and her mind accepted that none of it was a nightmare, that it was all real, and that if anyone was going to do anything to help not only her, but the two girls as well, it would have to be her.

Which meant she had to assess the situation. Telling herself once again — forcing herself to believe — that Emily was at least still safe, she turned her attention first to the blonde. What was her name? Lindsay!

That was it. Lindsay Mason, or Merrill, or something that began with an M. The girl looked reasonably healthy, and when their eyes met, Ellen saw a burning anger in them. And when Lindsay's eyes fixed on the figure in black, Ellen could feel her fury as clearly as if the girl had spoken out loud. *I'll kill him,* she seemed to be saying. *If I ever get loose, I'll kill him.*

But the other girl — the dark-haired, emaciated child with the dead eyes and gray complexion — seemed not even conscious of her surroundings anymore, let alone of what was happening to her.

Ellen's gaze returned to Lindsay again, who looked back, her eyes pleading now, and once again Ellen could read their message clearly: *Help us . . . please help us.*

Ellen tried to smile, but the tape on her mouth only tore at the skin of her lips as she moved them. Nor could she speak. Then, out of her desperation to communicate with the girl, an idea came.

And Ellen winked.

For a moment she wasn't sure Lindsay had even seen it, but then the girl's eyes flicked toward the black-clad figure for a second, then back to her.

And she winked back.

Ellen felt a surge of hope. She and

Lindsay had communicated, and they'd done it in front of their captor, right under his nose. If they could do that, they could find a way to escape. They just had to work together. Her mind began racing. The man in black had referred to her as "Mommy." So if she was the mother, then he must think of the girls as her children, so it was going to be up to her to take care of them, just as she had to trust that someone else's mother would take care of Emily until she herself got back. And she *would* get back. Somehow she'd stay awake and alert, and in spite of everything — in spite of the horrible taste in her mouth, the splitting headache from whatever drug he'd given her, the horrible pain in every part of her body — she'd find a way to prevail.

Maniac though he might be — and obviously was — in the end, he was still a man. And Ellen knew all about men. Reaching deep into the depths of memory, she retrieved the scraps of anger she'd felt toward Danny Golden, every wrong he'd done her. She examined each of them like jewels, then piled them together as if they were a hidden treasure that would renew not only her fury, but her strength as well.

Then she focused that fury and strength upon their captor.

He was standing next to the table now, holding a steaming kettle. As he started slopping scalding water into the tiny cups, Ellen assessed the possibilities.

If he expected them to drink, he would have to unbind at least one of their hands.

And if he did, and the water were still hot enough —

The vision of him screaming in agony as the boiling water struck his eyes, then recoiling from her to stumble blindly around the tiny chamber in which they were imprisoned, seemed to double her strength, and hope surged through Ellen once more. But then, as he poured water into Lindsay's cup, he looked over at her and stopped.

He set the kettle on the table.

"What's this?" he asked.

Ellen could almost feel his eyes fixing on the small tattoo of a bird that perched high on her thigh, a souvenir of that first weekend with Danny, when she'd managed to get tattooed and knocked up all in the same day.

"Who did that?" the black-clad man demanded. "Who did it?" He looked at the two girls, and Lindsay shook her head almost violently.

The other girl made no move at all.

"It shouldn't be there," she heard the man saying. "Mommy never had anything like that!" His eyes once again flicked between the two girls who sat bound to the chairs opposite Ellen. "And someone's going to have to be punished for this," he added in a voice so soft and menacing that her skin crawled as if something dark and cold had touched her soul. "Someone's going to have to be punished for everything!"

Then the man was rattling around in some kind of drawer or cabinet behind her. Though she could not see what he was doing, Lindsay could, and Ellen watched the girl's eyes for some clue as to what might be happening.

A moment later, as Lindsay's eyes widened in an expression of horror, Ellen had to fight for breath again.

And again she struggled with her bonds, but her legs were securely taped and her wrists so tightly bound that her hands were going numb.

"This," the man said. "I can use this, just like —" His voice broke and he fell silent. Then he reappeared, holding an ancient, rusting paring knife. "Yes," he said, his voice trembling as he gazed at the blade. "I remember this."

Ellen was afraid she was going to faint. But she couldn't. She had to hold it together, had to deal with whatever was about to happen.

But when he started to carve her leg with that dull, rusty blade, the blackness closed in around her peripheral vision like a swarm of bees.

And no amount of her will could keep it away.

CHAPTER FORTY-FOUR

Something is wrong.

I can *feel* it, feel it as if it were something physical.

It's the same feeling I used to get when I was a child, a strange tingling on the back of my neck when someone was watching me.

Or, more specifically, when one single person was watching me.

That person never watches me anymore, of course — I haven't set eyes on her in years — if she even still exists, it is no longer of any consequence to me.

And yet the feeling I have been experiencing the last few days is the same: the hair on the back of my neck begins to rise, as the hackles of a dog rise when it senses danger. But there seems to be no pattern to it. I have experienced it upon first awakening, and occasionally as I let myself drift into the arms of Morpheus when my day or night has come to an end.

Yet perhaps I am wrong. Perhaps it is only in my head, nothing more than a result of my recent carelessness.

And I readily admit that I have been careless.

The thing is, I truly believe my carelessness has been deliberate, for the very risks I have been taking have made everything I do that much more exciting. So perhaps it is nothing more than paranoia.

Yet how can I be sure?

But of course the answer is simple: I must be vigilant.

I must tune my senses to detect the first hint of any danger whatsoever, and determine its source the moment I feel it. There will be mistakes, of course — for now, instead of dealing with what I can readily control, I find myself forced to deal with what I have no control over whatsoever.

I do not like that.

I do not like it at all.

Still, what choice do I have? If my instincts are correct, and I truly am in danger for the first time since I was a boy, I must defend myself.

It is sad, though, for this should be a time of great rejoicing. I should be overcome with happiness. I should be shouting from the rooftops. But instead, this dank cloak of suspicion hangs over my head and blocks out the sunlight.

I am unable to enjoy myself, unable to bask in the glow of my accomplishments.

Perhaps, though, I'm wrong. Perhaps this strange sensation of an unseen watcher truly *is* merely a function of my recklessness last week.

Perhaps it is me, punishing myself.

Yet how can I know? For some reason, I find I barely trust my own instincts, though they have never failed me before. Yet those very instincts are now warning me of unseen danger.

I feel walls closing in on me. I am a prisoner of my own foolishness.

I don't know what to do next. Shall I abandon all and begin again, somewhere else?

I am afraid to do anything.

I am afraid to do nothing.

I am afraid my fear will turn to fury, and then all control will be lost.

And if control is lost, then everything is lost.

For the first time in her life, Kara wished she was the kind of person who took naps, but though her body now felt as exhausted as her mind and her spirit, she knew that retreating to her bed wasn't going to change anything. Even if she slept — which she knew she wouldn't — when she woke up, Lindsay would still be missing and Steve would still be —

Even in her mind, and in the loneliness of the house, she still cut her thought short before thinking the word. But not thinking it wouldn't change anything, any more than a nap would, so she paused halfway up the stairs, stood perfectly still, and said it out loud.

"Dead. He's dead, and nothing in the world is going to change that." The word echoed almost mockingly in the stairwell, but Kara steeled herself against reacting. She might feel like crying, but she wasn't going to. Instead she went back to polishing the already spotless banister, applying enough force to the dust cloth to make her wonder if it was possible to actually dust the finish right off the wood. She banished that thought, too, and kept polishing until she came to the top of the stairs.

Across the hall, the door to Lindsay's room stood open. It was the one room she hadn't touched today, and now she closed its door, determined that it, at least, would be unchanged when Lindsay was finally back home.

The buzzer on the dryer sounded, and Kara automatically turned back to the stairs, to go down and fold the last load of laundry. But she abruptly changed her mind. It was mostly Steve's things, and they'd just have to wait, at least until she made up her mind whether to put them in boxes and take them to Goodwill or fold them up and put them back in the dresser, even though she knew it wouldn't bring Steve back.

She pushed open the door to the master suite and stared at the stripped mattress; the clean sheets were down in the laundry room, neatly folded. But if she went down to get them, she wouldn't be able to ignore Steve's clothes cooling in the dryer, and then —

And then she'd start crying again, no matter how many promises she'd made to herself.

Ignoring the unmade bed, she picked up the remote control and clicked the television on. The sound came on before the picture.

"— was discovered alone in her house after her mother disappeared sometime after ten o'clock last night."

The picture suddenly popped up on the screen, and Kara gazed at the image of a little girl, no more than five years old, her eyes wide with fear as she was carried to a van by an attractive woman wearing a police uniform. The little girl was crying, and Kara bit her lip as she watched. The camera cut away to a cool blonde in a well-tailored suit who was standing in front of a small house. A For Sale sign was clearly visible on the front lawn, and as the reporter spoke, Kara felt her blood running cold. "According to neighbors, Ellen Fine became afraid there was someone still in her house when she and her daughter returned to it after her agent had held an open house yesterday afternoon."

Kara's heart began to race and she leaned closer to the set.

"Police searched the premises, but there was no evidence of an intruder."

No evidence of an intruder.

Just like her own house, after Lindsay disappeared.

Her hand was on the telephone before the broadcast was over. Andrew Grant's business card, with his home number written on the back, was on her nightstand. She took a deep breath, got herself under control, and dialed. As she waited for the detective to answer, she stared at the photograph of Ellen Fine that was now on the screen. She was a pretty woman who couldn't be more than thirty and looked vaguely familiar. But before Kara could ruminate on the woman who'd vanished, the detective answered the phone.

"Is your television on, Sergeant Grant?" she asked without preamble. "Because if it isn't, you'd better turn it on. Channel 5." There was silence for a moment, then she heard the detective breathe a single, quiet word.

"Shit."

Finally, at last, she had his full attention.

Andrew Grant rang Rick Mancuso's doorbell and hoped to God that Mancuso was going to have all the right answers to his questions. Not that it mattered whatever Mancuso had to say, it was going to be a long Sunday afternoon. He'd wanted to put Kara Marshall and her phone call on the back burner until tomorrow morning when he'd be back in the office, but there was no way he could; not, anyway, if he wanted to sleep tonight.

So he'd put in a call to Sean O'Reilly at the Smithton Police Department, but O'Reilly was already into the disappearance up to his ears and there was nothing else for him to do but grab his gun and shield and head over to Smithton.

In the briefing, flares went off in his head when the name Rick Mancuso had come up, and he'd laid out the whole Lindsay Marshall case for O'Reilly. O'Reilly had shrugged. "I already talked to him, and I think he's clean. But hey — if you want to lean on him, there's no way I can stop you, is there?"

So now he was leaning against the real-estate agent's doorbell. When Mancuso finally opened the door and he showed the agent his badge, Mancuso nodded as if he'd been expecting to see another detective and opened the door wide, inviting him in.

They sat on stools at a neat kitchen bar. For a single guy, Grant thought, Mancuso kept a tidy house. Too tidy? "So here we are again," he began, his manner carefully amiable, at least for now. "Another open house, another abduction. Any idea why your name keeps coming up?"

Mancuso shrugged. "It's a pretty small community. I can't be the only guy who was in both those houses." Grant said nothing, but kept his eyes steadily on Mancuso's, and finally the agent sat up straighter. "What do you want from me? I don't know anything about it. When I left Ellen Fine's house yesterday, it was all locked up. I don't even have a key — she wouldn't give me one. That's why I had to ring the bell when I went back today." His eyes narrowed truculently. "I've already told the other police the same thing a dozen times."

"Did you keep a logbook from yesterday?"

"Of course. And the Smithton cops have it."

Grant's cell phone rang in his pocket. He fished it out, glanced at the caller ID screen, and flipped it open.

"Grant?" the caller said. "It's Sean O'Reilly. Listen, we just found a report that there was another disappearance after an open house."

"Tell me you're kidding."

"I wish I were. Happened over in Mill Creek about three weeks ago. A nineteen-year-old girl named Shannon Butler. Vanished in the middle of the night. No clues. She's still gone — listed as a missing person. Looks like maybe we've got something hinky going on."

"I'll get back to you." Grant closed his phone and fixed Mancuso with his hardest stare. "You ever work open houses in Mill Creek?"

Did Mancuso hesitate before he shook his head? Grant wasn't quite sure. "Too far away," the agent said.

"Not that far," Grant countered. "You've never showed property there? Never gone to an open house there?"

Now Mancuso looked less certain. "Hey, I'm not going to say never —" he began, and Grant stood up.

"Grab a jacket," he said. "I think we need to talk down at the station."

The blood drained from Mancuso's face. "Am I going to need a lawyer here?"

"Did you do something you don't want to tell me about?"

"No, of course not."

"Then why would you need a lawyer? C'mon."

Grant didn't know what Mancuso had to do with all of this, but he'd bet all his years as a cop that if he dug deep enough into Shannon Butler's file, he'd find Mancuso's name.

CHAPTER FORTY-FIVE

Make it stop, Ellen prayed silently. *Dear God, just make it stop.* But no matter how hard she prayed, the agony in her leg seemed only to grow worse. When she'd first seen what the man had done, when she'd first looked down at the raw, bleeding muscle that lay exposed where the man — the *monster* — had cut the small tattoo away from her thigh, she'd barely believed it could have happened at all. But as she watched blood ooze from the gaping wound and felt the pain radiate out from her thigh until it had spread through her entire body, the truth quickly sank in. It wasn't a man who had taken her at all.

It was a maniac.

Which meant she'd have to deal with him as a maniac.

It was that realization, almost even more than the pain where he'd hacked her skin away, that made her want to simply give up, to fall back into the unconsciousness from which she'd awakened only a few hours ago.

Or was it only a few minutes?

And what did it matter anyway? Even if she fell back into the blackness, she'd only wake up again to the nightmare that was not only hers, but that of the two girls as well. So she'd forced aside the urge to escape back into unconsciousness, closed her mind to the agony in her leg, and tried to clear her head.

She was no longer in the room with the table and chairs. After he'd cut her leg — and after finishing with the hideous parody of a tea party — he'd carried and dragged her down a steep flight of stairs, through some kind of tunnel, and into a cold, dank chamber with bare mattresses on the floor and manacles chained to the walls.

A dungeon.

He manacled her wrists, then left her alone, not even bothering to replace the tape he'd torn from her lips for the "tea party."

A few minutes later he brought Lindsay in, and manacled her as well.

He was gone longer after that, and when he returned, he carried the other girl — holding her almost tenderly — and when he put her down, she didn't move.

Was she unconscious or —

Ellen didn't allow herself to think it.

The monster — for that's what she now knew he was — chained the unconscious girl as securely as he'd chained Lindsay and her.

At last, he'd finished securing the girl, taken his light up a set of wooden stairs and vanished, leaving them in absolute, claustrophobic blackness. Then all the nightmarish fears that Ellen had ever experienced came roaring back.

Now she found it almost impossible to breathe. Panic rose inside her as the darkness closed around her, and for a moment she almost gave in to it, almost began screaming and thrashing.

Instead she concentrated on slowing her breathing, forcing herself to relax her body, limb by limb. She blocked out the blackness, instead visualizing a perfect day at the beach.

And there, in her mind's eye, she saw Emily, playing happily in the sand.

The panic surged forth again.

Relax, or you'll hurt yourself. As long as you're here, there's nothing you can do for her. And it isn't just Emily, either. Think about Lindsay. If you can't help Emily, at least you can help Lindsay and —

What was the other girl's name? The question itself seemed to turn the tide against the panic, and finally she began to think.

She took a deep breath, and the panic further loosened its grip on her. "Lindsay?" she said, her whisper sounding to her like a shout in the silent darkness. When there was no response, she repeated the single word, more loudly this time.

A moment later there was the sound of chains rattling somewhere to her right. "How do you know my name?" a faint, almost lifeless, voice asked.

"I saw your picture on television. My name's Ellen Fine."

More rattling.

Ellen imagined the girl struggling to sit up. "Your mom is hunting for you."

"You saw my mom?" A little more life in the voice now.

"She's been on TV, trying to find you."

There was a silence, then: "H-How long have I been here?"

Instead of answering the question, Ellen countered with her own: "Who's the other girl?"

"Shannon," Lindsay whispered.

The name meant nothing to Ellen. "Does he give you anything to eat or drink?"

"Sometimes. But I don't even know —" Lindsay's voice caught, and Ellen could hear her choking off a sob. When she spoke again, her voice was hollow and she made no attempt to mask her fear. "I don't even know what time it is, or what day it is, or anything else. I just —"

Her voice broke again, but this time Ellen was ready. "It's going to be all right," she said. "We're going to get out of here — there are three of us and only one of him. We can do it if we have a plan, and if we work together."

No response. Then, in the quiet, Ellen could hear Lindsay crying, a sound that brought back memories of Emily, frightened of a nightmare, sobbing in the darkness of her room.

Only this was not a nightmare.

This was real.

"Listen to me, Lindsay," Ellen said. "It's going to be all right. We're going to get out of this."

There was a sniffle, then Lindsay uttered a single word. "How?"

Desperately, Ellen cast her mind back to the moments after she had awakened to the surreal scene in the room with the tiny table and chairs and the grotesquely leering smiles she'd seen on all the faces around her. And she realized what they had to do.

"We have to give him what he wants."

"But I don't know what he wants," Lindsay moaned.

"Of course you do," Ellen told her. "Think of the smiles, Lindsay. And think of what he said. He called me Mommy, and he kept talking about how happy we all were. Don't you see? He wants a happy family. He wants us to be his family, and he wants us to be happy. So here's what we're going to do . . ."

Slowly, uncertain if Lindsay had enough energy left even to understand, let alone follow it, Ellen began to explain her idea.

Andrew Grant raked his fingers through his hair, tried to slow the thoughts that were tumbling chaotically through his mind, then leaned back in his chair and took a deep breath. There were a million things that had to be done, but if they weren't done in the right order, everything could — and undoubtedly would — turn into a disaster.

With the third deep breath, he felt his mind begin to clear, and he began to assess the situation.

For the moment, the powers-that-be had

given him interjurisdictional authority, which presumably meant the guys in Smithton would have to cooperate with him, at least until the FBI guys arrived. And, for now at least, the guys in Smithton had given him everything he'd asked for, though what they had wasn't much. Still, it was enough that he'd at least be coherent at the press briefing scheduled for nine o'clock.

According to the big clock on the wall, it was now 8:38.

It was going to be a long night.

First things first.

Seventeen minutes to figure out exactly what he was going to say, and then . . .

Then it would be a *very* long night.

A couple of patrolmen who had been called in more for show than because anyone expected them to do anything to night were grumbling in a corner, and half a dozen reporters were already in the lobby, glancing impatiently at their watches every few seconds as they waited for the briefing to begin. To Andrew Grant, they looked like nothing more than a flock of circling vultures waiting to descend on a corpse, and if he made one false step, the corpse they descended upon could be his. Eyeing them balefully, he decided that maybe the briefing would start on time and maybe it wouldn't.

The telephones had been ringing steadily since word of Ellen Fine's disappearance had gotten out that afternoon, and they hadn't slowed yet. The reporters seemed to have put two and two together at least as quickly as the two police departments involved, and into the evening the local talk radio stations had done their best to whip the public into a frenzy. It worked: apparently everyone on Long Island had seen someone who looked "suspicious" at an open house sometime over the last year or so.

The talk jockeys had even come up with a name for the guy: Open House Ozzie. Well, maybe if it got bad enough, they'd both wind up in one of Ann Rule's books, and he would become a character on a TV miniseries.

More likely, he'd get fired for being the obtuse dunderhead he now felt like. Why couldn't he have at least listened to Kara Marshall, instead of insisting her kid had just decided to take off?

The office walls seemed to be closing in on him.

He took his mug to the coffee machine, filled it with the dregs of the lunchtime coffee, then took the curse off its bitterness with a double shot of sugar and powdered cream and slowly made his way back to his desk. Stirring the sludge in his cup, he relegated his mistakes to the back of his mind so he could concentrate on getting it right from here on out.

The first priority, of course, would be to keep anyone else from vanishing from their own homes after an open house. He needed to get the word out that three abductions had taken place after open houses on Long Island — within fifteen miles of each other, in fact — in the past month.

And this was Sunday night; for all he knew, another abduction had taken place today, making it four. He needed a detail to work on that. O'Reilly and Murphy could handle it, along with the guys who first responded to Shannon Butler's disappearance in Mill Creek.

He scrawled a note on his yellow pad.

The next thing was to find Shannon, Lindsay, and Ellen. He'd handle that one personally. Rick Mancuso remained at the top of his list of probable perps, but primarily because he didn't have any other names on the list so far. Mancuso had been cooperative enough, but the guy didn't have an alibi for any of the nights after the disappearances had happened.

Which didn't mean nearly as much as the general public thought it did.

Still, there was no reason to hold him.

And so far, at least, there weren't any bodies, so it was just possible — and now he knew he was grasping at straws — that all three victims actually had just taken off.

And pigs could fly, too.

Taking yet another deep breath, Grant signaled to one of the guys who'd been called in from their Sunday dinners. "I want every logbook from every open house from every agent in a thirty-mile radius. For the last month or so." The patrolman, who'd only been with the department for three months, gaped at him.

"But that'll take all night."

Grant rolled his eyes. "So people won't go to bed. Too bad. Just do it."

As the patrolman went off to find a phone, Grant set two more patrolmen to work on the local agents: faxing, calling, and following up on everybody who had signed in at the Fine, Marshall, and Butler open houses. Not, of course, that this guy would have signed in, but you had to go through the motions, and who knew? Maybe the guy wasn't nearly as smart as Grant thought he was.

He sipped his coffee and winced at the nastiness of it while he prayed to the gods of caffeine that it would keep him sharp through the night.

Then he turned his attention to his third priority: dealing with the press while at the same time keeping the spotlight off himself.

This was going to be a media circus. Once the FBI arrived, it became their baby, and they didn't have far to come. They'd be here by morning, telling him and everybody else what to do. Between now and then, he would be in the spotlight, and he'd better look good.

Or, in the best of all possible worlds, find those girls.

Grant checked his watch. Five minutes left. He could feel the energy rise in the building as the briefing room filled up, and in a couple more minutes he'd be at the podium, his lieutenant sitting in the audience, observing him.

If he was lucky. If he was unlucky, the chief himself would have come down to watch.

Shit.

He took a last gulp of the mud in his coffee cup, grabbed his legal pad, and stood up to go deal with the press, which until today had never been more than old Marguerite Gould, who delighted in making public every minor disturbance Smithton and Camden Green and every other town on the north shore ever experienced, even if it was only a dog running loose in the park. Tonight, Marguerite probably wouldn't even be able to get a question in edgewise.

Billy Ferguson poked his head around the corner.

"Sarge?"

"I've got a briefing."

"I know," the patrolman said, "but look at this here." He held out the guest book from the Butler open house. "Mark Acton — you know, the agent who held the Marshall open house?"

Grant's attention was instantly riveted on the kid. "Yeah?"

"He was at the Butler open house."

Goose bumps rose on Grant's arms. *Acton was a real weasel.* "Was he at the Fine open house?"

The patrolman shrugged. "I don't know. If he was, he didn't sign the book."

Grant's eyes narrowed and his lips tightened into a hard smile. "Go get him."

"Yes, sir." The young man's face disappeared.

413

Feeling better now, Grant shrugged into his jacket, smoothed his hair, and picked up his yellow pad. Now, at least, he had a real suspect.

Mark Acton — a guy who had given him a bad feeling the moment he met him. And if there was one thing he'd learned over all the years he'd been a cop, it was this:

Always trust your feelings.

The light woke Ellen. That and a moan from Shannon, the first sounds she'd heard from the girl.

He was back.

Ellen's heart began to hammer in her chest again. How long had it been? Minutes? Hours? Not days, but how could she know, really? Not that it mattered. The only thing that mattered now was to keep her mind clear and stick to the plan.

Whatever happened, she had to stick to the plan and pray that Lindsay had not only understood, but had the strength and the will to go along with it, too.

Banishing the last tendrils of sleep that clung to her mind, and ignoring the knot of fear forming in her belly, she sat up on her mattress, tucked her legs beneath her and leaned on one arm, trying to make herself look as relaxed as if she were lounging on a picnic blanket. The wound in her leg shot a stab of pain through her as she dragged it across the coarse mattress, but she stifled the scream that rose in her throat as the light from the trapdoor opening illuminated the man in silhouette. Then it went dark again for a moment, until he turned on a beam of light. She squinted into it as he came down the stairs and moved toward the dark chamber. As he approached, she spoke.

"Is that you, honey?" she asked, hoping her voice didn't sound as artificially bright to him as it did to her. "How was your day?"

The man stopped in mid-stride and turned to her, his grotesque mask smiling at her even in the indirect illumination of his flashlight.

"Did you bring something I can make for dinner? I haven't had a chance to get to the store, and the girls are hungry."

The man reached into the darkness, and a moment later the dungeon was flooded with light from a naked bulb overhead. Now Ellen could see the madness in his eyes. "Be quiet," he said, but she thought she heard a hint of uncertainty in his voice.

"Don't be like that, sweetheart. The children need to be fed. That's why they haven't been happy the last few days."

Suddenly the man's eyes were blazing. "Stop that. Stop that! *You're ruining everything!*"

"Daddy?" Lindsay's voice sounded so tiny, Ellen almost didn't hear it at all.

The man wheeled around, but instead of unshackling Lindsay, he went to Shannon, undid her chains, then picked her up and walked through the door into the tunnel.

"He didn't tape her mouth," Lindsay whispered.

"Maybe he doesn't think he has to," Ellen whispered back. "And maybe he's right — maybe she can't speak anymore."

A moment later he was back, leaning over Lindsay.

Ellen heard her whisper something to him, then he unlocked the shackles from her wrists and jerked her to her feet. As he guided her toward the mouth of the tunnel, she made no move to resist.

Was Lindsay going along with her plan, or had her will finally given out?

When he came back again, Ellen smiled up at him, but just as she started to say something, he slapped her hard, then muffled her yelp with a hand clamped over her mouth, pressing so hard that when she opened it to sink her teeth into his palm, they sank into her own lips instead. As the taste of blood filled her mouth, he pressed a length of duct tape across her lips. Doing her best not to react against the slap and the stinging of her cut lip, Ellen forced herself not to resist as he put a noose around her neck. Only after he'd tightened it did he loosen her chains. When she was free, though, he yanked on the rope, clearly irritated.

Giving no sign that anything extraordinary was happening, Ellen got to her feet, forced herself to ignore the agony in her leg, and walked alongside him through the tunnel.

The two girls sat at the little table, their hands and legs tied as usual, but for a change they did not have tape on their mouths.

Lindsay's eyes met Ellen's for an instant before fixing on their captor. "Don't tie up Mommy," she said, her voice perfectly even. "I need her to brush my hair."

Ellen offered a silent prayer of thanks as Lindsay actually managed to smile while speaking the last words.

The man gazed first at Lindsay, then at her, and Ellen felt a tiny flicker of hope. But then he shook his head, and she knew she hadn't managed to act as convincingly as Lindsay. "She's not here for *you*," he said, the softness of his voice somehow increasing its menace. "She's here for me, like she always should have been!" He pushed her down hard in the same tiny chair she'd occupied earlier, taping her legs to those of the chair. Just as he was finishing, a barely audible voice drifted across the table, and Ellen's pulse was suddenly racing.

"I love you, Daddy," Shannon whispered.

The flame of hope that had all but died inside Ellen a moment ago suddenly brightened. Shannon wasn't unconscious, and she'd heard, and understood, and was playing along!

But then the man cried, "Don't call me that!" Crouching low so his face was almost touching Shannon's, his voice shook with fury. "I'm not your father! Don't you dare call me 'Daddy'!" He glowered at Ellen. "Why don't you do what you're supposed to do? Why don't you ever do it?"

Ellen shrank back as he came around to her, pulled a red marking pen from his pocket, grabbed her hair and jerked her head back. She felt the pen moving over the tape that covered her mouth, and a moment later he roughly released her hair. "There! Mommy looks the way she always looks, no matter what might be happening. Keep smiling, Mommy! Just keep smiling, and act like everything's just fine!"

Ellen nodded again, but now he seemed to have lost interest in her, moving around to Lindsay and gently stroking her hair. "You want me to brush your hair?" he whispered. He stroked Lindsay's head one more time, then ran his fingers down Lindsay's cheek, and Ellen could see the girl trying not to cringe as his whisper turned to a snarl. "Or is this what you want me to do?" His eyes fixed on Ellen once more. "You never saw, did you? But this time you'll see! This time I'll make you see!"

Ellen froze, certain that any reaction she might show would only make things worse.

"She's so beautiful," the man said, his fingers trailing down her neck and her shoulder. "At least on the outside."

"Daddy?" Lindsay whispered.

"Don't call me that!"

"I — I'm sorry," Lindsay stammered. "I just want you to love me as much as I love you."

The man's eyes fairly glittered. "Love?" he asked, his voice dropping once more to that menacing whisper. "Is that what you thought? Is that why you always smiled?"

Lindsay nodded, apparently oblivious to the danger in his voice. "Don't you want me to love you now?"

Ellen froze. What was Lindsay saying?

Then Shannon spoke. "Me, too," she said.

Don't, Ellen silently commanded. *Figure out a way to make him untie me. But don't do this! Don't!*

The man was gazing at the girls through glazed eyes.

"We love you," Lindsay said, her voice taking on a seductive tone that utterly belied her age. "Won't you let us show you how much?" Now her voice dropped to an enticing whisper. "Please?"

The man produced a knife from his pocket — the same rusty, bloodstained knife he'd used on Ellen's leg earlier, and slit the tape on Shannon's legs and arms. Then he helped her to her feet.

Though she was so weak she could barely hold her head up, Shannon reached out toward Lindsay. "Her, too," she whispered. "We both love you . . . both of us. . . ."

The man's eyes gleamed. "Yes," he said. "It's time you showed Mommy how much you love me, isn't it?" He turned to Lindsay, but before he could cut the tape that bound her, Ellen saw Shannon's body tense, and in that instant she knew what Shannon was going to do.

No, she silently pleaded, again trying to reach out to Shannon with her mind, but knowing it was useless. *Wait until Lindsay is loose!* But it was already too late. Before even one of Lindsay's limbs was free, Shannon mustered what little strength she still had and struck out at the man, her foot catching his groin.

He doubled over and fell to his knees, and now both Lindsay and Ellen were struggling against their bindings.

Shannon threw herself onto the man and started to pull his ski mask off, but the surgical mask tied over it held it just long enough. Enraged by the attack, he lurched to his feet and slammed his back into Shannon, crushing her to the wall. Ellen heard a gasp as air exploded from the girl's lungs. Shannon's grip loosened and their captor shook her off, letting her fall to the floor in a broken heap.

"Your fault," the man rasped, wheeling to glower at Ellen once more. "See what they did? And they call it 'love.' But it's not love! It's not!" As Lindsay Marshall screamed, his foot lashed out at Shannon, smashing into her ribs. Then, as Lindsay screamed even louder, he drew his foot back and struck again, this time crashing his boot into Shannon's head so hard her neck snapped.

As Shannon lay still on the floor, and Lindsay's screams gave way to choking sobs, he loomed over Ellen again, breathing hard, his eyes glinting with fury. "Your fault," he whispered. "All your fault." He leaned closer, and terror gripped her. *Emily, Emily, Emily. I'm going to die, and I can't even say good-bye to my baby.* "You failed! You! *You didn't do the only thing you were supposed to do!*" He jerked furiously on the noose around her neck, and she felt her breath cut off and her eyes bulging.

The light in the room began to fade.

Then, from above her, there was a howl of anguish, and abruptly the tension on the rope was gone.

"I hate you," the man whispered. "I hate you all, and I never want to play with you again!"

He vanished down the steps that led to the tunnel. Ellen coughed through her taped-up mouth, choking, trying desperately to fill her lungs with air. It took almost a full minute, breathing heavily through her nose, until the red globes cleared from her vision and her panic began to subside. She looked up then and met Lindsay's eyes across the table.

Neither of them dared look down at Shannon. *What have I done?* Ellen thought. *Dear God, what have I done?*

CHAPTER FORTY-SIX

Kara sat immobilized at her desk in the morning light, a mug of tea going cold next to her. Spread before her were all her lists of things to do, of people to call. There were stacks of flyers with Lindsay's glowing face on them, a file folder full of life insurance papers, and a fat folder with unpaid bills.

All of it needed her attention. But instead of doing anything, she just sat there, staring dumbly at the mess, not even finding the will to pick up her mug of tea, let alone deal with everything that had to be dealt with.

But she had to deal with it.

All of it.

The checks had to be written, and the policies had to be gone through, and the flyers had to be distributed. She knew that. A thousand people had told her so.

Life had to go on.

She knew that, too.

She picked up a pen and looked at the desk, trying to decide where to start.

But all she could think of was the dream she'd had last night.

And it had been a dream. It had to have been a dream.

She dropped the pen in the middle of the desk and put her face in her hands.

It hadn't been a dream. She'd heard Lindsay's scream of terror as clearly as if Lindsay had been in the next room. In fact, she had shot out of bed, out the bedroom door, and into Lindsay's room before she was awake enough to remember that Lindsay was no longer there.

But the scream had been so real. It reverberated in the walls of the bedroom, and as she listened to it, she'd *known*.

Lindsay was alive and she was in trouble. Trouble so frightening that she was screaming in terror, screaming for her life, screaming for her mother.

And here she sat, at her desk, with her head in her hands.

She felt beyond despair — beyond desperation.

Almost — but not quite — beyond hope.

Nobody was going to believe that she'd heard Lindsay scream in the night. They'd call it a dream, and a mother's dream was not going to motivate any law enforcement officer to ramp up the search.

But it hadn't been a dream.

Her first impulse had been to call Patrick. He would understand. He would be able to help her. But it was the middle of the night, and Kara knew she had to learn to stand on her own. Patrick had been a wonderful help, but he couldn't hold her hand every minute of every day.

She had to start getting through the days and nights by herself, starting with this one.

If she took the day one hour at a time, she could get through it.

She looked at the clock on the desk and set herself a goal: in the next sixty minutes, she would write checks for the most urgent bills, shower, get dressed, and have something to eat.

While she was eating, she would plan the next hour.

Only when those two hours were gone would she plan the next.

And if she made it successfully through the day, as a reward she'd call Patrick and report her progress. Just the thought of his understanding eyes and warm smile gave her strength.

She picked up the pen, desperately trying to ignore the echo of Lindsay's scream still reverberating in her head, and opened her checkbook.

The doorbell rang even before she could look at the balance.

Her heart caught in her throat.

News! It had to be news!

With her bathrobe flapping about her legs, Kara ran down the stairs and threw open the door, certain it would be Sergeant Grant.

Instead, a somber-faced man in a dark suit stood on the porch with a package; in front of the house she saw a black Lincoln Town Car. A chill came over her as she realized what the package was. She signed the form the man offered her, took the box, and retreated back into the house.

The chill tightening its grip on her, Kara pulled off the brown paper wrapping, and the stabbing pain in her chest took her breath away as her suspicions about the package were confirmed.

Stamped in red all over the box were the words HUMAN REMAINS.

SUMMERS FUNERAL HOME was printed at the top of the label.

Steve's ashes.

Dear God.

Kara's knees weakened and she sank to a dining room chair. In her head, she could hear herself screaming right along with Lindsay.

On the table in front of her, next to the box, was the cordless phone.

With a trembling hand, she picked it up and dialed Patrick.

CHAPTER FORTY-SEVEN

"Good Lord," Patrick Shields breathed as he gazed at the box that still sat on Kara's dining room table. "They actually made you sign for it?"

She nodded as a sigh of both exhaustion and relief escaped her lips. Though it changed nothing, just having Patrick in the house was making her feel a little better.

"Unbelievable," Patrick went on, his eyes — always so warm and comforting before — now darkening with anger. "I gave them strict instructions. I don't see how I could have been any clearer. I told them —"

"It doesn't matter what you told them," Kara broke in. "And that's not why I called you anyway. It's just — it's just everything, Patrick!" Hesitantly at first, but then speaking faster and faster, until her words were pouring out in a torrent that reflected every emotion she was feeling, Kara told him what had happened since he'd brought her back to the house yesterday. "I just don't think I can do it," she said when she finally ran out of steam, both verbally and emotionally. "I don't think I can handle any of it. And the thought of tonight —" Her voice broke as she choked on the last word, and she shook her head in helplessness. Patrick gently placed his hands on her shoulders and looked directly into her eyes.

"I know exactly how you're feeling," he told her, now without the tiniest vestige of anger in his voice or his eyes. "Oh, Lord, do I know. So the first thing we're going to do is simple. I'm going to take you back to Claire's."

Kara shook her head again, but this time there was nothing helpless in the gesture. "Not Claire's," she replied, a little too quickly. "It's not that she hasn't been wonderful to me — she has. But — oh, I don't know. It's like she's handling me with kid gloves or something. As if she's —"

"Afraid you'll break," Patrick finished for her, speaking exactly the words she'd been about to utter. "I know what that's like. I got the same thing to the point where sometimes I just wanted to smack her!" His lips compressed into a grim smile. "And it's not just her, either — it's everyone. But what can you say? It's not like they don't mean well. It's just that they don't have any idea what you're going through."

"So what do I do?" Kara asked, barely aware that she'd spoken out loud.

"Come to my house," Patrick decided, speaking before he even thought about it. Seeing Kara about to protest, he held up a hand. "I don't know why I didn't think of it in the first place," he said, then grinned. "But of course, I did. I just didn't suggest it, and I know exactly why I didn't do that, either. After all, what would people think? What would the neighbors say? What would Claire say? Worst of all, what would Neville Cavanaugh say?"

"Neville? But he's like your butler or something, isn't he? Why would you care what he says?"

"It's not really so much what he'd say. It's the way he'd look." Patrick twisted his face into an exaggerated parody of the expression of an extremely disapproving servant. "Neville wouldn't actually *say* anything. He'd *imply*. There would be a distinct chill in the air. You have no idea what it's like — staff can be far worse than parents. They have ways of letting you know how much they disapprove without ever being anything less than perfectly respectful. Which I'm sure you'll see in about fifteen minutes. Go get your bag."

"Patrick, I can't!"

"Of course you can. What you can't do is stay here. Not yet. Not by yourself. Now stop arguing and go get your bag."

Less than fifteen minutes later Patrick pulled his Mercedes to a stop in front of Cragmont. Leaving her bag in the trunk of the car, he led Kara up the steps, pushed the huge oaken door open, and ushered her the full length of the main hall and into the library.

"First, let's fix you a drink," he said. "Something hot, I think, with plenty of brandy in it." But instead of going to the bar that was sunk into one wall, he pressed a button on the wall, then lowered himself into one of the wingback chairs opposite the sofa on which Kara was perched as her eyes darted around the large book-lined room. A small smile played around his lips. "Will you just relax?" he said. "This isn't some kind of museum, despite the way it looks. It's where I live. In fact," he went on, his voice taking on a wry note, "I was sleeping on that very sofa until the last week or so."

As Kara leaned back, Neville Cavanaugh appeared at the library door. His eyes fixed inquiringly on Patrick for a moment, but when he noticed that his employer was not alone, his demeanor instantly changed. The temperature in the room seemed to drop by several degrees, and Kara pulled a cashmere throw onto her lap.

"A hot Grand Marnier toddy for Mrs. Marshall, please, Neville. And perhaps just a touch of brandy with some water for me." As Neville silently began fixing the drinks, Patrick turned his attention back to Kara. "I still think I ought to have a word with Summers," he began, but Kara was already shaking her head.

"It's not that they did anything so terrible. The thing is, when the doorbell rang, I actually thought they'd found Lindsay." Her eyes began to glisten. "Isn't that stupid? I actually thought it was Sergeant Grant coming to tell me they'd found her."

Patrick leaned forward and took her hand. "It isn't funny — it's perfectly natural. I don't know how many nights I sat right here in this room, waiting. Just waiting for someone to come home. Listening for the door to open and Renee or one of the kids to call out in the hall." He shifted his weight in the chair. "Have you been watching the news this afternoon?"

Something in his voice made Kara's heart skip a beat. "The news?" she echoed. "No, I —"

"It appears there was a third girl. Taken a month ago from Mill Creek."

Kara stared at him. "Open house?"

Patrick nodded as Neville turned away from the bar and a moment later set a tray with two glasses on the coffee table. Patrick picked up the steaming one and handed it to Kara, then took a sip from the other.

"H-Have they found her?" Kara asked, her tone making her meaning crystal clear.

Patrick shook his head. "But at least the police can't keep pretending that Lindsay just ran away. Not with three people gone, and one of them having left a small child. And now there are two more places to look for clues. He must have left something behind."

As Neville turned and left the room, Kara drained half her drink. "I feel like I ought to call Sergeant Grant."

"There's a phone on the desk," Patrick said, his eyes on the closed door through which Neville Cavanaugh had just passed. "Go ahead and use it if you want. I'll be right back." He followed Neville into the foyer.

"Neville?" he called, but his servant had already disappeared into the kitchen wing of the house. When Patrick caught up with him, he was standing at the large island in the center of the room, upon which stood a half-frosted cake. As the kitchen door swung closed behind Patrick, Neville turned, his eyes widening as he saw his employer. Patrick frowned uncertainly as his own eyes shifted from his servant to the cake, then back to the man. "I hope that's not a birthday cake," he said. "Never liked that stuff."

"For Mrs. McGinn's grandson," Neville said. "At Beech House," he added as Patrick's frown deepened. Then: "Is there something I can do for you, sir?"

"Mrs. Marshall's bag is in the trunk of the Mercedes. Put it in one of the guest rooms."

Neville's left eyebrow rose a fraction of an inch. "Here?"

"Where else?" Patrick countered, his gaze fixing on the servant.

Neville hesitated. "If I may say, sir —" he began, but Patrick cut him off.

"You may not."

Turning away from Neville's cold disapproval, Patrick returned to the library and closed the doors.

★ ★ ★

Kara stifled a yawn as Patrick reached for the Grand Marnier. As he lifted the bottle and held it toward her glass, she shook her head. "No, thanks — no more for me. I don't usually drink anything except a glass of wine or two, and never this late."

"One more will help you sleep," Patrick replied, pouring a generous shot into the snifter that sat next to her empty dessert plate. It had been hours since he'd picked her up, hours during which they'd done little more than sit in front of the fire Patrick had lit on the hearth in the library, eating off TV trays when Kara said she didn't want to leave the warmth of the mahogany paneled room even for supper. Now, as the last note of the clock striking ten faded away, he smiled at her. "You need a good rest. And believe me," he added wryly, "I know how much this can help, even if it's nothing more than blunting the pain during the darkest hours."

"I don't think anything will help," she said. "And after last night, I'm not even sure I want to sleep." Still, she sipped the liqueur, then gazed at the flames through the clear amber liquid. Despite her words, she felt the alcohol taking the edge off the most painful of her roiling emotions, and even thought it might be starting to warm that spot in her soul that had grown so cold these past two weeks. Or, if not thaw it, at least it felt as if the freeze were no longer spreading. "This *is* good," she sighed, taking another sip and actually managing a smile. "I just hope you're not giving me a brandy habit."

A faintly sardonic smile passed over Patrick's lips. "There are worse habits."

"I suppose." She set the snifter down and stretched. "I think it's bedtime for me."

"Neville's set up one of the guest rooms. I'll show you."

She took his hand and let him help her to her feet, feeling woozy as she stood. Reading her dizziness, he steadied her with an arm around her waist. "Are you all right?"

She nodded, hoping she wasn't too drunk to negotiate the stairs. But once steadied, she had no problem following him out of the library, through the foyer, and up the grand staircase.

Patrick paused at a closed door. "This was my daughter Chrissie's room," he said. "It's still hard for me to look inside." He fell silent, his eyes fixed on the door. "But 'hard' is no excuse for not facing things, is it?" He opened the door and switched on the light.

Kara gazed into a room that looked for all the world as if its occupant would be back at any moment; a pair of shoes were under the desk, obviously kicked off and forgotten, and a jacket lay on the bed as if waiting to be hung in its proper place. "How old was Chrissie?" she asked as the silence grew uncomfortable.

"Nineteen. Home from Oxford for the holidays."

Kara bit her lip as she saw the suitcase on a luggage rack and the pile of textbooks on the desk. *This is how Lindsay's room would look in two more years,* she thought. *Her toys behind her and her future in front of her.*

The pain the thought brought must have been clear in her face, because Patrick took her elbow and drew her gently away. "You look absolutely exhausted. Come on." He clicked off the light and closed the door behind them. "This was the girls' bath," he said as they passed another closed door, "and this was Jenna's room." He touched the door with his fingertips, but instead of opening it, opened the door across the hall.

"I hope this will be all right for you."

The room was at least twice as big as the master bedroom in her own house, with two overstuffed chairs upholstered in flowered chintz flanking a large fireplace. A fire had been lit, and a robe laid out on the end of the bed. "This is beautiful," Kara said, moving to one of the four large windows. Moonlight illuminated the lawn that flowed down to the shore of the Sound, and sparkled on the water. "May I open a window?"

"Of course."

She lifted the heavy casement and breathed in the fresh salt air. "Heaven," she sighed as her head cleared and she began to feel a little better.

"I'm just down the hall if you need anything in the night," Patrick said. "Don't hesitate. Really."

"I'll be fine."

His eyes fixed on her for a moment, as if he was assessing the truth of her words. "Then I'll say good night," he finally said.

A moment later the door softly closed behind him.

Alone, Kara turned back to the window for another breath of the sweet, fresh air flowing in from the Sound, and though the last of the brandy-induced haze lifted, exhaustion began to close in on her again. *Don't think about it,* she told herself. *For tonight, just don't think about any of it.* Leaving the window wide open, she started toward the door to the adjoining bathroom, but before she'd taken more than half a dozen steps there was a soft rapping at the bedroom door.

"Come in," she called, certain it was Patrick coming back to tell her something. "I haven't even started changing yet." When the only response to her words was another discreet tapping, she went to the door, opened it, and found Neville Cavanaugh holding a small tray. It held a cup of what looked for all the world like the hot milk her grandmother used to make her when she was a child.

"To help you sleep," he said, echoing the exact words her grandmother used to say.

Kara opened the door wide and he set the tray on her nightstand. "How thoughtful. Thank you."

The servant straightened up and regarded her with a serious face. "I'm so very sorry about your husband and daughter." His eyes seemed to bore into her for a moment, and then, abruptly, he turned away. "Sleep well," he said. A moment later he had vanished from the room and closed the door.

Alone again, Kara took off her clothes, put on the robe that had been left on the bed, and went to the bathroom. Everything she could possibly need was laid out on the marble counter that surrounded the sink, right down to a fresh toothbrush, still in its box. But as she began to brush her teeth, Neville Cavanaugh's words kept echoing in her mind.

I'm so very sorry about your husband and daughter.

Perfectly normal words that she must have heard a hundred times in the last week.

I'm so very sorry about your husband and daughter.

The same words almost everyone she'd seen had spoken in one form or another.

I'm so very sorry about your husband and daughter.

Then what was it about Neville Cavanaugh's words that bothered her?

I'm so very sorry about your husband and daughter.

She climbed into bed.

I'm so very sorry about your husband and daughter.

She reached for the cup of warm milk.

*I'm so very sorry about your husband
and daughter.*

She picked up the cup.

I'm so very sorry —

And then it came to her.

It wasn't the words at all.

It was the way he'd said them.

Neville Cavanaugh had spoken the right
words, but he hadn't sounded sorry at all.
Instead, he'd simply spoken the words he
knew he'd be expected to say.

Kara raised the cup to her lips.

I'm so very sorry —

As Neville Cavanaugh's cold voice came
back again, Kara Marshall put the cup
back on the nightstand, untouched.

CHAPTER FORTY-EIGHT

Paralyzed!

She was paralyzed, and she couldn't breathe, and she was blind!

A wave of panic rose inside Lindsay, and she instinctively opened her mouth to scream, but instead of hearing her terror erupt in a howling cry, her mouth filled with air and her head felt like it was going to explode.

Then she began to choke.

Now the wave of panic towered higher, and as she struggled to control the choking and regain her breath, her gorge began to rise and her mouth was filled with the bitter taste of bile.

She was going to drown!

She was going to throw up, and choke on her own vomit, and drown!

The thought triggered a reserve of energy buried deep inside her, and she made herself swallow, made herself force the contents of her stomach back down through her esophagus. But even as the bile receded from her throat, her body began to tingle from lack of oxygen.

Why couldn't she breathe?

Tape!

There was tape over her mouth.

She focused her mind, willed herself to banish the panic, drove away any thought but the need to breathe and slowly released the air in her mouth through her nostrils and sucked a fresh breath in through her nose, down her throat, into her lungs.

The wave of terror that had all but killed her subsided.

She took a second breath, then a third.

Her mind began to function again.

Not blind, she told herself. Just in the dark.

And not paralyzed, either

Just taped to the chair — her arms to its arms, her legs to its legs. But at least the burning pain she'd felt earlier — the pain she'd thought she couldn't bear at all — was gone.

But she had borne the pain, and was still alive, and could still think, and —

A faint sound, nearly inaudible, slithered into her consciousness, and for a moment she wondered if she'd heard it at all. But then she heard it again, and knew what it was.

The door at the far end of the tunnel was opening.

Approaching footsteps, clearly audible, moving closer.

Asleep, Lindsay told herself. *Pretend to be asleep and he'll leave you alone.*

Then, out of the darkness, she had what seemed a vision — no, not a vision, she realized, but a memory.

Of Shannon, unconscious, sprawled on the floor.

Sprawled on the floor, and being kicked — kicked until her neck was broken, and her head slammed against the wall like a rag doll in the hands of a furious child.

And if she pretended to be asleep now, it would happen to her, too. So she would be awake, and face whatever new chapter in her torture was about to begin. But her mouth was so dry her tongue had swollen and felt like a wad of cotton, and every time she blinked, her eyes felt as if they were coated with sand.

Maybe, after all, it would be better to die.

He was coming up the stairs now, and once again the terrible panic to which she had awakened only a few moments ago threatened to overwhelm her.

No, she silently cried out to herself. *Be strong. Be stronger than Shannon. Be stronger than* him!

Again the panic receded, but the cold terror in Lindsay's soul only tightened its grip as first a beam of light and then the dark form of her tormentor rose out of the trapdoor in the floor.

"Good morning," he said, the softness of his voice carrying a menace that made Lindsay's heart falter.

Now she saw that he'd brought a large box with him.

"It's a special day," he said as he set it on the table. "A special day for all of us!" He ripped the tape from Lindsay's mouth, and she gasped in pain, but choked off the accompanying cry that might give her captor satisfaction.

The flashlight went out, and a moment later he began to light candles, until the chamber was filled with flickering illumination. As the light grew brighter, Lindsay saw Shannon's body, still lying on the floor, her head in a pool of dried blood. A cry rose in her throat, and she squelched it before any sound could escape, and turning away from Shannon, caught sight of Ellen Fine.

Ellen's eyes were fixed on her, boring into her, and though her mouth was still covered with tape, Lindsay understood the message Ellen was trying to convey as clearly as if she'd spoken it aloud.

The plan, Ellen's eyes were saying. *Don't forget. Give him what he wants, and wait.*

Forcing herself to act against every instinct inside her, Lindsay twisted her lips into a smile and whispered a single word through her parched lips. "Please?" The man's eyes fixed on her, and she managed to utter three more words. "I'm so thirsty."

"This isn't your party," he said, his voice hard. "This is my celebration."

Lindsay glanced at Ellen, whose eyes were open and watching.

When the room was lit by nearly two dozen candles, the man opened the box and began removing its contents, carefully placing each object on the tiny table.

A birthday cake, complete with candles.

Party hats, the kind of brightly colored, foil-covered cones Lindsay and her friends used to have at all their birthday parties.

Toy horns, and whistles from which paper tongues extended when you blew them.

And finally, small paper plates, plastic forks, and napkins that matched the plates.

The man arranged everything on the table, looked at Ellen, then at Lindsay. In the flickering candlelight, the grotesquely scrawled smile on his surgical mask seemed to come alive, making Lindsay's skin crawl as he leered at her. "It's my birthday," he said. "So we're going to have a party!"

He picked up the little hats and put one on, bringing the elastic band down over both his masks, giving him the look of a maniacal clown that Lindsay knew she would see in her nightmares for the rest of her life.

Wordlessly, he put a hat on her head, then one on Ellen's, and Lindsay was barely able to control her urge to twist her head away from his touch.

When the hats were secured to both of them, he lifted Shannon's limp body from the floor and placed it in her chair.

She toppled forward, her lifeless face smashing onto the table.

"Sit up!" he demanded, pulling Shannon's body straight. But as soon as he let her go, she fell forward again. Wordlessly, he pulled her up once again, and this time wrapped a loop of tape around her chest to keep her upright.

One side of Shannon's face was flattened

from where it had been pressed against the floor for hours, the blood that pooled in it giving it the look of a bruise.

One of her eyes was open, staring blankly at Lindsay.

Lindsay turned her eyes away as their tormentor put a party hat on Shannon's head and drew the elastic under her chin.

"Isn't this fun?" he asked, his voice going cold as he turned toward her. "Are we all happy?"

Lindsay forced herself to smile, feeling her lower lip crack as it stretched, and all she could think of was water.

But there was no water.

There was nothing but the cake, and the grotesque hats, and the terrifying figure whose visage was now looming only a few inches from her eyes.

"You're not smiling," the man whispered as he jerked her head back by her hair and leaned still closer to her face. She tried to look away, but he spoke again, his whispered words lashing at her like tiny whips. "Look at me!" His voice trembled with fury as he ripped off a length of duct tape and slapped it over her mouth, then used an almost ruined red felt-tip marker to scrawl the smile he'd just demanded. Then, his anger unassuaged, he put another length of tape over Lindsay's eyes, and drew two new ones on the tape, smearing her smile as he worked so it twisted upward into a grotesque sneer.

When he was done, she sensed him pulling back, admiring his handiwork. "Better," he said. "Now you look happy."

As Lindsay tried to sense what was happening, her tormentor turned to Ellen. "Are we all happy?" he asked.

Doing her best not to betray her fear, Ellen managed a nod.

"Very well, then," the man said. He flicked his lighter on again and began to light the candles on the cake. "I hope you brought me presents," he said. "You know how much little boys like their presents." When all the candles had been lit, he stood back and admired the macabre scene. "Good," he crooned. "Good."

Lindsay, blinded and muted by the tape over her eyes and mouth, sat absolutely still, silently praying that by doing nothing, she might escape her captor's notice, at least for a moment or two. Then he spoke again, and she knew her prayers had been in vain.

"Sing," the softly menacing voice demanded. "It's time to sing!"

Her heart began to race as she thought

of what he might do if she didn't comply. But how could she? Not with —

A searing pain ripped across the lower part of her face, and for a moment she thought her lower lip had been torn away along with the tape. Then the tape across her eyes was stripped away, too, taking most of her eyebrows and lashes with it. Despite her determination to show no fear, a whimper rose in her throat, but even as it escaped her lips, the man who loomed above her began singing.

"Hap . . . py . . . birth . . . day . . . to . . . you . . ." He enunciated each syllable as if it were a separate word. "Hap . . . py . . . birth—" He cut the song off mid-word, his eyes flashing as he glowered at Ellen. In a blur of motion, he reached out and ripped the tape from her mouth as furiously as he'd torn it from Lindsay's seconds ago. "Now you can sing. Now we can all sing." His hand moved, and it was a second or two before Lindsay realized what he was doing: conducting, as if he was the choirmaster and she and Ellen Fine the choir.

She heard Ellen clear her throat, and though Lindsay wasn't sure she could muster up even a single sound, she was terrified of what might happen if she didn't.

"Sing!" the man demanded. "Sing to

me!" Suddenly, he picked up the burning cake and thrust it into Lindsay's face. "Sing!" he shouted as she recoiled, the burning candles scorching her brows. "Sing!" the darkly leering figure demanded again. "Hap . . . py . . . birth . . . day . . ."

Her cheeks were stinging from the hot wax that had splashed onto them, but she forced herself to ignore the pain. "To you," Lindsay picked up, willing her barely audible voice into unison with Ellen.

The man nodded, then pushed the fiery cake toward Ellen.

"Louder!"

Lindsay and Ellen struggled to find the strength to continue. "Happy birthday to you," they sang together.

The man wheeled and thrust the partially crushed cake at Shannon. As Lindsay watched helplessly, Shannon's hair sizzled and began to burn, filling the air with acrid smoke and the stench of burning hair.

"Sing!" he demanded as Shannon's hair continued to burn.

Lindsay and Ellen raised their voices higher as the flames consumed Shannon's hair, but as the flames died away and they came to the end of the song, so too did their voices.

"Sing it again!" their torturer demanded. "Louder!"

Despair began to overcome the determination that until now had made Lindsay's terror almost bearable. She knew there was nothing she would be able to do to satisfy this creature who had snatched her from what should have been the safety of her home, and in the end she — and Ellen — were going to die. Die here, in the flickering candlelight, like Shannon had died before them.

No one was going to come for them; no one was going to save them.

Lindsay looked at Ellen, but Ellen's eyes had gone almost as blank as Shannon's.

"Sing!" the man howled. "Louder! Louder!"

Knowing it might well be her last act, Lindsay sucked in a breath and tried to sing along.

CHAPTER FORTY-NINE

Kara tossed restlessly in the unfamiliar sheets on the unfamiliar bed and breathed deeply of the sweet, fresh, but equally unfamiliar ocean air. Utterly unable to sleep, she opened her eyes to gaze once more around the perfectly decorated guest room that looked almost magical in the moonlight pouring through huge windows that overlooked the Sound. Given the luxuriousness of the satiny sheets, and the almost cloudlike support of the bed, she should have fallen asleep the minute she first snuggled into the warm cocoon the down comforter provided. But she hadn't; indeed, rest seemed far away — no more attainable here than it had been last night at home. But at least here she was somewhat removed from the agonizing memories of her own house, and could lie in the soft warmth of the bed and think about what she might do next.

But all she could think about were Steve and Lindsay.

Steve, who would never be back, and Lindsay, who —

She cut the thought off, but it was already too late. Slowly, over the last week, she had come to accept the reality of Steve's death, but the thought that Lindsay, too, might already be dead was far too painful to dwell on, even for a moment.

She closed her eyes and tried to think of her family's happiest times. All kinds of images rose out of her memory: summer days frolicking on the beach, and Christmas shopping in Manhattan, a day that always ended with dinner at the Sea Grill at Rockefeller Center, where they would all watch the skaters twirling on the ice beneath the great glittering Christmas tree.

The week five years ago when they'd gone to Orlando and seen every square inch Disney World had to offer.

And Lindsay's birthday parties, always filled with dozens of her friends.

Even now Kara could picture those occasions as clearly as if they'd happened yesterday. She remembered Lindsay's first birthday, when her daughter wore a little pink ruffled dress and sat in her high chair, wide-eyed, a big piece of angel cake all to herself, while the adults all sang.

Happy birthday to you, happy birthday to you . . .

The memory was so vivid she could almost hear it now, more than fifteen years later.

Happy birthday, dear —

Suddenly, it seemed she was actually hearing their voices, and she sat bolt upright in bed, listening.

She turned to the open window.

Nothing but the sound of the surf and a few gulls crying in the night.

As a chilly breeze wafted over her, she lay back down and pulled the comforter close around her body. Of course she hadn't heard anyone singing "Happy Birthday." It was a trick played on her by an exhausted mind. If she could just get to sleep . . .

She closed her eyes and tried to calm her mind.

She breathed slowly and deeply, concentrating on the freshness of the salt air.

Happy birthday to you —

The lyrics rose in her mind again, faint, but not so faint that they didn't sound real.

She got out of bed and went to the

window. The wind had picked up, and she could hear the clatter of rigging from sailboats bobbing on mooring buoys just offshore blending with the sighing of the wind through the trees.

Somewhere, a cat yowled in either fear or fury.

And, all but completely masked by the other sounds, she was certain she could hear what sounded like voices singing.

Could it be? Or was she finally losing her mind?

She stood at the window, trying to sort out the possibilities. Had her mind actually gone around the bend, or was it possible that someone — a neighbor? — was truly having a birthday party in the middle of the night? Impossible.

She listened again, straining to hear, but now all she heard was the wind, and the rigging, and the birds.

But she knew all possibility of sleep was gone.

She pulled on the robe Neville Cavanaugh had left on the bed for her, slipped her feet into her shoes, opened the door and stepped out into the silent hallway.

The immense house nearly overwhelmed her with its massive, solemn presence; the only sound was the steady ticking of the grandfather clock in the great foyer below.

Standing there, her eyes were drawn to the door across from her own.

Jenna's room.

Crossing the broad hallway, she turned the handle and slipped inside the girl's room, then closed the door behind her.

When she turned on the light, she saw that it was a mirror image of Chrissie's room, and not so different from Lindsay's, except for its generous proportions.

Kara moved slowly through the room, looking at all the things a teenage girl values: stuffed animals, CDs, posters of singers.

And books. Like Lindsay, Jenna was a reader.

Kara went to her bookshelf, thinking that if she could find something to read, it might help her sleep.

She scanned the titles until she came to a volume at the very end of the shelf that bore no title at all. She pulled it out and opened it.

A photo fell from the front of the book to the floor. As she bent to pick it up, she realized what the book in her hand was.

Jenna Shields's diary.

Straightening up, she stared at the script that covered the first page. Jenna's hand was even and nice. Kara flipped quickly through the pages. Jenna had filled her diary not only with the events of her young life, but with her dreams as well.

Had Lindsay kept a diary? If she had, she'd hidden it well enough that neither she nor the police had been able to find it.

Jenna hadn't hidden hers at all. In fact, she'd left it right on the bookshelf where anyone could have found it.

And now Kara had.

She bent down again and picked up the photo, and her heart chilled.

She must be wrong, she thought. It had to be a trick of the light. She took the picture over to Jenna's desk and turned on the study lamp to see the photograph more clearly.

It was of the entire Shields family: Patrick, Renee, Jenna, and Chrissie.

And Jenna Shields looked enough like her own daughter that she and Lindsay could have been twins.

Eyes blurring with tears, Kara looked away, wiped them with the sleeve of her robe, and thinking she must have been mistaken, looked once more at the photograph.

But no. It was almost as if Lindsay herself had somehow slipped into this photograph of a family that was not her own.

Instead of putting the photo back in the journal, Kara slipped it into the pocket of her robe, then replaced the book on the shelf exactly where she'd found it, turned out the lights, and stepped out the door.

Fully awake now, she didn't want to return to her room, so she slipped as quietly as possible down the massive staircase, through the marble foyer, and into the conservatory.

Hoping the alarm system wasn't turned on, she unlocked the French doors and went out onto the terrace overlooking the lawn and the Sound. The grounds were bathed in silvery moonlight, the air crisp and clean, and the sky ablaze with stars. A perfect night.

A perfect night that was shattered by a muffled shout.

The shout of a man!

Transfixed, Kara strained her eyes to see into the darkness, searching for the source of the shout.

Then she heard another sound.

Singing?

It *was* singing.

Once again it sounded like "Happy Birthday."

Unconsciously clutching the lapels of the robe tightly around her neck, Kara started down the steps toward the lawn.

They were going to die.

Shannon was already dead, and now they were going to die, too, and it was all her fault.

She'd failed!

How could it have happened? When she'd devised the plan — when she'd explained it so carefully to Lindsay and Shannon — she was sure it would work. There were three of them and only one of him, and even though Shannon had already been half starved to death, she and Lindsay should have been able to overpower this man. But they'd failed.

Now, as she watched the surrealistic scene swirling around her, Ellen Fine realized why it had failed.

Their captor was utterly, completely, insane.

A lunatic, waving his arms in the flickering candlelight and demanding that all of them — even Shannon — sing to him.

Sing to him!

How much time had she wasted thinking she was dealing with someone whose mind was even faintly rational?

And now Shannon was dead, Lindsay was on the verge of dying, and if she didn't do something soon, she herself would die, too. And even if they all died, it still wouldn't be over. This . . . miscreant, this lunatic, this *monster,* would only find new victims to torture in their place.

But he didn't even know that he was torturing them.

He thought he was loving them. *Loving them!*

Loving them, as he held them captive in the darkness, barely feeding them, not allowing them to slake their thirst. Maybe none of it was real. Maybe it actually was a nightmare. Maybe this tiny chamber with its undersized furniture and thick coating of filth and stale musty air that was now so smoky her eyes were stinging and running wasn't real at all.

Maybe it wasn't the man who was insane. Maybe it was her! Maybe she was hallucinating all this, hallucinating the candles and the cake and the song that seemed to go on endlessly and —

One of the candles on the cake flickered as it burned down to the frosting, and the man abruptly stopped singing. "Wish time," he said, his voice turning cold as his eyes fixed on her. "And I'm going to wish for the same thing I always wished for."

He tilted his head toward the ceiling, and Ellen realized he was drawing in a deep breath, puffing up his lungs like a six-year-old boy about to show off at his own birthday party. Finally, when his lungs were full, he bent over and blew on the candles, the ski mask bulging out under the force of his pent-up breath.

But it wasn't enough — more than half the candles remained lit.

He blew again, and then a third time, and finally the last candle sputtered out.

As his eyes moved malevolently from Lindsay to her, her fury and frustration finally overpowered her terror.

"Happy birthday!" she screamed, the words rasping as they erupted from her swollen throat. "Happy birthday, and go to hell!"

His head snapped up and he glowered at her, rage burning in his eyes.

"Why don't you just die?" Ellen cried, her voice trembling. "You're never getting your wish, so why don't you just die and go to hell!"

The blow came so fast, Ellen had no time to turn away. His fist slammed into her jaw hard and she felt it dislocate, the pain so intense she lost her breath as a fiery red glow of agony enveloped her. Still taped to the chair, she toppled over and her head crashed against the floor.

Emily. Oh, Emily. Only the thought of her daughter kept Ellen from letting herself slip into the unconsciousness that was the only thing that could assuage the pain.

Then he was kneeling next to her, and Ellen braced herself for the next blow. But instead, when he leaned close, his lips next to her ear, he whispered, "You're supposed to help me. Why didn't you help me? That's all I wanted — just for you to help me. But you didn't help me — you let them do whatever they wanted, and I had to pretend like I liked it! So now we all have to pretend. Every one of us . . ."

Ellen tried to pull away, but when she moved her head, a stab of pain shot from her broken jaw and a faint scream escaped her lips. She saw the duct tape back in the man's hands, and in mute paralysis watched helplessly as he tore a long strip from the roll.

As he pressed the tape over her mouth, the pain in her broken jaw burned through her, the shattered bones grating on each other. And for the first time since this nightmare began, Ellen found herself silently praying for the release of unconsciousness.

Unconsciousness, or even death.

As she lay helpless on the floor, the man rose to his feet and moved toward Lindsay. Crouching low, he reached out and gently began to caress her breast. "Now you're going to know what it was like," he whispered, and his fingers tightened on Lindsay's nipple. "Now you're going to feel everything I felt, and we'll see how you like it!"

As his fingers dug into Lindsay's body, and the agony in her own threatened to overwhelm her, Ellen Fine clung to the one thought that could give her the strength to keep on living.

Emily . . . Emily . . . Emily . . .

CHAPTER FIFTY

Nothing, Kara told herself. *You heard nothing, because there's nothing to hear.*

Yet even as she silently repeated the words, the sounds of the night enveloped her, seemed to close in on her with every step she took as she left the terrace steps and moved into the darkness that lay over Cragmont. The waves lapping on the shore, the wind sighing and whistling among the trees and in the eaves of the unfamiliar buildings scattered over the grounds, all of it seemed to warn her to go back to the house, whispering that there was nothing here for her to see.

Nothing, at least, that she would want to see.

She glanced nervously back over her shoulder, but the silhouette of the great house looming against the even darker blackness of the sky did nothing to reassure her, and for a moment she almost imagined she could hear the groaning of whatever vast unseen mechanism it was that drew the stars across the sky.

But the singing — if singing it had truly been — was gone, and as she drew the robe tighter around her against the chill and darkness of the night, Kara was no longer sure she had heard it at all.

Off to the left, almost invisible against a backdrop of hedges, the Shields family mausoleum crouched in the darkness, and Kara paused to gaze at its limestone walls.

She shuddered.

Could the sounds she'd heard, which she'd been so certain were voices singing, possibly have come from inside it? She remembered, then, what Patrick had told her about waking up a couple of weeks ago to find himself inside the mausoleum, cold and shivering in front of the crypts that held all that was physically left of his family.

Had he been drawn back there tonight? Could it have been Patrick she'd heard, keening his grief alone in the confines of this cold stone structure? Kara hurried forward and a moment later stood before the wooden door that was the mausoleum's entrance, its great panels appearing even larger than the doors of the house itself.

A heavy lock hung from a hasp, and even without touching it, Kara knew it was firmly latched.

As she stood on the crypt's cold stone steps, the night sounds deepened and once more seemed to circle closer. She stepped away from the mausoleum, but even when she stood in the middle of the path that led back to the great open lawn, the first tendrils of claustrophobia began to crawl around her.

She turned back to gaze at the mausoleum, and a vision of Steve's ashes — still on the dining room table in her deserted house — rose before her eyes.

She shuddered again.

Don't be silly. Don't be hysterical. Nobody is singing out here, and there's no way Patrick or anybody else is inside the mausoleum.

She turned around, intending to start back toward the house, but a small building off to the left caught her eye.

A building that appeared in the darkness to be an almost exact miniature of the enormous main house that stood at the top of the gently sloping lawn.

As she gazed at it, Kara realized what it was.

A children's playhouse.

The playhouse where Chrissie and Jenna would have played when they were little girls.

Perhaps even where Patrick and Claire had played when they were children, too.

Kara stepped off the path and started across the grass, which was glistening with dew in the moonlight. Though the dampness quickly found its way inside her loafers, she barely noticed the chill in her feet.

She drew closer.

The playhouse had been boarded up, its door and windows covered with heavy plywood.

Of course. After the tragedy, Patrick would have been no more able to bear the sight of the playhouse than he could his daughters' rooms.

Kara gazed at the building for a while, shivering at the memories that must lurk in its closed-off corners. A wind came up then, flapping the robe that was all that covered her bare legs and jerking her out of her reverie. Turning away from the playhouse as she'd turned away from the mausoleum a few minutes earlier, she resolutely headed back toward the house.

But just as she was mounting the steps

to the terrace and the conservatory beyond, she heard it.

Muffled, but distinct.

A shout!

The shout of a woman!

Kara whirled, goose bumps rising on her arms, and then her grandmother's voice echoed in her head: *"Someone's walking on my grave."* She banished the thought as quickly as it came, and strained her ears, listening.

Nothing.

Nothing but the waves and the wind, whispering in the darkness. Quickly, she hurried up the steps, crossed the terrace, and turned the handle on the door, but before she could push it open, it was pulled from within.

Neville Cavanaugh stood in the partially open doorway, fully dressed, gazing down at her, his eyes cold and suspicious. Flustered, she blurted out the truth before she even thought about it: "I heard noises." His expression didn't change, though he opened the door wider and stepped back so she could come in. "Like singing," she went on. "I thought it was . . . Oh, God, it sounds so silly now, but —" She faltered, but Neville only raised his eyebrows and waited. "I thought someone was singing

'Happy Birthday,' " she finally managed. "And someone was yelling."

The man's expression seemed to darken. "From where?"

"Down by the . . . by the mausoleum, I think."

After a moment, he closed and secured the door behind them. "Shore birds," he said. "They make all manner of queer sounds in the night. And there are peacocks on the next property. Sometimes it sounds like babies crying, sometimes like —" He hesitated, then his lips curved into what Kara assumed was his idea of a smile. "Sometimes I don't know what they sound like. And there are stories . . ." This time his voice faded away, and Kara thought he would go on, but instead he only shrugged. "Birds and animals make strange noises in the night. After a while you stop hearing them at all."

Birds! All it had been was birds. Kara felt utterly foolish, and hoped the dimness in the conservatory hid the burning flush in her face.

"Will you be needing anything?" Neville asked her.

Kara shook her head, left the conservatory, and hurried up the stairs. Back in the guest room, she closed the door behind her, twisted the key in the lock, slipped off her wet shoes, then slid under the covers of the bed, her robe still wrapped tightly around her. As she lay in the darkness, the servant's words came back to her.

Birds . . . birds and animals . . . After a while you stop hearing them at all.

But if he hadn't heard them at all, what was he doing, wide-awake, fully dressed, prowling the house in the middle of the night?

Lindsay felt herself fading away, drowning in something she no longer understood. Everything around her had turned surreal — the candles all had halos, grotesque shadows whispered to her in unintelligible words from the dark corners of the ceiling, and sounds reverberated in her head until they were rendered meaningless.

Nothing was real.

All she wanted to do was slip into that blissful unconsciousness where there was no pain, no fear, no terror, where nightmares were something from which she would awaken, and when she awoke, her mother and father would be there to hold her and kiss away her tears.

As the sirens of unconsciousness crooned their song, she began to let herself slip

472

away, singing with them for a while. But whatever words she was singing became as meaningless as the whisperings of the shadows that lurked in the corners. She heard someone yell, but, too tired, too depleted, too exhausted even to respond, she couldn't even raise her head from where it hung on her chest.

Like Shannon's had . . .

Then the dreams started — the bad dreams — and even though she knew she was still awake, she couldn't move or talk or fend off the red-eyed monsters that were growling at her from the dark.

She twisted against her bonds and tried to rise up through the layers of sleep, to fight the dreams that weren't dreams at all, but her strength was finally gone.

Now the fear itself began to consume her, the fear she'd been fending off since the moment the nightmare had begun. Was it the red-eyed monster that was stalking her? Was there nothing there at all except fear itself? But if that was all there was, why wouldn't it go away? She wanted it to go away — she was so tired of being afraid, she couldn't stand it any longer. She wanted to face things, to ignore the fear, but she didn't know how to do that anymore.

The world was made of fear.

Thick, impenetrable, suffocating fear.

Fear that was killing her.

She had to get away from it, had to escape from it. . . .

She began closing herself down, drawing back, away from the fear, away from her body, away from everything.

And slowly, as she pulled away from the fear, things changed. Somehow she had escaped her own body, and now she was looking down, gazing down from somewhere high above. Far below, she watched as the black-clothed beast that had imprisoned and tormented her sliced away the gray tape that held her hands and ankles to the chair.

She watched as he lifted her body and lay it with an odd gentleness on the table.

With an almost idle curiosity, she watched him part her legs.

And then, in an instant, the odd sense of detachment ended and she was back in her body, and she knew exactly what was happening, and the terror that had threatened to utterly destroy her moments before flashed into fury, a fury that jerked her out of the lassitude that had held her paralyzed, a fury that filled her with a keen, razor-edged consciousness and a sudden influx of strength.

Adrenaline surging into every fiber of her starved and ravaged body, Lindsay drew a great breath and screamed.

She screamed for Shannon and for Ellen, for her mother and her father, and for whatever god might be listening somewhere. She screamed and howled with every scrap of energy left in her, and heard the sound crash back at her off the ceiling and the walls.

And then a hand was clamped over her mouth and the scream was silenced.

"No one hears it," a hard voice whispered. "After a while, no one hears the screams at all."

A scream ripped through Kara's mind and she jerked bolt upright in bed before she even came fully awake. For a moment she felt disoriented, but as the vestiges of sleep fell away, her mind began to focus. She was still at Cragmont, still wearing the bathrobe Neville had laid out for her. But she no longer felt welcome — now she felt like an intruder, and it was the house itself that made her feel that way.

It was the house that was giving her nightmares.

Yet she had just been awakened by a scream — a scream she could still recall.

Lindsay!

Kara swung her legs off the bed, shoved her feet into her loafers, and went to the bedroom door, listening for a moment before she opened it. Hearing nothing, she cracked the door open.

All was dark and silent, but it wasn't a comforting darkness or silence.

Rather, it was the kind of silence that told her there was something else — something dangerous — lurking just beyond the range of her senses. Part of her wanted to close the door and go back to bed, but a stronger part told her to find Patrick, to tell him about the scream that had awakened her.

But had it been a scream? Or had it been nothing but a dream? Yet it seemed so real. *So real.*

She needed to talk.

She needed to talk to Patrick.

Opening the door wider, she turned to the right, walked silently down the corridor to Patrick's bedroom and knocked softly on the door.

Silence.

She knocked a little louder, and when he still didn't answer, she hesitated, almost went back to her own room, then changed her mind. Grasping the crystal knob on the door, she twisted it and pushed the heavy door open.

A fire had burned to embers in the fireplace opposite the bed.

A bedside lamp glowed dimly, and the linen in the huge bed had been carefully turned down, just as her own had when Patrick brought her to her room.

But his linens remained untouched. "Patrick?" she whispered, and his name seemed to echo as loudly as if she'd shouted it.

She went to his bathroom door and knocked lightly.

No answer.

She turned the handle and opened the door slowly, but the light was not on and she knew he was not here. Still, she flipped on the light and looked around.

Toiletries laid out, it was as ready for Patrick as the bedroom, and as empty.

The library. Patrick said he'd been sleeping in the library, where only a few hours ago she had sat in front of a fire, sipping a glass of Grand Marnier, the horrors of the world shut out, even if only for a short while. Was that where he'd gone to sleep tonight?

Kara left the bedroom and made her way down the dark hallway, shivering as she passed the closed doors of Patrick's daughters' rooms.

Halfway down the stairs, a noise stopped her cold and her heart began to race. But as the big grandfather clock in the foyer began to strike, she realized that the noise had been nothing more than the winding of its gears. Hurrying down the rest of the curving flight of stairs — grateful that whatever noise she might make would be covered by the striking of the clock — she paused on the bottom step until it finished chiming four.

As the last deep note faded away and a cloak of silence fell once more over the house, almost muffling even the ticking of the ancient clock, Kara darted across the foyer and rapped on the great double doors that led to the library. "Patrick?" she called softly, and once more her voice seemed to fill the silent house with its echoes. "Patrick, it's Kara!"

When there was no answer, she knocked again, then a third time.

Why wouldn't he wake up?

Was he ill?

"Patrick!"

Still no response.

Had something happened to him?

Turning away from the library doors, she peered up into the vastness of the foyer. In the near-blackness of the night, it looked even bigger than it was, and everything about it — the dark mahogany paneling, the shadowy corners beneath the soaring stairs, even the heavy draperies that nearly covered the French doors leading to the terrace — had taken on a sense of hidden danger.

Good God, Kara told herself. *Get a grip!*

But even her silent words couldn't quell the panic rising inside her.

Wanting, needing to get outside, she pushed away from the library doors and moved toward the French doors at the back of the foyer. Pushing one of the heavy draperies away, she fumbled with the lock until it finally snapped open, then stepped out onto the terrace and took a deep breath of the fresh ocean air. The panic that had seized her a moment ago began to loosen its grip. But only for a second.

She pulled the French door closed behind her and started along the terrace toward the library, thinking she might be able to get in through the French doors. A moment later she was trying the handle of the first of three sets of doors. It was locked, but through the heavy draperies drawn across the inside of the doors, she could see a faint light within the room.

Someone was inside.

"Patrick?" she called, pressing close to the door, pitching her voice loud enough so it would penetrate not only the glass, but the curtains as well. When there was no response, she rapped on the glass and called louder. "Patrick, wake up. Let me in!"

Still no answer.

She banged harder. Where else could he be? He had to be inside! He had to be!

Should she call for Neville? But just the thought of the man's strange presence made her abandon that idea. She moved to the next set of French doors, with no more success, and then on to the last set.

All of them were locked. She was about to start banging on the glass again when her eyes fell on a small wrought-iron plant stand that stood just beyond the last set of doors. She hesitated, but only for a moment. She picked it up and swung it against the small pane of glass next to the lock on the French door.

The pane shattered, a few shards falling to the terrace but most of the glass dropping to the hardwood floor inside the library, the sound muffled by the drapery.

Knocking away some sharp fragments stuck in the frame of the broken window, Kara slipped her hand through and unlocked the door, then opened it and pushed aside the draperies.

The room was dark except for a dim green-glass-shaded lamp on the desk.

Hesitantly, as if the house itself were somehow a threat to her, she stepped into the library, immediately feeling it close in around her. When she spoke, her voice had dropped back to a whisper. "Patrick?"

Her eyes found the sofa in the dim light. The cashmere throw that had kept her warm only a few hours ago was now folded neatly and lay atop it.

An ember dropped from the grate in the fireplace, sending up a shower of sparks, and Kara jumped at the sound.

But there was no sign of Patrick. *How could he have left a room that was locked from the inside?*

The desk lamp illuminated only a small fraction of the enormous room, and she edged around the back of the sofa toward the light switch. When she flipped it and the overhead chandelier went on, she found herself looking at something that made no sense at all. The enormous Oriental carpet that had covered the far third of the library earlier was folded back, revealing the hardwood parquet floor.

Curious, Kara moved closer, and just beyond the fold in the rug, almost hidden in its shadow, she saw something else.

An open trapdoor.

She stared at it, her mind whirling. Why was there a trapdoor in the middle of the library floor? Was that where Patrick had gone?

She took another step toward the yawning hole in the floor, then stopped. What was she thinking? It was four in the morning, and Patrick was gone, and she'd found a trapdoor that led God-alone-knew-where.

She reached for the telephone on the desk, her hand shaking as she picked up the receiver. As her finger hovered over the keypad, she struggled to remember the number the detective had given her — the number where he could be reached at home. But now, when she needed it, not only was it gone, but even his name had vanished from her mind.

911!

That was it — she'd just dial 911 and someone would come. But as she stabbed at the first of the three keys that would summon help, another scream ripped through the darkness.

And ripped through her heart.

Lindsay!

This time she knew it was no dream.

This time she was sure it was Lindsay, and her blood ran cold as she realized where the scream had come from.

She heard the scream again, and with it, all the fears and the panic that had threatened to overwhelm her only moments ago dropped away. Grabbing a poker that stood by the fireplace, she stared down the steep flight of steps that led from the trapdoor into the darkness below.

Every instinct she had told Kara to go back, to turn away from the steps leading down into the dark pit beneath the library floor. If she just picked up the phone, someone far stronger than she — someone who would know what to do — would be here in a few minutes. But Lindsay's scream was fresh in her mind, and she knew it had been no dream, no trick of the night or her imagination.

This time her daughter's scream had been real, and she was not about to question herself or hesitate. Gripping the poker tighter, she moved down the steps until she reached the bottom. Except for the shaft of light from the library above, the blackness surrounding her was complete.

A flashlight. Why hadn't she thought to find a flashlight?

But there was no time to go back now — Lindsay was down here somewhere, and she had to find her. She stepped out of the shaft of light and her eyes gradually adapted to the shadows. She came to a wider area then, the walls seemingly falling farther away, and strange, almost surreal images began to emerge out of the darkness.

Thin mattresses on the floor.

A bucket near each of the mattresses.

Scanning the ceiling, Kara saw a lightbulb hanging a few feet away, groped above her and found a string. She pulled it, and in the suddenly blinding light, found herself standing in what appeared to be a dungeon.

The stench of it filled her nostrils, a wave of nausea rising in her belly as her eyes took in the chains and shackles bolted to the concrete walls. Again, her instincts told her to turn around and flee back up the stairs, but once again, the memory of Lindsay's scream checked her panic and pushed her deeper into the strange chamber.

How was it possible? How could Lindsay be here? This was Patrick's house — the house she'd come to for refuge, and protection, and —

And Lindsay was here! She could feel it now, feel it deep in her soul.

But not in this room, not in this dark dungeon.

Yet not far away, either.

Kara's eyes darted around the chamber, searching for some way out other than the trapdoor she'd come down, and a moment later she found it. A small door, constructed from thick oak, set into the concrete wall at the far end of the grim room.

Carefully, she picked her way through the litter strewn over the floor until she got to the door. It was barely ajar, and she reached out with a trembling hand to pull it open.

Ahead of her lay a tunnel, barely high enough to stand up in, just wide enough to let her pass.

In the distance she saw a dim glow, no more than a faint brightening of the blackness that filled the tunnel. How far away? Twenty yards? Fifty? A hundred?

Her hand tightening on the poker so hard her fingers hurt, she started toward that light.

Where did the tunnel lead? As she moved through the darkness, feeling her way along one of the rough walls, she again recalled Patrick telling her about waking up in the mausoleum with no memory of having gone there. Was that where the tunnel led? She tried to gauge not only the distance ahead, but the direction as well. And then, as the light grew brighter, she knew.

The playhouse! The miniature copy of Cragmont itself that stood near the woods between the house and the mausoleum.

The playhouse whose door and windows were boarded up.

Certain she knew what lay ahead, Kara quickened her step, and as the light at the end of the tunnel grew steadily brighter, it began to pulse oddly, almost as if it were energized by a beating heart.

Lindsay's heart!

"I'm coming," Kara whispered. "I'm coming." She quickened her pace, but not enough to risk tripping on the uneven floor of the tunnel and twisting her ankle. When she was still ten or fifteen feet from the source of the light ahead, she heard something and stopped short.

Voices.

She listened, and in the dim light saw what lay ahead.

Another set of wooden stairs, like the ones that had led from the library down into darkness and the dungeon, only this flight led up. Taking a deep breath, Kara moved slowly and silently to the foot of the stairs. *Lindsay,* she said silently to herself as she gazed at the open trapdoor overhead. *That's all you have to think about. Find Lindsay and get her out of here.*

As quietly as a wraith, she mounted the stairs.

What she saw as her eyes cleared the floor was even more surreal than the dungeon she'd come upon earlier. A few feet directly ahead of her, a pair of bare legs were duct-taped to chair legs that had been fastened to the floor with angle irons. Above the legs, she saw a table, also bolted to the floor.

Kara's eyes shifted, and she saw a figure looming at the end of the table. A figure clad in black.

Then she rose into the room, and the full reality of it made her reel. In the pulsing glow of dozens of candles, two women were tied to miniature chairs. One of them was gazing at her with eyes so empty, Kara knew in an instant she was dead, and the other one's eyes were filled with a terror unlike anything Kara had ever seen before.

But they were smiling! They were both smiling!

A choking cry emerged from her throat

when she saw Ellen's mouth covered with duct tape, upon which a grotesquely hideous grin had been drawn.

And then she saw Lindsay.

Her daughter was on top of a table as small as the chairs around it, and between her legs stood the tall, black-clad figure, a hideously grinning surgical mask hiding his face.

A partially crumpled birthday cake — the cake she'd seen earlier in the kitchen, she realized — sat on a side table, its candles melted down to blue blobs. And suddenly she knew.

Neville! That was why he'd been skulking around the darkened house! That was why she'd felt him watching her! He'd taken her daughter and —

"Lindsay!" Her child's name burst from Kara's lips in an anguished scream.

Lindsay began to struggle on the table, unintelligible cries bubbling from her lips.

The black-clad figure wheeled around, his hands rising as he backed away from Lindsay.

Kara raised the poker. "Get away from her," she said, her voice low, but carrying enough menace that the figure lurched backward.

"It's not my fault," the man whispered.

"Untie her," Kara demanded, her voice rising. "Untie them all!"

"It's *her* fault," he whimpered, cowering back against the wall. He was pointing at the dead girl now.

A blinding fury surging inside her, Kara swung the poker at the cowering figure. "Untie them!" she screamed as she brought the poker around, its sharp spur aimed at his head. But he ducked away, and the spur intended for the skull of the monster who had taken Lindsay sank deep into the wall instead, hitting it with such force that when Kara tried to pull the spur out, she lost her grip on the poker. Then the man was upon her, wrapping his arms around her, pinning one of her arms to her side.

With her free hand, Kara reached up and slashed at his face with her fingers, trying to sink her nails into his eyes. But again he twisted his head away at the last second, and her fingers closed not on skin and flesh, but on the knitted yarn of his black ski mask.

She yanked hard, jerking away not only the ski mask, but the surgical mask as well.

In the strangely pulsing light of the guttering candles, Kara found herself staring into the face of Patrick Shields.

CHAPTER FIFTY-ONE

It was the house itself that awakened Neville. Even before he opened his eyes, he knew that all was not well, that somewhere in the house, something was terribly wrong.

It was a feeling he'd had more and more often over the last few months, when he'd listened to the silence, then risen from his bed to prowl through the house, checking doors and windows, making certain his employer's realm was secure. Indeed, he'd already made his patrol once this night, and found Mrs. Marshall coming in from the terrace with strange tales of hearing sounds she couldn't possibly have heard. Of course, he reassured her that it had been nothing more than shore birds, sent her back to bed, then finished his tour of the mansion before returning to his own room and his bed.

He'd slept.

But now he was awake again, and something felt wrong. Then, before he'd thrown the covers back and reached for his robe, he heard it.

The sound of breaking glass.

Instantly, his mind began cataloging the possibilities. Perhaps it was nothing more than Mr. Shields dropping a brandy snifter after trying to medicate himself through another sleepless night. Or perhaps one of the old family photographs that covered so many of the downstairs walls had fallen from its mount.

Except it hadn't sounded like either a dropped glass or a fallen picture.

It sounded like a breaking window.

Slipping into his robe, Neville hurried silently along the corridor and down the dark stairway that led from his apartment to the kitchen, still trying to convince himself that whatever the sound had been, it was nothing serious.

But even as he moved through the kitchen into the dayrooms, the house whispered that something evil lay nearby.

Emerging into the vast entry hall, he slowed his step and listened, but heard nothing but the ancient clock's eternal ticking; all around him the house was dark and quiet.

Just as it should be.

Yet still he heard it whispering to him, telling him that all was not as it seemed. Neville crossed the hall and slipped into the conservatory, where only a little while ago he'd met Mrs. Marshall, but now all was well in that room, too, and beyond its great glass doors, a lightening sky signaled the coming of dawn.

And by that light, he could find no broken windowpane whose shattering might have disturbed his sleep.

Neville Cavanaugh moved silently on.

The library doors were locked, which told him that Mr. Shields was once again sleeping there instead of in his room. He raised his hand to rap softly at the door, then changed his mind: if his employer was asleep, he didn't want to awaken him, at least not until he had discovered what was amiss.

He turned away from the library and moved to the massive, circular table that stood in the center of the foyer, its intricately inlaid mosaic surface still half obscured by the profusion of yellow tulips that Mr. Shields's sister had picked.

The tulips that were now past their prime, and should have been thrown away a week ago. Neville stood quietly, seeing neither the faded tulips nor any other visible thing, for his mind was focusing on the house itself. He knew that if he waited quietly, it would tell him of its ills.

It always had; it always would. He understood its subtleties — knew every inch of its molding, every scar in its paneling, even every vein in every slab of its marble, as well as every pleat in every curtain.

He knew every creak, moaning joint, and settled beam. As the decades passed, he had kept this house, and this house had protected him. He thought of himself and this house as partners; they understood one another.

And this night, things were not right with the house.

He could feel its ills deep in his soul.

He waited for the impressions to become more specific, but his impatience clouded any psychic message he might have gleaned, and finally he strode to the staircase and mounted the stairs, his slippers soundless on the marble treads.

The doors to the girls' rooms were closed, as always.

The guest room door, though, was open, and when he peered inside, he saw only the empty bed, the bedding itself in disarray.

So Mrs. Marshall was up and about again, and no doubt it had been she who broke something. Certain there was nothing else to be found up here, Neville quickly went back down the stairs, searched the rest of the day rooms, and finally stepped out onto the terrace, using the same door in the conservatory through which he'd admitted Mrs. Marshall a while ago. The air was chilly, and Neville clutched at the lapels of his robe with his fingers as he moved down the length of the terrace, checking each of the French doors in turn.

He saw the breech in the last set of doors that opened into the library. A pane of glass next to the doorknob had been broken — smashed in with one of the wrought-iron plant stands of which he had never approved, and for the reason that now confronted him. The plant stand lay on its side in front of the door.

So there *had* been an intruder.

Neville pushed open the damaged door and stepped into the library, closing it behind him, and as the latch clicked into place, he knew that here, in this room, was the source of the distress that had awakened him.

It wasn't merely the pervasiveness of Mr. Shields's grief or the aroma of Mrs. Marshall's cheap perfume. No, it was something far darker, far more disturbing. But what? The room was vacant and cold, the fireplace barely sustaining a few faintly glowing coals.

Then he saw that the Oriental rug in front of the desk was folded back.

Frowning, he approached it, and stared at the gaping trapdoor.

For a moment all he could do was peer in astonishment at the hole in the floor, barely able to believe his eyes. How many times had the carpet been rolled back over the years? How was it possible that he hadn't known that a trapdoor was there? As he stared at it, and saw how perfectly the door would drop back into the deeply grooved parquetry design of the floor, he realized that the entire floor had been designed to disguise this trapdoor; closed, it would be all but invisible.

But where did it go?

His brow furrowing deeply, Neville Cavanaugh hurried toward the kitchen in search of a flashlight.

CHAPTER FIFTY-TWO

"Patrick!"

The voice seemed to come from far away.

It was calling his name, screaming at him: "Patrick!"

And again, louder: *"Patrick!"*

Patrick wanted to answer, but it was as if he was asleep and couldn't wake up; as if someone were calling him in a dream, and even though he wanted to respond, to call back, he couldn't.

He couldn't do anything; couldn't speak, couldn't move, could barely even breathe. It was as if he was bound in something, as if spiderwebs were wrapped around him, webs so fine he couldn't see them, but that nonetheless held him in their grip.

The voice came again, howling out his name, and Patrick struggled to free himself from the bonds at least enough to speak, to let whoever was calling to him know that he was there. And he *was* there, he knew it. He was not asleep, though he felt as though he was; not caught up in a nightmare, though it seemed as if a nightmare was what it had to be.

The voice screamed his name yet again, and his mind began to focus. There was light all around him; but not bright light, not the light from the chandelier in the library or the lamp by his bedside.

Candlelight.

That's what it was: candlelight. Glowing all around him, bathing the room in a warm, golden glow.

Now the room itself came into a strange kind of focus. A small room, with small furniture.

The playhouse! That's where he was — the playhouse halfway down the lawn, where Claire and her friends —

Claire!

Was that who was calling him? He looked around, trying to see if his sister was there, but he couldn't quite see out of his own eyes. Something seemed to be blocking his vision.

"Go back to sleep!" a new voice whispered, and this time Patrick recognized it right away: it was his own voice. But how could it be, since he hadn't spoken and

wasn't asleep? The voice inside him spoke again: *"Go on. Go back to sleep. You want to go back to sleep. I know you want to go back to sleep, and so do you. So do it. Do what you want to do, and then I will do what we want to do, just like I always have."*

As the voice whispered to him, Patrick felt himself starting to relax, to obey it and drift into the dark and gentle quiet of sleep.

But then he heard the other voice calling to him again. Not Claire's voice, but a familiar voice, a voice he knew.

A voice he liked.

"Patrick! Patrick, what are you doing?"

Kara!

Kara Marshall! That's who it was. And he was holding her, his arms wrapped so tightly around her, he was hurting her. But what was she doing in the playhouse? No one ever went into the playhouse anymore, not since he'd boarded it up. Even his daughters had never been allowed in the playhouse. But now Kara was here and —

"She doesn't belong," the other voice — the voice inside him — said. *"She shouldn't be here, and neither should you. Go back to sleep and let me do what we want to do. Go back to sleep, and I will*

make everything all right. And no one will ever tell."

Tell? Tell what? He shoved Kara aside and twisted his head as she crumpled to the floor. Then, for an instant, it seemed that the hand covering his eyes fell away, and he saw the girl sprawled out on the table, lying on her back, staring up at him with terrified eyes.

Why?

Why was she afraid of him?

Then he saw the girl in the chair, the girl whose head was lolling over, the girl who wasn't moving at all.

And another one.

A young woman, who looked familiar. She was bound to one of the little chairs — the chairs Claire and her friends had sat in when they were children.

When they were children, and they'd brought him in here, and —

The vision of what had happened here so many years ago began to take shape in his mind, and he wanted to turn away, to disappear back into the cradling arms of unconsciousness, where the terrible memories of the past could do him no harm.

"That's right," the voice in his head urged him. *"Go to sleep, Patrick. Let me deal with it. I dealt with it then, and I've dealt*

with it all our life and I will deal with it now. And you won't be any part of it. Not any part of it at all!"

As the voice whispered to him, and Patrick felt the bliss of unconsciousness wrap him in its comforting darkness, he was barely aware of yanking from the wall the heavy iron poker that Kara Marshall had swung at him a moment earlier.

Kara could hear Patrick's voice, but the words made no sense. Who was he talking to? Since he'd let her tumble to the floor, he hadn't looked at her. Now, with the poker gripped in his right hand, he was gazing around the room as if he didn't know where he was. And when he spoke, the words didn't make any sense. Deal with what? What was he talking about?

Then she saw something in his eyes change, and it was as if she was looking at a completely different person. This wasn't the Patrick Shields she knew. This wasn't the man who had been at her side so much of the last two weeks, lending her the strength to cope with everything that had happened to her. His features were the same, but this wasn't Patrick. It couldn't be!

"Patrick!" she screamed again. "Patrick, for God's sake, help us! Help me!"

The face looming above her winced as if something had struck it, and then she saw something different in the eyes again.

She saw Patrick. . . .

As Kara's voice pulled him back again from the brink of the blissful oblivion of unconsciousness, Patrick saw the macabre scene around him in terrible clarity, but this time he shut out the dark whisperings inside his head and let the images — and the memories they called up — speak for themselves.

The memories he'd buried so deep and for so long that he'd forgotten they were there suddenly leaped up at him, dancing and weaving in the flickering candlelight in a dark ballet he wished he could turn away from but knew he could not.

In his mind, he went back to the last birthday party he could remember being held in this playhouse. He'd been six, and his real birthday party — the one his mother held for him — had ended hours ago. He'd been in his room when Claire came to tell him she had a special present for him — a present she and her best friend had in the playhouse.

He'd followed her eagerly, wondering what the present was, and when they were in the playhouse, there were candles burning.

Just like now.

And Claire's friend had been lying on the table.

Just like Lindsay Marshall was lying on the table now.

"We're going to play house," Claire explained as she locked the door with the key, then put the key in her pocket. "Only we're going to play it the way real grown-ups play it."

He hadn't understood at first, but then, when Claire started taking his clothes off, he began to understand.

Then Claire started touching him, and so did her friend, and then —

He didn't want to remember any more of it, didn't want to remember all the things they'd done to him, the way they'd tied him to the table so he couldn't fight back, or even move. It wasn't just his arms and legs they'd tied. No. They'd tied thick twine in places they shouldn't have touched him, and then pulled it tight.

So tight he could still feel the agony in his groin.

But they hadn't stopped even then.

They'd put things in him, too — a broom handle and pop bottles and —

He wanted to shut it out, but he couldn't. As the terrible memories of what had happened in the playhouse so many years ago — not only on his birthday, but so many times afterward — began to unwind in his mind, Patrick felt his sanity beginning to unwind as well. And now the voice was whispering in his mind again, telling him things he didn't want to hear. But he could no more stop listening to it than he could stop remembering everything that had happened now that the memories had returned. *"We liked it,"* the voice whispered. *"Didn't we like it?"*

"No!" Patrick howled. "It was wrong! It was all wrong!"

"But we didn't stop!"

"She made me," Patrick whimpered, cowering back from the kaleidoscope of images and memories that were not only all around him, but exploding in his mind as well. "Claire made me! She and —"

"We liked it!" the voice screamed. *"We loved it!"*

"It was wrong!" Patrick howled. "Mommy should have —"

" 'Mommy' didn't care," the voice snarled. *"Look at her — she's sitting right there, but she's not doing anything, is she? She's just smiling and being happy!"*

The voice was right! The woman bound to the chair, who looked almost exactly like his mother when he'd been a little boy, was just watching silently, smiling at what was happening.

But she wasn't smiling, not really! The smile was just painted onto the tape that covered her mouth.

"Kill her," the voice in his head commanded. *"She wouldn't help you then, so kill her. Kill her now!"*

Patrick's fingers tightened on something in his hand, and he looked down curiously at the poker he was gripping. *Where had it come from?*

"Patrick! Why are you doing this?"

He looked down at the woman on the floor. What was she doing here? Her face seemed vaguely familiar, but in the confusion whirling in his mind, he couldn't quite place her. Was she a friend of his parents?

Or had Claire brought her?

But it didn't matter who she was — if she was a friend of Claire's, she was going to do the same terrible things to him that Claire and Susanna did, and even if she didn't, she would know.

She would know all the terrible things that had happened.

He raised the poker high.

"Patrick, listen to me!" the woman on the floor shouted. "It's Kara!"

Kara . . . Kara . . . Kara. The name echoed through Patrick's mind and seemed to bounce off the walls of the tiny playhouse. Suddenly he felt as if he were suffocating. The ceiling was way too low, and there wasn't enough air, and there were too many candles, too much fire.

Too much fire, like —

Now a new memory burst out of his subconscious.

Last Christmas, in the house in Vermont, the house that had burned.

And now, in the flickering glow of the candlelit playhouse, he could see it all. His girls — Jenna and Chrissie. In their rooms, lying in their beds, deep in sleep. He'd stood at their doors watching them in the moonlight as they slept.

"We had to do it," the voice whispered in his head. *"They were going to tell on us. They were going to tell their mother what we were doing to them —"*

"Not *us!*" Patrick bellowed as the full memory of what he'd done to his daughters exploded in his mind. *"You!* It was *you!"*

"I am you!" the voice taunted. *"I've always been you, doing all the things you*

wanted to do but were too afraid to do! You're a coward, Patrick! You've always been a coward!"

And finally all the confusion in his mind cleared away, and the playhouse seemed to fade around him. He was back in Vermont, watching as his house and his family were consumed by flames.

Flames from the fire he himself had set.

Flames that had been smoldering inside him ever since he was a boy, and Claire had brought him here, and his nightmare had begun.

His perfect nightmare.

A nightmare so perfect he'd shut it out completely, even while he'd lived it.

All because of —

"We have to kill them," the voice commanded him. *"If we don't, they're going to tell, just like Jenna and Chrissie were going to tell! We have to, Patrick! Do it!"*

Patrick raised the poker high, its spur hovering over the head of the woman on the floor.

"Kill her!" the voice howled.

And the poker started its downward arc . . .

"Patrick!" Kara tried to scuttle away, but there was no place to go — she was already pressed against the wall. But as the poker moved toward her, she lunged away, and it slammed into the playhouse's miniature sideboard instead of her head. As the sideboard shattered, the candles it had supported flew across the room, hot wax spattering everywhere. Patrick raised the poker and swung again, but again Kara ducked away, lurching against the table. More candles crashed to the floor, and now the thick paper covering the windows caught fire, and as the flames began to spread, Patrick paused in his flailing, staring mutely at the growing blaze. Then his eyes shifted to Kara. His lips were working, but the confusion of words that had been pouring from his lips stopped.

"I loved them," he whispered, his eyes still on Kara. "Believe me. I loved them." Then, as the flames seemed to reach toward him, Patrick Shields vanished through the trapdoor in the playhouse floor.

As Lindsay screamed in terror, Kara tore at the tape that bound Ellen to the chair, ripping at it with her fingernails until finally one foot came free. Then she went to work on one of her daughter's wrists, until finally Lindsay was able to jerk her hand loose, roll onto her side and, with her free hand, tear away the tape that bound the other hand. Kara dropped down to the floor to untape the woman's legs.

"I'll do that," Lindsay yelled, jerking her other hand free and ripping the tape from her wrist. "Put out the fire!"

But the fire was now engulfing the tiny chamber.

Patrick shambled through the tunnel, the poker still clutched in his hand, the memories of everything he'd done threatening to overwhelm him with every step, to push him over into an insanity from which he knew he would never recover.

Nor even want to recover.

But not yet . . . not yet.

Not quite yet.

The tunnel seemed to go on forever, but then he came to the door at the other end, and found himself gazing at Neville Cavanaugh.

For a moment the two men stared at each other blankly, then Neville reflexively stepped back. "Mr. Shields, what are you —" he began. Then he heard screams echo through the tunnel and saw the yellowish glow of fire piercing the blackness at the far end. "Dear God, what have you done!" he cried as the shouts echoing in the tunnel grew louder. Seeing the insanity in his employer's eyes, he took another step back.

"Not me!" Patrick howled. Blindly, he raised the poker and slashed it down, sinking its iron spur deep into Neville Cavanaugh's skull. "Not me," he said again, his voice breaking. "It was never me."

Stepping over Neville's body, he lurched across the concrete floor of the basement and staggered up the stairs, into the library, then out through the open door to the terrace.

For a moment he stood perfectly still, gazing out over the broad lawn that swept down to the water. Off to the left he could barely make out the shape of the mausoleum, which was almost hidden by the smoke curling out from the playhouse.

He dropped the bloody poker on the flagstones, and the last details of the nightmare he'd suppressed for so long came starkly into focus.

It hadn't been a nightmare at all.

It had all been real, and now he remembered.

He remembered everything.

He looked one last time at the playhouse, where flames were leaking out around the plywood he'd long ago nailed over the windows.

Then he turned away.

There was one last thing he had to do.

CHAPTER FIFTY-THREE

The tires of the Mercedes-Benz shrieked in protest as Patrick hurled the big car through the curves of the winding roads that would take him to his destination. The only car he met along the way pulled off to the side long before he tore past it, and he was barely aware of the driver's blast of a protesting horn. As he negotiated one turn after another, some small part of his mind guided him along the route as the rest of his consciousness tried to cope with the memories that were still boiling up from his subconscious. His rage and his horror at all the things that had happened kept growing, building upon themselves, until not only his mind, but his whole body, felt as if it might explode.

By the time he slewed the car into the long driveway that led to Claire's house, tears were streaming down his face and his throat hurt from the howls of anguish and fury that had filled the car during the short drive. The car lost traction on the gravel drive as he slammed on the brakes, spun around, and came to a stop with its rear end laying waste to more than half of the rose garden that had been Claire's pride and joy for more than a decade.

Giving the horn three long blasts, then adding two more to be certain Claire would wake up if she was asleep, he got out of the car. Leaving its lights on, the engine running, and the driver's door open, he took the steps to the broad porch of the big shingled cottage in two quick strides and a moment later was punching at the doorbell, then pounding on the door. After what seemed an eternity but couldn't have been more than a few seconds, he stepped back and bellowed his sister's name. "Wake up, God damn you!" he shouted into the faint light of a false dawn. "Get down here and open the door!"

He was about to resume his pounding when the porch light flashed on. Then the door opened and his sister appeared, clutching her robe close around her neck.

"Patrick?" she said, appearing confused. "Patrick, what's wrong? My God, do you know what time it is?"

Instead of answering, he shoved through

the door, catching Claire off balance and making no move to catch her before she tumbled to the floor. He towered over her, his face scarlet with rage, his eyes glazed, his body quivering.

"Patrick," Claire gasped, instinctively trying to pull herself away from him before she got up. "What are you —"

His right foot lashed out, catching her just below her left breast. "I killed them!" he roared. "I killed them myself!"

As the pain from the kick slashed through her, Claire scrambled away and got to her feet. "What are you talking about?" she gasped, pressing her hand against her chest and bending over against the pain.

"Renee!" Patrick howled. "And Jenna, and Chrissie, and that girl, and —" His voice broke, he choked on his own sob, but then he went on. "How many others?" he demanded. "How many?"

Claire stared at him, trying to fathom what he was talking about. Then the light from the chandelier caught his eyes and she saw the insanity that gripped him. Shifting her gaze away, she scanned the foyer, searching for something — anything — with which to defend herself.

There was nothing.

"Patrick, calm down," she said, backing away as he moved toward her. "Tell me what —"

"You *know* what!" he roared. "How could you do it? I was a little boy! What kind of monster are you? I was only six! That very day, I turned six, and you and —" His voice broke and he reached toward her.

Claire's eyes narrowed as it finally became clear, and she took another backward step. "Patrick, slow down. All that was years ago and —"

But Patrick didn't want to slow down. He wanted to hurt Claire the way she'd hurt him. He moved closer, close enough to see the fear in her eyes.

The fear and something else.

Guilt. It was in her eyes, and the knowledge that she knew exactly why he was here further fueled his rage.

Claire turned then and ran, darting up the stairs, her bathrobe streaming behind her.

Patrick bolted after her, stumbling on the staircase, then regaining his balance and charging up again.

Claire got to the master bedroom and tried to close the door, but he was right behind her and shoved his way into the room. She backed up again; the fear in her eyes had turned to abject terror.

"It was only a game," she said, searching for something that might mollify her brother. "We were just playing a game! We were children —"

"It wasn't a game," he said, his eyes bleak and his voice harsh. "It was sex, Claire. It was sex and torture! You tortured a little boy, Claire. A little boy who was your own brother!"

Once again Claire's eyes darted around the room, this time searching for a means of escape. But there was no escape, not without getting past Patrick, and he was too big, and too strong.

Far bigger and stronger than he'd been back then, all those years ago, in the play-house.

And now he was furious, too.

Turn it back, she told herself. *Make him think it was his fault.* "You wanted to do it," she hissed. "You liked it, Patrick. You loved it! And you were lucky Father never found out — if I'd told him you raped me, he'd have killed you!"

Ignoring her words, he moved closer.

Claire turned, scrambled across the bed, and fumbled with the nightstand drawer. "Get away from me, Patrick," she said, trying to keep her terror out of her voice. "I'm warning you —"

But it was already too late. Lunging at the bed, he threw himself on top of her, then twisted her around so she was lying on her back, his legs straddling her, his weight pinning her to the mattress. She kicked and struggled as she kept reaching for the drawer in the nightstand, but it was useless.

As she struggled even harder, Patrick saw the desperation in her face, and it somewhat eased his pain to see that now she would feel what all the others had felt, all the others who had suffered because of what she'd done to him. He could feel the blood pumping through her arteries under his hands now, feel her heart pounding and her chest heaving. His hands moved to her neck and his fingers closed around her throat. She was still thrashing beneath him, her face turning red, her eyes bulging. Then her lungs began to spasm as she struggled for air, and he could feel her larynx and esophagus collapsing under the pressure of his fingers.

No more was he the little boy molested by his big sister and her laughing friend.

No more was he stripped naked, bound to a table, and forced to submit his body to his sister's desire.

"No more!" he screamed, releasing the

last of the pent-up fury and outrage that had split him in two so many years ago.

Claire's face had turned from red to purple, and her struggles had lessened, yet still he squeezed. And then, finally, she stopped struggling.

Her arteries no longer throbbed, her chest no longer heaved.

And still he squeezed.

He squeezed until his hands ached as much as his heart, until his own lungs began to heave with sobs.

He squeezed until tears fell from his eyes into the dead, wide-open orbs of his sister's.

They trickled into her mouth and onto her cheeks and through her hair.

His tears.

The tears he'd held back, just as he'd held the memories at bay.

Finally, his tears as spent as his rage, Patrick rolled off Claire's still body. For a few minutes he lay on the bed next to his sister, then wiped away the last of his tears.

It was time to finish it, finally and forever.

Opening the drawer he hadn't let Claire reach, he took out the small pistol she'd bought after Phillip Sollinger had left her ten years ago.

He gazed at the gun for almost a full minute.

Oh God, I'm so sorry, he said silently to himself as he put the gun to his temple.

As his finger began to squeeze the trigger, one last memory rose in his mind.

The journal.

The journal written by that other person, the secret person who had hidden inside him all those long years while he himself was hiding from the past.

The journal that was locked in the bottom drawer of the desk in the library.

The journal that, perhaps, would explain it all.

His finger tightening once more, Patrick Shields pulled the trigger.

CHAPTER FIFTY-FOUR

Andrew Grant was only vaguely aware of the brightening dawn outside the window of the small apartment he'd called home since his wife had thrown him out five years ago — not because of another woman in his life or another man in hers, but because of the kind of behavior he was indulging in right now. Not only was the small dining room table covered with copies of every report, note, and photograph that might be even peripherally relevant to the open house cases, but so also was the couch, the coffee table, and every other flat surface. All night, he had been sifting through them, moving relentlessly from one report to another, prowling through the mass of interviews, observations, and speculations like a hungry tiger sniffing for prey it knows is there but can't quite pin down. But he was close, though it was his gut telling him he was almost there rather than his brain.

An invisible person.

That was what it boiled down to. Someone who could blend into even a small crowd so perfectly that even people who remembered he was there couldn't quite recall what he looked like. That left out all the real-estate agents he'd talked to, and all the clients they'd brought with them. And all the couples who had gone through the houses, too. And all the singles who'd signed in — whoever he was looking for wouldn't have signed the agents' books at all. But at all three of the open houses he was now investigating, at least one person — and at the Marshalls', three people — had remembered someone being in the house at the same time they were, though they couldn't recall anything about him. "One of those guys you just don't notice, you know?" someone had said. "Like a waiter when you're at a restaurant. You know he's there, but you don't even look at him."

A waiter . . .

What the hell did *that* mean?

His gut told him it meant *something,* but *what?*

As he reached for the mug of cold coffee he'd left on the windowsill, the police scanner in the kitchen, which had been droning intermittently all night with reports of domestic violence and drunken driving, suddenly came to life with a report of a fire. But it wasn't the fire itself that caught Grant's attention — it was the location: 35 Flinders Beach Road.

The coffee mug instantly forgotten, Grant went to the dining room table and picked up one of the twenty-odd reports he himself had made on this case over the last two weeks, this one in reference to the reward that had been offered for information about Lindsay Marshall. He stared at the name and address of the donor: Patrick Shields, 35 Flinders Beach Road.

Now Grant's mind was racing. This wasn't the first fire Patrick Shields had been involved in. Just last Christmas the man's skiing cabin in Vermont had burned, killing his wife and both his daughters.

That fire had been deemed accidental, but now, as the address of tonight's fire was repeated on the scanner, Grant's skin crawled. One fire might be accidental. But not two.

He picked up his jacket from the chair by the door, and in less than a minute was driving out of the building's garage, his mind racing.

Two girls and a woman had died in the

fire in Vermont, and now two girls and a woman were missing.

And Patrick Shields's house was once more burning.

But Patrick Shields? It made no sense — almost everything about Shields was memorable: he was good-looking, and always expensively dressed in the kind of clothes whose quality even he could spot instantly. And not just spot, either — actually notice, and wish he could afford.

But it wasn't just that. At least until his wife and children died, Shields had always possessed the kind of self-confidence that only old money brings, which again always commanded attention.

Nothing like a waiter at all. The notion of Patrick Shields serving anyone —

Suddenly, the last piece of the puzzle clicked into place for Grant.

Serving . . . *servant!*

The word exploded in his mind like a bomb, and he switched on the siren and the flashing light of the bubble gum machine on top of the car and hit the accelerator.

Neville Cavanaugh.

A man who had spent most of his life being invisible!

Ten minutes later, Grant swerved into

the driveway of Patrick Shields's estate and skidded to a stop amidst two Camden Green police cruisers, an ambulance, and two fire trucks. But the house, looming high against the dawning sky, showed no signs of fire.

Getting out of the car and following the hoses the two fire crews were pulling around the end of the house, Grant stopped short when he saw the source of the flames. It wasn't the house burning, but a far smaller structure, no larger than a child's playhouse. And even at a glance, he was certain that neither the structure nor anyone who might be inside was going to survive. Already, smoke and flames were pouring up through a gaping hole in the roof, and as the firemen turned on their hoses, the entire roof collapsed. He saw the firefighters flinch as a storm of sparks and flames shot toward the sky, the fire feasting on the oxygen that flooded through the structure's fatal wound.

As they began to douse the blaze, Grant looked around for Patrick Shields, but saw neither the estate's owner nor Neville Cavanaugh. Was it possible that somehow *both* of them were inside the disintegrating playhouse?

Grant broke into a run as he started up

the lawn toward the house. He'd come to the steps to the terrace that ran along the rear of the house when a set of French doors burst open and Kara Marshall stumbled out, pulling someone behind her. A moment later a third figure appeared, followed by a stream of smoke. All of them were choking and coughing.

Grant yelled back over his shoulder for blankets as he raced up the steps, and as the walls of the playhouse tumbled into the inferno that the fire hoses were just beginning to defeat, policemen and EMTs began swarming toward the house.

Lindsay Marshall collapsed into Grant's arms just as he reached her, and he gently lowered her onto the terrace. While a policeman covered her with a blanket and an EMT began checking her for injuries, Grant recognized Ellen Fine, shivering in the morning light, wrapped in a blanket as another of the EMTs tended to her.

He turned to Kara Marshall then, who was crouched close to her daughter, clutching Lindsay's hand and gently soothing the girl's forehead. "It's all right," Grant heard her whispering. "You're safe. It's all right."

Kara clung to Lindsay's hand even as the attendants gently eased the girl onto a stretcher and carried her to the ambulance. There, they wrapped her up in yet another blanket and strapped her to the gurney. Another crew was doing the same thing with Ellen Fine. Kara stayed with her daughter, her fingers constantly caressing Lindsay's hair, her face, her thickly blanketed shoulder. "It's okay," she kept saying, as much to herself as to her daughter. "It's over."

"I just want to go home," Lindsay whispered.

"Soon, sweetheart." Kara smoothed a strand of hair back from Lindsay's forehead. "Very soon."

As the attendants began to slide the gurney into the ambulance, she felt a hand on her shoulder and turned to see Andrew Grant standing behind her. As their eyes met, he took a clean handkerchief from his pocket and offered it to her. Kara took it, wiped the soot and sweat from her brow, then blew her nose. She crumpled the handkerchief and was about to get into the ambulance with Lindsay when Grant spoke to her.

"It was Cavanaugh, wasn't it?" he asked.

Kara paused, then turned to face him, shaking her head.

Grant frowned, looking puzzled. "Shields?"

For a long moment Kara said nothing, her mind filled not only with the confusion of getting Lindsay and Ellen out of the playhouse and into the tunnel before the roof fell in on them, but on the madness that had culminated in the fire. Finally, she nodded. "He — He killed Neville Cavanaugh, too, I think. And another girl — her name was Shannon."

"Shannon Butler," Grant breathed, but Kara barely heard him.

"I know it was Patrick," she went on. "But it was someone else, too. Someone not at all like Patrick Shields." She fell silent for a moment, and when she spoke again, her voice was hollow: "I don't know what happened. Isn't that strange? I was there, and I really don't know what happened, and I don't think I'll ever know. All I do know is that whatever it was, it's over."

One of the EMTs shut the door, then Kara scrambled in the other door, and a moment later the ambulance pulled away. As Grant stood watching, another ambulance pulled to a stop, to take Ellen Fine to the hospital, and then all that was left was the smoldering wreckage of the playhouse.

Feeling more tired than he'd ever felt before, Grant turned away, Kara Marshall's words still fresh in his mind. Later today he'd go through the house, searching for the answer to the question she hadn't quite asked, the answer that Kara herself obviously thought he'd never find: what exactly had happened?

Maybe she was right — maybe he never would find out.

Then, as he was starting toward the car, his cell phone came alive and he listened as an impersonal voice told him what had just been found at Claire Sollinger's house, not far away. Sighing deeply, he started the engine. Kara Marshall, it turned out, had been absolutely right about one thing.

All of it, now, was truly over.

ABOUT THE AUTHOR

Perfect Nightmare is **John Saul**'s thirty-second novel. His first novel, *Suffer the Children*, published in 1977, was an immediate million-copy seller. His other best-selling suspense novels include *Black Creek Crossing, Midnight Voices, The Manhattan Hunt Club, Nightshade, The Right Hand of Evil, The Presence, Black Lightning, Guardian,* and *The Homing.* He is also the author of the *New York Times* bestselling serial thriller *The Blackstone Chronicles,* initially published in six installments but now available in one complete volume. Saul divides his time between Seattle, Washington, and Hawaii. Join John Saul's fan club at www.johnsaul.com.